To

Jonathan, Rebekah, Kristina, Christopher, Benjamin, Tiffany, Eli, Claire, and all the sons and daughters of light striving to walk by faith in a world that walks by sight.

Never settle for less. While most paths have some truth to them, not all paths lead to life. There is but one. As it turns out, the path is a person. He came for you.

Now, go and be His fragrance to the world and love as He loved. There are those who will hear and believe.

ACKNOWLEDGMENTS

Who I am and everything I write flows from the people who have congregated in my soul since birth—family, friends, and others who entered my life along the way. I am especially grateful to those who introduced me to Christ, taught me about the life of faith, and mentored me throughout the years. I have met some of these people. Many I have not. They have influenced me through words from a distance.

I am eternally thankful to those who pointed me to Jesus, especially Billy Graham, David Hunt, and Gene Block.

I am indebted to those who fueled my infant faith, men like Roy Paulson, George Bonnema, Mr. Den Herder, Pastor Caley, and Dr. Grady Spires, Don Mostrom, and Bernie Grunstra from Camp Peniel in upstate New York. Many of these men have graduated from this world and now behold Jesus face to face. I look forward to seeing them again and thanking them properly.

Then there are the men who challenged me to move on from the milk of faith to the meat. Once again, some of them I have never met. I list only a few here, namely, Chuck Colson, Francis Schaeffer, A. W. Tozer, John Eldredge, Tim Keller, Chuck Swindoll, Bill Bright, Paul Lindberg, Stanley Oawster, Chaplain Glen Bloomstrom, Gary Setterberg, Norman Plasch, Arlan Rolfsen, and Steve Unruh. I leave unmentioned the names of mentors who influenced me through the words they wrote and the lives they lived centuries ago.

I would not be writing at all if it was not for the influence of authors in my youth, such as Edgar Rice Burroughs, Jules Verne, Louis L'Amour, and John Bunyan. As I grew older, other writers influenced me like J. R. R. Tolkien, G. K. Chesterton, Charles Dickens, Chaim Potok, C. S. Lewis, Randy Alcorn, Frank Peretti, John Lennox, Sigmund Freud, Frederick Nietzsche, James Michener, Fyodor Dostoevsky, Tom Clancy, Lee Strobel, Nabeel Qureshi, and Scott Peck. All these authors opened doors to rooms I had never entered before. Although I do not embrace the beliefs or philosophies of all these writers, they now sit at a table in my heart, some as acquaintances and some as dear friends. Jesus stands at the head of the table.

Also, God has brought beautiful biological children and spiritual sons and daughters into my life over the years to teach me how to love, serve, lead, and mentor. They are catalysts for much of what I write. I love these young people deeply.

I am thankful to Nancy, my faithful wife and the humblest servant I know, who has encouraged my writing and tolerated the many hours I lived in another world. I am also grateful to Travis Dye, a friend who early on read my manuscripts and inspired me to keep writing.

Above all, of course, I write because of Him. Jesus Christ has been my best friend since He tracked me down at seventeen. Everything has changed for me—inside and out—since the day He delivered me from the kingdom of darkness and transferred me into the kingdom of His Son. To Him be the glory and the honor and the praise. He alone is worthy. I live to speak His name to men and women so that they, too, might know His love and experience inexpressible joy.

"If the whole universe has no meaning, we should never have found out that it has no meaning: just as, if there were no light in the universe and therefore no creatures with eyes, we should never know it was dark. Dark would be without meaning" - C. S. Lewis, *Mere Christianity*.

"I believe in Christianity as I believe that the sun has risen: not only because I see it, but because by it I see everything else" - C. S. Lewis, from a paper presented to the Oxford Socratic Club entitled "Is Theology Poetry?"

"The people dwelling in darkness have seen a great light, and for those dwelling in the region and shadow of death, on them a light has dawned" (Matthew 4:16, ESV)

Table of Contents

PROLOGUE

In the Dead of Night

The night is moonless—as dark as a cave. But not as dark as the intent of the lone figure staggering through the stone gate of the cemetery. A dense fog whipped onward by an icy wind churns across the adjacent lake and over the lawn of the massive church. It glides into the graveyard and clutches the headstones with skeletal fingers.

The night feels heavily ominous. Thick with a sinister presence. It mirrors the man's dark deeds—the one already done and the one soon to come.

The intruder in the place of the dead stumbles several times as he gropes his way through the inky night. He struggles past grave after grave, shivering violently, but not from the midnight air. What courses through his veins is colder than the wind.

When he reaches the place of his summoning—a dim mound of freshly excavated dirt in the far corner of the cemetery—he collapses to the ground. The burden he is carrying falls from his shoulder and strikes the sod with a dull thud. Panting from exertion and dread, he remains on his knees in the damp grass wishing he was anywhere but here.

Somewhere in the night, a gurgling cry pierces the darkness and the man's body tenses. He stops breathing and listens as if to detect the approach of a specter. His eyes narrow as he peers through the blackness. Nothing. The cemetery is eerily quiet except for the lone raven.

The fog is wet on his exposed neck as he gropes around in the burlap sack he carried with him into the graveyard. He extracts a small shovel and slowly turns to face the mound in front of him. Making out the dark form of wildflowers placed on the grave, he snatches them with frozen fingers and throws them aside. Then, sucking in a long breath as if it will be his last, he begins knifing the blade into the burial earth that had been deposited on the grave less than twelve hours earlier.

He should know—he had attended the funeral.

As cold beads of perspiration roll down his face, he wishes he had thought of another way to hide the morbid deed he had committed. But nothing else had presented itself to his insane mind. So here he is. Alone. Trembling. Dedicated.

A loamy smell fills his nostrils as his shovel bites into the deathly blanket of dirt. On any other occasion, he would have found pleasure in the earthy redolence that elicits memories from his childhood on the farm. But not on this night.

Most of an hour passes before he removes the fresh soil that had cocooned the coffin in the ground. He does not need to remove as much dirt as at some burial sites since the omnipresent rock of the region prevented the grave from being dug to the customary depth.

For an eternity, the lone figure stands transfixed before the open grave. He is panting from the exertion of his shoveling—and from fear. Creeping appendages of fog wrap themselves around his legs like the tentacles of a devilish octopus intent on dragging him into the underworld.

Finally, clenching his teeth, he lies down on his stomach and extends his upper body over the dark hole. Pausing half in and half out of the grave, he listens to the night for a long time. Silence. Again, he is listening for something that does not inhabit the world of the living.

Satisfied that he is alone, he reaches into his pocket and extracts a candle, a small box of matches, and a turnscrew. He knows that the next five minutes will place him at the greatest risk of detection. *But who would be out in the cemetery in the middle of the night?* his muddled brain asks itself.

Only dead people, it answers as the man begins to shiver.

He reaches down and places the squat candle on top of the casket he cannot even see. Then he lights the wick with a wooden match, and light rushes into the rectangular hole. Finally able to see, he sets about removing the screws that secure the lid to the casket box.

This part of his mission takes longer than expected. His uncooperative fingers are shaking as if he is lying on the January tundra at the Arctic Circle.

When all the screws have been removed, he pushes his upper body out of the hole and gets up on his knees. He rubs his sweaty palms on his pants as his wary eyes survey his surroundings. The chilling breeze rattles a brittle leaf from last autumn that is still stubbornly clinging to its host.

The man's eyes dart up at the sprawling branches above him, and he imagines long arms reaching for him—the accused one. The guilty one. Inviting in the daylight, clothed as they are with young blossoms, the branches appear macabre in the night.

With great effort, he tears his eyes away from the arboreal appendages and stares down into the gaping mouth of the grave. He imagines that at any moment, the writhing branches above him will descend, vulture-like, and rake the back of his neck with razor-sharp claws. He shivers so violently that his teeth chatter in his head.

Sighing raggedly, he reaches into his pocket and pulls out a clothespin that he promptly attaches to his nose. Without hesitation, he lies back down on his stomach and extinguishes the candle between his thumb and index finger. Immediately, darkness rushes back into the space vanquished so briefly by the meager light of the presumptuous candle.

The man pauses long enough for his eyes to adjust to the darkness, then attempts to lift the coffin lid with his hands. The mahogany-wood cover initially resists him but then surrenders to his efforts. He lifts it back against the far wall of the rectangular abyss.

When an icy hand reaches out and claws his arm, the man shrieks and recoils as if bitten by a rattlesnake. Scrambling to his feet, he staggers away from the grave. His lungs gasp for breath as terror gurgles up his throat. His wild eyes stare through the darkness of the night, expecting the corpse to climb jerkily out of the hole like a marionette's puppet on strings. The clothespin is still attached to the man's nose, but he gives it no thought.

Frozen by panic, he stands there for several minutes, his eyes boring holes through the slithering fog.

Finally, when nothing unnatural appears over the edge of the grave, he wills his feet to move back toward the exposed coffin. Step by step, he creeps forward and again kneels next to the gaping black orifice as if worshipping a god in the underworld. He fumbles for a match as a cold chill plunges down his neck and into his bowels.

After splintering five matches against the flint of the matchbox, he manages to strike the sixth one into a flame. Biting his lower lip until he tastes blood, he leans forward slowly and peers over the edge of the hole with his fragile light. He spies a small tree root protruding from the wall of the grave about two feet down.

The grave digger curses himself for being a cowardly fool and drags the back of his hand over his forehead that is pouring out perspiration.

The respite from horror is short-lived because the circle of light generated by the quavering match spills down into the open coffin and illumines the alabaster face of the reposing cadaver. The man glimpses the lifeless countenance for but a moment before the match extinguishes in his hand.

Jerking violently away from the grave for a second time, he stares up into the night sky and curses his bad fortune. He had sworn to himself long before he set foot in the cemetery that no matter what else happened, he would avoid looking at the recently interred corpse.

Attempting to purge the image of the death mask from his mind, he struggles to his feet. As quickly as his shaking legs will move, he wobbles over to the burden he had carried into the cemetery under the dark of night.

Quickly, he unwraps the object that prompted his graveside visit from its cloth covering and drags it over to the waiting mouth. As gently as possible, he rolls it into the grave and hears it thump onto the alabaster face beneath that is framed with a white lace bonnet.

His mother was always fond of bonnets.

He reaches down and arranges the newly deposited addition to the coffin so that it fits adequately in its final resting place. Finally, he depresses the wooden lid as far as it will go and then pushes himself out of the twice-fed mouth. Throwing the screws onto the lid of the closed coffin, he grabs his spade.

Driven by dread and half out of his mind, the lone figure shovels the dirt back into the hole with feverish urgency. Reburying proceeds much more quickly than the earlier excavation. Soon the job is finished. The man carefully grooms the pile of dirt on top of the grave as well as he can in the darkness and deposits the wildflowers back atop the mound.

Standing next to the grave, he bends over at the waist and rests his hands on his knees. He is panting like a rabid creature. His body is drenched in sweat, and he can feel the dirt caked on his arms and hands. His tongue works around nervously in his mouth and slides over his lips. His heart thuds heavily as if beating its way out of his chest. For a fleeting moment, he succumbs to madness: he imagines that his chest is a grave, and his heart is buried alive inside of it.

The man shakes his head to rid his mind of the horrible image. He is only marginally successful.

Eventually, he stands up and collects his burlap sack and the cloth that had shrouded his burden—a burden that he will never again carry physically. No, never again *physically*. The fear that creeps into his brain now like a haunting phantom is that he will carry the burden *inside* himself until the day he dies.

Squinting through the dark, his eyes examine the burial scene one last time. A*m I leaving anything behind that will betray a disturbance of the gravesite or might incriminate me of this ghastly deed when the sun rises? No, he decides, everything appears as it did when I arrived.* He had even remembered to deposit the matches in the grave before he replaced the dirt.

It is over, then. He has accomplished his hideous mission. Now no one will ever know what he had perpetrated on this night.

The man stumbles ten feet away from the mound and grabs one of the four saplings that grow near the grave to steady himself. He drags in repeated breaths as he attempts to steady his shaking body and calm his galloping heart.

As he stands there in the night, an unwanted thought creeps into his head. "Two in one," it whispers. Then a second later, "Two in one box." Then, "Two, one."

When the demonic thoughts cannot be exorcized despite his best efforts, he abruptly pushes away from the tree and plunges through the darkness. The only thought his frenzied brain can form is that perpetrating his evil act must have opened his mind to intrusive attacks.

Is guilt the gateway to the voice of a prosecuting attorney whose accusations will never cease?

He hurries out of the cemetery as fast as the darkness and the fog permit. He strides down the deserted hill and across the lawn until he reaches the basement door of the imposing church. He stops there and listens for a moment, breathing as quietly as his exertions and anxiety will allow.

Eventually, he turns the cold brass knob and opens the door. Then, steadying himself with one hand on the cold stone wall, he makes his way down the steps into the inkiness below. It is even darker in this stygian dungeon than in the accursed cemetery.

At the bottom of the steps, groping, he deposits the shovel in a small tool closet. His fumbling fingers then extract the candle from his pocket, and he lights it after countless attempts. With feet heavy with fatigue, he makes his way across the dirt floor of the basement.

When he finally arrives at the subterranean room that functions as his study away from home, he enters and sets his candle on a small wooden table whose only companion in the gloom is a matching wooden chair. Shuffling to the corner of the room, he falls to his knees and dislodges a stone where the wall and floor meet. Behind the slab is a recess in the wall that contains a tin box. He extracts it from its hiding place and carries it back to the table. It feels five pounds heavier than the last time he lifted it.

He opens the box with fingers that still tremble and takes out a book that he sets on the table. Then he reaches back into the box and removes a pen and a bottle of ink.

Before he begins to write in the leather-bound journal, he shuffles through the pages and finds the entry he had written several months earlier.

The flame of the candle grudgingly sheds enough illumination for him to read the words he had recorded in February. They were the last words he had written before his recent dark deeds were transacted.

I was once a good man. Good in the sense of not being bad—at least not bad to the observing eye. Maybe not good in the sense of loving God with a single heart, whatever that means in truth. But I did not disobey my deity intentionally or grievously. I worked hard at whatever I laid my hand to and paid my taxes and loved my family with faithfulness. I kept the rules...until...I decided to conduct—innocently, I once thought—My Experiment with Desire, as I have come to call it.

At that juncture, I committed myself by willful intention not to resist any of my passions but to surrender to them as they arose.

At first, desire seeped into my heart like the trickle of a fragile stream, quite manageable to resist. Gradually its intensity increased until it crashed in like a wave from the ocean. But the wave always went back from whence it had come.

My desire, like a seed, grew into a sprout and then a plant. But the plant was still so small that I could crush it under my heel.

I allowed myself to pursue liquor and drugs. I frequented places that previously my nagging conscience would not have permitted me to enter. I began cavorting with women and soon pursued unrestrained carnal pleasure with many of them. I stepped over a line I had never crossed before. I trespassed into previously forbidden territory.

And then I met her. It was not like I had never seen her before. In fact, I had encountered her several times in the community in years past. But now, she stirred up something new, something untamed within me that had not been there before. What accounted for this change of affection? Had she changed, or had I changed as I abandoned myself to my desires?

Even as I write, I am arriving at the belief that she was not more attractive than she had been before. No, it was something in me that had changed. My lust had been fed so regularly in recent months that the furnace of this desire was aflame day and night. If truth be told, my passions grew until they spilled out of the furnace like some fiery flow of molten steel that I could not stem.

M. D. was beautiful to my eyes. The more I was in her presence, the more my desire was aroused. I fed it with the secret imaginations of my mind. Eventually, the plant of lust grew as big as me and then so large that I lived under its shadow instead of it under my shadow.

My passion became unbridled, and I wanted her even if I had to take her—even if she was the wife of that unsettling man, P.D. Violent imaginations began to inhabit my mind day and night.

No! I am not that man!

Yes, I am that man, or, more accurately, I have become

that man.

What does it matter that I am that man?

I am loathe to admit it, but the truth is that I have become a slave to a demanding master. I am at its beck and call. Day and night. I desire what I should not want. Will I go back to where my mind and heart once grazed like a contented stallion in his own field?

Alas, I fear it is too late to reform my heart. I have ventured beyond the boundary, as it were, too many times. I have fed my desire. Imagined it. Rehearsed it. Is this what they call sin? The rut I have worn in my heart by countless journeys down the same path is so deep now that I go there without effort. I am no longer me. It is me.

I have no instrument of deliverance at my disposal. There is no weapon to parry the sword of desire that attacks my soul. No! Yes! I will have what I want. I will. Why should I not? Who is lord over my heart save me?

A stilling voice whispers to me that I have veered from the ancient path, from the road that I was meant to take. But, alas, that voice at present is so Lilliputian in stature to my desire that I heed it not. It has been eclipsed. Replaced. Yes, for good or ill, a new master now sits on the throne of my heart. I have rationalized away the last remaining boundaries until the final outlying defenses have been breached by desire.

The pagans have overrun the castle.

I no longer bow to any authority. I sail on open seas that have no limits. Choice is captain, now. Desire and passion and lust are my cartographers.

What of the moral compass? It has been cast overboard. I now am directed by a new compass. No one—neither parent nor constable nor reverend nor mentor—shall have sway over me ever again. I am the captain of my soul. I am free to choose my path! Anything that is pleasurable is good, is it not?

How can anything that fills me with such happiness—fleeting as it can sometimes be—how can it be wrong? What could be more desirable and beautiful than the climax of sensual pleasure and the elation of hedonism? I curse the rules and swear allegiance to what I want. After all, commandments are only soft rules, are they not? Recommendations, at best. In the end, I decide what is right and wrong for me!

Admittedly, I confess one last time, before I can do so no longer, that I am not entirely free. Yes, I am loosed from the rigging that in times past steered me to seek a required anchorage in the haven of suffocating obedience to a wrathful God. Now I am no longer restrained by these cables and chains!

But make no mistake: I am still under the authority of a master. Just a different one. It calls me to do whatever I wish—even at times with reckless abandon to life and limb and integrity. (What is integrity anyway besides an agent of parochial restriction and confining legalism?)

I am free, then, on one account, and enslaved on the

other. I no longer am at liberty to say no to my desires. I am, as it were, in a trance—irresistibly summoned—dedicated to desire and wanton lusts and immediate gratification of appetites above all other callings. I am the sailor lured in by siren voices that cannot be silenced.

Will my ship be wrecked against the jagged rocks of these tempting sirens? I think not. I am confident I will see the rocks coming and avoid running aground.

My experiment is revealing to me that, in the end, all mankind will serve one master or another. When we cast off the chains of the moral code, we will find ourselves bound to another code. Thus, my freedom does not lie in being liberated from every master but in choosing which master I am willing to serve.

I am the one who chooses my compass setting. No other being holds that right. Not even God. I am the captain who chooses when I will steer to port or to starboard.

Or am I? Who else would it be?

Sailing by a new compass ~JLS

25 February 1899

Here the two-month-old entry ends.

The man entombed alone deep in the bowels of the dungeon stares at the final words of his previous entry for a long time. Minutes pass. Then he covers his face with hands soiled by dirt and death. Furious emotions roil in his body.

He attempts to draw a deep breath to settle himself, but the muscles in his abdomen are as tight as steel cables, and he cannot. Uninvited words hiss in his brain, accusing him without mercy. He fears that the condemnation is going to accost his mind until it drives him to insanity.

He squeezes his head between his hands and rocks back and forth on the chair in the small pool of grim light.

Hours pass.

Finally, the man dips his pen into the ink and begins his next entry with the words, "It is finished."

CHAPTER 1

Arrival Day

The sun is a blazing warrior riding fiercely atop its azure steed when Jack Sutherington navigates his ink-black Jeep Wrangler into the parking lot of the Academy. He finds a place to park in the busy lot and, with the tired sigh that follows the conclusion of a ten-hour drive, turns off the ignition.

Leaning forward and peering through his dusty windshield, he gazes through the broken curtain of majestic oak trees and observes a gray structure climbing skyward. The castle-like edifice is constructed of an assortment of beveled stone blocks that speak of another age.

To the right of center, a Roman portico dressed with fluted pillars incongruously clings to the castle from the dark ages. Set back in the deepest shadows of the portico, Jack spies an arched double door constructed of heavy hewn timbers riveted together with thick iron strapping—no doubt the main entrance to the building.

His eyes travel away from the portico, and he observes a half-dozen stained-glass windows three stories high that interrupt the impregnable flow of stone blocks. The majestic windows give the structure an appearance of a basilica wed to a fortress.

When he continues to scan to his left, Jack's eyes fall on a giant octagonal turret bursting forth from the corner of the castle. The impressive tower is replete with arrow loops that would afford a clear view of an approaching enemy. Dentated battlements decorate the lip of the tower six stories above the ground.

Ignoring the stained-glass windows and the Roman portico, Jack stares at the massive structure and lets his imagination drift. He envisions a medieval castle, ancient and enchanted, dropped from the sky here into the heart of the Midwest. If the stones of this castle could speak, tales would undoubtedly be told of blood and death, of courage and conquest, of fierce campaigns between the embattled residents of the fortress and besieging armies.

In Jack's mind, the only things missing are a lumbering wooden drawbridge manipulated by massive rusty chains and a moat populated with forbidding crocodiles.

Of course, it is beyond Jack's physical eyesight, totally outside his limited mortal ken, to know that past clashes have indeed occurred in and around this castle-church—albeit invisible ones—and that furious battles will be fought here in the days and weeks to come. Some will involve Jack and his soon-to-be-new-friends.

A few will threaten his life.

Jack stretches his road-weary body and steps out of the Jeep that still carries Colorado mud as a stubborn stowaway on the underside of its black fenders. Many students his age are gathered in small clusters in the parking lot or are making their way toward the imposing fortress. He has fifteen minutes before he is scheduled to check into campus housing, so he decides to inspect the grounds of the small school known as the Teleios Academy.

He jogs across the old cobblestone road that runs in front of the imposing flagship castle to stretch his stiff legs. Then he slows to a walk and saunters over the rich green lawn toward the shore of the lake that borders the campus on the south.

Under the canopy of a towering oak tree, he stops about twenty feet from the shoreline and surveys the body of water. A slight breeze ripples the surface of the lake, and a thousand diamond ballerinas pirouette across the blue dance floor.

On the far side of the lake, maybe two miles away, a multi-level structure rises above the surrounding landscape. Jack assumes this building must be the Silver Bay Lodge hotel that is owned by the Academy. He has been informed that most of the students are employed there during the school year to defray their tuition and living expenses.

Out of the corner of his eye, Jack sees a miniature silver horse leap out of the water and then hears it smack against the lake's surface. By the time he turns to look, the fish—he presumes—has already disappeared, leaving only a rippling ring in the water.

Just then, as he is staring out over the lake, Jack feels it. Unfortunately, it is not an unfamiliar sensation. He has felt it many times before. When it descends on him in the darkness of the night, it is a foreboding that someone is in the room. It is a presence, and not a desirable one. Something sinister is watching him.

When it manifests during daylight hours, he experiences a heaviness in his chest that triggers anxiety and, occasionally, dread. At the moment, he feels like he is in one of those horror movie scenes where the world around him suddenly becomes distorted and unreal. More than once in the past, he has wondered if he has a dissociative disorder like derealization. But in so many ways, it seems very different than a mental illness.

It is difficult for him to dismiss the sense of fear and hypervigilance that the presence generates. He is embarrassed to admit that at the age of twenty-four, such things still bother him. Nobody knows that he has been harassed by it since the day his father died fifteen years ago. He is alone with it. He has never been able to shake it. It comes when it wishes and leaves when it wishes. He is at its mercy.

Jack inhales a deep breath and lets it out slowly. He runs his hands through his shoulder-length, straw-blonde hair and chews on his lower lip. Then he strides down to the shore of the lake and follows it as it curves to the east.

As he walks, he notices that the mighty castle on his left is connected to an equally huge four-story stone edifice that looks more like an old university building. The structures appear harnessed together like two gigantic draft animals in a yoke.

Attached to the side of the academic building is a much smaller two-story dormitory. Its small rectangular windows stand in pedestrian contrast to the mammoth stained-glass windows of the castle and the tall arched lancets of the edifice. Although constructed of the same gray blocks as the larger structures, the dormitory's contemporary style betrays it as a more recent addition to the school campus. It is connected to the edifice by a small, enclosed walkway that reminds Jack of an umbilical cord.

As he studies the rectangular dormitory, he notices that the building ends abruptly against the shoulder of a hill, shoving up against it.

Jack walks past the dormitory to the bottom of the hill and begins to climb the moderately steep slope. When he reaches the top, he finds himself in a forest of trees so foliaged that he cannot see the sky. As he continues to walk, he arrives at a break in the trees where he can look down on the flat roof of the dormitory twenty feet below him.

From this vantage point, he notices that the two-story dormitory is shoe-horned into what looks like an abandoned stone quarry, undoubtedly the source of the stone blocks that compose both the parent and the child structures. The end of the dormitory building as well as a twenty-foot length of its side opposite the lake, are built directly up against the quarry wall and so are windowless.

As blind as Samson after the Philistines gouged out his eyes, Jack remarks to himself and smiles wryly. I *hope my room has eyes to see. What are the odds of me ending up in a blind room, anyway?*

Jack wipes the perspiration from his forehead with the back of his hand and then uses his sleeves to wipe his eyes. Even with hiking shorts and sandals on, he feels overheated under the presence of the late August sun that is rallying its slowly waning strength against the gathering coolness of autumn's siege.

Jack takes one last look at the dorm, and the imposing citadel that overshadows it like a small mountain then turns and continues to advance through the phalanx of silent soldiers. Eventually, he begins to descend the hill on the other side of the dorm opposite the lake.

Halfway down the slope that is more gradual than on the lakeside, he sees a cemetery. *Surprise, surprise,* he thinks to himself. The old graveyard is enclosed by a chest-high wall that is, predictably, constructed of the same gray stone that is the flesh and bones of the other three structures.

What is the word? Jack asks himself. *Ubiquitous. Yes, this stone is ubiquitous,*

On closer examination, he notices that the stone cemetery wall is interrupted intermittently by wrought iron fencing whose vertical bars appear to be relatives of the ramrod trees he encountered in the forest. Unlike the forest sentinels, however, that are guarding the world of the living, the cemetery sentries are guarding the world of the dead.

Randomly, Jack briefly ponders why there are fences around graveyards. *Are they there to keep things out or to keep things in?* He smiles to himself at the thought.

Descending to the stone and wrought iron wall, he follows the perimeter of the cemetery as it parallels the dormitory and the towering edifice that is yoked to the castle. Soon he arrives at a wide double-gated entry that is standing open. Tall grass has grown up around both halves of the gate. Jack imagines a giant foot kicking in the gate and leaving it forever open to symbolize that death does not have the last word.

Above the open portal is a black wrought iron arch with a sign that reads, *The dead will be raised imperishable.*

Jack gazes into the cemetery and observes row after row of ancient headstones. The silent monuments are mottled with lichen spots that look like leprous passengers. The gravestones lean, cockeyed, in every direction like a battalion of soldiers weary of standing at attention for more than a century.

Jack thinks about entering the cemetery and doing some exploring but changes his mind when he retrieves his phone from his pocket and notices that it is past his check-in time at the dorm. He immediately retreats to the parking lot, where his vehicle awaits him.

"I have an ominous feeling about this putrid mortal," the gravelly voice utters from the deep dark that surrounds the world of light, only a whisper away.

"Yes, he shines far too brightly," rasps another voice that sounds more like a guttural hiss.

"T*his place is flooded with shining ones on this day*," a third fallen one growls. "*They are coming back, and this place will soon be alive again.*"

"Fool! Do not speak that word that word!" a forbidding voice screams from the darkness. The voice belongs to a leader among his fellows who

has been cursed with verbal redundancy as an eternal consequence of the Great Rebellion. "*We are here to communicate death, not life! Do you hear me do you?*"

"*I do, my lord*" the voice replies obsequiously.

"*Jack Sutherington!*" the lord spits out the name."*Jack from from Colorado. The image-bearer made his way here even after we placed formidable objects in his path to prevent such a thing from happening to prevent it. He is such a fool! Like the rest, he is walking dust, decaying flesh that decaying flesh that will die one day and raise a stench down to the gateway of hell itself. We will live forever, but he will die and be consumed. By the worms, he will die!*"

"*What should we do with him?*" the gravelly one inquires with derision dripping from his words.

"*At all times, keep a sentry on him at all times,*" the dark lord commands."*He must not meet her. We may lose her then, when she is so close to being veiled in darkness forever, we may lose her. No, he must not meet her.*

But if he does, she must die as surely as the prince of darkness rules this pathetic outlying province pathetic province called earth!"

Jack groans audibly when the upperclassman leads him down the hall and into the ground floor room in the far corner of the dormitory. Both sides of his room butt up against the stone quarry, as evidenced by the rough sculptured surface of the two walls. His room has no eyes to the outside world. It is dark and sightless. He will be like Samson, after all.

"Not so fast," Jonathan says in response to the new student's displeasure. "You may have no windows, but you do have the most special room in the whole dorm," he says, nodding his head slowly.

"Special?" Jack asks with a tilt of his head as he eyes the upperclassman.

"Yes, most special." Jonathan stares at Jack with an enigmatic smile playing on his lips.

Jack returns the stare for a while before impatience gets the best of him, and he says, "Okay, I give up. What's so special about this room?"

"Sorry to arouse your curiosity and then bail on you," Jonathan says in a feigned apologetic tone. "I don't have time to show you now," he says. "It would take too long. We need to get your stuff in here straight away so you can get over to the welcome session for newbies. I'll explain the mystery of the room to you after you get back here tonight. I'm just down the hall," he says, gesturing with a tilt of his head.

As Jonathan moves toward the door, he says over his shoulder, "You simply won't believe it."

By the time Jack opens his mouth to speak, the other young man is out of sight. "You have to show me?" he asks the empty room. "I won't believe it? What are you talking about, dude?"

Half an hour later, Jack's belongings are stowed on or next to the lower bunk bed. He is examining the two quarry walls around him to see what could be so special about his room when another man appears in the doorway and announces, "Hey, looks like I'm your roomie, homie." The voice is accented and inviting but infused with a subtle hint of challenge.

Jack turns and studies the olive-skinned man standing in the doorway. He is half a foot shorter than Jack's 6'2" frame with a wiry build that belies his strength. He has closely cropped black hair and a teardrop tattoo below his right eye. His neatly trimmed mustache and goatee frame straight, white teeth that are currently on display in his broad smile. A very fine, almost imperceptible white scar travels down his left cheek and disappears into his facial hair.

Jack reaches out his hand to welcome his new roommate. "Hola, I'm Jack. And who are you, homie?"

"Yo soy Armando. ¿Tú hablas español?" he states as he shakes Jack's hand.

"Poquito," Jack replies. "Enough to know that you're Armando." Jack turns and motions like an orchestra director with his arm, "Mi casa es su casa. Welcome to the blind room. No windows!"

Armando laughs winsomely and says, "I grew up in a place where not having windows was a good thing."

Jack does not understand what his new roommate means but nods his head slowly. "I'll help you get your stuff in here—amigo. We've got fifteen minutes before the welcome session for new students."

"Sounds good, Juan," the other man says with his wide grin. "Yes, you will be Juan to me."

Jack smiles at his roommate and says, "Just so you know, this room may not have windows, but it's very special. Just don't ask me why it's special because I have no idea."

It is Armando's turn to nod his head slowly, quizzically. Soon they are both striding down the hallway to retrieve his belongings.

Jack and Armando walk to the end of the dorm and through the narrow umbilical cord hallway that opens into the huge four-story academic building. Once in the larger structure, they follow signs directing them to the meeting room for incoming students.

As they make their way through labyrinthine hallways and up seemingly endless flights of stairs, they are soon joined by a handful of other new students headed for the same destination. A girl next to them with long blonde hair glances over and says with a pleasant smile, "Nothing like being a freshman for the third time."

Jack tilts his head and smiles at the young woman whose cheeks transform into dimples when she smiles, and her green eyes shine. He is about to reply to his fellow student when they enter a large room on the fourth floor that juts out from the rest of the building like a small peninsula. Half the room is a classroom equipped with long tables, while the other half is a lounge area with several overstuffed chairs and couches situated around a large coffee table. A rich red carpet, feather-soft under Jack's feet, gives the room the feel of an elegant private study.

Centered on the back wall of the room is a huge stone fireplace with a mouth six feet wide and four feet deep. It is constructed of smoothly beveled stones that ascend to the fifteen-foot ceiling and boasts a thick stone mantle that runs the full length of the fireplace. Although it lacks a hearth, the floor in front of the fireplace is covered with paving stones. Resting on top of the pavement is a stack of logs patiently awaiting a colder season to be pressed into service.

Between the small stained-glass windows set into the three walls of the peninsula hang large paintings depicting familiar biblical events. The six paintings are embraced by ornate gilded frames that look like they belong in a museum.

Gazing from picture to picture, Jack sees David running toward Goliath, Esther standing before King Ahasuerus, Daniel praying with lions all around him, Adam and Eve fleeing God's presence in the garden, Abraham standing knife in hand over Isaac on the altar, and finally, Moses parting the Red Sea, his staff raised high toward the stormy sky.

While he is examining the fierce intensity of Moses' face, Jack hears a pleasant female voice invite the students to take a seat in one of the folding chairs that have been arranged in a half-circle three-rows deep.

Jack shifts his gaze to the front of the room and sees a woman dressed in an ankle-length denim skirt with a colorful scarf tied around her neck. He is surprised to see two pieces of jewelry resting against her robin-egg blue blouse—a cross and a peace sign. The woman has a youthful face and long silver hair that flows over her left shoulder. Her face and hair communicate competing messages: one says she is thirty while the other says she is sixty. Whichever one is true, she appears to be a pleasant woman, Jack decides. Her smiling face radiates joy.

Jack grabs a chair in the front row next to Armando and then turns to look at the other newcomers. He estimates that about two-dozen new students are present.

The radiant woman steps behind a small lectern in the front of the room. Beside her stands a middle-aged man with curly dark-brown hair and matching facial hair. His mustache and beard are neatly trimmed. His eyes, set back in deep caves, are intimidating beneath his overhanging forehead. Unlike his female counterpart, his face looks grave.

The woman gazes around at the new students and says, "It's so good to see you all! We're so pleased to have you here at the Teleios Academy. Please know that every single one of you is meant to be here. The faculty on campus," she says gesturing to her colleague next to her, "prayed over your applications for weeks seeking the will of our Lord. Rest assured that all of you gathered here in this room are the answers to those prayers!"

"Dr. Livingstone is correct," affirms the man with intense eyes. His voice is incredibly deep and strangely soothing. He speaks slowly and precisely as if each word is selected with great intention. "None of you is here by accident," he states. "You're here on purpose for a purpose."

He pauses briefly, then says, "Before we go any further, though, I want to ask our Savior to be with us tonight." The man bows his head and speaks a brief prayer that communicates a consistent theme of gratitude for the pursuing love of God.

When he is done, he looks up and says, "My name is Dr. Milner McNeely." He gestures toward his associate and adds, "Dr. Livingstone and I are going to circulate a handout that introduces the classes you will be taking this term along with the names of your professors and the location of your classes. Then we'll briefly explain the salient components of this unique program here at the Teleios Academy. We'll close with a brief community time during which you will meet the members of your micro-cohort.

"By the way, the name of the Academy is pronounced Te-lay-os. As some of you may already know, this Greek word means complete in the sense of having reached full growth or maturity. In other words, the Academy exists to grow all of you toward increasing spiritual maturity; toward becoming more like Jesus."

When Jack receives the course handout, he glances at its contents.

COURSE	INSTRUCTOR	CLASSROOM
Practicing Presence	*Miriam*	*River Room**
Warfare and the Enemy	*Windsor*	*Catacombs*
Weapons	*Greenlay*	*Aquarium*
Love	*Livingstone*	*Greenhouse*
Why Atheism?	*Hawkstern*	*Fireside Room*
Grave Whispering	*Fagani*	*Cemetery*

Armando leans toward Jack and points his finger at the classroom column. "Do you see this, man? The Aquarium? What's that? A classroom located underwater? And then there's the Catacombs, the River Room, and the Greenhouse. What is this place anyway, a botany school?" he inquires, smiling.

Dr. Livingstone appears to have heard Armando. "The class locations may sound exotic," the silver-haired professor explains. "In fact, this whole post-graduate program is marvelously unique. As you already know, you will not be graded here at the Academy by conventional metrics because you are here to grow in ways that transcend mere academics.

"Take note, for example, of my class focusing on love. Not your ordinary class. But I can almost guarantee that you will leave this program seeing everything in this world from a new perspective, and not because of us but because of Him."

Dr. McNeely slowly scans his young audience and interjects in his deep bass voice, "Just to add to what Dr. Livingstone has already said, be sure to log into the Academy website for directions on how to get to your classrooms. Some of them are in exotic locations, as you can see. By design."

The professor pauses to distribute another handout entitled Program Elements. When everyone has a copy in their hands, he says, "Please walk with me through this list of academy components that are in addition to your regular course work."

Dr. McNeely looks down at his notes and announces, "Component number one is called Spelunking. This element of the program is the inspiration of another professor on our faculty, Dr. Alan Greenlay, a member of the National Speleological Society. Some of you know that this organization was created by cavers in the United States and pertains to the exploration of cave systems around the country. Here at the Teleios Academy, Dr. Greenlay has inspired us to apply this practice of spelunking to the exploration of the human heart."

The professor looks up and says, "After all, it was Jesus Himself who said, 'Don't just clean the outside of the cup. Clean the inside as well.' Accordingly, during your time here at the Academy, our goal is to facilitate your efforts to 'go inside the cup,' as it were, with an experienced spelunker under the guidance of the Holy Spirit."

Before Dr. Livingstone reads the second element of the program, she dons reading glasses that are attached to a silver chain. Now she has three chains around her neck, Jack observes. As she bends her head down to read the handout, her silvery hair slides off her shoulder and is suspended in the air. It is then that Jack notices that her hair extends almost down to her waist.

"The second element is referred to as the *Cave of Dread* or alternatively, as I like to think of it, as the *Cave of Presence*," the melodious voice says. "More will be said about this unique experience as we approach it in the weeks ahead. Students will engage in this component one at a time and only once during the academic year. The Cave of Presence is a highly individual experience that nonetheless may have significant ramifications for the whole community."

"The third aspect of this program," Dr. McNeely interjects, "is simply referred to as Prophecy. A wise woman by the name of Miriam is our resident prophetess," he says as he gazes out on his audience of new students. "On different occasions throughout the year, she may be moved by God to communicate a message to you. This message is most often not foretelling but forthtelling. She will confide in you a prophecy she received from the Holy Spirit that is expressly intended for you by name. These words can have—dare I say, will have—a profound impact on your life now and in the future."

"Next," Dr. Livingstone announces, "is a component we call the Personal Narrative. Each of you will be asked at some point in the school year to share your journey with God. This narrative sharing represents an opportunity for your micro-cohort to know you better and for you to review your personal growth up to this point in your life."

Dr. McNeely clears his throat and then says, "The last element of your experience at the Academy is tripartite. It entails three aspects that have been carefully engineered for you to be in the world working with and loving other people. This three-pronged component consists, firstly, of employment at Silver Bay, the hotel owned and operated by the school on the other side of the lake. As you already know, your employment at the hotel pays for your tuition at the Academy. You can't beat that, can you?" The professor says with something that could be mistaken as a sparkle in his dark eyes. "You may request a waiver to work at another location as long as you know that your tuition will be your responsibility if you choose that option."

Dr. McNeely consults his notes and then looks up. "The second part of this program element involves volunteering in the community primarily with the homeless people who live under the Lexington bridge two miles from campus. This outreach focuses on food distribution, education, providing medical care, and sharing the love of Christ with men and women and children who have no stable home."

"Lastly," the professor says, "the third prong of the social outreach is simply called, *Into the World.* Alternately, we refer to it as the *Tip of the Spear.* Somewhere along the way, while you are here at the Teleios Academy, you will be called—not by the faculty but by God—to reach out and love someone off-campus. Some of you may already know who that individual is. Most of you don't have a shadow of an idea who this person is going to be. Trust me," he says, "God will reveal who it is during the academic year."

Dr. McNeely glances over at Dr. Livingstone and inquires, "Is there anything else you want to add, M.B.?"

The professor with the silver waterfall nods her head and says, "Be alert to two things while here at the school." She pauses and slowly scans the room. "First, students tend to have a lot of dreams while they're here at Teleios. Some of you may experience this phenomenon. Don't dismiss them out of hand.

"Secondly," she informs the students as she fingers the cross dangling from her neck, "for years, rumors have circulated around the campus that might simply be urban myths. On the other hand, they might be worthy of your Sherlockian skills. Some of these rumors involve a murder, a treasure, and a secret cult that worships darkness."

Dr. Livingstone pulls yet another handout from her file folder and begins to pass it around. She has a warm smile on her face. Jack loves her smile. It is full of compassion.

"At this time, we would like to divide you into your micro-cohort groups," she says brightly. "Please move your chairs to the locations in the room I have indicated on this sheet. Share your names, where you're from, and why you're here. When you're done, feel free to head down to the Agatha Room for the first supper."

"As opposed to the last supper," Dr. McNeely adds without cracking a smile.

So, the man does have a sense of humor, Jack thinks to himself.

Before he receives the handout, Jack turns to Armando and says with a grin, "I'm assuming we're in the same micro-cohort since we're roomies—homies according to you."

Armando collects his handout and scans it as he passes several on to Jack. "Yes, we're together in a group with some other strange people named Stewart, Aliyah, Emily, and Rachel."

Jack stands up, and his attention is immediately drawn to the Moses painting once again. The leader of the Exodus is standing on a huge boulder with his staff thrust toward the heavens while the Israelites cross the Red Sea in the background under a lightning-rent firmament. His face reflects the red-orange light of the pillar of fire that burns nearby. His hair and beard are wind-swept.

"That's our spot over there," Armando announces as he nods toward the corner of the room. "Let's grab six chairs and set them up next to Moses."

By the time their chairs are in place, the four other students have made their way over to the corner of the room. Sitting down, the six newcomers smile at one another but say nothing.

After glancing around at the others, Jack says, "I can get us started. My name is Jack Sutherington. I'm from a small town northwest of Denver. Lived there all my life. So, why am I here?" He pauses and examines the lofty ceiling for a while.

Eventually, he looks down at the others and says, "Ever since I heard about this academy three years ago, I was intrigued. Then a year ago, I heard God clearly tell me to apply. I didn't hear His voice audibly, of course, but I heard Him speaking clearly inside my heart. I knew He wanted me here. I want to become what the academy catalog refers to as an uncommon believer in Jesus—mature and strong in faith."

After Jack is done speaking, the five remaining students take turns sharing about themselves.

First to speak is Rachel, the auburn-haired girl from Ledyard, Connecticut, whose pleasant face is covered with freckles and who speaks in a distinct accent that Jack immediately recognizes as Bostonian. She talks rapidly and drops the "r" at the end of her words. *She must have grown up in Boston and later moved to Connecticut,* Jack thinks to himself.

Then there is the smaller girl, Aliyah, who appears to come from a Muslim background due to the black hijab she wears on her head. The young woman has a heart-shaped face and fine features. She reveals that she is from southern Thailand. Like Rachel, she also speaks in an accent, but hers is not as pronounced as Rachel's. Jack ultimately decides that it sounds less like an accent and more like tonal variations. She speaks animatedly about her desire to grow in her faith. She informs the members of her micro-cohort that they can call her Aly.

After Aly comes Emily from Ft. Myers, the girl with the long blonde hair and the dimpled laugh. She also has the radiantly green eyes that Jack noticed earlier in the hallway. In contrast to Rachel, she speaks more slowly and softly.

Stewart from Two Harbors in northern Minnesota speaks next. He drones on for several minutes about growing up on the shores of Lake Superior, where he searched for agates and unique driftwood and always participated in the annual smelt fishing. He also talks about several famous shipwrecks that lie deep beneath the cold waters of the gigantic lake. He is a veritable storehouse of facts but comes across to Jack as dry and academic.

Armando shares last. He informs the other students that he was originally from La Puente near Los Angeles and attended college at Washington State, where he majored in entrepreneurship. He mentions rather enigmatically that he hopes to develop a product someday that will remotely neutralize traditional guns and prevent them from firing.

All five students share reasons similar to Jack's concerning why they enrolled at the Academy—all of them except Emily, who seems strangely vague about her rationale for being at the school.

After everyone is done speaking, Jack considers each of his fellow micro-cohort members. He decides that Aly with the hijab is determined just by the way her mouth moves with such deliberate motions. Emily is unhappy because even though she smiles a lot, her green eyes are deep wells of sadness framed by her long blond hair. Stewart is an intellect because he speaks from his brain, not his heart. Armando is guarded because he, occasionally at least, has an edge to his voice as if he is defending himself before accusers. And vivid Rachel with her rich auburn hair, freckles, and many words is hiding something. Her easy smile and loud laugh function as a protection to keep something in—or something out.

Jack decides that he likes them all. Every one of them is interesting and appealing in their own way, even Stewart with his black horn-rimmed glasses, neatly combed hair, and crooked smile that curls upward in the right corner, exposing his large front teeth. He has five pens and two mechanical pencils in his front shirt pocket, securely and methodically ordered in a plastic shirt protector.

All six students in the micro-cohort have been summoned to the Academy to grow in ways they cannot begin to fathom at this early juncture in their journey. Only the passing of days will reveal to them the extent and means of their personal and corporate growth that will transform them all. An unseen hand will wisely direct their steps even through the valleys of darkness that lie ahead.

CHAPTER 2

Down into Darkness

The Agatha Room is the church's old fellowship hall located on the ground floor just off the huge sanctuary. It is large enough to seat a thousand people instead of the one hundred plus students who are gathered for supper on this first night of the semester. Far above their tables, the ceiling hovers over them with its large octagonal-framed cupola that invites light into the room through its translucent glass panes.

This old building is an architectural wonder, Jack observes to himself. Even now, as he smiles and chats with the nine other students at his table, his eyes travel over the old walls of the room and fall on an inscription chiseled into the stone mantel above the doorway. It reads, "Whoever comes to me shall not hunger and whoever believes in me shall never thirst."

Jack's eyes return to the people around him. As he scans their faces—some serious, others bright with laughter, and still others deep in thought as they listen to their peers—he experiences a deep conviction that they have been brought together for an amazing adventure. There is a plan, still unknown to them, that will unfold in the days ahead. Coming here to the Academy is going to define their lives until the day they die.

Jack feels something warm flow through his body like a summer breeze. At that moment, Jack thanks God for loving him. Does anything else really matter?

A half-hour later, Jack, Armando, Stewart, and Jonathan gather in the ground-floor corner room of the dormitory. It has already been dubbed the blind room by the two roommates who will be living there during the academic year. Jonathan has a backpack slung over his shoulder.

"So, do you want me to reveal to you what's so special about your room, or would you prefer safe and boring lives?" the upperclassman asks with a smile.

"Come on, man, stop dragging this out," Jack replies with feigned disgust. "Show us already!"

"Okay, don't tell me I never warned you," Jonathan says. Then he adds, "There are some doors in life that should never be opened. You sleep better if you keep them closed and locked."

"Yes, like never opening the door to Quantum Physics," Stewart says matter-of-factly as he adjusts his black-framed glasses. "Or maybe even Ochem. I think my life would've been better if I hadn't invited those entities into my life."

There is a short pause, and then Stewart clarifies, "Well, maybe not better, but easier. Yes, far easier. But I must concede that after I had studied these sciences for several years, Quantum Physics and Ochem eventually became increasingly understandable to me. Relatively speaking, that is."

The three other young men eye their suddenly loquacious classmate with mild surprise. Up to this point, Stewart had hardly spoken a word since introducing himself in the Fireside Room. Jack's early estimation is that the young man from Minnesota does not seem to be particularly adept at social interactions. Even now, after delivering his tangential interjection, he stares back at them, his large, boyish eyes peering out from behind his horn-rimmed glasses.

Jack finally comments, "'Relatively speaking'—is that supposed to be an Einsteinian pun?"

Stewart cocks his head to one side and ponders Jack's words for a moment. Then his face brightens almost imperceptibly, and in a flat tone, he replies, "I wasn't making an intentional reference to Einstein's law of relativity if that's what you are alluding to. I only meant that compared to other more difficult topics, I found Quantum Physics and Biochemistry less challenging than they had been at the outset. Compared to—"

Jonathan's impatience gets the best of him. "Hey, plebes, let's get on with this. Life and death and adventure wait for no man. In this case, I think it's primarily adventure." He turns and walks over to the bunk bed and announces, "We need to move the bed and roll back the rug."

Jack and Armando glance at each other, then simultaneously shrug their shoulders and scramble over to do the bidding of the upperclassman. They quickly push the bed aside and roll back the carpet, exposing a hidden door set into the floor.

"Is this what I think it is?" Armando asks in amazement, raising his dark eyebrows as he eyes the exposed portal.

Jonathan smiles and nods his head slowly.

"I thought trap doors were only for haunted houses and World War II hiding places in Amsterdam," Jack comments. "Where does it lead?"

Jonathan looks him directly in the eye. "Only one way to find out." He bends over and struggles to open the small, hinged door. Armando helps him lift it up against the wall of the dorm room. The gaping, black mouth belches a wave of dank, rancid air. All four men make disgusted faces, and Armando exclaims, "Ay, caramba! Something died down there!"

Jack feels the familiar dark heaviness settle on his chest that he had felt down by the lake, and he shivers involuntarily.

"Something's down there," he mumbles as he stares down into the black hole.

"I don't disagree with you," the lanky guide says. "I'm not going to lie to you. I've only been down there once, two years ago now, but I had dreams about it for months afterward."

Armando's brown eyes grow large, and he repeats with trepidation in his voice, "Dreams."

"Okay, they were technically nightmares," Jonathan admits. "So," he says, elongating the word, "I should warn you—there will be a cost for going down there."

"A cost?" Armando asks as he runs his hand over his short-cropped black hair. "And nightmares? And something down there? Maybe we should think this over a bit more," he says, nervously glancing at the other men. His index finger massages the teardrop tattoo below his right eye.

"Is there a cave beneath us?" Stewart inquires impassively, seemingly unruffled by the prospect of what lies below.

"The shaft descends down to an old stone quarry beneath the dorm," Jonathan answers. "Supposedly, the foundation of this building was laid on the floor of the quarry."

"So, we won't be going that far down then?" Stewart inquires. "We'll hit the quarry floor five or six feet down?"

"One would think so," Jonathan replies, "but that's not the case. It goes much deeper than that. Those of us who have been down there—professor Greenlay in particular—believe that the shaft descends into a channel cut into the quarry floor by the stone extractors back in the 1800s. The channel accesses an old cave system."

"It sounds evil down there," Armando says as he continues to massage the teardrop below his right eye. "I still get a freaked out by my 'Bloody Mary' experiences from childhood. I hate dark places and mirrors."

"Well?" Jonathan asks as he scans the faces of the new students. "Do you want to go down there or not? It's do or die time, men."

Jack shrugs his shoulders and says, "Let's do it. We don't always want to be safe and bored. Life's too short." He hopes he sounds more confident than he feels. He has never liked dark places either, especially since—

"Speak for yourself, ese," his roommate says nervously.

"Ese? Where is that coming from?" Jack asks, glancing sidelong at Armando and laughing.

"Sorry, vato. I regress into my barrio lingo when under stress."

"It sounds more like gang nomenclature to me," Stewart reflects with two fingers on his chin. "When I studied the history of gangs in America in my contemporary history class, we learned that such references are an acceptable way to show affection to homies in the set while retaining the macho dignity of a gang member."

The other three men glance at each other and shake their heads in unison. "Is there anything you haven't studied, Stewart?" Jack asks.

The young man opens his mouth to answer, but Jack quickly adds, "Don't answer that, Mr. Intellect. Rhetorical question." Turning to Jonathan, he says, "I assume you have flashlights in your pack, so let's get going."

"Yeah, but not without a prayer," the upperclassman responds.

Jonathan prays briefly, asking Jesus to give them protection "in the valley of the shadow." Then he turns and disappears down the shaft.

The three other adventurers—one of them very reluctant—follow Jonathan into the intimidating mouth and venture down the narrow throat. They descend into the darkness on an ancient iron ladder attached to the quarry wall. The further they go down, the colder and damper the rungs feel against their fingers. The air becomes cooler as well. Soon there is no light except for the diminishing square of illumination far above their heads.

"How far down is it?" Armando asks from somewhere above the other young men. "I've counted forty rungs so far."

"Only thirty-three to go," Jonathan's muted voice speaks from the darkness below. "I'm already at the bottom."

Soon, all four men are standing in the near blackout at the bottom of the ladder.

"We are down here, Juan!" Armando exclaims with his noticeable accent. "We are deep!" Jack thinks his roommate sounds very nervous.

Jonathan begins rummaging around in his backpack. A few seconds later, he pushes a small flashlight into the hands of each man. Soon, bright beams of light cut through the darkness and illuminate the men's surroundings. Jack hears an audible sigh of relief from Armando.

"I don't think flashlights are adequate for our purposes," Stewart's analytical voice resonates in the penetrated darkness. "We need lanterns or an old-fashioned torch. Our cell phones might even serve us better."

No one responds to the young man. His comments are beginning to sound like white noise to his peers. Instead, Jonathan says, "I'll lead you down the passage, but I don't want to go too far. Tonight's just going to be an introductory foray." None of the new students disagree with the upperclassman.

For half an hour, the four men venture through the dark tunnel that is as quiet as a tomb except for the scraping of their feet. Initially, the walls appear sculpted by human tools. Later, they become noticeably smoother as if formed by a softer agent like water. Here and there along the way, side passages branch off from the main tunnel and lead into darkness. The floor of the main passage is surprisingly even but damp.

Jonathan eventually stops and directs the narrow beam of his flashlight down one of the dark side tunnels. "Someone claims that one of these passages actually leads back to the citadel basement," he says. "You probably don't know it yet, but one of your classes will be meeting in what's called the Catacombs. It's located in the cave system beneath the church basement. There aren't any actual tombs down there as you might expect in a typical catacomb. Somebody just started calling it the Catacombs, and the name stuck."

"That's good," Armando comments in the dark gloom of the underground passage. "I mean, that there aren't any tombs down here."

"I believe this rock is limestone," Stewart interjects as he trains his flashlight on the wall of the tunnel, "with some striations that are not familiar to me. And," he says, turning to squint at the three other men in the darkness that is surgically vivisected by four beams of light, "I've noticed that the ceiling of the tunnel varies from approximately seven feet to twenty feet in height. In the places where it's not as high, there are black smudges on the ceiling that appear to be the smoke of torches. Other people have been down here whether in recent years—or maybe a hundred years ago."

"Maybe even other students, decades ago," Jack offers.

Armando's voice quivers so slightly that no one notices it but him. "I'm ready to go back," he announces in an ostensibly nonchalant manner. "I—I want to get some sleep before the big day tomorrow."

"Not yet," Jonathan replies. "There's one more thing you have to see."

Armando begins to comment that they probably don't have to see anything, but when Jack and Stewart turn and follow Jonathan down the tunnel, he has little choice but to do the same. He has no desire to be left alone in the dark belly of the snake.

As they move forward, all four men notice that the relatively smooth tunnel floor is descending at a steeper angle and becoming narrower to the point that their elbows are scraping the damp walls on either side. The air is becoming even colder and thick with moisture.

After what seems like a long time, Jonathan halts the small party and says, "Look over there." He trains his meager beam of light on the wall of a small tunnel branching off to their left.

The other three men gather around the upper classman and focus their lights on the wall before them.

"What are they?" Jack asks as his eyes attempt to make out a half dozen faded images on the side of the tunnel.

"No one knows for sure," Jonathan replies. He does not look at Jack but continues to stare at the wall as he adds, "However, some of these symbols—I don't know if you can make them out—seem to depict an upside-down cross and a goat's head with long horns. Both symbols are often associated with Satanism."

The three freshmen glance at each other in the suddenly creepy tunnel. Jack notices even in the gloom that Armando's eyes are large with discomfort while Stewart's eyes remain in their fixed impassive state, unreadable and, he thinks to himself, almost android in nature.

"So, this cave system was frequented by Satan worshipers," Jack comments.

"That's the oral tradition," Jonathan affirms.

"Or is being frequented," Armando adds. "Maybe they still come down here. Maybe they're down here right now," he says, his eyes, if possible, even larger than before.

The young men fall silent for a while and listen for unwelcome sounds in the subterranean shadow world. Jack feels the cold heaviness as it weighs on his chest. Right on cue, the four students hear a noise from a long way off that sounds like a rock dropping to the floor.

Jack abruptly turns to Jonathan and says, "Is this a setup? Do you have someone down here to scare the snot out of us as part of some hazing ritual?"

Even before the upperclassman can reply, Jack reads the tightness in his shadowed face and knows there is no deception on his part. "I'm not sure what that was," Jonathan says slowly. "Supposedly, there's an underground river that runs somewhere through the cave system. Maybe the water dislodged a rock or something."

"It's time to go back," Armando says with strong conviction. He pauses and then speaks a thought that just entered his mind, "Did any of you hear where the sound came from—in front of us or behind us?"

No one answers.

"Great," Armando says, "just great. Now we don't even know if it's safe to go back the way we came." His shadowed face is etched with worry.

"Maybe someone came into our dorm room, saw the open trap door, and decided to explore down here just like we're doing," Jack offers. "Whatever the case may be, we have to go back the way we came, right?"

"Yeah," Jonathan agrees, "it's the only way out. At least the only way I know. But we'll be fine, guys." He doesn't admit that secretly he is as ready as Armando to be done with their adventure into the river of ink. The unexpected noise has him a bit rattled as well. He anticipates more nightmares.

"Before we head back," the tall man says as he glances back and forth in the gloom, "I want to inform you of one last thing. If you keep going down this tunnel—I don't even know how far since I've never gone further than where we're standing—you'll find the passage blocked by a pile of rocks."

The upperclassman looks at the men with narrowed eyes and adds, "Dr. Greenlay doesn't know if it's a natural cave-in or if the pile was intentionally made by people who wanted to close it off. No one has attempted to clear it. Just thought I'd let you know in case you want to tackle the job on a rainy day."

"What could be on the other side?" Armando inquires with a little too much intensity in his voice.

"Who knows?" Jonathan says in the murky passage. "Speculation over the years covers a lot of ground—everything from a hidden treasure to a secret rendezvous for the worship of the Devil, to an ancient crypt, to a shaft that leads down to the center of the earth."

"Wow, speculation has been creative," Jack comments with a laugh.

"On the other hand, the closure of the tunnel might simply be due to the poor integrity of the ceiling which eventually precipitated a total collapse," Stewart offers. "Although I would imagine that such a collapse would be much more common in a man-made tunnel than in a naturally formed passage. I read in National Geographic—"

"Well, whatever the cause," Jonathan interrupts, "the tunnel is shut. If you guys decide to clear the passage someday, maybe Dr. Greenlay will give you extra credit," he remarks with a smile. "But for now, let's head back to the world above."

As the four men turn and begin to retrace their steps back up the narrow passage, they realize just how much the path of the cave had descended. Soon they are all breathing heavily and sweating profusely. Every time they encounter an intersecting tunnel, they shine their flashlights into the darkness to check for the presence of anything undesirable, whoever or whatever that might be.

Several times on the return journey, one of the students comments that he hears something, and they all pause to listen. Most often, it is Armando who claims to have heard a phantom noise in the darkness. Every time they stop, they hear nothing.

After forty-five minutes, the four men finally reach the ladder leading back to the world above. Jonathan leads the way up just as he had led the way down. Jack is the last to ascend. Against his own mental admonishments, he repeatedly glances down into the dark shaft beneath his feet to see if anything is climbing up behind him, ready to claw at his legs. With great relief, the four men step off the top rung of the ladder one by one and onto the floor of the dorm room.

After they replace the trap door over the portal and move the rug and bunk bed back into place, the explorers pause long enough to catch their breath. Stewart, who surprisingly recovers from the exertion the most quickly, reaches out of habit for an imaginary pencil behind his ear and comments, "Before I came to the Academy, I researched these grounds a bit. In my perusal of the history connected to the church, I discovered that this dormitory was built fifty-seven years ago when the Unitarians employed it briefly as a small college and seminary."

For the first time that night, Stewart has the attention of his three listeners.

"Before the Unitarians purchased it, the church and the adjoining four-story edifice were the only buildings here—not to mention the cemetery, that is. Since the dorm wasn't built yet, the quarry lay exposed to the naked eye. A person could walk directly from the lake to the cemetery back then if you took a course a little west of the quarry."

The Intellect pauses and adds, "Tonight, as we already know, we went far deeper than the quarry floor."

"And a lot farther back into the hillside," Jack observes as he interlaces his fingers behind his neck.

"Yes, we must have been two miles deep into the tunnel," Armando states, looking much more relaxed now that they are back above ground.

"The torch smoke on the ceiling and walls certainly suggests that the cave system has been known to people for some time," Jonathan comments. "Maybe for hundreds of years. The question is who went down there and why."

"It was probably the Satan worshipers," Armando says as he absently fingers his goatee.

"Maybe one day we'll know," Jack offers.

If a voice could glower, this voice sounds like what a glower might look like on a grotesque face. *"You must continue to strike the weak one where his armor is fatally compromised. He poses as someone strong but inside, he is as weak as a child. Yes, he is a poser. Continue to brand that idea onto his mind until his brain stinks with the foul smell of seared flesh. Until he knows nothing but the lie that he is weak and shameful—clearly not a man."*

Another voice rumbles in the darkness like a giant millstone thundering over a wooden bridge, "*We have been sledge-hammering that deception into his mind since he was thirteen; plunging it into his mind and heart like the knives that ushered his brother out of the world of light and into the realm of death. We will not falter in gashing him open. We will gnaw at him where he is vulnerable until our jagged teeth tear at his bones and suck out the marrow. He is weak. He is exposed. We will relentlessly emasculate him until even his pin-cushioned, heroine-veined stepmother appears more valorous than him. Yes, the one who was once called Syko Loco will be brought low."*

He could set his clock by it if he owned one. Two hours after he had drifted into a fitful sleep, the dreaded current of electricity tears through his brain. It is the familiar, despised mega-jolt that makes his head feel like it is exploding, like he is sitting in the electric chair and the high voltage has been switched on. He throws himself on the floor, gasping for breath while his heart races wildly in his chest.

Frantically, he tries to remember where he is so he can at least comfort himself with the grounding feeling of being in a known place. But all he can discern in the darkness is where he isn't—he knows he isn't in his bedroom back home in Colorado. All is dark. He is alone. Lying on the cold floor on his back, he runs trembling fingers through his hair and grinds clenched fists into his raging forehead as he stares up into the darkness.

Eventually, he experiences a brittle comfort as he breathes heavily on the floor. Always the floor—the solidity of the floor. It is his only retreat when the dreadful voltage arrives, his sole refuge when the nightly visitor rips through his body, setting ablaze every nerve ending.

Almost his only refuge.

As he drifts back into a fitful sleep on the floor of the dormitory, he mumbles to his best friend, "When I am afraid, I will trust in you."

He has another hiding place, after all.

CHAPTER 3

Presidential Welcome

The next morning, Jack and Armando venture through the enclosed walkway from the dormitory to the four-story academic building otherwise known to the students as the Edifice. They navigate several hallways that feel ancient with their stone flooring and dark wood paneling until they reach the Agatha Room.

Aly, Emily, and Rachel are already sitting at one of the round tables beneath the towering ceiling consuming waffles and yogurt and drinking coffee. Stewart is either regaling them or lecturing them—to Jack, it looks more like the latter—about wormholes and multiverses, so it appears less of a social time and more about listening to "the Intellect," as Jack is beginning to think of him.

Smiling to himself, Jack sits down next to Aly. The woman's hair and the edges of her heart-shaped, fine-featured face are hidden beneath her hijab. Besides the head covering, she is wearing black pants and a white blouse decorated with vivid purple orchids. Her olive skin is lighter than Armando's, almost a honey wheat tone. She is a smaller woman—maybe 5'2" and 110 pounds.

When the three women are done eating and listening to Stewart—who has entirely ignored his breakfast—they get up from the table and make their way across the worn paving stones of the Agatha Room toward the double door at the far end that leads to the sanctuary. The convocation they will be attending is designed for everyone—new students, returning students, professors, staff, and any parents who wish to attend. All are welcome to join the formal launching of the new academic year.

When he enters the sanctuary—the castle he viewed from the outside just yesterday—Jack is immediately captivated by its sheer volume. The actual footprint of the sanctuary is expansive, but the ceiling is what captures his attention the most—it towers so far above the floor that it renders the large Agatha room small in comparison.

What magnifies the mammoth size of the space is that the plaster on the ceiling has been removed, exposing a complicated constellation of huge wooden timbers designed to shoulder the massive roof. The timbers remind Jack of the squared Lincoln Logs he played with as a child, only a hundred times larger.

In the center of the ceiling high above the sanctuary, a large glass dome reveals the mingling of blues and grays in the morning sky that portends a gathering storm. Looking up at the circle of light, Jack has the eerie sensation of being at the bottom of a well, looking up at the world above.

The plaster on the walls of the expansive room has also been removed, exposing the hewn stone blocks beneath. For the second time since his arrival at the Academy, Jack feels like he has been thrown back hundreds of years into a medieval castle-church. The arched stained-glass windows he saw yesterday prismatically produce rainbows in the air and dapple the floor and the wooden pews with pastel paints.

At the back of the cavernous room, a choir loft replete with a massive organ is set high above the floor. On the wall behind the organ stands a pipe platoon of vertical soldiers that vary in size from large flutes to small telephone poles.

In the front of the sanctuary, a long, elevated platform serves as the floor of the turret that lumbers upward like a towering titan. Everything about the room cries majesty and glory. If the original architects had hoped to inspire the presence of divinity in this place, they have succeeded admirably, in Jack's opinion.

As the members of the micro-cohort walk quietly toward their seats, Jack fails to notice that Rachel is not with them but sitting on the bench in front of the massive organ.

The five students settle into an old wooden pew not far from the dais in front of the sanctuary. Seated in large carved-wood chairs on the raised platform are seven administrators and faculty members. None of them is dressed in academic regalia or other garments consonant with the high atmosphere that the church sanctuary exudes. On the contrary, they are wearing clothing that would look at home in a university classroom.

As he surveys the small group of leaders sitting in the footprint of the giant turret, an organ chord suddenly rends the atmosphere and reverberates through the sanctuary. Instantly, Jack feels like he has been transported to the throne room of heaven. If he had thought that the physical presence of the sanctuary alone evoked a sense of God's presence, now he is fully persuaded. He rises to his feet and joins two hundred other individuals as they sing the hymn, "A Mighty Fortress Is Our God."

How apropos, Jack thinks—*a mighty fortress. Yes, our God is a mighty fortress, far mightier than this imposing castle-church.*

When the final majestic chord crashing from the king of instruments ceases to reverberate off the walls of the throne room, everyone sits down.

The leaders seated on the wooden chairs in the turret take turns standing at a raised lectern on the left side of the platform. Students are welcomed, introductions are made, people speak, more hymns are sung, prayers are prayed, special acknowledgments are announced.

Half an hour later, Dr. McNeely takes his place at the highest lectern to deliver the keynote address. Though he is all of six feet tall, he looks small as he stands at the bottom of the massive turret. Jack notices in his program that this professor who helped to welcome new students the previous evening is also the president of the Academy.

The professor-president stands silently in the raised pulpit for a long time, his eyes looking down at his notes. Eventually, he looks up, and his eyes slowly scan every face in the sanctuary. When he finally utters the words, "I can't do this," complete silence falls over the majestic room.

To everyone's shock, the president turns and descends the steps from the lofty pulpit and then continues down the steps that run the width of the platform until he reaches the floor of the sanctuary. Now he is so close to the students and the other members of his audience that he can touch them. Jack can clearly see the man's face with its neatly trimmed brown beard and eyes that are set deep beneath the shelf of his protruding forehead. They burn like fires in small caves. His appearance is sinister.

"That's better," the chief administrator of the Academy comments in his deep baritone voice that does nothing to temper his intimidating countenance. "I'm not as much a priest or a prophet as I am a shepherd. I feel much more at home down here, closer to the sheep." There is another long pause.

"I feel totally inadequate to address you today," the man says as his intense eyes scan the sanctuary. "But that's the point, isn't it? It's not about me. It's about Him. I'm the jar of clay through which He communicates His truth, so I dare not remain silent. My only hope is that the words that proceed from my mouth this morning will be more His than mine."

The president touches the corner of one of the small eye-caves with his index finger and clears his throat. Jack thinks he hears thunder grumbling in the distance.

"There are those who insist that the God we serve is opposed to human desire," Dr. McNeely begins slowly. "They claim that He is God of the negative—the God of 'no.' 'Don't do this!' He cries. 'Don't do that! Stop desiring that object or that person! Extinguish that hunger or that want. Cease being human. Become a fawning automaton! Stifle yourself and your desires,' God demands."

Dr. McNeely pauses and then says, "I suppose one could argue that these people are not entirely wrong in their assertions—obviously, there are things in this world that God doesn't want us to cultivate affections for.

"But neither are they anywhere close to being right. They fail to see that the one we serve is a God of the *positive*. Most certainly, He doesn't want us to desire less. Oh, no. He wants us to desire more! To say it another way, He doesn't want us to settle." The professor speaks the last sentence with a poignant pause after each word.

"You may remember the first line of T. S. Elliot's poem, 'The Waste Land:' 'April is the cruelest month, breeding lilacs out of the dead land.' Well, let me tell you," the professor says with energy, "settling for less in this world is worse than being forever imprisoned in the cruelest month that hints at the coming of a sweeter season but never actually delivers on its promise."

The president strokes his beard slowly with the fingers of his right hand and takes a deep breath. "So many people in this world settle for the cruelest month when they could have July," he says. "It's as if, after surviving an interminable winter, they have no knowledge of the warmth and beauty of summer with its iridescent butterflies and cochineal hummingbirds. Instead, they settle for a depressing tundra with a few wilted plants that serve as false harbingers of a summer that will never come.

"These men and women might even believe that summer is a myth and that what they're experiencing in the existential moment is all there is. So, their desperate fingers cling to the few pleasures to be found in the cold, forever half-gloom of the cruelest month."

At that moment, Jack sees a flash of light out of the corner of his eye. When he looks up at the dome overhead, he sees that the blue is gone, supplanted by gunmetal. The dark clouds glare down into the sanctuary, their puffy faces full of hostility. The unconditioned air of the massive room is thick with humidity.

"Rosalind Russell once quipped that 'Life is a banquet, and most poor suckers are starving to death,'" the professor comments with a smile as he removes his jacket and throws it onto a nearby pew. "Settling for less is like starving to death when the banquet is spread out in front of your face. Why in the name of all that's holy would you settle for less when there's more right under your nose?"

The president pauses and touches the corner of his right temple again. "What are the ways we settle for so much less on this planet when banquets are waiting to be enjoyed? There are dozens of ways—so many that I can't list them all. Today, I will mention four examples of settling, and develop one."

An explosion of thunder crashes against the old castle like an ocean wave against a breakwater, rattling the glass in the cupola far above the sanctuary floor. Jack cannot imagine being anywhere safer in a storm than in this impregnable fortress.

The speaker turns and walks over to the central aisle. As he slowly makes his way down the blood-red carpet between the pews, he says, "First of all, during our eighty years on this planet, many women and men settle for experiencing life with only one set of senses. They are content to interact with the world around them through their physical senses only when there is available to them a quiver full of spiritual senses capable of accessing a whole different dimension of reality. Is it any wonder that so many people are bored and empty or even contemplating suicide? They simply don't possess the faculties to explore a whole other aspect of reality, the one that's eternal and ultimately fulfilling.

"Secondly," the professor says as he glances up at the huge balcony, "every human on this planet apprehends God in one of three ways. Some men and women settle for believing that there is no God at all. He is simply a figment of the human imagination. Others believe that God is an impersonal pantheistic entity who flows through all creation—trees, rocks, water, animals, humans, and everything else in the universe. Then there are those who see God as a separate, personal Being who made everything and therefore is above and outside of His creation.

"A simple metaphor to clarify these three perspectives that we refer to as atheism, pantheism, and theism is to view all of humanity as actors in a play. The pressing question that demands an answer is who wrote the play. Many of us settle for believing that there is no playwright at all—meaning that we're alone in the universe—or that the playwright is merely an impersonal force that does not see us or love us. How empty it is when humans settle for these two inadequate beliefs about God.

"Of course, theists believe there is a personal God who wrote the play, constructed the stage, and created the actors. We are not alone in the universe but were made to have a relationship with the Divine Playwright that is more intimate than any you can have with a human—even your best friend."

The president stops and looks first to his right and then to his left. After a lengthy pause, he says, "The third way we settle for less in this universe is by exchanging greater things for lesser things, superior for inferior. We're like a child who naively trades a thousand feet of prime lakeshore property for a pretty stone because he does not comprehend the value of a property deed. The rock is so observable, so shiny, so smooth against his skin. Like that boy, physical pleasure in our hands seems so immediately attractive to our earthly senses that we cannot delay our gratification for one that is further off and perceived by a totally different constellation of senses.

"Those of us who love God know we're all made to worship something," the professor says as he looks back at Jack and the other members of the new cohort. "It's built into our DNA. We all wittingly or unwittingly choose something to worship whether it's our own bodies with their firm abs, toned pecs, and physical beauty, or a favorite sports team, or nature, or money, or material possessions, or pets, or another man or woman, or power over others, or—you name it. Humanity is capable of being sadly indiscriminate when it comes to worship. Incredibly, there are even some who worship feet or inflatable animals. Talk about bowing down to idols! Talk about settling!"

The speaker compresses his lips together tightly, and they disappear into the jungle of his beard. Then he admonishes, "Please be wise about adages such as, 'Tomorrow is overrated.' Advertisers and philosophers today encourage us to settle for fleeting pleasures at the expense of eternal adventures and priceless treasures. Do you have eyes to see this deception, men and women?

"And don't be seduced by the words of the Roman poet Horace who said, 'Carpe diem, quam minimum credula postero,' which loosely translated means, 'Seize the day, putting very little trust in the future.' This aphorism is married to the belief that the material world is all there is, so 'go for the gusto' and indulge your physical senses before you croak because there ain't nothin' to live for after you're buried six-feet under, or your ashes are scattered to the wind."

The president of the Academy walks back to the front of the sanctuary. "Here again," he says, turning to face his audience, "we encounter settling for lesser things over greater things because we don't believe in life after death; we don't see the spiritual world all around us. 'Today is all there is,' we arrogantly declare. 'This physical world is the total of existence.'"

Dr. McNeely glances up at a lightning flash that briefly sets the glass dome on fire with brilliant radiance. Then he looks back down and says, "The fourth and final way you settle for so much less in your brief lifetime occurs when you fail to see that you're born a warrior into a universal conflict and instead settle for believing that you're merely an evolved beast frittering away a meaningless life in an accidental world.

"If we embrace this mentality, we're back at the 'seize the day' credo where we don't see life for what it is. We live as if our destiny is simply to experience as much passion as we can during our eighty years on this planet before we return to the dust. We're a mere hedonistic mist that appears ever so briefly in the universe, and then—poof—we're gone, never to be seen again!

Fortunately for us," the speaker says as he dabs at his forehead with a handkerchief, "God clearly informs us that He created us and that He has a purpose for our lives. He announces to all who believe in Him that He will miraculously create new hearts within us replete with spiritual eyesight, hearing, taste, touch, and smell. Then, we will hear His call to join the underground resistance and battle against the powers of darkness that currently control both the material and spiritual realms we inhabit—and I'm not referring to human powers here. We're not called to go to war against them but to love them and speak the good news to them."

The school administrator pauses for a moment and then announces, "Not only will God develop new spiritual senses within us to help us perceive the war going on around us; He also will equip us with spiritual armor and weapons so we can engage our opponent who is not made of flesh and blood.

"This enemy is far more powerful and frightening than a mere human. Fictional magic with its wands and potion is futile against the prince of darkness," he warns, his deep voice rising in volume. "Lightsabers are objects of fantasy while our enemy is as real as this sanctuary that rises up all around us.

"So, never forget," the professor says with urgency, "your life in this world is anything but ordinary; unless, of course, you settle for a mundane existence. God calls you to the great adventure. He calls you to the battle. He comes to open your eyes to see that life is far more than what you experience with your physical senses.

"Do you believe this? Will you choose not to settle for a severely limited view of the universe that restricts reality to the material and the mortal?"

Dr. McNeely makes a steeple with his fingers and touches it to his lips. "I'm not a big movie watcher," he confesses in a calmer tone, "but once every blue moon, a movie captures my attention. Several years ago, a friend of mine suggested I watch The Matrix, a science fiction flick that came out in the late 90s. I took his advice and found myself intrigued by the movie.

"To summarize the plot, this futuristic movie follows a small band of men and women whose eyes have been opened to see that the everyday reality humans believe they are experiencing is, in fact, an illusion. They discover that they are being held captive by machines that possess artificial intelligence. These machines dupe humans into believing that they are going about their normal lives when in truth, their bodies are confined to pod-like incubators while their brains are manipulated by a computer program. Only a few humans who have escaped the control of the computer-generated reality perceive that they are enslaved."

"My point here," he says as he scans the huge sanctuary that could accommodate two thousand more people, "is that the storyline of this movie provides a chilling parallel to what is occurring in the world we currently live in.

"Of course, we're not enslaved by machines possessing artificial intelligence that manipulate our brains. Rather—" here the professor pauses for a long time and his eyes burn more brightly—"rather, we're enslaved by spiritual forces of darkness that deceive us into believing that we're nothing but earthly creatures living in a terrestrial world whose only purpose is to eat, drink, sleep, have sex, get rich, acquire things at the mall or online, play video games, be entertained, watch football, binge on TV series, and worship one of the things I just mentioned. We're deceived into settling for so little when God has created us for so much more!"

Jack hears heavy rain beating on the roof of the sanctuary far above. The retreating thunder that had been growling for a long time has fallen silent.

"For those of you who have seen the Matrix, my question for you is this: What will you choose to believe? Will you take the blue pill and settle for enslavement to deception, or will you take the red pill and join the underground band of warriors whose opened eyes perceive that all of us have been enslaved by spiritual powers of darkness?

"God's Word speaks clearly about this insurgency against the unseen enemy: 'For we do not wrestle against flesh and blood, but against the rulers, against the authorities, against the cosmic powers over this present darkness, against the spiritual forces of evil in the heavenly places. Therefore, take up the whole armor of God'—which includes all the spiritual senses—'that you may be able to withstand in the evil day, and having done all, to stand firm.'"

The professor clears his throat and laughs. "We're not talking *Star Wars or Harry Potter* here, men and women. I'm not referring to a frolicking Sci-fi romp through the universe or fictional powers and potions. I'm talking about a real battle between light and darkness unfolding in the world you currently live in if—if you have eyes to see it. If.

"Okay," the president says, qualifying, "*Star Wars* and *Harry Potter* and *The Matrix* and *The Lord of the Rings* and the countless superhero movies out there all contain distant rumors and rumblings of this unseen tension between light and darkness. Their limitation is that they are fiction. Their strength is that they point to the non-fiction reality beneath the material world that inspires them.

"This Academy exists because all of us here believe that God's Word exposes the existence of this universal strife," Dr. McNeely says. "Scripture informs us that we're born into a world at war. Because we have this word of truth, we're not limited to hearing whispers of the supernatural in a fiction book or left to wonder why our hearts are so passionately aroused by cosmic tales of titanic conflicts that unfold on the silver screen. Oh, no. The Bible informs us that we're living smack-dab in the middle of this battle with darkness. Whether we choose to embrace it as reality or not, we're up to our eyeballs in it.

"Tragically, many people trudge through a lifetime without giving a single thought to this truth. *A lifetime.* They're seduced into believing that only the material is real."

The professor falls silent for a long time. Fingers of rain thrum on the roof and the glass dome of the medieval castle. The pause is so long that some students begin to wriggle with discomfort. Dr. McNeely massages his mustache with the thumb and forefinger of his right hand as if contemplating what to say next.

Finally, he says gravely, "Students, listen very carefully to what I'm saying here: We're not born to drift through this world with a depressing aimlessness and chronic restlessness that, at best, can only be briefly medicated by drugs, alcohol, sex, novels, extreme thrills or even the escape of sleep. God calls our hearts to come awake so that we might join the resistance; so that we might fight with our brothers and sisters around the world against the darkness that desires to rob every human of a purposeful life and convince them to settle for only fleeting passions that blaze briefly but then dissipate into nothingness. Talk about a war of the worlds!"

The speaker lifts his chin slightly, and his jaw tightens with passion. "The very reason most of you have matriculated at this school is that you desire to be uncommonly brave, highly trained frontline warriors in the resistance. You have chosen not to settle for the drudgery of living as oblivious civilians who don't know or even care that a war is raging beyond their sight and hearing. Ignorance is bliss—or deadly."

Dr. McNeely smiles as he walks back toward the platform and then turns to gaze at the men and women in the pews. "So, why do people settle for so much less?" he asks. "Maybe they're unaware of God's existence, blinded by the veil that the enemy pulls over every human eye. Possibly, they struggle to embrace God's existence because they have internal resistances that might be intellectual, more often emotional, and most often rooted in pride and rebellion. They might love something else more than God and refuse to surrender it—an idol of some type; or they could fear the personal consequences of believing in God, convinced that the suffering and loss they might experience will cost them too much."

The president pauses and, one after the other massages the corner of both eyes. Then he says in his reverberating bass voice, "My challenge to all of you today is to never settle for fleeting, ultimately empty pleasures when you can know the God who created the universe with its two hundred billion galaxies.

"Our Milky Way galaxy alone is 100,000 light-years in diameter. Did you know that it would take the Voyager spacecraft two billion years to travel the entire length of our galaxy? How amazingly huge is that! But our galaxy is small compared to the Hercules, a galaxy that is 1.5 million light-years across!

"I don't know about you," the professor says, shaking his head, "but I don't have nearly enough faith to believe that such a gargantuan outer space came about by accident. If the universe was indeed created by an intelligent designer, a truth I believe with all my heart and mind, then this Creator is mammoth. But I challenge you not to seek God just because He's incomprehensibly large. Seek Him because He is loving and personal as well, appearing in this world wearing our skin in the person of Jesus Christ. Is there anything better than friendship with the awesome Creator who made everything and puts breath in your lungs?"

The professor pauses briefly and then lifts both of his arms toward the lofty ceiling. "Let your amazing adventures at the Academy begin," he announces loudly. "You'll never forget the next two years because they'll take you far beyond this world!"

As the audience in the sanctuary applauds the president's speech, Jack glances down the scarred wooden pew and sees Aly. She is leaning forward, and her eyes are shining. As he watches her, the young Thai-Saudi woman lifts her hands slowly to her head. They hesitate and hover there for some time. Eventually, she carefully removes her hijab as if it is woven glass. With small, purposeful fingers, she gently folds the black cloth on her lap with ceremonious finality. Then she bows her head and closes her eyes. Jack is so captivated by the moment that he does not hear the closing benediction.

"*She is such a betrayer!*" a grating voice mutters from a layer of reality not perceived by human senses. "*She turned her back on her faithful mother, her proud father, and her heroic brother. She'll pay for this act of betrayal. She and every member of the 'scimitar society' must understand that vacating the faith will be punished without mercy."*

"*He will soon find her!*" another voice growls icily. "*He will appear and deliver justice to this traitor who dares to abandon the faith.*"

"*Yes,*" the last voice intones as its owner smiles horribly. "*She will be dead within the month.*"

As the convocation attendees stand up and move toward the doors, Dr. Livingstone announces in a loud voice that is all but swallowed up by the cavernous sanctuary, "First-year students, remember that classes begin tomorrow. Also, be sure to check your individual schedules. Some of you begin spelunking tonight."

CHAPTER 4

Rachel's Spelunking

Shortly after supper, Rachel leaves her classmates in the Agatha room and negotiates a maze of wood-paneled hallways decorated with striking paintings and elegant statues ensconced in niches in the walls. She pins her short auburn hair behind her ears as she ascends six flights of stairs to the top of the huge building that huddles between the sanctuary and the dormitory. The stone steps are smooth and slightly concaved by use. Rachel wonders how many hundreds of thousands of feet have ascended and descended these stairs over the previous century.

Eventually, she finds herself standing at the half-closed office door that has a name-bar affixed to it that reads, *M. B. Livingstone*. She is breathing quickly and is reminded yet again that she needs to lose weight and work out more often. Whatever happened to that season in her life when she exercised multiple times a day?

Ignoring the accompanying accusations—they are cutting and condemning and ever so familiar—she knocks quietly on the heavy wooden door that must be at least ten feet in height. Even as she stands there alone in the hallway, she feels the invisible presence of shame flow like burning lava down her body all the way to her toes. She is totally covered by the creeping filth. Her cheeks flush with warmth, and she knows they must look as red as a pair of ripe September apples.

A voice that sounds to Rachel like gentle rain on rose petals invites her to enter. Some of the invisible shame inexplicably lifts from her spirit as she walks into a room that looks more like a farm kitchen than an academic office.

Colorful flowers arranged in ceramic pitchers and copper vases rest on several small tables in the room. The walls are decorated with pictures of golden fields, shining ponds, rusting water pumps, and framed needlepoint designs. An old spice rack hangs on the back wall of the office beneath a weathered wooden sign that reads, "A cheerful heart is good medicine." A sweet aroma of apple spice lingers in the air, dispensed by candles burning on several small shelves attached to the walls.

Dr. Livingstone stands up and embraces Rachel in a gentle hug. More shame sloughs off the young woman's soul.

"You have a homey office," Rachel says in her Bostonian accent that has not been completely erased by her years in Mystic. "I remember wanting to bring barn wood into my dorm room at college, but my roommates thought I was crazy," she announces with a loud laugh that belies her anxiety. "They accused me of being a country hick."

"Roommates," the professor says with a gentle wave of her hand. Then she exclaims, "Rachel, you did an amazing job playing the organ today. You made that old instrument come alive like I've never heard before! You're quite gifted, young lady."

Uncomfortable with the compliment, Rachel shrugs and says nothing. Then she abruptly glances at the professor's nameplate and asks, "What does M.B. stand for?"

"Well, you get right to the point, don't you?" Dr. Livingstone remarks with a smile on her lips and in her eyes. She chuckles softly and confides, "I grew up with—unique parents. That's a euphemism for eccentric. It was the sixties, and they were living in San Francisco and moved easily into the hippie culture. They wore extreme bellbottom jeans, psychedelic tie-dye shirts, and vests with fringes. My mother even had the granny glasses though her vision was perfect," she remarks with a shake of her head.

"So, it was quite natural for them to christen their first child with a hippie name. M. B. actually stands for Moon Beam. My brother was named River. Some people confused our names and called me Moon River, which you don't know is the name of a song made famous by a dead man named Andy Williams. It was all very humorous.

"By the way," the smiling woman adds, "all the students at the Academy eventually call me Embee, so feel free to do the same."

Rachel has already learned from some of the women in her dorm that the professor is commonly referred to by her initials. She has also been told that Embee often wears long dresses with lace or denim jackets with matching pants. Even now, Rachel notices that the woman sitting in front of her is wearing large loop earrings and her two necklaces—the cross and the peace symbol.

Before Rachel can ask her next question, Embee anticipates it and says, "I wear a cross, yes, and a peace symbol as well. Why the peace symbol? I don't wear it because I'm an aficionado of the 60s and the hippie culture or because I have deep admiration for Gerald Holtom, its purported designer. No, I wear it because when Jesus died, he broke the power of the cross, the power of death. My peace sign is a personal symbol of Jesus' conquering death for all of us."

"Cool," Rachel responds as her eyes scan the room. When she opens her mouth to ask another question, her mentor interrupts and says, "Rachel, this time is for you. Let's focus on you, okay?"

"Is this therapy?" Rachel blurts out abruptly as she looks at her mentor. "I mean, are you going to shrink me?"

Embee laughs softly and folds her hands on her lap. "This is not therapy, although it incorporates aspects of it. Remember, we call it 'spelunking,' as silly as that term may sound. It's a time for me to listen to your heart and be a mirror that reflects you back to yourself so you can know yourself more objectively. I do this under the direction of the Holy Spirit, by the way. That's what makes our time distinctly different than secular therapy. The master Counselor is here with us to teach you whatever you need to learn about Him and yourself. It's all about growing you and glorifying Him."

The auburn-haired young woman from Mystic looks at the professor and remarks dryly, "So, the point of all this is to know myself better? Sounds a lot like therapy to me. My mother sent me to several counselors in the past."

"Before we travel down the road too far, Rachel, I want to invite God to lead our time together," the professor states. Without further comment, she bows her head with its flowing silver locks and says, "Holy Spirit, be present with us tonight. Give me the ability to hear what Rachel is saying as well as what she's not saying. Lead us to her heart. Above all, help both of us to hear what you're saying. In the name of Jesus, Amen."

When Dr. Livingstone looks up, she sees that Rachel is smiling broadly.

"What is it, Rachel?"

"I always smile stupidly when I'm nervous," the twenty-four-year-old woman confesses. "See, you already have some material to work with," she adds with a muted laugh.

The maternal listener nods and looks directly into Rachel's eyes. "I've reread your application to the Academy in preparation for our time together tonight. Since I'm not big on grilling you with lots of questions, let's just jump in with any thoughts you have about being adopted. Several of your comments about that experience are intriguing to me."

Rachel has always talked a lot. It comes natural to her since her mother has always been an excellent example of the behavior. Even more than that, Rachel's loquacity serves as a smokescreen to hide her deep emotions. Her habit is to talk a lot but never reveal much about herself. Tonight, however, she is disarmed by her caring listener and quickly raises the blind that typically covers her heart. For the next seventy-five minutes, the adopted woman from Connecticut via Boston talks almost non-stop about what it was like growing up in her family.

Eventually, Embee Livingstone announces that she needs to bring their spelunking session to a close but that she wants to summarize what Rachel shared before they wrap up.

"What you told me tonight," Embee begins, "is that your adoptive father was an emotionally distant man who was highly dedicated to his job as an anesthetist. Your adoptive mother confided to you at a young age that your father ideally had wanted a boy and was disappointed when they settled on you. She instructed you to perform well in everything you did to gain your father's attention and approval.

"Unfortunately, her admonition led you to believe that you wouldn't be loved unless you were perfect. In addition to that, your musical and academic efforts were largely ignored by your more athletically-focused father."

Rachel nods her head slowly. Encouraged, Dr. Livingstone continues her summary.

"Although you were closer to your adoptive mother than to your adoptive father, that changed when she unexpectedly became pregnant and had a baby shortly after your seventh birthday. At that point, your mother became highly invested in her biological daughter, Celeste, and largely ignored you.

"An even sadder complicating event was that your sister developed severe asthma when she was young, so your mother spent many nights sleeping in Celeste's bedroom, away from you. You were banned from your sister's room because your anxious mother feared you might expose her to germs that would result in a respiratory illness and potentially lead to Celeste's death."

Embee pauses, her eyes suddenly sad, and looks at Rachel. "Meanwhile, you spent all your nights alone in your room. Your only companion was your favorite stuffed animal and the food you snuck into your room to comfort yourself. Not surprisingly, as a teenager, you struggled briefly with anorexia and later with bulimia. You engaged in binge eating and purging—most frequently at night in the solitude of your bedroom."

Embee stops talking, and Rachel looks down at her hands. She thinks they look thicker than they should be. Eventually, she looks back up at her listener and replies, "Yes, that pretty much sums up my life, at least in broad brush strokes."

"Now, before you leave tonight, Rachel, I want to share a few observations with you," the woman with the silver waterfall confides softly.

The auburn-haired student nods her head slowly and crosses her legs.

"Always remember that what happens to you in life is not nearly as important as how you respond to it," Embee says with eyes that shine with earnestness.

Rachel is so hungry for words from a mentor that she literally leans closer to hear what the professor is going to say next.

"I suspect that the pain triggered by your adoptive parents was exacerbated by the fact that you already felt unwanted by your birth parents." Embee speaks slowly as if uncertain that all her observations are accurate.

"Feeling unloved by two sets of parents led you to protect yourself from the acute pain that accompanies rejection and abandonment. So, you built a wall around your young heart to prevent yourself from getting hurt any further."

At this point, Dr. Livingstone pauses and tilts her head to one side. "Ironically—and sadly," she comments with furrowed brows, "your protective wall today prevents anybody from getting close to you. So, while you very effectively protect yourself from harm, you also protect yourself from love."

Rachel is unusually quiet as she absorbs the words from her mentor. She presses her fingers together and scans the walls of the quaint office before she finally looks at the professor and announces, "I don't think you're wrong."

Dr. Livingstone sits up straight and leans toward her student. With passion in her eyes and urgency in her voice, she says, "At the beginning of it all, young lady, Adam and Eve lived in perfect relationship with the Triune God. All was right in the world. Peace, love, joy, and intimacy all converged like beautiful threads in a tapestry of shimmering glory. Nothing in all creation disturbed the holy dance between God and His two image-bearers."

Embee's gaze drifts away from Rachel and, with unseeing eyes, she stares over her mentee's shoulder. "But then the deceiver came," she says so quietly that Rachel strains to hear her. "The father of lies...the tempter... the first rebel who was so full of pride and defiance against the Lover of his heart. This hater of God and humanity successfully tempted our first parents to disobey their loving Creator."

The silver-haired woman looks back at Rachel and says, "So it was that what I call the *Devastating Separation* descended on the universe. *The Great Divide* rose up, and a previously unimaginable divorce ripped apart the tapestry of love and glory. In its place, a heavy blanket of darkness and death fell over the Cosmos."

The older woman sighs and says, "Rachel, God created us for amazing love and intimacy—to be known to the depths of our hearts; to never experience loneliness or abandonment. Never! But then the dividing wall rose up. Shame and pride became our father and mother.

"Ever since that terrible day, our default position has been to rebel, to run away, to hide from the divine lover of our hearts."

Embee pauses as she plays with the large loop dangling from her left ear.

Then she announces, "Never underestimate the damage caused by our disobedience in the Garden, Rachel. Never. It changed everything! After that awful day, we abandoned the divine playwright only to serve an imposter.

"Yes, thanks be to God, He sent His Son to deliver us from sin and death, but we must be aware that every day we still fight the battle against separation. You're familiar, Rachel, with three of its offspring: Rejection, abandonment, and aloneness."

The professor tilts her head to one side again and touches her chin with her long index finger. "Our most natural response is to build walls, my daughter. It's in the DNA of our fallen nature. The mortar that holds these walls together might be anger, sadness, fear, abandonment, contempt, shame, pride—even grief.

"Rachel, you must identify your walls with their cementing mortar and tear them down at all costs. Yes, at all costs. Even if it's the most difficult thing you'll ever do, you absolutely must tear them down. They have the power to separate you from God and others for an eternity."

Dr. Livingstone, who has now become Embee to Rachel, sits back in her chair and thoughtfully steeples her long, slender fingers. "Okay, then," she says, "let's conclude the same way we began the night. Let's talk to the One who collects all your tears and puts them in a bottle," the professor says in a warm tone that reaches out and emotionally hugs the younger woman.

"Lord Jesus," the mentor begins, "I thank you for Rachel Biandi. Your Word informs us that she is fearfully and wonderfully made, and her heart is precious to you as you tell her in Isaiah 43."

"Sadly, sometimes in this world, the people who bear the name 'parent' do not have the supplies we need. They are unable to be present for us with the love we yearn for. So, we turn to other things to comfort ourselves—and you know how well that worked for me, don't you, Daddy," she says with a chuckle.

"You've come to heal all the wounds that Rachel has experienced from others but also to reveal the unhealthy ways she has responded that only magnify her pain and isolation. Empower her to open the door of her heart so you might fully enter in. Amen, Father."

After the prayer, Rachel thanks her professor and quickly exits the kitchen office. She hurries down the stairs in the growing darkness and finds an empty room just off the Agatha dining area, where she collapses to the floor. Even before her knees touch the floor, she begins to weep uncontrollably. The only words she can choke out are, "Abba, please don't leave me, too. Please don't."

Back in the dorm, Jack, Armando, Stewart, and Jonathan have just finished planning their next adventure into the underworld beneath the blind room. Jonathan is ready to walk out the door when Jack asks him, "By the way, what can we expect from the Windsor Warfare class tomorrow?"

The upperclassman snorts and chuckles. "Dr. Windsor is one tough dude, and he's the perfect man for the job."

"What's that supposed to mean?" Armando inquires.

"He's the right professor for that class—the whole warfare thing," Jonathan replies. "Believe it or not, the man spent thirty years in the military retiring with the rank of colonel. If I remember right, he was in the 101st Airborne. He just retired five, maybe six years ago. Rumor has it that he still has a fragment of a .50 BMG bullet lodged in his back from a sniper rifle in Fallujah."

Stewart adjusts his glasses and opens a file cabinet in the basement of his brain. Then he launches into a commentary that Armando receives as condescending.

"The 101st Airborne Division is also known as the *Screaming Eagles.* They're a specialized light infantry unit that can mobilize at a moment's notice. They've come to be known as the *tip of the spear.*"

"I'm out of here," Jonathan interjects abruptly as he glances at Jack with a shrug and then heads toward the door. When he reaches the hallway, he remarks over his shoulder, "A word to the wise: you don't want to get on Windsor's bad side. He's a cross between a pit bull and a wolverine. But if you ever find yourself in a battle, he's the man you want leading you into harm's way."

That night as he tosses on his bunk bed in the dorm room, Jack has nightmare after nightmare. In the last one, he sees a hundred robed and hooded figures gathered around an altar with four horns, one in each corner. The fire that burns on the altar is green, and it casts grotesque shadows on the surrounding walls of a cave. A choking cloud of smoke clogs the subterranean room. Jack hears a deep voice growl, "*The man will be stricken where it hurts the most. The fallen ones will strike him directly in the heart.*"

The figure who had uttered the threat throws back his hooded head and unleashes horrible laughter that reverberates off the rock walls of the cave. Then the terrible creature snaps its head in the direction where Jack is standing and stabs a long, withered finger toward him.

At that moment, a surge of electricity explodes in Jack's brain, and he throws himself onto the floor.

CHAPTER 5

Windsor's War

After breakfast in the towering Agatha Room, the micro-cohort—consisting of Aly, Rachel, Stewart, Armando, Jack, and Emily—along with the other members of their macro-cohort, move toward their first academic experience of the new term. The class, which focuses on spiritual warfare, meets in a room beneath the sanctuary. Jack, who is in the lead, doesn't even bother to grope on the wall for a light switch since Jonathan had informed him that there is no electricity in the Catacombs. Instead, he carefully descends the steps into the nether gloom using his phone flashlight.

"What's up with this?" one young woman asks as she follows Jack down the steps. "Why do we meet in some creepy basement for the warfare class?"

"Yeah, it's seriously dark down here," another student comments.

"I think that's the whole point of it," Jack says over his shoulder.

"What do you mean?" a third student asks.

"Our warfare is with darkness," Jack replies. "So, what better place to study darkness but in the darkness."

When he reaches the bottom of the steps, Jack's flashlight reveals what looks like a dungeon. It is a large room, but not tall—no more than seven feet in height. The floor is dirt, and the walls are stone. The air is damp and earthy. Soon, Jack is joined by more than two dozen other students.

"So, where do we go from here?" one of them asks.

The students' flashlights rake through the darkness in search of a classroom door or a sign pointing them toward their destination.

"Let's spread out and see what we can find," Rachel suggests.

"I'll go this way," Jack says, directing his light straight ahead toward a dim passage leading off the main room.

Jack makes his way across the dirt floor and enters the narrow passage. He penetrates fifty yards into the tunnel before it occurs to him that he is no longer in the basement beneath the citadel. He has undoubtedly gone well beyond it.

"Wow, no wonder they call this place the Catacombs," he comments to the student behind him. "It just keeps going and going."

A voice from behind him agrees. He recognizes it as Emily's. Turning to greet her, Jack sees that Aly and Rachel are also behind him. Rachel laughs and comments with sarcasm in her voice, "I've had lots of bad dreams where I can't find my classroom on the first day of school, but this is ridiculous."

Everyone laughs, and Jack says, "You can say that again."

Without a moment's hesitation, Rachel said, "I've had lots of bad dreams where I can't find my classroom—"

"Okay, Rachel, ha, ha," Emily says.

Just then, Jack sees a glow in the distance. "Hey, gang, what's this?" He picks up his pace and soon finds himself standing at the entrance to a room on the right side of the passage.

"Congratulations! You've located your objective," a voice booms from inside the room. "Welcome to Warfare 101, where careful reconnaissance is critical to victory."

Jack enters a gloomy room illuminated on every side by oil-fed lanterns set in niches cut into the walls. As he scans the room, his first thought is to wonder how the basement is ventilated since the oil lamps generate carbon dioxide as they burn.

If Stewart were here, he would know, Jack thinks to himself with a smile.

As he walks deeper into the dungeon classroom, Jack notices four long tables and a small army of old wooden chairs situated around them. In the front of the room, his dark face melting into the dim surroundings of the cave, he sees a figure standing as straight as a flagpole. Moving toward the man who is dressed in khaki pants and a sky-blue shirt, Jack says, "Dr. Windsor, I presume."

"You have presumed correctly," the professor replies curtly. "And I presume you are Jack Sutherington."

Jack stops and cocks his head to one side. "You know my name," he observes.

"I make it a point to know all my people," the man says. *He speaks like someone who makes it a point to know a lot of things*, Jack thinks to himself.

By this time, other students are flowing into the gloomy underground bunker and filing into the rows between the tables. Jack turns and follows suit. He finds a chair between Armando and Emily and sits down. Before long, everyone is seated at the four long tables.

Armando leans over to Jack as he unzips his backpack. "Can't say I've ever attended class in a cave before," he quips to his roommate.

"That makes two of us—probably all of us," Jack replies with a wry smile.

Dr. Windsor begins to pace slowly back and forth in the front of the room. He looks straight ahead. His hands are clutched behind his back. The professor is several inches over six feet tall, thin, and fit. His boots thump against the dirt floor. He says nothing for a long time.

Students begin to squirm as the man continues to walk in front of the cave classroom without uttering a word. Jack senses that he is not a common man. Oddly, he elicits both fear and comfort within Jack. He agrees with Jonathan that this is the man you want leading you into battle.

Eventually, the professor stops pacing and turns to face the students. "A ruse de guerre," he announces—"literally translated as a 'ruse of war'—belongs to a classification of warfare that entails military deception."

The man's voice is strong in timbre and loud in volume. "These components of deception usually involve creative, highly intelligent, even unorthodox stratagems by which an enemy seeks to gain an advantage over a foe. A classic albeit mythical example of military deception appears in Virgil's Aeneid. As you may recall, the Greeks finally gain the victory over the stubbornly resistant city of Troy through the insertion of the Trojan horse.

"Real-life examples of deceptive stratagems involve the use of spies, ambushes, false radio messages, and other types of disinformation." He ticks the examples off on his fingers as he walks back and forth.

"Article 23 of the Hague Convention of 1907 prohibits ruses that are considered perfidious or treacherous, and therefore unworthy of noble warfare," the professor declares in his no-nonsense voice. "Not that enemies are always found in compliance with these articles, of course. Integrity is often in short supply during wartime."

Dr. Windsor continues to pace in front of the room. More accurately, Jack perceives that the ex-military professor is marching slowly. His strides are uniform, crisp, and rhythmic.

Eventually, he paces closer to the table in the front of the room and eyes each individual student as he walks by. For the first time, Jack gets a close look at the man's stern, slightly pocked face with its rock-hard jaw and bloodless lips. Everything about his body appears square and orderly.

"It is essential for you to know from the outset that our spiritual enemy is absolutely not noble," the professor states as he lifts his chin slightly. "He does not adhere to established rules of warfare. Quite to the contrary, he will use any means at his disposal to discourage you, defeat you, destroy you, kill you. Do you understand this, people?" The man's words are not so much a question as they are a statement. He is commanding them to understand this truth about the enemy.

At that moment, Jack feels the familiar but unwanted presence settle, uninvited, on his chest. It is the same sensation he experienced when walking by the lake and exploring the tunnel. He glances around at Armando and Emily, but they appear oblivious to the strange phenomenon. He finds it unusual that he is encountering the heaviness so often at the Academy. It is almost as if evil is more concentrated on and under the campus.

"In this class, we will address warfare and the enemy," the retired colonel states. "The mere fact that you are attending the Academy and sitting in this classroom renders you a high priority target. Make no mistake: You are in the crosshairs of the enemy. Do you understand this, people?

"The prince of darkness will leave men and women alone, even believers in the Almighty God, if he considers them of little threat to his purposes. But if one person begins to stand against the powers of darkness, the enemy will promptly send ten messengers from the pit of hell to defeat the brazen image bearer by any means at his disposal, none of them fair or predictable."

The flickering flames of the oil lamps cast undulating shadows across the room and over the professor's face. The whole scene feels strangely surreal to Jack. He shivers involuntarily and attempts to take a deep breath.

Dr. Windsor comes to a stop in front of the table and holds Jack's eyes prisoner with his intense gaze. "During Operation Desert Shield, I flew deep into Iraqi territory in an Apache helo and helped to cut the accursed serpent in half. I witnessed the carnage on the Highway of Death. I later served in Afghanistan and had several run-ins with IEDs and enemy snipers, not to mention countless RPGs."

The Screaming Eagle looks away from Jack and moves on to scrutinize Armando with his dark eyes.

"I've seen a lot in my lifetime, men and women; a lot of war, blood, and death. But I want you to know something that you must never forget. In the spiritual campaign between light and darkness, you are engaging a far more dangerous enemy with so much more at stake.

"In the battles that are fought in the material world, the worst that can happen is that people die physically. Don't get me wrong, that type of war is hellish, and death on the battlefield is often horrific. The sights, sounds, and smells are terrible. But in the spiritual battle that rages in the universe, people's souls and eternal destinies are at stake. The potential carnage is incalculable."

Dr. Windsor compresses his already bloodless lips and looks around the room, his countenance grave. The intensity of his gaze makes it appear that victory or defeat will be determined by the accuracy of his surveillance.

"Well, now you've heard it," he finally comments. "Now you know the reason for this course—to be aware of the enemy, firstly, and then to learn how to engage in spiritual warfare. So, let's get underway, people. You did bring your FMs with you today, I'm assuming." Again, the retired colonel is not asking a question so much as he is issuing a statement of expectation.

Everyone in the room begins to glance around at their classmates in adjacent chairs, wondering what this FM is that they are supposed to have with them.

"What's an FM?" Jack hears Armando inquire of the professor.

"Your Field Manual, of course," Dr. Windsor replies with a hint of impatience in his voice and consternation chiseled into his black-granite face. "You do know what an FM is, I would hope."

Everyone is at a loss until Stewart speaks up. "Are you making a veiled reference to our Bibles? If that's the case, I have mine right here in my backpack." The bespectacled intellect addresses the man before him as a familiar peer instead of someone to be respected or even feared.

Stew, you clearly lack social awareness, Jack thinks to himself as he cringes at his classmate and then observes Dr. Windsor for his reaction.

"Yes, young man, I'm referring to the Word of God," the retired officer says with surprising evenness. "The United States army has written doctrinal manuals that address every issue imaginable for soldiers out in the field. These manuals address survival skills, leadership development, operations—otherwise known as the fundamentals of fighting a war—and even skills relevant to identifying and disarming a booby-trap."

The professor pauses to make sure he has the attention of all his enlisted personnel before he adds, "As followers of Jesus Christ, you also have a field manual written by God Himself."

Jack nods his head in agreement as his eyes drift down to the man's khaki pants. He can't help but notice the perfectly straight crease running down the front of both legs. The black boots that they partially overlap are so shiny that Jack imagines he could see his face reflected in the mirror-like toes. The heels of the boots are almost touching, and Jack has the passing thought that the man looks like he's participating in a stationary drill on the parade ground.

"The truth you must always remember about field manuals," the colonel continues in a commanding voice that is only two levels below a bark, "is that they are meant for the field. They must not be gathering dust on the coffee table in your cozy, sunlit living room. It's essential that you take them everywhere you go to ensure your readiness for battle.

"When I was in the army, I carried my military field manual with me wherever I went. I took it with me in the Humvee when I was out doing reconnaissance. I also owned a handy pocket-size version that I carried in my cargo pants pocket. I rarely went anywhere without it.

"In the same way, you must never be without God's field manual so you'll be prepared for every eventuality you might encounter in spiritual battle."

Thirty pairs of eyes rivet on Dr. Windsor as he strides over to one side of the room. "I'm a man under authority," he asserts. "I'm under the generalship of Jesus Christ. You're under my authority. People are or will be under your authority one day. Do you see the pattern here, people? There's a hierarchy in the universe, a hierarchy built on authority, obedience, and respect. It goes without saying, of course, that authority must be earned."

The professor who helped subdue a physical enemy while in the army strides across the dirt floor to the other side of the room. He comes to a stop next to one of the gas lanterns that illuminates his face.

"Our current culture is not distinguished for its love of authority," he announces as he turns to face the students. "On the contrary, we are living in a world of choice, a world of individual rights. There are no absolutes in this world except the one that insists there are no absolutes. People demand what they want when they want it. If anyone denies them what they want, they're accused of violating their rights.

"No, our culture is not about obedience to authority," the retired colonel states. "Even morality is considered relative. There is no universal standard, people. There is no Field Manual. There is no absolute truth. It's all about pluralism and relativism. Truth is what you choose and what I choose it to be. Again, it's all about personal choice—about truthiness instead of truth.

"How do you think an army would function with no central authority and no FM to direct it?" the officer inquires of his troops as he scans the gloomy war room. "The result would be total chaos. And so it is that our current culture is in total disarray and retreating further and further from the frontlines every day."

The man pauses as he looks around the room, his eyes radiating purpose. At that moment, Jack notices that everything about the man is straight. His back is straight, his teeth are straight, the crease in his pants is straight, even his truth is straight as an arrow.

"Dr. Greenlay will venture further into the topic of the Word of Truth, so I'll leave that to him," the straight man says. "Suffice it to say that we need an authority in this world to direct our steps, and that authority is the Word of God. It's through a careful study of this Field Manual that we gain a clear understanding of warfare and the enemy as we move forward in this world."

The remainder of the first Warfare class is spent examining 2 Corinthians 10 in God's Field Manual. Dr. Windsor focuses on the three verses that refer to the battle for men and women's minds. He explains that the words found in this section of the FM inform the believer that even though they live in a physical world and are physical beings, they wage war with a weapon that is unlike the physical weapons of this world.

The professor teaches that instead of rifles, tank howitzers, bombs, and other explosive weapons, the ordnance that believers in Jesus wield is the powerful truth of God that exists not to destroy life but to give life. It is a weapon that, if used correctly and wisely, can tear down fortresses of falsehood that defy the absolute truth of God. It neutralizes all false arguments and every ungodly thought inserted deep within the minds of every human.

Professor Windsor concludes the class with one final challenge from 2 Timothy 2.

"If you didn't know it before today, people, I'm here to inform you that you've all been born into a war," he announces slowly as he looks down his straight nose at his students. "You, along with every other human being on this planet, must make two choices in this war. The first choice is whether you're going to trust in Jesus Christ as the God of the universe or if you're going to trust in yourself instead. This is the first crossroad we all encounter, the intersection where we decide whether to turn right or left.

"If you've chosen to believe in Jesus at the first crossroad, the second choice is whether you're going to live in this world as a civilian or a soldier. Civilians claim faith in Jesus but live like practical atheists. They do not walk by faith but by sight. They focus primarily on the things of this world instead of the command of Jesus to seek Him first. They stand on the sidelines because they're afraid to offend anybody. They value the praise of men more than the commendation of their general. As a chaplain once told me, they practice their faith in Jesus as if it is an extracurricular activity instead of their very life."

The colonel lifts his chin and again looks down his straight nose at his audience, but without arrogance. "Do not choose to be civilians, people," he admonishes. "Choose to be soldiers. Step up on the side of Light to fight the battle of the universe that makes Star Wars look like what it really is: a comic book.

"The war I speak of is real. To fight in it as a soldier of the Almighty

God is to engage in the most exciting adventure a human can experience. Yes, you will learn how to destroy every rebellious thought that stands proudly and willfully against God. Yes, you will learn truth and wield it with confidence. However, you will also learn something even more powerful. You will learn to internalize the force that created the universe, namely, the Lord Jesus Christ."

The professor pauses and makes eye contact with every student in the uneven light of the dungeon classroom. Then he asserts slowly, enunciating each word crisply, "You will live by Jesus' words in John 13 (ESV) where he says, 'A new commandment I give to you, that you love one another: just as I have loved you, you also are to love one another. By this all people will know that you are my disciples, if you have love for one another.'

"Do you hear the full meaning of this commandment?" Dr. Windsor inquires of his students. "We are called to be soldiers in a war, but our munitions are not hatred and judgment but mercy and love. We are called by Jesus to love even our enemies. He calls us to be revolutionaries who will transform the world by love and by the written word of truth."

When his admonishment has been uttered, the retired colonel falls silent and bows his head briefly as if in prayer. Then he looks up and dismisses the class with the enigmatic words, "We are done here, today, people. Come to class next time with *full battle rattle*."

The students sit transfixed in their chairs as they attempt to decipher the professor's parting message. They are motivated to understand him since the academic leader has already earned their full respect. In the end, it is Stewart, once again, who comments to his classmates, "I believe Dr. Windsor means that we need to bring our Field Manuals next time as part of our standard-issue equipment so that we can be fully prepared for spiritual warfare."

The light of recognition brightens the faces of the students in the room. Having understood the meaning of full battle rattle, they pack up their gear and file out of the subterranean war room to begin their trek back up to the world of light.

As one student exits the Catacomb classroom, Jack hears her quietly comment to her classmate about the total absence of Wi-Fi in the "bomb-shelter classroom."

When Jack finally turns to leave, he hears a voice call his name. He glances over his shoulder and sees the ex-officer summoning him with a nod of his head. Jack follows Emily to the end of the long table, then turns and approaches his professor.

Not sure what to expect, he stops in front of the man and says, "You wanted something, sir?" Unlike some of his classmates who have grown up in the south or served in the military, Jack rarely, if ever, addresses an authority with the word, "sir." But there is something different about this man.

Standing close to the professor, he sees the wrinkles creased into his face by the passing of time and the early invasion of white hair into his dark eyebrows and temples.

The colonel's eyes are so penetrating that Jack finds it more comfortable to look down at the perfect creases that descend to the shiny boots. When he finally does look back up again, he decides that the professor's eyes are two bullets fired at him with great velocity but somehow arrested before they could physically strike their target.

"You sense it, Jack Sutherington," the officer's voice speaks to him, as cold as steel.

Jack swallows hard and stammers, "What do you mean?"

"You perceive the darkness, young man," he says. "I saw it in your face today."

"What are you talking about, sir?" Jack inquires, his voice shakier than fifteen years ago when he was standing in front of an irate store owner following his first and last attempt at shoplifting.

"The more you perceive the presence of evil, the more you draw fire," the colonel insists in his sternest voice, almost angry in tone. His dark face is austere and foreboding.

Jack opens his mouth to ask for clarification, but the man's flinty eyes bore through him, and he scolds his student in a severe tone, "Don't be a fool, Sutherington! Wear your Kevlar. Wear it all the time, even when you're sleeping. There will be no respite for you. You're a target, and you're too soft!"

The ex-colonel and present-day academician stares at Jack for a moment longer. Then he turns sharply on his shiny black boots and strides away. Jack is left shaken and angry.

"*The man knows,*" a voice moans from the corner of the gloomy room. "*He sees it in him.*"

"*He sees it in him just as I first saw it in him down by the water,*" a second voice announces. "*He is a threat to our objectives.*"

"*We've known that for weeks, even months now, you fool,*" a third voice berates his fellow murderer. "*We know he's here by the design of the One of the One.*" Even before he is done talking, the speaker's whole being trembles, but he will never admit to himself it is fear that he feels at the thought of the Name above all names.

"*We must destroy him!*" the first being announces. "*We must separate his spirit from his body now!*"

"*You know we don't possess the power or the authority to kill his body to kill*," the third voice sneers. "*Instead, we must lure him to do himself in. We must tempt him into darkness so that he will come to believe that he is disqualified to serve disqualified.*

"*Shame and accusation have historically been effective with this worm. He has a chink in his armor he has. He has a soft spot that we must exploit yet again. It is a wound in his spirit that we must hammer must hammer like a bullet wound in his chest. Go and pound on it viciously pound on it. Both of you, go!*

"*Strike, hammer, batter, pummel and bash the ancient wound until he falls once again! No more will he be a soldier no more. He may even be reduced to something less than a civilian something less! Jack the crack! Jack the hack! Jack the tack! We will reduce him to a shadow of a shadow of himself.*

"*Image bearer? Ha! We will make him into a sack of bones. We will reduce him to a bone bearer instead of an image-bearer. Sticky, creaky, crumbling bones that break at a touch from our wicked digits that break. Jack the sack! Jack the sack of bones!*"

Raucous laugher rumbles in the dimension that exists somewhere between the material world and the heavenly realm.

Later that night, Jack is cruelly awakened by the familiar shock wave that tears through his brain. He jumps out of his bunk bed, gasping for breath. For a short time, he has no idea where he is. This time, mercifully, it takes only a few seconds for him to remember. Groaning, he collapses on his knees next to his bed and prays.

"How much longer, Lord?" he whispers into the darkness so as not to awaken his snoring roommate. "How much longer?"

When his racing heart slows to a trot, he crawls back into bed and immediately encounters the strong temptation of an old counterfeit comfort—the old broken road that offers a temporary escape from anguish and deep aloneness. The battle is fierce, but he resists—at least on this night.

CHAPTER 6

Silver Bay Lodge

The Kodiak bear is all of ten feet tall with paws the size of frying pans. Its mouth gapes as wide as an oven revealing huge teeth that can rip apart a small automobile. The long fangs are stained red with blood. The claws are even more impressive than the fangs, shooting out of the paws like razor-sharp knives. Usually fearless, Aly gasps and lets out a small cry when she rounds the corner and spots the 1500-pound killing machine.

When no one else makes a move to help Aly, Armando jumps between the small woman and the behemoth. "I will protect you, maiden in distress!" he cries in a chivalrous, accented voice.

The knight in shining armor holds his ground for several seconds, then doubles over in laughter and exclaims, "The bear is in a glass box, Aly! It's stuffed, or whatever you call it when an animal is preserved after death. Your life is not in danger," he announces, elongating the last word for humorous effect.

Aly removes her small hand from her mouth and rolls her eyes at Armando. "Thanks for announcing my stupidity to the entire civilized world," she says in a rare display of sarcasm. The guests in the lobby who had stopped to witness the shock of the young woman snicker and then move on about their day.

"Don't worry, Aly," Rachel says, touching her classmate's arm, "it surprised me, too."

"For future reference," Stewart informs Armando, "the correct term to describe the science of preserving a deceased animal's body is taxidermy. I have often referred to an animal so preserved as taxidermied. You may not find this word in some dictionaries, but it is frequently used as an adjective to describe the body of an animal that has been preserved through the art of taxidermy. Thus, you would correctly refer to this bear as the taxidermied polar bear."

Armando stares at his intellectual friend and then says, "If you tell me how to talk correctly one more time, Stew, I just may have to taxidermy you." He is not smiling as he speaks.

"Hey guys," Emily says, breaking up the tete-a-tete between Armando and Stewart, "we have to keep moving if we're going to be on time."

"Yeah, let's get going, guys," Jack agrees as he grabs Armando's arm and pulls his roommate forward.

As they pass through the lobby of the Silver Bay Lodge Hotel, Jack takes in the ambiance of the impressive room. He hears the squeaks and groans of the wooden floorboards beneath his feet. He smells the freshly varnished knotty pine wood that decorates the walls and the cathedral ceiling far above his head. He sees the lobby rising upward through all three stories of the lodge, the upper levels crowned with a wooden balustrade that encircles the rising lobby shaft on all four sides. He tastes the leathery flavor of the old bear skins hanging from the walls. In his imagination, he feels the breeze of history whispering around him, stirred by the men, women, and children over the past one-hundred and fifty years who have walked through the very same lobby.

Jack's eyes drift over the wagon wheel chandeliers adorned with eight lanterns apiece and down to the huge fieldstone fireplace whose mouth is black from years of smoke. His gaze then shifts to the massive floor-to-ceiling latticed windows at the far end of the lobby that afford a stunning view of the lake glistening in the distance. The still waters are painted rose-pink by the artist known as the rising sun.

Jack awakens from his reverie when the group of prospective hotel employees turn into a broad hallway that leads to several party rooms. Above the second room is a nameplate that reads, Lakeside Seminar Room. A small sign stapled onto a pinewood post directs them to the orientation meeting they have been summoned to attend.

Jack, Armando, Emily, Aly, Rachel, and Stewart sit down together at a long table on the right side of the spacious room. Like everything else in the lodge, the table and chairs are constructed of small pine logs, and the floor is covered with dark-stained pine planks. About twenty other students are in the room. Jack recognizes all of them from classes across the lake at the Academy.

While he is scanning the room, his roommate leans over to him and asks drolly, "Why do they call it knotty pine anyway? Did it do something bad? Get it? Naughty pine?"

Jack makes a face at his friend and groans.

Armando opens his mouth to make another comment, but the words are never spoken.

"Good morning," a man in front of the room says in a voice that Jack can only describe as tight as if his words are traveling up through a very narrow throat to reach the outside world. The man is dressed in an old-fashioned three-piece suit with a watch chain dangling from the vest pocket. His face is somewhat severe, with a sharp chin and a pointed nose. His eyebrows arch upward like steep rooftops. There is a smile on his face, but it, too, appears tight, feigned, and—sharp.

Jack does not trust the man.

"My name is Steve Slotter," he begins. "I'm the general manager of the Silver Bay Lodge Hotel. I've served in this capacity for five years now," he says with his tight smile. "You're here today for your new job orientation.

"As you may already know, 90 percent of our employees at the lodge come from the Academy, including both current students and graduates. Your employment here keeps the hotel afloat while also defraying the cost of your tuition. Most of you will work enough hours here each year to fully offset your tuition as well as your room and board expenses.

"Such an arrangement is a rarity in the academic world—unless you factor in work-study programs. Almost never does a college tuition reimbursement program employ a hotel as its work destination. I can think of only two others in the nation."

The man hooks his thumbs in the waistline of his trousers and announces, "The Silver Bay Lodge Hotel has been in existence since 1867 in some iteration or another. Of course, remodels and upgrades have been part and parcel of the lodge's history. The most recent occurred in 1988, a few years before the Teleios Academy was founded. The occasion for this large addition and accompanying renovation was a fire that caused damage throughout the structure. Although the damage was primarily smoke-related, it did compel the owners to entirely gut the lodge and pursue widespread updates even to the infrastructure.

The entire electrical was updated as well as the plumbing," Mr. Slotter explains. "For the first time, a sprinkler system was embedded into the ceilings of the lodge. Also, an outdoor irrigation system was installed to keep the grass, flowers, and other flora healthy and appealing to the guests.

"Fortunately, the walls of the lodge were all constructed of large pine logs that had to be sanded to remove smoke damage, then varnished and sealed—not a small job, mind you, but less costly than demoing and replacing tons of sheetrock. At great expense, an entire third floor was added to the existing structure to bring the total number of guest rooms to ninety-one."

The general manager pauses to stroke his sharp chin and lick his lips. Then he says, "Fortuitously for us, the prior owner did such a poor job anticipating the final cost of this huge project that he ended up walking away from the lodge. The bank that carried the mortgage had to sell it on a short sale.

"Few people were interested in buying the lodge because they thought it was outdated and, frankly, an unappealing option compared to the modern hotels in the city. The Academy was one of only three entities that offered a closed bid for the lodge. One outside investor whose unstated intent was to raze the hotel and build a condominium was warded off by the city council. Fortunately, one member of the council smelled a rat and intervened and got the state to declare the lodge a historical site that could not be torn down. Subsequently, the Academy won the bidding for the lodge and—voila—here we are today."

Mr. Slotter pauses and runs the fingers of his right hand over his chin. At that moment, Jack notices a large gold ring on the man's finger. He looks more closely at the object and sees a cross affixed to the ring. *A man of faith*, Jack thinks to himself. *It's always exciting to see someone who's not ashamed of his faith.*

"It's essential to remember that when you're employed in a hotel, you're engaged in the hospitality industry," the general manager informs the students. "You're here to host people who are coming to the hotel to eat, drink, sleep, and even be entertained. It takes many hands to make all those things come together in a way that's efficient but also appealing enough to bring people back again for a future stay. My staff will train you in the weeks ahead how you will play an integral part in driving this cruise ship forward."

The man pauses momentarily, and his lips stretch into a tight smile. "I like to think of this hotel as a seagoing vessel, so be prepared for me to use nautical terms when I describe it."

The general manager turns toward a woman just rising from the pinewood chair behind him and says, "I'm now going to turn to my cruise director, Julie Wilson, to describe the various hospitality positions you will fill on this ship."

As Julie strides forward, Jack notices that the woman is young and bright-eyed. Her quick smile and the quickness of her movements communicate a vibrant energy that seems especially suited to her position as the cruise director of the USS Silver Bay.

Steve Slotter sits down in the chair that Julie just vacated while the young woman assumes a position in front of the new lodge employees.

"Welcome!" she announces with a smile the size of Texas and a southern accent to match. Her mouth opens so wide that Jack thinks he can count every one of her glistening teeth. "All of us who work here at the lodge affectionately refer to it as our second home. So, understandably, we're tickled to have y'all on board with us!" The energetic woman exclaims.

Armando leans over to Jack and whispers, "Obviously, she drank the nautical Kool-aide. Personally, I think she's just sucking up to Steve the Slaughterer."

Jack laughs on the inside and replies, "Maybe."

"Here, at the Silver Bay Lodge Hotel, we enlist people to fill many important positions," the cruise director says with great verve. Unlike the steady rooftop eyebrows of Steve Slotter, Julie's eyebrows bob up and down like a dinghy on heavy ocean waves.

"Since two restaurants are located on board this ship," the cruise director announces, "we need frontline personnel such as hosts and hostesses, bus boys, and servers, as well as behind-the-scenes food preparation staff. Bakers are needed as well as line cooks all the way up to the executive chef. Since the Silver Bay offers catering and banquet services, additional staff are needed to float those boats."

Julie Wilson brushes strands of brown hair from her red-rouge face and proclaims with impressive energy, "In addition to the restaurant personnel, of course, this vessel requires support staff who will conduct the typical operations of a hotel. These positions include maintenance workers, cleaning crew members, sales and marketing personnel, front desk clerks and reservations clerks, and management positions such as the HR department and bookkeepers. Last, but not least, of course, is the grounds crew. All these positions are essential to the smooth operation of the lodge," the cruise director says with conviction.

The young woman pauses a moment for effect as she scans the room, her chin raised by boundless positivity. "Always remember, crew members," she says as she swings her fist in front of her—"'a chain is only as strong as its weakest link.'"

"I'm fine being any link in the chain except for the grounds crew link," Armando mutters to Jack. "Just wait and see, Juan—I'll bet I get stuck with the grounds crew. God always puts me in a position that I hate most. Then I might be the weakest link in the chain if not the most bored one."

Julie glances down at the notecard in her hand and then looks back up at her audience. "At this time," she says with a beaming face, "I will assign positions at the lodge to y'all that best suit your skillset as per the information gleaned from your applications to the Academy. Many of you come pre-trained due to prior experiences in the work world. Accordingly, we have done our best to place you in positions that draw on your previous employment experiences.

Mind you, these positions are not set in cement," the woman qualifies reassuringly, "just a place to start. And how important it is simply to start. Some of the positions on board this ship are reserved for upperclassmen and graduates who are veterans of the day-to-day operations of the lodge. So, do not fret," Julie announces, "none of you new shipmates will be assigned stressful positions such as chief officers or directors of departments.

"Okay, here we go," Julie says in a slightly higher-pitched voice as she smiles brightly. "I'm so excited for all of you newcomers! I know you're going to absolutely love working here as members of the crew!"

One by one, the cruise director reads off the names of every student in the room along with their corresponding position at the lodge.

When Emily's name is called, and she discovers that she is assigned to the dual positions of HR assistant and restaurant hostess, Jack gives her a thumbs-up and an encouraging smile. Stewart is named to the book-keeping staff, a respectable position in Jack's mind and one that will fit his socially challenged personality. Confident Aly ends up as a reservations clerk as well as a desk clerk while Rachel is assigned the impressive position of assistant director of banquet and catering services.

When Jack's name is called, Julie excitedly explains that he will be the assistant manager of the grounds crew as well as a member of the in-house maintenance staff. Jack is not surprised since much of his work history has been at a camp where he has done every job from middle and high school counselor to cleaning bathrooms and painting tin roofs.

Armando's name is the last one called. When Julie announces that he will work both in pool maintenance as well as on the grounds crew, the ex-gang member throws his arms into the air and issues a low groan. Julie does not look up at Armando, but the color in her already rouged cheeks rises as she repeats her earlier statement that none of the positions are necessarily permanent.

Armando elbows Jack and says with exasperation, "What did I tell you, ese! Condemned to grounds crew! God must be trying to humble me. I thought I was humble enough already, but obviously, I'm wrong. A few months ago, I was a big hitter in R&D for a company in the Northwest. Now I've been demoted to pulling weeds and yanking hair out of pool filters."

Jack smiles at his friend and says, "Hey, look at the bright side—we'll be working together, at least some of the time. That's a good thing, right?"

Armando mumbles his dispirited reply, "Nice try, Juan," and stares at his shoes.

Julie looks up, and her eyes scan the faces of the students. She avoids Armando's crestfallen countenance. "At this time, I will direct you to the various locations where you'll begin your job orientation," she announces. "Some of you will actually begin training today for your assigned positions."

The cruise director claps her hands together several times and displays her brilliant smile. Then she announces, "Congratulations to all of you! Mr. Slotter and I hope y'all immensely enjoy your time as crew members on this ship." Jack thinks Julie sounds a bit too excited, as if she is announcing the winner of an all-expenses-paid cruise around the world.

Five of the six members of the micro-cohort congratulate each other on their new assignments. Only Armando remains silent, disheartened by the news of his assignment. In an attempt at encouragement, Stewart comments to his peer, "Working on the grounds crew will at least get you outdoors. My job will keep me secluded inside the lodge all year long."

Armando shrugs his shoulders and turns to Jack. "I'll be okay, bro," he says with a grimace. "Worse things have certainly happened to me in the past—I just can't remember them right now. Part of the problem is that I don't know anything about lawn care or pool upkeep. I blow up the false stereotype that all Hispanic men living in LA are naturally gifted at lawn maintenance. The only phrase I know about taking care of the grounds is from the Lord of the Rings. It's in the first movie when Gandalf tells Samwise Gamgee, 'It's a little late for trimming the verge.'"

Jack laughs and says, "Stewart is right. Our jobs will get us outside a lot. Just think of those beautiful summer days when we'll be out in nature."

"I suppose this means we'll have to rake leaves and shovel snow," Armando comments with a sigh.

"Leaves, yes," Jack replies. "Snow, not very often. They don't get much white stuff down in these parts. Certainly not like out west in Colorado or up in northern Minnesota."

A few minutes later, the two young men find themselves descending creaky pinewood stairs into the basement of the lodge. Armando mumbles something to himself about going down below deck to the engine room of the cruise ship. Then he comments in a grousing tone, "I thought just like California, they didn't have basements in this part of the country."

"I think you're partially right," Jack says. "Many houses around here don't have basements. Maybe the lodge has a basement so guests can seek shelter during a storm."

The orientation meeting is as boring as Armando fears. While the four new recruits sit on wobbly workbenches in the cavernous basement, Zeke Caldwell, the director of the grounds crew as well as pool and lodge maintenance, drones on and on about trivialities relating to carpentry, electrical systems, plumbing, general upkeep of the building, lawn care, flowers, bushes, trees, and even bird feeders.

Toward the end of his lecture, Zeke speaks about pool maintenance.

He intones on and on again, only this time about optimal chlorine levels, proper pH balances, and how to keep all the various chemicals maintained in a "perfect harmony because a healthy pool is a happy pool."

"Hey," Jack says in a hushed voice to his roommate, "look at the positive side—maybe when you're out cleaning the pool, you'll meet some young and single women who love Jesus."

"Finally, an upside to the day," Armando says, brightening.

"I heard that, guys," Zeke says crossly. "Haven't I already made it crystal clear that there'll be absolutely no fraternizing with the guests! Do you savvy?"

"Yes, we savvy," Armando replies but this time with a growing smile on his face. To Jack, he says quietly, "I may not be able to fraternize, but I certainly should be able to evangelize! Beautiful women need to go to heaven, too."

Jack smiles at his suddenly ebullient friend and says, "I think you're going to make it very interesting around here."

Just then, Zeke holds up a socket wrench, and Armando whispers to Jack, "What's that?"

CHAPTER 7

Aly's Narrative Night

Seven days pass. Following supper in the Agatha Room, the micro-cohort gathers in the forest that grows thick on the hill above the dormitory. They are in a small clearing protected by the tall, ramrod-straight guardians Jack encountered his first day at the Academy. The air is hot, but a breeze whispering through the trees brings a hint of coolness. The leaves create a thick curtain above and around the small group, closing out the rest of the world. Jack cannot see the lake or the massive sanctuary turret from the secluded clearing. They are in a safe refuge, a womb ripe for the cultivation of faith.

The six students along with Dr. Milner McNeely, are sitting together on the benches of a small three-tiered amphitheater around a central paved floor on this late summer evening in September. The circular theater is a hundred feet in diameter and is constructed of the same gray stone found in the walls of the castle church, the academic citadel, and the dormitory.

As Jack looks around at the small company of believers, he feels a growing sense of camaraderie. He is confident that the six members of this micro-cohort will soon become a tight group driven by a common—or uncommon—purpose, as Dr. McNeely has said.

Jack glances at Emily, the intriguing young woman with the long blonde hair and the scintillating green eyes that are diminutive treasure chests hiding both treasure and mystery. He looks away from the woman when Dr.

McNeely reigns in the playful chatter of the five other students and introduces the purpose of the evening.

"Welcome, students, to the first Narrative Night of the fall term," the professor announces in his bass voice. "Initially, those of us on the professorial committee were going to draw on C.S. Lewis and call these monthly sharing times the Chronicles of Night—a word play on *The Chronicles of Narnia,* of course. Accordingly, we would have referred to tonight as the *Chronicles of Aly Night.*

"However, a chronicle is a written account, whereas these testimony times are oral accounts of a person's life. Accordingly, the committee scrapped the chronicle idea and went with the narrative theme since students will be narrating on these nights, not reading a written account."

Dr. McNeely grimaces and comments, "Now, didn't you all want to know that obscure, totally inconsequential detail."

The president of the Academy pauses to allow a different emotional tenor to settle over the group of seven, then says, "I have found these narrative nights to be profoundly special. Whenever a person willingly allows others to see into her heart, she is giving them a great gift. These times are also a direct blow to the enemy whose chief purpose is to separate men and women from their Creator and from each other.

"These accounts are especially sacred because those who share them speak of the Savior who rescued their lifeless bodies from the bottom of the river and revived them to new life. I invite you to treasure these narratives that describe the journey from the kingdom of darkness into the kingdom of the Son."

Dr. McNeely clears his throat and nods at the young woman sitting in front of him on the first stone tier. "Without further fanfare," he says with smiling eyes, "I want to welcome you to the narrative night of Aliya

Ahmed, otherwise known to us here at the Academy as Aly."

All eyes in the micro-amphitheater focus on Aly as she stands up and moves to the center of the small circular floor. She is as small and light as one of the leaves on the trees behind her and is wearing white pants, a black blouse, and, significantly, no hijab. Her jet-black, glistening hair swirls softly around her honey-hued face and rests on her shoulders. Her hazel eyes are large and luminous, and her nose is a button, as cute as a child's. She clears her throat quietly and smiles self-consciously. Then she begins her story, and what a story it is.

"Sawasdee Ka, to all of you," she says as she presses her delicate hands together under her chin and bows her head to her audience. The girlish voice that proceeds from her mouth contends with her intense eyes to define her personality. "I'm so happy to be a part of this micro-cohort! I look forward to getting to know all of you. Tonight, though, it's your turn to know me." The smile on Aly's face grows larger.

"I'm going to start before the beginning," she informs her listeners, "years before I was born.

"The story begins when my mother decided to leave Thailand to go to university, and my father left Saudi Arabia to go to university as well," Aly says. "It so happened that my parents attended the same school in Los Angeles called USC.

"One day in an accounting class, they met and soon discovered that they enjoyed each other very much. Less than two years later, they were married. Obviously, it was not an arranged marriage, a practice that can still happen in my father's culture. I came along after my older brother was already walking and talking. Later, my two sisters joined us. For the most part, we were a happy Muslim family.

"I have features of both my parents," Aly admits with a bright laugh.

"My Thai mother is responsible for my lighter skin and the Asian features of my face while my father gave me my Arab eyes. He also makes me moody and a fighter. My lighter skin helps me to fit in back in Thailand since many of the women there want light skin. Some of them will even use umbrellas—you might call them parasols—on sunny days to keep their skin as white as possible."

Aly brushes a wayward black ringlet of hair from her petite cheek and says, "After graduation and after working for several years in America, my parents decided to move to Saudi Arabia to the city of Tabuk where my father's family still lived. I was three years old when we moved. My father did administrative work for a company that provided services to the large air force base in that area.

"While we were in Tabuk, my father's more conservative Muslim faith grew and overruled my mother's moderate practice of Islam. As a result, my brother and sisters and I all attended a Sunni madrasas school that closely observed Sharia law."

Aly clears her throat and gently probes the top of her head with the fingers of both hands, possibly in search of her hijab, Jack thinks to himself.

"When I was ten years old, my parents decided to leave Saudi Arabia and establish our family in Thailand. We moved to the city of Yala in the Yala province that is in the far south of Thailand near Malaysia. My father began managing a rubber factory there owned by my mother's father. He was very successful.

"In Yala, all of us Ahmed children attended the conservative mosque. My brother and I especially—not so much my sisters—increasingly embraced the conservative faith. We soon became so radical in our beliefs that we began logging on to Arabic forums that were devoted to Sunni Islam. Mahmoud and I posted strong religious opinions on the forum and engaged in frequent online debates. I became interested in Islamic history and theology and advanced well beyond my female peers and even most of the boys. My father's pride in me only fed my desire to grow in the faith even more."

Aly looks away from her fellow students and stares off into the distance. When she turns back, her large eyes communicate a mix of joy and sadness. "Then, one day, I logged onto my favorite forum and read an unusual message. A woman named Esther—I assumed that wasn't her real name after I began reading her words—was talking about Jesus. I knew only a little about the controversial prophet from the teachings of the Quran.

"Esther blasphemously proclaimed that Jesus was God," Aly informs the micro-cohort. "As a Muslim, I had always been taught that Jesus was a great prophet who entered this world by way of a virgin birth. However, I certainly was never taught that He was God. Only Allah is God and God is one. Tawhid is the name of the powerful Muslim doctrine that taught me that God is a monad."

Jack looks away from Aly, and his eyes drift to his four other classmates from his perch atop the third tier. Rachel is nibbling on a chocolate bar. Emily is stroking her long golden mane. Armando is absently rubbing the tattooed dots on the skin between his thumb and forefinger. Stewart is staring at Aly with a face as alive as a mannequin. In their own way, they all appear to be locked into the words of their classmate.

"For months, I fiercely debated Esther," Aly confides to her listeners. "I accused her of committing shirk, the sin of idolatry. I condemned her for exchanging the great and transcendent Allah for Jesus, a mere man."

Aly pauses and looks down at the ground. "I'm ashamed to admit that I even threatened her with violence. Without a doubt, that was the voice of my father and brother speaking through me. Yet, it was my mouth that uttered the words and my heart that burned with hatred."

The small woman shifts her weight from her left foot to her right and says, "After a while, Esther began showing me the inconsistencies in Islam. Prior to her teaching, I thought I was so smart and knew everything about the Quran and the prophet. Esther began to reveal things to me that I had never noticed before—or maybe didn't want to notice. Most importantly, she showed me that the monadic God, Allah, did not have love at the core of His being because He was alone before the creation of the world. So how could love be a strong aspect of His being if there was no 'other' to love before He created mankind?

"In contrast to Allah," Aly explains with growing passion in her voice, "Esther taught me that Yahweh, the God of the Christian faith, is a Triune God, three persons in one. She showed me that the Father, Jesus the Son, and the Spirit were all part of the one Godhead. For a long time, I resisted the concept of the Trinity because I stubbornly believed that it meant that there were three Gods; and I could never accept three Gods since my monotheistic Islamic beliefs would not permit a theology that was suspiciously polytheistic."

Aly sighs deeply, but a wide smile brightens her whole face when she announces, "Then one rainy day eighteen months ago in Yala, I quietly surrendered to Jesus. I didn't even see that moment coming until just before it happened. In the end, it was His love that won me over—and the fact that He was so 'knowable' as opposed to Allah, who was so...transcendent, so distant.

"As a Christian now, I still believe that God is the greatest possible being who is far above us in His holiness; however, I'm also convinced that He condescended to enter our world in the person of Jesus so that we could know Him personally. How foreign that idea was to me, initially. How beautiful that truth is to me now!"

Everyone in the small circle, including Professor McNeely, begins to clap for Aly. Even as he applauds the Saudi-Thai woman, Jack notices that two individuals in the small amphitheater seem less enthusiastic about their classmate's journey to faith. Stewart's impassive face does not surprise him that much. Emily's hesitant and measured celebration captures his attention, though.

"A few weeks after I told Esther about my faith in Jesus, her posts abruptly stopped," Aly says, her voice suddenly grave. "I never heard from her again. It wasn't until several months later that a blogger in Iran mentioned that she was dead. He reported that her father had drowned her in the river behind their house when he discovered that she had abandoned Allah and his prophet, Muhammed."

Rachel gasps and covers her mouth. Dr. McNeely groans and shakes his head slowly. Jack stares in disbelief at the follower of Allah, who had become a lover of Jesus. What father could do that to his own daughter? Was it even possible? Jack could not begin to comprehend such a monstrous thing. Armando's face had transformed into a molten mask of anger—maybe even hatred.

Aly wipes a single tear from her cheek and says, "I hid my new faith from my family, of course. I'm sure they suspected something was different about me. They just didn't know what. I continued to grow in my faith as I visited websites where I could learn more about Jesus."

The radiance streaming from Aly's heart-shaped face fades a bit when she informs her audience, "Everything was fine until six months ago. That's when my brother entered my room while I was gone and hacked into my computer. It didn't take him long to discover that I had adopted a new faith.

"When I returned home that evening, Mahmoud was irrational with anger," Aly reports with troubled eyes. "I had never seen him that enraged before. My own brother, who I had always idolized, suddenly hated me. He demanded that I repent of my apostasy before the sun rose the next morning. If I didn't, he insisted that he would tell my father. He even threatened to kill me, a response that's not inconsistent with how some Sunni family members deal with apostasy—especially in certain countries where the imams are more radical. Witness what happened to Esther in her Sunni culture."

Aly shakes her head, and waves of black hair wash over her cheeks. "I was terrified and didn't know what to do," the young woman reveals as she chews on her lower lip. "I'm ashamed to say that I wasn't as brave as Esther. Like the disciples on the Mount of Olives when Jesus was arrested, I ran.

"That very night," Aly confesses, "when the house was quiet, I took all the money I had saved from my job and slipped out of the house. I walked my motorbike for half a mile before I dared to start it for fear that my brother would hear me.

"I rode in the dark for more than two hours to the city of Hat Yai, where my cousins lived. I wept the whole way. At times, I could barely see the road through my tears. I feared that I would never see my family again."

Aly pauses and blinks long black lashes over her large hazel eyes. Then she says, "I rode straight to the airport in Hat Yai and purchased a ticket to Bangkok. Fortunately, I owned a passport due to my family's annual trips to Saudi Arabia to visit my father's parents. I gave the key to my motorbike to the first young woman I saw in the terminal building. She took it and stood there stunned as I walked away. I didn't want to leave any evidence that Mahmoud could use to trace me to the airport," the runaway explains.

"I flew from Bangkok to Los Angeles where I contacted one of my mother's college friends who I knew was not sympathetic with radical Islam. She allowed me to stay with her for many months. I found out for the first time that she was a believer in Jesus, just like me. She's the one who recommended the Academy to me. When she put me on the plane to the Midwest, she swore that she would never utter a word about where I had gone or that she had even seen me."

Aly's petite fingers probe her hair again as she says, "So here I am in the middle of America after I had been quietly living in southern Thailand only six months ago." She pauses and then admits, "My two persistent worries are that I'll never see my family again and that my brother is radical enough that he might believe it's God's will for him to find me and kill me." Another tear slips from her eye and makes a glistening trail down to her rosebud lips.

Rachel, who is sitting close to Aly, gets to her feet and walks over to the young woman. She wraps her arm around the Narrative Night speaker and whispers something into her ear. Then she returns to her seat.

Dr. McNeely clears his throat and inquires, "Do you think your brother is capable of pursuing you all the way to America?"

Aly's eyes drift away from the professor and focus on something in the woods. She is still staring into the trees as she slowly nods her head. "Mahmoud is extreme. Some of his friends in the provinces of Pattani and Songkhla and many back in Saudi Arabia are jihadists. They are prepared to do violence to anyone who forsakes Islam."

The young woman's eyes refocus, and she stands up straight. She raises her chin, and the muscles in her jaw grow taut. "But I do not fear what humans can do to me. As Dr. Windsor taught us, I have the Field Manual to guide me and comfort me."

Aly pauses her narrative to stoop down and pick up a small purse from the ground by her feet, from which she extracts a Bible. "See, I have the compact version Dr. Windsor talked about. He carried his FM in his

Humvee. I carry mine in my bag."

The young believer in Jesus smiles, and the light from her face brightens the dusk that is descending on the small group in the woods. Everyone in the amphitheater laughs at Aly's heart-felt show-and-tell.

"I have a deeper hunger for the words of this Field Manual than I ever had for the Quran," she claims excitedly. "It gives me joy and fills my heart like nothing else has ever done. Recently, I memorized the Gospel of John."

Aly displays her small Field Manual and then clutches it close to her chest. "I carry three truths in my heart every day, now. First, I believe that Jesus is God along with the Father and the Spirit and that He is the way, the Truth, and the Life. No one comes to the Father except through Him. And therein lies my double blasphemy: Not only do I believe that Jesus is God, but I also believe that He is a member of the Holy Trinity. I can no longer embrace Islam because of those beliefs, and, of course, Islam can no longer embrace me.

"The second truth I learned from John is that Jesus has given me His Spirit to be my counselor and my teacher," Aly continues. "That means that I have God living in me right now!" Even in the retreating light, Jack can see that Aly's eyes are dancing with joy. "Unbelievable!" she cries out. "How different from my experience with Allah who was always so far away and seemed forever displeased with me.

"I could talk about Jesus all night," the glowing woman announces with the elated laugh of someone who has been released from a lifetime of manacles and chains, "but I will spare you that. Instead, I'll tell you the third truth, which is that I now know, instead of worrying about it until the day I die, that I'm going to be with Jesus in heaven someday! I know it! I absolutely know it!" she exclaims as she rises up on the toes of her feet.

Aly must notice that everyone is staring at her with a look on their faces that says, "Yeah, we know that. The Bible tells us that clearly. What's the big epiphany in that?"

The small woman looks around at her audience and states, "You don't know, do you? Well, then I'll tell you. In Islam, we never know if we're going to heaven or not. Our eternal destination all depends on the will of Allah, and we can never know his will. Being granted entry to paradise or turned away depends on whether our good deeds outweigh our bad deeds in Allah's eyes.

"In contrast to this terrifying lack of certainty, the wonderful news found in Jesus is that I don't have to worry about being good enough to undo my sin. Jesus already paid the price. He took it away at the cross. He makes me righteous apart from my efforts so that I don't ever have to ever worry about being good enough to get into heaven!"

Dr. McNeely rises from his seat on the second tier of the amphitheater and steps down beside Aly. "Isn't it amazing what our God can do?" he exclaims. "Isn't it wonderful to hear a narrative about how the Shepherd pursues one of His lost sheep with relentless love and calls her to be His own? I have so many questions for this young believer, but we need to wrap up before it gets pitch dark up here. Let's pray for this brave woman," he says.

Within moments, everyone is standing around Aly, forming a protective hedge. Strangers a week ago, the members of the micro-cohort are now friends—brothers and sisters adopted by the same Father. They begin to talk to the God, who only months ago became Aly's Savior and best friend.

Jack is in the tunnel beneath his dorm room again. This time, he is with all the "Screaming Eagles"—a name the six students adopted for their micro-cohort members after the first Warfare class with Dr. Windsor. They are all standing around in a tight circle at the bottom of the ladder.

"What in the world?" Rachel exclaims in her mild Bostonian accent.

"Should we be down here?" Emily asks. She is holding her cell phone in one hand as she attempts to wrap her arms around herself to fend off the cool air.

"Where does it lead?" Aly inquires.

"We've only been down here once before," Armando reminds the newbies, sounding much more confident than the first time he was in the passage, "so we don't know much about this place."

Stewart adjusts his glasses and informs the female members of the spelunking expedition, "Jonathan informed us that one of the passages that branch off from this tunnel leads back under the citadel complex. He also told us that there are mysteries waiting to be solved down here and that he had nightmares for months after his first spelunking trip into this tunnel."

"Nightmares," Emily repeats slowly. "What kind of nightmares?"

"We didn't ask him what kind of nightmares," Armando responds impatiently. "Why do you need to know what kind?"

Jack continues to notice a pattern of defensiveness in his new friend whenever he perceives that he is being challenged. He is tempted to call out his roommate on his behavior but decides to wait until they are alone. Instead, Jack changes the direction of the conversation.

"How about if we do some exploring and see if we can find the passage that goes under the school," Jack offers. "We can split up into groups of two—one guy and one girl—and explore some of the tunnels," he suggests as he turns and winks at Armando.

The six students eye each other in the gloomy, dank tunnel. The only light at the bottom of the shaft is provided by their phone flashlights that illuminate the passage better than the small flashlights they had the first time around with Jonathan.

"Let's do it," Rachel agrees. "I'll go with you, Jack."

"Sounds like a plan," Jack replies.

After the other students have divided into their dyads, they all venture forward through the darkness of the tunnel, excited for their adventure.

"This passage actually reminds me of Hezekiah's tunnel in Jerusalem," Stewart comments, predictably, sharing yet another insight. "Have any of you been in Hezekiah's tunnel?"

Without waiting for an answer, the Intellect says, "When I was there three years ago, the tunnel was filled with water. At one point, it came up to my waist. That wasn't necessarily a problem except that some of the explorers with me were anxious about encountering a snake.

To be honest, I wasn't worried about snakes. I was more uncomfortable with the tarantulas that were scurrying around on the walls of the tunnel. Well, I guess they weren't 'scurrying.' Tarantulas don't move fast enough to describe them as scurrying. Crawling slowly is a better way to word it. I was certain one of them would jump—."

"Stewart, please don't say anymore," Aly interjects as she begins eyeing the walls of the tunnel with concern. "I hate snakes and spiders."

"Me, too," Emily adds.

Stewart remains in the only gear he seems to know. "Tarantulas actually are not to be feared," he drones on. "Their bite is no worse than a bee sting. It's far more devastating for individuals who are allergic to spider bites, of course. But overall, the brown recluse spider is to be feared far more than your common tarantula. The primary habitat of the recluse spider is found in the western United States as well as the central part. In fact," the Intellect pauses for a moment and then says, "come to think of it, it's actually not uncommon to find them in this region of the country."

"Really, man!" Armando exclaims in frustration as he shines his light directly in the Intellect's face.

Stewart continues, seemingly oblivious to the displeasure of his peers. "The recluse spider is distinctive because of the violin shape located on its cephalothorax. It has six eyes instead of the more common eight eyes that most spiders possess. The good news is that we rarely see recluse spiders because they like to hide in dark, secluded places."

"Like dark and secluded tunnels," Rachel says, "where we happen to be at this exact moment. Stewart, stop scaring us. Can't you talk about something else, like puppies or butterflies?"

"Don't get him started," Armando says sharply. "Remember how he lectured us about cicadas all the way back from the amphitheater the other night? The guy will talk forever about anything."

Jack opens his mouth to defend his fellow explorer, who seems largely untrained in the art of interpersonal communication. Before he can say anything, however, he notices a passage branching off to their right.

"Here's where Rachel and I veer off," he announces. Turning to the others, he says, "My phone has, let's see, 7:15. How about if we give ourselves thirty minutes to explore? No, on second thought, let's say forty-five to give us time to retrace our steps back to this spot. I'll leave my backpack here as a trail marker."

Jack pauses and then cautions, "Keep your eyes open because this place is entirely unknown to us. If you run into any...problems, just scream as loud as you can."

An hour later, the three scouting groups rendezvous at Jack's backpack in the main tunnel and debrief about their findings. Only Stewart and Emily have found anything of real import. The passage they explored—the one immediately after Jack and Rachel's—did indeed lead back under the church but only by way of a tunnel they had to navigate in very tight quarters.

At the end of the long worm hole, as Stewart called it, they had to push aside a heavy stone slab to exit the tight passage. Once through, they found themselves in another larger tunnel that eventually ascended to the dungeon beneath the church.

Aly suggests that they should all return to the citadel through the tunnel that Emily and Stewart had discovered. There are no dissenting voices, so the Screaming Eagles set out through the five-foot-wide passage to retrace the steps of their classmates.

After five minutes of walking by the light generated from their cell phones, Stewart announces that very soon, the passage will become much tighter. Sure enough, only a few minutes later, the tunnel begins to shrink in size to such a degree that the students bend over to protect their heads from the descending ceiling.

Eventually, they are forced to get on their hands and knees and crawl through Stewart's worm hole. The unyielding stone floor is painful for Jack's knees, but no one else is complaining, so he makes no comment about it. Football—Jack thinks to himself—*the gift that keeps giving.*

Soon, the six spelunkers come to a place where the tunnel narrows even further, and they have no choice but to squirm through it on their stomachs. Now everyone understands why their peer referred to it as the worm hole. This much smaller passage seems to go on forever.

Just when Rachel announces in a high-pitched voice that she is on the verge of a panic attack, the Screaming Eagles squeeze their way out into a much larger tunnel. As Jack crawls out of the tight passage, he looks up at Emily's dimly lit face and says, "Wow, you've been through that hole three times now. I didn't picture you as the type of girl who'd be up for that."

"What's that supposed to mean?" the blonde-haired green-eyed girl replies sharply. Jack is not sure if she is feigning irritation or genuinely aggravated by his comment. Uncertain how to respond, he laughs as he gets up and brushes off his clothes. "I meant it as a compliment."

Emily smiles at him then, and he assumes that the young woman is not genuinely upset. He opens his mouth to speak again, but the light of his phone falls on the thin stone slab lying on the floor of the tunnel.

They all train their lights on the jagged slab, and Aly comments, "It's possible that a person coming down this passage from the basement wouldn't even see this slab when it covered the mouth of the worm hole. It's not like it stands out from the other rocks down here in the dark."

"Why would anyone cover the mouth of the tunnel in the first place?" Rachel muses aloud.

"Good question," Armando says.

"There's only one logical answer," Stewart declares as he adjusts his glasses in the murky tunnel. "Someone wanted to hide the hole because they didn't want it to be discovered. And they didn't want it discovered because there was—or is—something on the other side they didn't want someone else to find."

"Like a treasure," Armando says, his eyes growing large.

"Maybe a treasure," Emily reflects. "Or possibly a secret." She speaks the word in such a way that it sounds like she is personally familiar with the word.

"A secret," Rachel repeats in her accented voice. "Who would want to hide a secret down here?"

"Someone who wanted to hide something where no one would ever find it," Aly offers in her endearing voice that hides a deep treasure of its own.

"Because if the secret were ever discovered, it would be very costly to that person," Jack adds.

"Wow," Armando exclaims, "we have the corporate mind of a detective!"

"Like Sherlock Holmes and Mr. Watson," Rachel interjects.

"It's Dr. Watson," Stewart corrects. Then he adds, "Or like Tommy and Tuppence Beresford, or Hercule Poirot and Arthur Hastings, or best of all, Elijah Bailey and R. Daneel Olivaw."

Everyone shakes their heads at the ambulatory encyclopedia standing in their midst except for Aly, who inquires innocently, "Who are all those people?"

"Famous detective teams," Stewart replies as the corners of his mouth turn up ever so slightly in the dark tunnel.

Since when does the man smile, Jack wonders to himself. *Maybe whenever someone is interested enough to ask him a question.*

"It looks like we have some exploring to do in our spare time," Armando comments, his straight, white teeth flashing in the gloom. "As if we have any spare time—and as if this is the place I would want to spend any of my spare time if I had any."

"Yeah, I guess we'll need to look for more stone slabs," Emily offers.

"Slabs might be his—or her—modus operandi for hiding things."

"Good point," Jack says with a little too much enthusiasm.

Emily's eyes find Jack's in the dark tunnel.

Hidden partially in the shadows, Rachel stares at her two peers and then looks away.

"It's possible that at one time, this worm hole was the only way to access the rest of the cave system," Stewart surmises. "This larger tunnel doesn't lead anywhere—it dead-ends two hundred feet from where we're standing. Emily and I scouted it out."

"Unless there was an entrance from the quarry back before the dorm was built over it," Armando parries, an edge in his voice. "You have to consider all options, Stew."

"Whatever the case may be, we'll clearly need to come back down here again," Jack proposes.

"Yes, maybe we'll find the treasure or the secret or whatever it is," Aly comments optimistically.

"If there actually is anything to find," Rachel qualifies.

"I'm up for a treasure hunt," Emily volunteers brightly. "If we look hard enough and long enough, I'm sure we'll find something."

At that moment, of course, Emily cannot know the prophetic power of her words. Indeed, there are many things they are going to find in the days ahead that none of them know anything about at the moment. Some they will wish they never discovered.

CHAPTER 8

The Titanic Dr. Hawkstern

Dr. Hawkstern does his name justice. Or at least close enough. Perched on his large, bearded face is a proportionately large nose that curls down sharply over his graying mustache like a bird of prey guarding its nest. There are no eggs in this nest, of course—only crumbs from the chocolate chip cookie that had been consumed before class. The man's eyes are small, almost beady—like a hawk. They dart back and forth as if searching for something to pounce on. According to Jonathan, the man's words are like talons, ready to attack and rip apart anything that is not wise enough or quick enough to scurry for shelter.

Most of all, the professor plays the part exceptionally well of looking stern. His eyebrows are foreboding gray clouds capable at any moment of emitting jagged flashes of lightning or deep rumbles of thunder. His forehead is corrugated steel.

Everything about the man is oversized, from his hands that are as large as grizzly bear paws to his barrel chest that heaves up and down like a ship navigating the crests and troughs of waves in a tempest. His pipe dangles from the corner of his mouth as if it is a permanent appendage attached to his face at birth like the trunk of an elephant. His beard is full and spills down his chest like a dirty-white avalanche. He is, as some might say, larger than life, and large he is, standing just over seven feet tall according to Jack's visual calculation.

Dr. Hawkstern stands next to the fireplace in the fireside room and fumbles through the papers and tomes he carried into the room in a leather briefcase the size of a small car trunk. He grunts and snorts like a starving bear foraging around in a fallen tree trunk, attempting to find grub worms. Apparently, he is having little success. He adjusts and readjusts his silver, wire-rimmed glasses that appear hammered out of iron by some medieval blacksmith and fumes some more.

Eventually, the giant professor lifts his head, not quickly but glacially. Initially, Jack wonders if the man's body is moving slowly for effect, but he and the other members of the cohort soon discover that this behavior belongs to the natural repertoire of the man's eccentric personality.

When his beady eyes finally lift from his hodgepodge of notes and books and rise to the level of the students' faces, they do not tarry there but keep moving. They don't stop their upward journey until they are gazing well above the students toward a spot on the ceiling in the back of the room.

Jack looks at Armando, who glances back at him. His roommate shakes his head ever so slightly and mouths the words, "We're dead meat, Juan." His face is so sincere with concern that Jack looks away quickly before he bursts into laughter. Such behavior would most likely not be received well by the professor who towers over them like the Eiffel Tower over the River Seine. Jack has already discerned that this is one of those classrooms where it is wise to be as invisible as possible. Some classrooms are meant for learning. This one is meant for honing survival skills.

"Good morning, students," the giant man growls loudly. "Although I dare say there is little about this day that is good."

He pauses, and all the students sit transfixed. Statues in the forum of ancient Rome would appear more alive than this group of fossilized students.

They are like unarmed Christians in the amphitheater facing a merciless gladiator—or worse, a lion insane with hunger waiting to rip them limb from limb.

Jack glances away from Armando and looks at Aly. Her chestnut eyes are large with emotion, and her small fingers squeeze her pen tightly as if to prevent it from flying out of her hand.

"This is the day that evolution has made," the professor finally announces, reciting his daily mantra. His voice is deep and reverberates through the fireside room. "We will embrace it and fearlessly shoulder the crushing boulder of despair and chaos that necessarily accompanies it. Certainly, you all agree with me, yes?"

Nobody breathes. None of the students know if the giant is asking a rhetorical question or if he is genuinely posing an interrogatory that he hopes will be challenged by one of his students who forever thereafter will be remembered as foolish or masochistic. Either way, they will come to a similar fate. Nobody in their right mind is going to venture out into the open field and trigger one of the Bouncing Betty mines that Dr. Windsor has referred to in his warfare class.

Jack pictures dozens of the small mines buried beneath the thick royal-red carpet of the fireside room.

A low, rumbling sound originates deep inside Dr. Hawkstern's chest and rises into his throat. The primitive noise surprisingly emerges from his lips in the form of intelligible words and not the primal growl anticipated by the edgy students.

"You theists all alike are cowards," the huge man announces. "Is it any wonder Nero fed you to the lions and lit you up as human torches?"

Jack and Armando exchange glances again. Jack cannot get out of his mind his roommate's earlier comment about dead meat. It seems amazingly appropriate in the current context.

Shaking his massive head, the titan slowly looks down to view his notes. Eventually, he says, "Today's lecture will address Rudolf Bultmann—a brilliant German theologian who sought to resolve the tension between science and religion. Some of you might want to ask me how he accomplished such an impossible task."

"Not in this class, I won't ask," Armando says quietly to Jack.

Dr. Hawkstern pauses and then suddenly breaks out into a ragged cough that sounds like point-blank cannon fire. He recovers shortly, but only after every student in the room is convinced that the professor will expire on the spot. Even the giant man's cough proves to be terrifying.

"Bultmann was wise enough to know that he had to make the Christian faith palatable to the modern scientific mind," the professor asserts in such a deep voice that Jack imagines that if the man sang in a choir, they would have to invent a name for a singing voice two levels lower than bass.

"Bultmann knew that the age of belief in literal miracles was done—kaput," the professor continues slowly. The giant man pronounces each syllable so sharply they could cut tin.

"Indeed, he was acutely aware that the ship of supernaturalism had sailed a long time ago during the Enlightenment. Science had already demonstrated that mankind was living in a closed space-time continuum where everything outside the realm of materialism was conjecture at best and irrationalism at worst. The god of the gaps was no longer needed or tenable."

Dr. Hawkstern's bear paws claw at the podium as he mangles the pipe in his mouth. He continues to direct his eyes to a spot on the ceiling in the back of the room. It strikes Jack that the stern visage of the professor and the one on Moses' face in the painting on the wall during the crossing of the

Red Sea are not entirely dissimilar.

Certainly, Moses had to be less intimidating than this man standing before me, Jack muses. Except when an enraged Moses descended from Mt. Sinai and threw the tablets with the Ten Commandments at the idolatrous Israelites and their golden calf. Yes, that might have been the one occasion when Moses' countenance matched the professor's current intimidating features.

"So, what was this sincere man to do?" Dr. Hawkstern inquires rhetorically of his reticent students.

"Well, I'll tell you what he did," the giant man exclaims as he strikes his huge fist on the podium so loudly that it sounds like the report of a gun. "He took it upon himself to demythologize the Bible. He didn't approach this task like some liberals who take the physical miracles and try to explain them to us. These theologians might say, for example, that Jesus' walking on the water was simply Him knowing where the sand bar was located or that His acclaimed resurrection from the dead occurred because He had never died in the first place. He swooned, only to be revived later."

The bear-man clutches his pipe with his left hand and manipulates it vigorously in his mouth as if attempting to extract one of his teeth.

"Bultmann took a different approach, a wiser tack," the professor announces. "This amazing man interpreted the stories of the Bible not for what is, but for what they could be. Instead of viewing them as actual historical events whose importance was rooted in their historicity, he viewed them existentially, a la Martin Heidegger.

"In other words, for the esteemed Rudolph Bultmann, it was not important whether Jesus literally rose from the dead or not. He believed that the event itself, the historical truth of it, was irrelevant and, of course, altogether impossible in the post-supernatural universe of the mid-twentieth century."

The large man pauses long enough to adjust the iron glasses on his face, then continues in his plodding, precise delivery.

"The only thing that mattered for Bultmann was what personal meaning the thought of Jesus rising from the dead evoked in the early believers. Yes, the meaning extracted by each person from the resurrection of Jesus is what matters, not the event itself. Individual subjective truth is what matters in this universe.

"So, you see, my foolish, misguided theists," the professor says with a shake of his massive head, "Bultmann knew that there was no need to explain away the physical miracles. He properly discerned that such an approach was erroneous. Instead of arguing about the historicity of the biblical events, he simply encouraged each person to extract from the events in the Bible nuggets of existential truth that might bring a ray of hope into their daily lives as they sought to attain their authentic selves.

"What massive brilliance!" the towering professor exclaims with such fawning admiration that Jack is convinced that the man would promptly bow down to the theologian, were Rudolph Bultmann in the room and not in his grave.

"Because of his efforts to demythologize the New Testament message, he made the Bible accessible to modern man," Dr. Hawkstern continues. "Indeed, his noble reconceptualization of how to approach the Bible rendered it a book that scientists and other intelligent people would now choose to read instead of dismissing out of hand because of its ludicrous supernaturalism. No longer did the intellectual man have to tediously stumble over the miracles because—to repeat—Bultmann jettisoned the mythical element."

The professor paws at the dirty avalanche on his chest and adds, "So, it was Rudolph Bultmann, the perspicacious man that he was, who determined that the absurd historical content of the Bible simply needed to be supplanted by personal, existential content and, voilà, all is fine."

At this point, Jack senses a wave of irritation swell within him that is almost strong enough to compel him to speak. He glances around the room to see if anyone else is feeling the same way. None of the stone countenances reveal anything until he looks at the girl from Thailand. Aly's jaw is moving up and down as if she is chewing something.

Dr. Hawkstern breaks into another paroxysm of coughing that shakes his whole body like a volcanic eruption might shake a mountain. Amazingly, his pipe remains attached to his mouth. During this second attack, the large man's face turns different colors—unnatural hues. The most noticeable of them is the light purplish shade that slowly migrates into his cheeks just before he recovers from the fit.

Jack feels a growing empathy for the imposing professor, who is as fragile as the human torches in the room.

"Do you need a cough drop?" Jack hears a voice behind him inquire. The voice belongs to Emily, the blonde-haired girl from Florida. "I have some in my backpack if you would like one," she offers.

The professor's hawkish eyes flit down from the ceiling and appear to fly over Emily's face—ever so quickly. Then they return to their safe refuge in the ceiling. The glance happens so fast that Jack cannot be sure that the giant man actually did look at Emily, especially when his habit so far has been to avoid eye contact.

The mammoth man mumbles to himself and takes a swallow of water from a bottle he extracts from inside the podium. The sound of his gulp fills the room—loud, like everything else about this man.

"Where was I?" he begins again after he clears his throat. "Ah, yes, we are to extract the authentic meaning from the Bible as a silversmith extracts precious metal from the dross. An example might be Jesus walking on the water. What meaning could be found in that story? Maybe that you can transcend the problems you encounter in life by choosing to have a good attitude or a thankful heart. Or maybe that you can visualize yourself walking on top of your problems. Do you comprehend what I'm saying about arriving at an existential meaning?"

Aly apparently has heard enough. She raises her small hand, a hand that Jack notices is shaking, whether, from anger or fear, he is not certain. Probably anger.

Without moving his eyes from the ceiling, the imposing professor growls in his deep rumbling voice, "What is it?"

"Does Bultmann believe along with the intellectual scientists you have referred to that the universe is a closed system?" Aly inquires curtly but with obvious restraint.

"Why, yes," Dr. Hawkstern replies as his billowy eyebrows collide violently above his nose. "Of course, he does."

Aly raises her chin a bit as she comments, "So, Rudolf Bultmann was an atheist. If the universe is closed, then not only are miracles an impossibility but so is the existence of a God who is outside the universe."

"Yes, I believe Bultmann was an atheist, although he might not assert that position if he were here to represent himself," the professor replies in words that are precise and clear despite the pipe in his mouth.

"What if I believe that we live in an open space-time continuum where miracles do occur, and God does exist?" Aly asks.

"Prove it!" the large man retorts without hesitation as if he has been waiting for someone to be lured into this ambush.

Aly hesitates for a moment, momentarily cowed by the professor's intense reply. Eventually, she says, "Few historians today deny that Jesus existed."

The dirty avalanche beard shakes as Dr. Hawkstern begins to chortle. "Neither Bultmann nor I doubt that Jesus ever lived, young lady. Of course, we believe that He walked this earth like the rest of us homo sapiens. We just don't go so far as to say that He was a god since the supernatural doesn't exist. It is the mythological element in the Bible that we cannot embrace. We believe that only what we can see and touch is real. Materialism rules the day for rational men and women."

By now, the classroom is coming alive. The atheist titan in the front of the room has awakened a passion in even his most intimidated students. Jack cannot help but wonder if Dr. Hawkstern's pot-stirring personality is one of the reasons the school hired the professor to teach at the Academy.

"Can you prove there is no God?" a student from the larger macro-cohort inquires of the towering atheist.

"No, no, no," he chides. "Damnation and drumsticks! The burden of proof is on you, my friend. Show him to me right now, and I will believe," the professor says, raising his arms toward the ceiling in a gesture of feigned homage.

"God is spirit, not flesh and bones," another student parries. "We cannot see and touch him. Besides, He is not at our beck and call. We are at His."

"The point is that the burden of proof is on God," the polar bear with the white fur covering his head and face growls in response. "If He exists, why doesn't He present Himself to me? Here I stand, waiting. Reveal yourself to me, Jesus, and I will believe," the huge man says mockingly.

The professor begins to move and talk more animatedly as the energy in the room begins to grow. His eyes, however, are still trained on the ceiling in the back of the room.

Jack raises his hand and observes, "Aren't you limited by your world-view, Dr. Hawkstern? Since you presuppose that the world is a closed universe, of course, you won't believe in God or miracles. Your assumption predetermines what you must believe."

The professor snorts and then snaps, "Aren't you dictated by your worldview as well? You presuppose that the world has a spiritual element, so you necessarily believe in the existence of God and miracles. Your Weltanschauung is just as limiting as mine, with the one glaring difference that it is built on fantasy and folly. You'll get nowhere with that argument, young fool!"

The classroom falls silent before the professor's harsh rebuke.

At that moment, Jack recognizes this man for what he is, namely, a bully. He defends himself and his position with smoke and fire and a booming voice and pounding fist. Jack is reminded of the scene in the *Wizard of Oz* movie where the wizard is hiding in a curtained booth all the while pulling cords and levers and pushing buttons to intimidate his visitors with the huge luminous head that emits bursts of fire and speaks with a threatening and resounding voice.

The remainder of the class period settles into unchallenged lecturing by Dr. Hawkstern, punctuated by occasional coughing episodes.

When the class is over, Jack thinks he sees the titan glance briefly at Emily.

Several weeks pass and the six members of the micro-cohort find themselves sitting around a table in the Agatha Room. Only with great effort does the feeble light of the dying day filter through the large cupola above. Supper has been consumed, and the exhausted students finally have some space in their demanding schedule to relax together. Students sitting at the tables around them are engaged in animated conversation and spirited laughter.

"Have you heard that Dr. Windsor's wife is ill?" Emily inquires of her friends.

Stewart nods his head knowingly. "I've been told she has a recurrence of ovarian cancer. She's on her third round of chemotherapy."

"That doesn't sound good," Rachel says with a sigh. "My great aunt died of that when she was like in her fifties."

"Does anybody know her prognosis?" Aly asks.

The six students glance around inquiringly at their peers. They all shake their heads.

"We should do something for them," Jack says as he feels a dark shadow settles over his eyes. Death. He sees death. He smells death. *Why does death always have to raise its ugly head? God, why does everyone have to die?*

"I think that's a wonderful idea," Emily says, her perpetually muted eyes coming alive—at least for a moment. *They are a brilliant green even when dimmed by mystery,* Jack thinks.

"Where is she?" Armando inquires. "At home?"

"She's at Memorial hospital downtown," Stewart answers.

The dark-haired, olive-skinned young man from La Puente shakes his head and then turns to look at the Intellect. "How is it that you seem to know everything?" he asks with an edge to his voice. "Are you a walking search engine full of facts but no heart?"

Stewart's eyes briefly hold Armando's gaze, then fall away to the floor. He is silent.

"Let's do this," Rachel announces in a loud voice, interrupting the tension at the table. "Let's find out when visiting hours are and go see her. We can bring some flowers and a card. If she's been released from the hospital already, we'll visit her at her house."

"Can you plan that for us, Rach?" Jack asks of the auburn-haired woman sitting next to him. "Just let us know what you find out, okay?"

The young woman stares at Jack for a few seconds before she replies, "Yeah, I can do that." The wave of red that drifts into her face is lost against the red of her hair and the freckles that populate her face.

Heavy with grief, the group falls silent. Everyone is lost in their own thoughts.

Eventually, Stewart steals a look at Armando out of the corner of his eye and says, "There's one more thing I've heard—not about Mrs. Windsor—but about somebody else. Do you want me to tell you or not?" There is no sarcasm in the man's voice, no anger. As usual, his head deals only in information, not emotion.

"Go ahead," Emily says gently. Sad eyes, warm heart, Jack thinks to himself as he looks at the young woman. *Is that what my grandmother used to say? No, she would say, "cold hands, warm heart."*

"Last week, an upper classman told me that Professor Hawkstern has been divorced for twenty years and that he has one daughter," Stewart informs the micro-cohort.

"Why are you telling us this, Stew?" Armando asks, shaking his head. "It's nothing but gossip. I thought you were above that, man."

"It's not gossip," Stewart counters. "As far as I can discern, it's factual."

"Does she live around here?" Rachel interjects, attempting to diffuse the tension. "Dr. Hawkstern's daughter, I mean."

"No, Ben said they're estranged," Stewart answers.

"What exactly does that mean?" Jack inquires.

"It seems that shortly after the divorce, the daughter began acting out," Stewart replies. "She jumped into the deep end of the pool and began using drugs, alcohol—you name it. She hasn't talked with her father in twenty years. Apparently, she wants nothing to do with him. The professor has never recovered from the loss of his daughter. She was his one enduring affection in life—among many other non-enduring affections."

"I can't say I blame her if Dr. Hawkstern talks to her like he talks to us," Rachel observes.

"Yeah, if he talked to me that way, I'd uppercut him right in the nose," Armando says with a mirthless laugh.

"Harsh words, my friend," Jack cajoles, "harsh words."

"Okay, okay," Armando replies, raising his hands as if to parry Jack's words. "I wouldn't punch him. I'd just, ah, just give him a piece of my mind and then pray for the dude."

Everyone laughs except Emily. She is staring at her hands, distracted by something else. Jack comments that she seems a million miles away.

Emily looks up at him and says, "It's just sad, I suppose. It's so easy to look at it from the kid's perspective since we're in that age group ourselves. But I wonder how it feels from the parent's view of it."

Jack looks into Emily's eyes for a long time. They are deep wells, and he wishes he had a bucket and a rope. But he discerns that her wells are so incredibly deep that they are currently inaccessible. Her heart is out of reach.

"Hey Jack," Rachel says, interrupting his thoughts. "I've been meaning to ask you for a while now what's up with Dr. Windsor. Why is he so hard on you? The whole cohort has been referring to him as Colonel Crush behind his back ever since he began singling you out."

"I don't know," Jack says slowly, looking away from Emily and shrugging his shoulders. "I'm still trying to figure that out myself. He's made vague comments to me several times after class, but I don't quite understand what he's getting at. I haven't shown him any disrespect that I'm aware of. And here I thought he'd like me since I wear hiking boots that aren't all that different than his army boots."

The six students laugh and then move on to other topics. Soon, they leave the Agatha room and go their separate ways.

Stewart is coming down the steps from Dr. McNeely's office after his first spelunking session. It went sufficiently well, he thinks. Nothing too eventful was discussed. He reported that he had grown up in an "adequate" home where his father had two jobs, and his mother stayed home to raise the kids.

He mentioned that appearances were very important to his mother—how things looked on the outside, whether it was her house, her car, or her clothing. She wanted the world to perceive her as a good person. He also talked about the teasing he experienced in school, but who wasn't teased as a kid in the public school system?

Stewart concluded his time with the professor-president by sharing a few experiences he had at RTI, where he obtained his BS in engineering.

Looking back on his time with Dr. McNeely, Stewart is mildly curious why his spelunking guide repeatedly called his attention to one theme in his past. It was as if he was trying to draw something out of him. Stewart has no idea what that might be.

When he descends the last flight of stairs and enters the Agatha Room, a hand grabs his arm and pulls him through the doorway into the adjacent sanctuary.

After he recovers from his initial shock, he adjusts his glasses and finds himself looking down at a woman he has never seen before. Her hair is as white as snow and appears like rolling whitecaps driven forward by a strong gale. If her face has achieved a wrinkle for every year she has lived, the elderly woman must be well over a hundred years old. She reminds Stewart of a grandmother who might be found in the kitchen with an apron on and with the aroma of cookies and baked bread emanating from her whole person.

At the same time, she is different than a normal grandmother in several ways. Her eyes are far too intense, and her whole body vibrates with irrepressible energy.

Stewart begins to talk, but the woman promptly shushes him. "You speak too much," she scolds. "You must learn to listen more."

The elderly woman pauses and glances around the citadel conspiratorially as if to ensure that no one is eavesdropping on their conversation. "There are other ears in this room," she states with conviction.

Eventually, she leans her white head toward him and says, "Yes, you must listen more. In fact, you must listen to me closely in this exact moment. I have a word for you, young man from Minnesota," she says, her hazel-green eyes riveted on his face.

"I am Miriam, prophetess of the Most High God, the One who rules the universe in love and truth," the elderly woman announces. "The Spirit of God has sent me to warn you that you must come out of your hiding place, and you must come out now!"

Mesmerized, Stewart watches the woman's lively brows dance up and down, and her hands fly back and forth.

"You must come forth if you are to complete the task set before you, Stewart," she declares.

Stewart begins to ask the elderly woman how she knows his name, but she interrupts him with a gesture of her hand. "Quiet! There is a time to speak and a time to be silent. This is a time to be silent."

The prophetess fixes her fierce eyes on Stewart's flat eyes and exclaims, "Listen to what I say. Hear the words that God has for you. How can you love others when you remain in the cave? How can you be prepared for the test that is coming to you when you are alone? The times are dark, and you have been called. Open the door and come out. Come out, Stewart! Yes, you will encounter opposition, but you must come out!"

Stewart adjusts his glasses again and blinks his eyes hard several times to avoid the woman's uncomfortable gaze. He looks up at the glass dome far above his head and examines the azure skies pouring through the cupola. When he looks back down at the prophetess, she is nowhere to be seen. His eyes search the sanctuary, but the woman has vanished.

Shaken, Stewart asks himself, *What exactly did she mean, 'come out, come out of the cave, come out of the hiding place?' Is this related to my time with Dr. McNeely, who directed me to go deeper into one specific area of my childhood?*

His head spinning, Stewart stumbles out of the sanctuary and slowly makes his way back toward the dorm room where he lives by himself.

One thing he does know—Miriam was not referring to the cave beneath the church or the dormitory. No. He is convinced that she was referring to his heart. But what really is his heart, and where might he find it?

CHAPTER 9

Emily in the Cave of Dread

The six members of the micro-cohort trudge down into the catacombs in the company of Dr. McNeely and Dr. Livingstone. Both professors carry a powerful lantern to guide the small party through the dark underworld beneath the campus.

When they reach the bottom of the steps, they do a one-hundred-eighty degree turn and travel in the opposite direction of Dr. Windsor's Warfare classroom. They walk down the tunnel toward where Emily and Stewart discovered the secret wormhole several weeks ago. When they come to the location of the hidden passage, only Stewart spots it as they walk past, so effectively is the entrance camouflaged by the stone slab.

As they continue to move forward through the dark tunnel, Jack feels the floor begin to slant downward sharply. Simultaneously, the air grows cooler and thick with moisture. Emily glances alternately at the two professors and then at Jack. She looks nervous.

Jack estimates that they are well beyond the dormitory and the amphitheater when they finally come to a halt next to a small aperture mostly obscured by a large boulder. One by one, the two professors and the six members of the micro-cohort stoop down and enter the 3' by 4' doorway. The students are amazed at what they see on the other side.

The members of the small traveling party find themselves in a large cavern. By the light of the two powerful lamps, Jack looks around the room and sees that it is shaped like a giant cube, roughly forty feet high, forty feet long, and forty feet wide. It is not a cozy room. The only items that Jack sees in the large underground bunker are a folded futon mattress wrapped in plastic leaning up against the wall, a jug of water, and a small chemical toilet.

"Well, Emily, this is the place," Embee says quietly, almost reverently, as if she is in a holy place.

"The infamous Cave of Dread," Armando mumbles quietly but just loud enough for everyone to hear.

"Remember, Emily, it is referred to by that name because people are understandably apprehensive about sojourning down here alone," Dr. McNeely says reassuringly. "But even more importantly, people don't like being down here because it is a place where God reveals difficult things to them that nonetheless are essential for their growth."

Embee touches Emily's arm and interjects, "This cave is simply a place to be alone with God, a place to hear Him speak to your heart. Oftentimes, we are so adept at keeping ourselves so busy in our everyday lives that we rarely have time to examine ourselves or listen to the voice of the Holy Spirit. Eighteen hours down here affords a person not only quality time but also quantity of time to examine her heart."

"You won the lottery," Rachel quips to Emily with a nervous chuckle. "You're the lucky winner who earned the right to break in this place for our micro-cohort. God clearly wants you down here first."

Rachel hesitates just a moment and then says more empathically, "Look at it this way, Emily—it's like being the first to present in speech class. Once you're done, you can sit back with relief and watch the rest of us go through it."

Emily does not look comforted. "You did say I can quit any time I want, right?" she asks, turning her shadowed face toward the two professors.

"Yes, of course, my dear," Embee says, nodding her head. "We've discovered that it's beneficial to complete the whole eighteen hours, if at all possible, but if you must finish the exercise sooner, feel free to do that."

Jack suspects that Embee came close to repeating the same word Emily used—"quit"—but was careful to choose the word "finish" instead. *That's Embee,* he thinks, *always positive and encouraging.*

"Try to remember everything we told you in class today," Embee advises. "Since you look worried, I want you to hear it again: Your time here alone is an occasion to listen to God and hear what He has to say to your heart. Frequently, these cave sojourns reveal things that you'll never discover in the middle of the distractions of daily life. God has a way of speaking to us when we create space to hear His voice."

Dr. McNeely levels a serious gaze at Emily. "Also, be aware that you may very well encounter the dark side of your heart or even the enemy of your soul while down here. Such encounters can be challenging. But it's exactly at such times that Jesus walks the closest to us," He comments with quiet confidence.

"Do you have any questions for us, Emily?" Embee asks as she takes the student's hand into hers.

"How will I know when I'm done?" the young woman asks in a voice that quavers.

"All seven of us will come down and retrieve you," McNeely says in his bass voice.

"Okay, then I guess I don't have any other questions," Emily comments. "I just want this to be over."

Even though the striations of light expose her face unevenly, Jack observes that Emily is scared. Initially, he feels a strong compulsion to comfort her or rescue her from this place, but then it strikes him that maybe the young woman is not so much afraid of her external environment as she is afraid of what she might encounter inside herself while in this alone and undistracted place.

"I know you do, Emily," Embee comments. "Just do your best to take full advantage of this experience. Part of the power of this sojourn is knowing that we'll be up in the sanctuary praying for you all night long. All of us. You won't be alone. We'll be praying for the Holy Spirit to be present in powerful ways to teach you and to comfort your deepest fears."

Following a common practice at the Academy, the professors and students gather around Emily. Then, in a voice that echoes in the dark cavern, Dr. McNeely prays, "Jesus, we thank you for your example, how on various occasions when you walked this earth, you retreated to a lonely place—often at night. We know that at those times, you sought your father's face with all your heart. Be with Emily tonight as she also seeks you with all her heart. May she hear your voice clearly. Also, open her eyes so that she might examine her heart as never before. Reveal what you know will be helpful to your beloved daughter. In your holy name, Amen."

When the prayer is over, everyone says their goodbyes and offers the reassurance that they will be up all night with Emily, just in another location. Then they leave the cavern through the small doorway.

Jack is the last one to leave. He gently touches Emily's arm and says, "You won't be alone down her, Emily. Jesus is always with us in the valley of the shadows." Then he, too, turns and retreats from the cavern.

For a while, Emily listens to the sound of retreating feet shuffling over the stone floor of the tunnel. Then there is only silence. She is alone. They have taken all the light with them.

"I'm definitely not going to do this in the dark," she says out loud. Kneeling on the mattress that was unwrapped and laid out on the floor before the others left, she gropes in the blackness for the candle and the box of matches that Embee said were left for her. Eventually, she finds them and lights the single candle that generates only a feeble glow in the large cavern.

Initially, she is not convinced that the light is a good thing because now she looks up apprehensively into the dark vault above her and down the length and width of the gloomy room. The single candle sheds only enough illumination for her mind to imagine dark images in the corners of the creepy cavern.

For a long time, she sits on the floor of the Cave of Dread with her back against the damp wall. *I could sleep,* she tells herself. *Then morning will come quickly; this will all be done before I know it. But who am I kidding? I'm wide awake. It's only 7:00 at night, anyway.*

She sits in silence. She does not know for how long since she has no way to measure the passage of time. Phones and other time-keeping devices are verboten during the sojourn in the Cave of Dread.

A longer time passes. Nothing changes—on the outside, at least. On the inside, Emily senses a familiar tension building. She chooses to ignore it, ignore it as she has done for the past five years.

As she knew it would, the familiar sensation continues to gnaw away at her heart. In recent years, she has come to think of it as her dis-ease. She experiences the dis-ease as a combination of restlessness, desire, shame, aloneness, and abandonment. She must send it away.

On this night, it slowly grows in intensity until she is forced to stand up and pace in the gloom, candle in hand.

She longs for her comforter—her go-to coping agent that she discovered in college. She wants a drink, and not something soft. She wants something hard that will burn all the way down her throat and into her stomach, something that will quickly numb her pain—whatever it may be—and mute the mysterious dis-ease that chews on the edges of her heart.

Emily's thoughts descend to a basement room deep inside her heart that serves as a vault for her old memories. She remembers that she was raised in a home where her parents loved God and raised her to know God. She was sent to Sunday School and to Bible camp on the lake every summer. She attended a Christian college and participated in multiple mission trips, some domestic and some international. Before she was twenty-one, she gave her heart to Jesus and was baptized.

In subsequent years, Emily shared her testimony on many occasions and even encouraged her younger siblings in their faith journeys. Her relationship with Jesus seemed close and genuine. But somewhere along the way, during the ups and downs and twists and turns of life, she began to drift off the path. The drifting turned into straying and the straying into a full-blown flight from faith.

Then, one day, she discovered alcohol and fell off a cliff. The addiction was instantaneous. Since that first day after her senior year of high school, she had never thought about it long enough to figure out if the alcohol had caused her dis-ease or if the dis-ease inside her heart had led her to turn to alcohol as a comforter. Whatever it was, she had taken one drink and immediately was captured by a relentless craving. A deep desire within her awakened like a slumbering dragon, and she became its slave.

Five years into her journey off the path, Emily has learned that the dis-ease within her can be muted and even temporarily eradicated by alcohol. But then the excessive alcohol use spawns the emptiness that can only be subdued with more alcohol. Tonight, in the Cave of Dread, she feels the dis-ease ramping up, but she does not have access to her usual comforter. So, she paces back and forth in the dark cavern faster and faster to quiet the growing tempest within her. She stumbles several times on the uneven floor.

The tension within her begins to morph from the vague restlessness to something different. She feels an emotion. Sadness. She also sees a face in her mind but cannot identify it. Then something strikes her. She stops pacing.

She remembers that she was a daddy's girl since the day she was born.

Funny, how I forgot that, she thinks in her foggy brain. Soon she remembers why she had to forget that. She begins to pace again.

The truth is, she has been distant from her parents for years now. When she strayed off the ancient path and began traveling down her own road, she had to avoid them. She perceived them as too conservative, too overprotective, too judgmental, too ignorant, blah, blah, blah.

The alternative road she has traveled down for a handful of years now has taken her far away from everything she was raised to believe. So, now she avoids her parents for another reason: she believes they will be deeply disappointed in her choices, and worse than that, deeply disappointed in her as the daughter who used to be their good girl.

Emily believes that they will shame her—make her feel bad for what she has done and for what she believes. They will judge her. Yes, that's the primary reason she avoids them, she thinks. They are narrow people, and her life has become...broader.

But somewhere inside her befuddled mind, she wonders if she also avoids them...because...she feels guilty around them—even if they don't say a word. Her options, then, are to blame her parents for judging her or... or to admit to herself that she is acting in a way that generates guilt within her even apart from anything they might say.

She cannot allow the latter truth to linger in her mind because then she will have to admit that she is doing something bad. She may even feel compelled to give up what she is doing, which brings her pleasure and makes her feel calm. She absolutely refuses to do that.

Emily paces even faster in the damp candle-lit gloom as the emotion within her grows more intense. It chokes her throat while tears beat against the inside of her eyes, clamoring for release. Suddenly, she cannot breathe.

Meanwhile, back in the cavernous sanctuary above ground—like Emily's cavern, illuminated by only a single candle—it is 1:30 in the morning. All seven members of the support team are taking turns praying or reading Scripture. Aly prays that the Triune God will strengthen Emily in the darkness. "Dear God, wrap your arms around your precious daughter who needs to see that you are a good, good Father."

"Don't you see!" the voice chops out the syllables like a butcher knife cleaving bones on a wooden block (of course, human ears cannot hear it). *"All the lies we've been carefully wrapping around her mind like so many chains are under threat! They're in danger of collapsing like so many dominos! You absolutely must prevent a beachhead of intimacy from being established in her heart! Have you, in your idiocy, forgotten that the enemy of darkness loves a beachhead? As soon as he sets one foot on that strip of sand, it's only a matter of time until he takes it all back! Go at once and shove the truth back out to sea! It must not take root in her heart! Destroy every beachhead! Every single one!"*

Emily collapses to her knees on the stone floor of the cavern. A heavy curtain that has covered her heart for years is yanked aside for a moment, and she realizes that her path has taken her far from God and the people she used to love. How much she has lost! She has strayed away from them so she can pursue other loves and avoid facing the consequences of her poor choices.

The tension of the brief civil war within her becomes crushing.

She has placed herself in a position where she will suffer loss no matter which path she now chooses, but she is convinced that if she forsakes her current affections, she simply has too much to lose and too much to own. The pain and the guilt will be massive, as well as the fear of losing her comforter.

Just when her heart is about to break like the dam of an engorged reservoir, the candlelight in her hand is extinguished, and Emily finds herself in utter darkness.

For a long time, she kneels on the cold stone floor, disoriented. Eventually, she gets to her feet and carefully makes her way back toward the mattress, her arms stretched out before her in the total blackout. Briefly, she sees a mental video of her dad tying a blindfold around her eyes and placing a small baseball bat into her hands so she can swing away at the dinosaur piñata. It is her seventh birthday.

For a moment, she contemplates the idea of returning to her father as well as to her Father, but then she remembers it. No, she remembers them. She stumbles in the black cave and falls hard onto the stone floor.

Emily hears the familiar voice in her head that seems so ancient now as if it has been there from the beginning of time. It accuses her of being selfish, foolish, bad, sinful, evil. Her parents and friends will be ashamed of her; it reminds her for the millionth time. It tells her that no one who loves God would ever do what she's done. Then comes the familiar coup de grace: *Murderer.*

The accusation is spoken quietly. It rings with finality. It defines her.

Emily curls up into a ball where she has fallen. Soon she becomes as cold as the stone floor on which she lies—and just as hard. She feels nothing. She remembers nothing.

When the two professors and the five other members of the micro-cohort return to the Cave of Dread precisely at 1:00 p.m. the next afternoon, they find Emily sitting with her back against the damp wall of the cavern. She is in complete darkness. She seems fine and talks fine and looks fine. But both Embee and Jack know something has happened during her sojourn that Emily will not expose to the light. Something has transpired in the cavern during the night that is unspeakable.

Embee utters a silent prayer as they usher Emily away from the Cave of Dread. The professor prays because she is not unfamiliar with what can occur in the darkest and most inaccessible recesses of the human heart. She understands that the door of the soul can be slammed shut more tightly than a vacuum-sealed container and walled off more impenetrably than the thickest chromium steel barrier. She knows that mere human argument is powerless against both the darkness and the defenses that reign inside the human heart.

Only one light in the vast expanse of the universe can penetrate that impenetrable keep—the light above all lights and the name above all names.

CHAPTER 10

Stewart's Discovery

Stewart approaches Jack while he is sitting at a table in the library that is located on the fourth floor of the edifice.

"I found it!" he announces breathlessly. His voice is unusually animated, and his face is flushed.

"What exactly did you find, Stewart?" Jack asks with a valiant attempt at interest. The Intellect has shared so much information with him over the past two months that Jack has become largely inured to his peer's revelations. At the same time, Jack notes that Stewart's level of excitement is unprecedented, so he attempts to generate at least some genuine interest in his friend's discovery.

The bespectacled man from Two Harbors, Minnesota, holds up what appears to be a metal box that is shorter than a shoebox but a little wider. It is battered and scratched and looks to be very old. Unusually, Stewart's mouth is silent, but his face is beaming.

"What is it?" Jack asks as he leans forward and examines the box with narrowed eyes.

"Follow me," Stewart insists as he turns and disappears behind the nearest floor-to-ceiling book stack. Jack shakes his head and sighs. Then he gets up from his chair and follows his friend down the narrow aisle and into a small study room.

As soon as Jack is in the room, Stewart shuts the door and yanks down the mini blind that covers the single rectangular window set into the door. Then he carefully sets the box on the table in the middle of the room and proceeds to open the lid.

Leaning forward, Jack pushes his shoulder-length hair out of the way and peers into the box. The only thing inside is a book with a leather cover.

"I haven't even taken it out yet," Stewart reports, looking at his friend with eyes that shine with excitement. "I want this to be something I share with my trusted mini-cohort, beginning with you, Jack. I think it must be an item of interest since the owner took pains to hide it."

"Where in the world did you find it?" Jack asks as he stares at the opened box with mild interest. "More importantly, *how* did you find it?"

"Believe it or not, I discovered it in the Warfare classroom as I was applying a heuristic strategy," the Intellect explains. "You see, after Emily and I discovered the worm hole, I decided to search every cavern and passage in the subterranean space beneath the campus focusing on the juncture of the walls and the floor.

"As you've most likely surmised by now, I was looking for a stone slab like the one Emily and I discovered in the tunnel the other day. It took me three days, but I eventually discovered a loose rock in the classroom that covered a small hiding place carved into the rock."

"No way!" Jack exclaims. "Where?"

"In the far corner of the room. On the left side, nearest to Dr. Windsor's desk."

"You're kidding!" Jack says and then groans. "It's been right under our noses all along?" He pauses and looks down into the box again. "So, what is it?"

"Like I said," Stewart repeats patiently, "I haven't opened it yet."

"Yeah, so you said," Jack acknowledges. "Well, let's open it now. I'll be the witness who observes you crack the cover of the book. In fact, I'll videotape this whole thing with my phone." Jack rubs his hands together like a safe cracker's assistant before the combination to the vault is solved.

Jack smiles to himself as he watches Stewart lick his lips and then carefully extract the book from the tin box. "At least it doesn't look like it's going to disintegrate into dust between your fingers," he quips.

"I don't think it's that old," Stewart replies matter-of-factly. "Besides, it's been preserved in a relatively dry environment."

Jack smiles again at the man who just missed another opportunity to display social awareness. "It was a joke, Stewart," he comments with a small shake of his head. "Not everything is to be taken literally."

By now, the amateur archaeologist is so enthralled with his artifact that he does not even acknowledge Jack. *He probably didn't hear a word I said,* Jack thinks to himself.

Stewart carefully places the leather-bound book on the wooden study table and, with the care of a surgeon, removes the sturdy string tied around it. He slowly opens the cover, and a small landslide of dust and stone particles slides onto the table. Then the Intellect begins to examine its contents.

"It's just what I thought. It's not a book or a ledger. It's clearly some type of personal journal," Stewart observes.

"What does it say?" Jack asks, leaning in for a closer look.

"Well, the first page is some type of introduction," Stewart says as he scans its contents. "It reads, 'The private diary of JLS.' Sorry to be reading so slowly, Jack. The cursive is a bit challenging, although the ink is clear and robust."

The Intellect pauses for a moment and pinches the right bow of his glasses. Then he lowers his head close to the journal and begins to read again.

"'This account is not a seed calendar or a farm almanac or a business record. Rather, it is a personal journal in which are recorded the thoughts of JLS and the occurrences in his life. Let it be known that this diary commences on the date of 4 March 1899.'"

"Wow, all the way back to the nineteenth century," Jack comments, genuinely impressed. "But why would he go to the trouble of hiding a diary or a journal or whatever it's called?"

"Well, there's only one way to find out," Stewart says as his methodical eyes rise to meet Jack's. "We'll have to read the whole thing."

"How long is it?" Jack inquires.

Stewart's fingers carefully walk through the pages of the old journal. "Well, it's not completely full. I'd estimate that about two-thirds of it contains entries—so maybe seventy or eighty pages since the journalist writes on only one side of each page as far as I can see."

"Okay, so not a terribly long read then," Jack observes, rubbing the fingers of his right hand over the two-day-old stubble on his chin. "I like your idea of sharing this journal with the micro-cohort, Stew. It'll definitely help develop our esprit de corps."

Jack smiles since he pronounced the last phrase phonetically, so it sounds like he was talking about the spirit of a dead body. "I'll text the others and find out when they can join us. Then let's read this thing."

"Sounds good to me, Jack," Stewart responds. "Maybe we can read it together as soon as after supper tonight. We should all be back from the hotel by then."

The next morning, Jack heads out before dawn for his daily four-mile run. At the beginning of the semester, he had mapped out a course that runs along the lake for more than a mile, then up the amphitheater hill and through a less wooded seam in the forest. Once through the trees, the course runs down the hillside opposite the lake and eventually ends at the cemetery.

Although he feels a little uneasy running alone through the deserted woods an hour before sunrise, the course is far less worrisome to him than some of the isolated ones he would run back in Colorado.

When he completes his run at the arched gateway of the cemetery, he checks his time on his fitness wearable that features a barometric altimeter—helpful in Colorado but unnecessary in the Midwest. Satisfied with the result—sub-eight-minute miles—he pockets his phone and wanders a short distance into the cemetery while he catches his breath and engages in some post-run stretching.

Rose-colored light is brightening the eastern sky and beginning to spill over the horizon when his eyes fall on four large trees in the far corner of the cemetery that grow so close together that they appear to share the same trunk. It strikes him at the moment that maybe even trees come in quadruplets. He bends over and stretches his right leg one last time. Then he straightens and turns to leave.

To Jack's complete shock, he finds himself nose to nose with a man he assumes is the cemetery caretaker. The front half of the man's head is totally bald, but the sides and back are covered with long stringy hair that crawls down his shoulders like a living thing. His scraggly beard is very thin, with islands of pale skin peeking through. His nose is crooked as if it had been displaced in the past and never correctly repaired. His eyes are badly bloodshot. He is not a small man.

Before Jack can step away, the man jabs a finger into Jack's chest and growls at him, "Don't think I don't know who you are!"

Jack can only register that the man has uttered a double negative and should work on his grammar when he feels the searing pain of a knife penetrate his body between his ribs. His eyes open in horror, and he attempts to speak, but all that comes out of his throat is a gurgling groan.

The deranged man leans in close, his breath rancid in Jack's nostrils. "I know who you are, Jack!" he rasps, spitting out the name. "You ain't goin' to stop me now. I'll see you in hell, Jack Sutherington! But how sad for you—you're goin' to get there long before me!"

The terrifying man begins to laugh wickedly, exposing badly yellowed and crooked teeth. Then he gives Jack a rough shove, and he reels backward. Despite his best efforts to right himself, Jack stumbles backward and tumbles into a freshly dug grave. He hits the bottom of the hole so hard it knocks the breath out of him.

Even as Jack is gasping for air, the cemetery caretaker begins to shovel dirt on top of him. Panic grips him when he realizes that he is going to be buried alive. He tries to scream, but blood is filling his lungs, and he is unable to produce anything but a hissing sound. Then a shovel-full of dirt hurtles toward his face in slow motion and hits him with crushing force. Everything goes dark.

Jack feels the jolt of electricity crash through his body like a runaway train, and he throws himself onto the cold floor. He quickly rolls over onto his back. While he attempts to breathe, he hears Armando mumbling in his sleep, "Are you okay, ese? Don't worry, Juan, I'll protect you from those cholos." His roommate mumbles something else and then falls silent.

Jack struggles to breathe for a long time. He wonders how his heart can absorb the shock of it all. Finally, he turns over onto his stomach and buries his face in the rug.

"Why, God?" he cries out in a muffled voice. "Why? How much longer must I endure this suffering? I don't think I can take it anymore. Help! Please help me, God!"

Little does Jack know that his last four words are precisely what is needed to set in motion an invisible army that exists in a dimension beyond physical sight and hearing.

CHAPTER 11

Lighthouse Farm

The mid-October day is sunny and crisp. The air is laden with a whisper of autumn coolness, the smell of dry leaves, and the vague scent of crisp apples ripe on the trees. The six members of the Screaming Eagles micro-cohort are riding in the Academy van with windows wide open headed for the Livingstone farm. The rural road, wonderfully, takes them over rolling hills and around sharp corners and across small creeks as they penetrate deeper into the country and further from the city.

Thirty minutes after leaving the Academy, they turn onto a narrow gravel road that curves for another mile along with fenced fields and lazily grazing horses until they arrive at a wrought iron sign hanging from a post that reads *Lighthouse Farm*. Here they turn and navigate a long driveway framed on either side by towering cottonwood trees and waist-high hedges clothed with burning orange, red, yellow, and copper leaves. The crushed-rock driveway slants upward toward a quaint two-story house crawling with ivy and hugged by a large porch that reminds Jack of a Thomas Kincaid painting. A wind vane ruled by a black rooster perches atop the crown of the roof. On their left is a small sun-sparkled pond with an inviting wooden dock stretching out into the water.

When they reach the top of the hill, Jack parks the van on a small apron in front of the house and climbs out. He could not be more pumped about being in nature, him being a Colorado boy and all. His five passengers are quick to follow him out of the vehicle.

As Jack surveys his rustic surroundings, he hears Armando say, "Dude, I don't think I've ever been on a farm before. It seems so...so open and smelly. But where are the chickens and pigs?" he asks, looking around, bewildered.

Jack smiles broadly and slaps Armando on the back. "Not all farms have animals, my urban friend. Some only have crops like corn, beans, wheat, and alfalfa. I remember Embee saying that the only animals they have are a bunch of feral cats, a few goats, and a dog or two. I think her husband farms several hundred acres."

"And look," Armando observes, pointing at a structure adjacent to the house. "There's a barn, but it's not red. I thought all barns were red. That one's white."

This time Rachel educates her confused classmate. "Armando, you've obviously had a deprived childhood. Barns can be many different colors. Out in Connecticut, we even have some green and yellow barns. They don't have to be red. There isn't some universal agricultural edict that says barns must be red."

Armando opens his mouth to comment that he doesn't see a windmill either when Dr. Livingstone steps out of the farmhouse accompanied by a tall, thin man. On his head is a red baseball cap inscribed with the name of a defunct farm implement manufacturer. The matron of the farm is wearing a long print dress with a colorful yellow scarf tied around her neck. She has sandals on her feet, and her hair flows down over her left shoulder like silver water. Large gold earrings bounce and sway as she walks toward the cohort.

Dr. Livingstone still has a bit of hippie Moon Beam inside of her, Jack thinks to himself with a smile.

"Welcome, welcome!" Embee says in her inviting voice that is as bright as sunlight and as smooth as moonlight on still waters. Instantly, everyone feels at home at the farm nestled in the countryside.

"This is my husband Sam, otherwise known as Sunny," she says, squeezing the arm of the man next to her. "His name is spelled with a u, not an o."

The man is dressed in slim jeans and a sharp, grey flannel shirt that make him look like country with a splash of style. If possible, he is smiling even more broadly than his wife. It is a warm, easy smile that makes the students feel as welcomed as Embee's voice. Jack immediately knows how the man came by his nickname.

After the Academy professor introduces the students to her husband, Dr. Livingstone and Sunny lead a tour around the farm property, showing them the roundish pond that is stocked with bass and crappies and the white barn that is more of a bunkhouse than a shelter for animals or a storehouse for hay.

After a tour of the barn, Sunny leads them to a one-room cabin located on the edge of a heavily wooded riverbank that descends steeply toward what looks more like a big stream than a river—at least, at this time of the year.

Embee and her husband pause beside the diminutive cabin and glance at each other. The joy that had been radiating from their faces remains but is tempered by lines of sadness that appear around their eyes and mouths.

Dr. Livingstone gestures toward a golden cross planted in the ground next to the cabin. "Our first child," she informs the group in a quiet voice. "A boy. We named him Abraham. He was afflicted with a rare chromosomal disorder. He lived seven days and four hours in this world. He died in my arms in the swing under the oak tree. Over by the pond."

Embee falls silent and Sunny steps in where she left off. "We knew his spirit went home to be with Jesus," the tall man says in a strong voice but with a tear blazing its way down his weathered cheek. "But we still didn't want to leave him alone in the cemetery. So, we had the service down by the river and buried him here, close to us." He pauses and then adds quietly, "In honesty, we buried him close by for our sake."

Embee shakes her head slowly. "We were totally unprepared for how much grief we were going to experience for that little guy. After all, we had four months to prepare for his death. I never realized how precious life was until Abraham came to us and then left us. He taught us so much. Of course," the woman adds softly as she stares down at the flowing water, "the grieving was complicated by other...factors."

The matron pauses a moment and eventually turns a smiling face toward the small group. The tears in her eyes would lead people who do not know the professor to judge her smile as ingenuine, as a blatant contradiction to her smile. But everyone standing in Embee's presence beside the little grave is fully aware that the woman's smile and tears are not incongruous—that the joy inside of her will never be extinguished by even the harshest storms of life.

The Screaming Eagles already know that her joy is not mere superficial happiness whose existence is conditional—contingent on things around her going well for it to endure. No, her joy is a deep underground river that runs under and through every event in her life, both good and bad.

Sunny leads the small group away from the cabin and down a hill that opens out into a field covered with golden stubble. To the left, the hill slopes much more gradually until it meets the river.

"This is one of two fields I farm," Sunny announces. "The other one is across the river and up the hill on the other side. This year I planted corn and soybeans. As you can see, I've already harvested the crops. Just finished on Monday, in fact. Moisture levels in the corn were nice and low."

On the far side of the cornfield in front of them, a dense wall of trees brings the field to an abrupt halt. "We call that forest over there Deer Run since so many deers travel through there to get to the river," Embee says. "And this little glade we're standing in between the field and the river we call Fox Hollow."

The students follow Moon Beam and Sunny down a sloping path that leads to the river's edge.

"We call this area Lazy Beaver Bay because the river widens here and flows very slowly," Sunny says as he squints against the bright sunlight dancing off the water. "The river itself we call the Little Jordan since, like its namesake in Israel, it floods in the springtime with runoff from the heavy rains. Just like the real Jordan, she's a bit challenging to cross that time of the year. You sure wouldn't know it now, of course."

"What's that over there?" Emily inquires as she nods her ponytailed head in the direction of a golden retriever sitting eternally across the Little Jordan on top of the opposite bank. The canine figure appears to have been carved out of the trunk of a tree.

"Well, there's a story in that," Sunny answers as he pushes his red cap back on his head and adjusts the bill until it's in just the right position. "It's in memory of Summer."

"Who's Summer?" Aly asks. "I mean, I know Summer most likely was a dog, of course. But who exactly was he—or she?"

"Yes, Summer was one of our dogs," Sunny replies wistfully. "In fact, she was my favorite dog. We had two at the time—that was about twenty-five years ago when we first moved out here. It was around the time we had Abraham.

"Their names were Summer and Belle—sisters. Summer was older but not very obedient. Belle, the younger one, was much better at following directions. Every time we crossed the river and went up to the other field,

Summer would run on ahead, but Belle would stay by my side or next to the tractor."

Sunny gazes out across the flowing water toward the upper field. "One day—it was June, I think—I was going up to cultivate the corn; I told Summer to stay beside the tractor. Of course, she didn't listen. As usual, she hightails it lickety-split up the hill ahead of Belle and I and disappears," the tall man explains.

"Well, by the time I cross the river and get up to the top of the hill on the tractor, all I saw was Summer's tail disappearing into the woods on the far side of the field. I called and whistled and called some more. I even yelled out the name of her favorite treat. She didn't respond. She didn't obey."

Sunny yanks off his cap and runs work-worn fingers through his thinning gray hair. "I kind of had this funny feeling that I would never see her again," he says with a hint of melancholy in his voice. "And you know what? I was right. That tail of hers was the last thing I ever saw of Summer. She probably ran off chasing a squirrel or a rabbit and kept going and going until she was gone. Never did figure out what happened to her. Probably eaten by a pack of coyotes or a rare mountain lion passing through the woods."

Embee wraps her arm around her husband's waist and interjects, "When our six children were growing up on the farm, they soon learned exactly what we meant when we warned them not to be like Summer but to be like Belle. Obey, and things will go well for you. Disobey, and sooner or later, you will bring great harm to yourself like Summer did."

Sunny grabs the bill of his hat and repositions it on his head. He remarks, "I loved that dog almost like a child. It's sad to think that the momentary pleasure of running off after some rabbit was more rewarding than obeying me and living out her years in a family where she was deeply loved.

Goes to show that temptation is a slippery slope. It can lure even a dog into pursuing a fleeting pleasure that kills her in the end."

The students are quiet as they contemplate the sad demise of Summer simply because she didn't obey her master.

Dr. Livingstone arouses the members of the micro-cohort from their somber thoughts by announcing that it is time for class to begin and that she will now lead them to the outdoor classroom next to the farmhouse. She also informs them that brisket burnt ends, baked beans, corn bread, and peach cobbler will be waiting for them after class is done.

Everyone laughs when Sunny wryly suggests that they should all play hooky and go straight for the food—everyone but Aly and Stewart; Aly because she doesn't know the meaning of the dated word, and Stewart because he rarely comprehends humor in any setting.

As everyone retraces their steps through Fox Hollow and back up the hill, Jack looks over his shoulder and notices that Emily is lingering beside the river. He turns back and joins his classmate by the gently flowing water that carries leaf-boats on its back.

"I've been meaning to ask you," he says, announcing his presence to the girl with the golden ponytail, "what it was like."

Emily does not turn to look at Jack as she replies, "What are you talking about?"

"I think you know," Jack says quietly.

"You mean the cave," she responds while gazing up the river that wends its way quietly, silkily between the high banks. The young woman sounds far away.

"Yes," Jack says, nodding his head.

Emily's bottle-green eyes remain fixed on the river for a long time.

Finally, they travel over to Jack and glance at him briefly. "The Cave of Dread is a very personal experience," she says matter-of-factly. "As such, I plan to keep what happened there to myself."

"Well, if you haven't noticed, your personal experience in the cave seems to have impacted you a lot," Jack observes with zero critical intent.

Emily reaches down to touch a stick that is floating by, borne along on the silver sheet of the lazy river. "What do you see?" she inquires coolly as she stands up.

"You've been…" here Jack pauses, searching for the right words. "You've been quieter and…brooding. I think that's the right word. You've been brooding. And distant."

"Brooding," she repeats back to him mechanically. "You make me sound like a hen or a storm cloud." She laughs, but it is not a warm laugh.

Emily examines the detained stick in her hand as if it is an object of great importance. She does not see Jack shake his head in frustration.

"Okay, let's call it preoccupied," Jack observes. "You seem preoccupied with your thoughts—and not positive ones." He hesitates a moment and adds, "A part of you never came back from the cave, Emily."

"That sounds extreme," the young woman parries, frustration tightening her voice. She chooses not to look at Jack.

"Is it, Emily?" he counters. He directs his attention away from Emily and nods his head at a tree that has fallen into the river twenty feet upstream.

"See that tree?" he asks. "See how it has dammed up those branches and leaves?"

"Of course, I'm not blind," Emily replies with a shrug.

"I'm thinking you are like that tree," Jack suggests. "You have a dam inside of you that's holding you back. Hiding you. And I just...just want to see your heart."

For the first time in the conversation, Emily looks at Jack fully, her green eyes fiery. "You and every other guy I've met over the past decade!" she retorts with heavy sarcasm.

"Whoa," Jack responds gently. "What's that supposed to mean?"

Emily stares at him a while longer before she snaps, "You said you wanted to see my heart. Well, here it is!"

Jack holds her flashing eyes and says, "At the risk of you telling me that I'm stating the obvious, I'm going to venture to guess that you've been hurt deeply by certain men in your past."

The young woman with dimples that have not made an appearance since before her sojourn in the Cave of Dread stares at him a while longer and then looks away. "It's time for class," is all she says, and Jack knows that his attempt at intimacy has been masterfully fended off.

"I'm so happy you're here at Lighthouse Farm," Embee says brightly to the students sitting in a small circle under Abraham's towering oak tree by the pond. A swing still hangs from one of its lower branches. "In some ways, this annual gathering here is the highlight of my year at the Academy. I—"

"May I ask you the reason for the moniker, Lighthouse Farm?" Stewart inquires, interrupting. His face is expressionless, bereft of humanity. He is an artificial intelligence seeking more data to enter and store in his memory.

Jack shakes his head ever so slightly, feeling frustrated and amused at the same time. Once again, it is obvious that his fellow student is not interested in Embee or his classmates as people—not really. His sole desire is to satisfy his brain's voracious hunger to gather more information. Jack thinks to himself that this class with Dr. Livingstone focusing on love is the perfect one for Stewart. Love seems so foreign to the young man whose personality is so analytical.

"How good of you to ask," the professor comments as she smiles and leans toward Stewart. "It's a funny thing, really." Embee laughs as she steeples her fingers together thoughtfully.

"My husband and I thought about our names—Moon Beam and Sunny—and decided that whatever we called this rural property, it had to be about light. Besides, it's been our prayer since the day we were married that the Savior's love might shine through us to everyone walking in darkness. From the very beginning, we've wanted to be beacons leading people away from potential shipwrecks and toward safe anchorage in the love of Jesus. So, what better name than Lighthouse Farm?"

The matronly professor smiles at Stewart as she leans back in her white Adirondack chair to consult her iPad. After a glance, she sets it on one of the broad arms of her chair and says, "In class on Wednesday, we discussed how one reductionistic approach claims that love can be divided into two types: We can love people for what they do for us, or we can love people for who they are as creatures designed by God in His image.

"The first type reduces love to utility because it's innate in humans to love others in a mercenary fashion. Deep inside, we say, I will love you *if* you make me happy. I will love you *if* you don't make me angry. I will love you *when* your personality doesn't inconvenience me. I will love you *if* you do your part cleaning the house or the dorm room. *If. When. When. If.*"

The professor gently fingers one of her golden earrings as she looks at the students sitting in the small circle in their matching Adirondack chairs. "This type of love is not only utilitarian but also conditional," she asserts.

"It's grounded in performance and convenience.

"So, never minimize the interpersonal allure of convenience. People love others who don't take them out of their comfort zone or create unnecessary tension or make emotional demands on them. When our love is rooted in condition, we really only love others if they consent to be nice people pleasers."

Embee pauses and looks one by one into the faces of her six students. A bee flies lazily by Jack's ear. A large choir of cicadas generates a high-pitched buzzing down by the river. A crow caws loudly in a nearby tree. A light breeze wends through the backyard of the farmhouse and lilts the ends of Rachel's vivid auburn hair.

"Contrary to humans who love conditionally," the professor continues, "Jesus did not love us for what we could do for Him. He loved us with a love that entailed no condition, no selfish gain, and that pursued us when we were inherently inconvenient to Him. He loved us when we were in love with our idols and addictions. He loved us when we were sold out to hatred instead of forgiveness. He loved us even when we chose autonomy as our god instead of Him. Motivated by grace and love, He died for us even when we accused Him of being judgmental and wrathful."

Dr. Livingstone smiles and gently brushes a small grasshopper off her arm. "So," she says, spreading her open palms toward the students in the circle around her, "can one of you tell me what happens when we invite God's unconditional love into our hearts?"

Without hesitation, Aly interjects, "We're born again. Jesus enters into our hearts and changes everything."

The professor nods in agreement and remarks, "Exactly, Aly." She pauses and then says, "Some people claim miracles don't happen anymore, or that they've never occurred at all. Well," the owner of Lighthouse Farm says, absent-mindedly fingering the cross that dangles from her neck, "let me remind you that believing in God's Son and being born again is the most incredible miracle a human can experience."

The professor takes a swallow from her water bottle and then adds, "We sometimes forget that the moment we invite Jesus into our hearts, a spiritual transformation happens within us that's more amazing than any physical miracle. This new birth is more awesome than a blind person receiving sight, cancer miraculously disappearing from someone's pancreas, or a paralyzed person made to walk again. These physical miracles are nothing to be discounted, of course. But the new birth involves a change in our very nature whereby a new person is created within us who will live forever."

Embee looks directly into Stewart's eyes and says, "This miracle that happens when we open our hearts to Jesus' love is not fiction. We're not talking about becoming mutants with God-like abilities or superheroes with some type of amazing physical power. We're not referring to fantasy. Jesus literally, in real time, creates something new in us the moment we believe in Him! He creates a new Aly, a new Stewart, a new Rachel! What could be more loving and miraculous than that?"

Rachel rests her chin on an extended index finger and reflects aloud, "I never thought of it that way before, that the new birth is greater than any physical miracle."

Aly knits her fine brows and asks, "Can you explain the new birth a bit more? I don't think I've ever fully understood what happens at that moment."

Dr. Livingstone leans forward in her large chair, nodding her head and rose-budding her lips. "Jesus made it very clear when He spoke to Nicodemus that men and women need to be born twice in this world," the professor begins. "Obviously, we're born physically, delivered from our mother's womb. But Jesus declared that He was sent by His loving Father to give everyone who would receive it a second birth—a *spiritual* one. He says about these two births, 'Flesh gives birth to flesh, but the Spirit gives birth to spirit.'"

The rays of the sinking afternoon sun search out Embee's eyes, and she squints. "Even though the Light of the world—Jesus—invites us to be born again spiritually, He says that many men and women love darkness instead of light. Sadly, these people refuse to be born for the second time. They settle for being born only once—physically. They love their idols more than they love Jesus, and so they shun the gift of second birth.

However," Embee says as her somber countenance brightens, "those who love the truth and want to live in the light forsake their most tempting idols. They come to their senses and turn to Jesus, and the Holy Spirit conceives and births a new man or woman in them—a new spiritual self. Paul refers to this new birth when he writes, 'Therefore, if anyone is in Christ, he is a new creation. The old has passed away; behold, the new has come.'"

Dr. Livingstone's eyes scan the faces of the six students in the outdoor classroom. "But that's not the end of it, is it?" she asks with a knowing smile. "We've all experienced the most incredible relationship that comes after we've been born again. The Spirit of God Himself takes up residence in our newly born selves. God lives in us! God Himself lives in these jars of clay we call our bodies.

"The bottom-line truth that follows is that we don't see anything ever again from a worldly point of view. Since Jesus lives in us, we have His mind and His desires, and we are now able to experience and perceive the world with spiritual senses in addition to mere physical ones."

Rachel brushes aside strands of hair matted on her cheek and remarks, "God in us—that's what walking with Jesus is all about for me. It has meant so much to me in dark times to experience God living inside my heart. I've learned that I'll never be alone in this world, even on my worst days."

"Yeah, talk about having power inside of you," Jack agrees. "The God who created this whole amazing universe has condescended to live in us. No wonder Paul says, 'I can do all things through him who strengthens me[1].'"

"I know I've taken it for granted," Armando says as he rubs his small goatee. "I've never thought about being born again as such an amazing miracle even though it did absolutely change my life."

"Right on," Jack agrees. "When I became a follower of Jesus, I experienced that second birth. I didn't see an angel or hear a voice from heaven, of course, and my life didn't change in some magical second. However, within a month after I believed, I began to see everything differently. It was C. S. Lewis who said something like, 'I believe in Christianity like I believe in the rising of the sun. Not only do I see it, but by it I see everything else.'"

"Yes, Jack," Embee confirms, nodding her head. "He was referring to how the light of Jesus enables us to increasingly see everything more clearly as we look at the world through His eyes."

The professor pauses for a moment as she shades her eyes from the sun. Then she says, "Before we believe in Jesus, we are on our own in this world. We are living entirely separated from God's love. We are rebels set against the truth. We are serving the other master, whether we are aware of it or not. Somewhere deep inside, we know what's right and wrong and that God exists, but we're incapable of hearing the voice of God. Totally incapable. Darkened eyes cannot see light."

"But then the day comes," the woman says with a glow on her face, "that day unlike any other when we are presented with the good news that Jesus

---

1 Phil. 4:13 (ESV).

has not left us alone and empty in this broken world. He's here. He has come for us. He's pursuing us. He invites us to surrender to His love and become a member of His family. He invites us not to go it alone—sadly, like Summer did—but to leave the far country of sin and rebellion and return home to the one who created us for a life of loving intimacy with Him and others."

Embee sighs not with sadness but with the gravity of what she is about to say. "At that moment, we encounter the choice above all other choices." She pauses as her eyes scan the circle of students. Then, she says, "We can continue living in opposition to the one who came to give us abundant life, or...we can choose to believe that He is the Way, the Truth, and the Life and be born again."

Even before Embee finishes speaking her final words, Stewart clears his throat in his quiet, mechanical way that becomes obnoxious when repeated too often. No, the intellectual young man never does anything particularly loudly—just frequently. In fact, he rarely calls attention to himself beyond his analytical monologues that scroll briefly across the social interactions of daily life and then fade away like an irrelevant, transient mist.

So it is that the other students sitting in the small circle at Lighthouse Farm turn their eyes toward Stewart out of obligation but, in all honesty, not out of respect. No one is expecting to hear anything notable from the Intellect's mouth. He is someone who only requires assimilation from others, never accommodation, like the driver of a car that doesn't slow down or alter direction for a leaf on the highway but certainly will do so for a horse or a deer. The young man is a leaf that demands no adjustments from the drivers around him. They simply accelerate over him and keep going.

"Theoretically speaking," Stewart begins, his large dispassionate eyes peering out from behind his glasses as if from a bunker, "is it possible for a person to give intellectual assent to belief in Jesus as the Son of God but not experience the new birth? Or, maybe said more accurately, can someone experience the new birth but not actually sense the power of it because it never fully penetrates his heart?"

"Now there's a question," Embee replies thoughtfully as her brows furrow deeply. "But please indulge me in one question before I answer yours, Stewart. Is your question theoretical or personal?"

Stewart stares at Embee for a long time before he finally answers quietly, reluctantly, "It's theoretically a personal matter."

"Well, okay, then," the professor says, smiling and leaning toward the young man. "I take it from what you're asking that you've believed in Jesus but never felt like it made a noticeable difference in your life—if you can indulge me in my use of the word 'felt.'"

Stewart nods his head gravely and says, "I can. And yes, I have believed in Jesus and asked Him to be my Savior. I'm not like the demons mentioned in the book of James who believe that Jesus exists and even that He is the Son of God but never ask Him to be their Savior. However, even after I believed in Him as my Savior, I haven't felt anything different, to employ your word."

"Maybe that's because you never feel anything, Stew!" Armando interjects sarcastically. Jack isn't certain if Armando is speaking seriously or just trying to be funny. Either way, he's heard enough of these comments from his friend to believe that his roommate is being critical. He opens his mouth to tell his roommate to back off, but Rachel weighs in first.

"You know, Armando," she says in her voice that becomes more nasal when she is upset, "I think I speak for all of us when I say that we're getting tired of how you treat Stewart. It's like you're bullying him. What's up with that? Did he do something against you that we don't know about, and now you're living out a personal vendetta against him?"

Silence falls over the group. Embee sits back in her chair and says nothing, observing the group interaction.

"It's okay; I'm sure that—" Stewart begins to say.

"No, it's not okay, Stewart," Rachel blurts out. "We're people who have been born again and called to love as Jesus loved us. My goodness, if anywhere in the universe is going to be safe for a person to be known, it should be right here in this group. We're family!"

Another period of silence reigns. Both Armando and Stewart examine their shoes.

Finally, Jack decides to weigh in against his better judgment. "You've been beating up Stewart ever since day one, bro." Even as he says the words, he senses that they might be too much.

While Jack is still speaking, Armando jumps to his feet and yells, "Why is everybody ganging up on me?" He glares around at the group, his eyes flashing with anger. "I don't need any of you," he snaps. Then he turns and stalks off toward the river.

"Armando," Embee says gently to the retreating figure. The young man does not turn back.

Everyone sits in shock at the sudden fracture in their peaceful conversation.

Aly finally breaks the silence when she offers, "I've never seen him like that before. I know he can be edgy at times, but not like that."

"He just needs time to cool off," Dr. Livingstone advises. "I'll say a quick word of prayer for him."

As the professor begins to pray, Jack can't help but recall his roommate's words, "ganging up on me." Intuitively, he believes that those words are not accidental, that they carry significant weight. Somewhere, at some time in the past, Armando has been outnumbered…

"The walking-dust creatures we know as divine dung sometimes say, 'Kill two birds with one stone.'" The voice that speaks is sharp, eviscerating. *"You killed two souls with one fell swoop of your weapon, my fellow destroyer,"* it growls. *"Kill and destroy. Kill and destroy. Kill and destroy. This is our mantra and our mission. Now the grotesque biped named Stewart will never venture to share his ugly heart again. And the rage and distrust awakened in the idiotic gangbanger has destroyed the fragile bridge of intimacy that was being constructed at that accursed school. Two kills in one. Two kills in one. Two kills in one. I am so delighted to witness destruction and death times two!"*

As Embee is finishing her prayer, the sound of a dinner bell alerts everyone to the late afternoon meal. Jack promptly gets up and goes in search of his angry friend.

Stewart remains in his chair, paralyzed. He is still staring at his feet. In his head, he is listening to a voice that familiarly chides him. "You know better than to do that," the voice says almost soothingly. "You learned many years ago that when you attempt to reveal yourself to anyone, it never goes well. Never. Never. Never. They're all incapable of loving you.

"Besides, don't you remember—" Here, the voice turns from soothing to accusing. "You're not worthy of love. She taught you that."

Ninety minutes later, after devouring the delicious meal that Sunny grilled in the cozy wood-latticed patio behind the house, Embee invites all the students to accompany her and her husband down to the large fire pit at the edge of the field adjacent to Deer Run and Fox Hollow.

Minutes later, the Livingstones and the six Screaming Eagles gather around a growing blaze that reaches orange fingers toward the darkening, early evening sky.

Reluctantly, Armando had joined the others for the meal. Now the young man is perched on a tree stump next to Jack. His body is as stiff as the wood he is sitting on. He is quiet and detached. From the tops of his eyes, he sends probing glances in the direction of his peers apparently reading their faces for signs of residual resentment. Sunny feeds three large logs to the flames, and the fire begins to roar.

The six members of the micro-cohort along with the Livingstones, sit quietly in the growing dusk, staring thoughtfully into the fire. Frogs down by the river, self-designated heralds of the descending night, warble loudly. An evening breeze, like a rising tide on sun-drenched sand, intermittently glides coolly over their skin.

Aly breaks the silence. "Many Muslims believe in Shaytan—the devil," she speaks toward the fire. "We believe that"—she corrects herself and says, "They believe that he is from the race of jinn, not a human. Some think he was an angel named Iblis, but many disagree, saying that an angel has no free will and could not disobey God, his Creator. The Muslim belief is that Shaytan was made from fire," she comments as she stares into the flames.

Aly looks away from the burning logs that are stacked like a miniature tipi and directs her large, brown eyes at Jack. "What do you believe about Satan?"

Jack pokes at the fire with a long stick, sending a burst of orange embers into the air. They glow brightly for a few moments, then die into black ashes that waft upward carried by the hot updraft of the fire.

"When I was a kid, I remember visualizing Satan as a horned, tailed, goateed red devil who carried a three-tined trident," Jack reflects. "But when I gave my heart to Jesus, I began to read the Word of God and learned that he was not some cartoon figure but a real personality who lives to tempt, lie and accuse those who are created in God's image."

"In our Warfare class, Dr. Windsor says that Satan is an intelligent strategist," Rachel interjects. "He believes that Satan's most fundamental battle strategy against humans is to divide and conquer, to separate and destroy, to get people all alone and at the mercy of his accusing lies. Whereas God created the universe for intimate relationships, Satan seeks to wreak conflict, enmity, and divorce. He fights unceasingly to drive people away from God and each other."

It doesn't take long for everyone around the fire to begin eyeing each other with furtive glances. Eventually, the glances turn into knowing looks. In the end, it is Armando who speaks aloud what everyone is thinking privately.

"You can say it," he says quietly as he looks down and fingers the flesh between his thumb and index finger where three dots are inked into his skin. "I know the enemy was and probably still is here tonight."

He hesitates, then says haltingly, still looking down, "My heart spoke divorcing words tonight. I know they weren't from God. I so want to speak words that draw us together, not words that separate us. Sometimes I'm so dang quick to...to be critical."

"I believe without a doubt that Shaytan—Satan wants to undermine our group," Aly says. "After all, we've come to the Academy expressly to grow in our faith and become uncommon in the depth of our relationships with Jesus. Undoubtedly, the enemy will want to resist that."

"What do you believe, Embee?" Emily inquires. "I mean about the devil's efforts to destroy relationships." Jack notices that her words are not only inquisitive but have a challenging edge to them. Is he the only one who notices that?

The female proprietor of Lighthouse Farm leans back on her log stool and straightens her back. The cross and peace sign dangling from her neck mirror the orange flames that dance in the night air. Her eyes blaze no less brightly than the fire.

"I know his ways well," the woman replies with quiet intensity. "It was Peter who wrote, 'Your adversary the devil prowls around like a roaring lion, seeking someone to devour.' Truth be told, he hates all of us. In fact, he despises all humans—created as they are in the image of God—and will go out of his way to defeat us even to the point of luring us toward physical self-destruction."

The professor looks directly at Armando and says, "The enemy knows he can't have you now since you have forsaken him as your master and chosen Jesus as your Lord. Because you've miraculously been delivered from the kingdom of darkness, he will strive to oppose you even more intensely."

"How powerful is he, really?" Rachel asks.

Embee gazes at Rachel through the fire and says, "I think of him as an antagonist in a story. Certainly, he is the main antagonist in our story—or should I say, in God's story. But Satan does not write the story. Nor does he possess the power of a puppeteer. His influence is limited. We still get to choose if we want to believe his lies and sell out to him as our master.

"And most importantly," Embee adds with conviction, "we need to always remember God's words that tell us that 'He who is in you'—God

Himself—'is greater than he who is in the world,[2]' namely, Satan."

Sunny stands and stretches his tall, wiry frame. He coughs softly and adjusts the bill of his red hat. The Screaming Eagles have already observed that Embee's husband doesn't speak much, but when he does, he says something worthy of their attention.

"The prince of this world is the wedge-driver, the bridge-burner, the liar-teller," Sunny announces. "And yes, he is here tonight, make no mistake. But if we seek out God as our hiding place, the enemy cannot touch us."

Sunny's words are still floating off into space when a vivid picture paints itself in Jack's mind. The scene is somewhere by the ocean. Waves are crashing violently against the shoreline during a tempest. Jagged flashes of lightning tear through the dark clouds that rise upward like two gargantuan pillars supporting an anvil roof. A wild wind whipped forward by the towering cloud-warriors churns up forty-foot waves. The entire atmosphere is unstable and furious.

Standing on a promontory overlooking the monstrous waves is a solitary lighthouse that emits a single beacon of light. The storm is so huge that the lighthouse resembles a slender vertical pencil, and the beam of light it casts stubbornly across the fierce waters is a sliver. In his mind's eye, Jack imagines the lighthouse as a loving father extending his hand to his lost daughter, who wavers with rebellious uncertainty in a boat sailing near the wave-thrashed shoreline.

Jack closes his eyes and says a prayer for the young woman who he senses is torn between sailing into the dangerous storm and seeking refuge in the haven of her Father's love. He prays that she will choose to return to her wooing Father instead of turning her back on His love and recklessly abandoning herself to the terrifying tempest.

---

2 1 John 4:4 (ESV).

Don't be Summer, Jack whispers softly to himself as he looks up and gazes again at the woman who has captured his heart, prickly as she can be. *Emily, don't be Summer! Choose to be Belle!*

CHAPTER 12

The Journal of JLS

It is the evening after the excursion to Lighthouse Farm. The six members of the Screaming Eagles are gathered around a table in the Greenhouse Classroom perched on top of the four-story edifice that adjoins the old castle church. The sun has retreated below the horizon, and a growing darkness is taking possession of the glass room that years ago was abandoned as a center for horticultural studies and now serves as a classroom dedicated to the study of koine Greek and Old Testament Hebrew. Stewart is just beginning to read from the journal of JLS that lies open before him.

3 March 1899: I am chronicling my impending journey

on these pages. I ask myself, "Self, why would you desire to keep a written record of what you have chosen to do?" My answer is because I am an amateur scientist and philosopher; ergo, I wish to document for myself the progressions or regressions, if you will allow it, that I experience during the course of my forthcoming experiment.

Let me begin today by documenting the fact that I am presently joined in holy matrimony to my wife, Martha, who has borne three children to me. But despite these four blessings, my soul is restless. I am a ship anchored in a safe harbor but wish to set sail for the open sea. I am an eagle perched safely atop the nest but desire to soar away high and far to see what I can see.

I have always been noble. I have practiced the Christian religion since I was a youth. I was baptized and confirmed inside the sacred walls of my father's church. I grew up obeying my parents and conforming to the rules of society. I have not knowingly willed to do wrong by practicing theft, cheating, slander, taking God's name in vain, or coveting my neighbor's wife.

In a word, I have been good—a God-fearing man. Yet, I feel empty and accosted by the unrelenting restlessness. I would far more readily identify as a Stoic than a hedonist in my outward practices. My hidden affections, however, pull me in another direction. They threaten to undermine everything I have valued up to the present time.

I made the decision late the previous evening when alone in my study (I specify that I was alone since I have observed that my restless affections noticeably burgeon in intensity when I am removed from the company of others). I decided to raise the anchor that has kept me in the familiar harbor, to throw myself off the nest, open my wings and ride the winds of fate to wherever they might take me.

Nay, I will not intentionally seek out the wanton pursuit of self-indulgence. I will merely not extinguish my strong desires as they arise within me. I will allow my passions to speak even though they be contrary to my upbringing and the commandments of God. I will conduct this experiment to discover if, perchance, my restlessness will abate when my desires are freely fed. If this abating does occur, then I will subsequently claim that being good and pursuing obedience to God is simply making guilt and law my master when I could be free to enjoy the liberties of the flesh.

I will commence my experiment tonight at midnight. I will record my ongoing observations in this personal journal as often as I am at liberty to do so. I dare not keep this journal within the walls of my home for fear of discovery. I will, therefore, bury it in the labyrinth beneath the church. May fair winds blow my way and guide me to fulfilling destinations. ~JLS

There is a brief silence among the members of the micro-cohort until Armando offers, "Well, that's a candid journal."

"That's the purpose of a diary, silly," Rachel counters. "A diary is for true confessions, a place to write things you wouldn't want anyone to know. Am I right?" the brunette inquires, looking around at her circle of friends.

"Couldn't tell you," Jack replies with a shrug of his shoulders. "Never had a diary."

"Me either," reports Armando. "When I was a boy, I did keep a journal where I recorded some events and observations like how many tacos I ate at my Abue's house—sorry, my grandmother's house—but never had a personal diary that's as transparent as our Mr. JLS."

"You guys are impossible," Rachel says, shaking her head in feigned frustration. Jack and Armando smile at each other, happy to be members of the fraternity of men.

"So, who is this guy, anyway?" Emily inquires. "He seems like he wants to keep his identity hidden along with his experiment."

"These entries are one hundred and twenty years old," Aly points out, her large almond eyes shining out from under the hoods of her long, thick eyelashes. "How will we ever find out his identity, and, even more importantly, do we even care to know?"

"Wow, Aly, you sound more like a guy," Armando quips. "I thought girls were always curious."

"Not necessarily," Stewart relates. "Carl Jung's disciples have done research suggesting that while most men have more *animus* in their psyche than *anima*, sometimes it is reversed. Personality assessments show that some women have more animus than *anima* while some men have higher levels of *anima* resulting in a stronger manifestation of opposite gender traits."

Rachel stares at her bespectacled counterpart for a moment before she comments, "That's...informative, Stewart." Then she turns to the others and says, "I think we should just keep reading the diary several entries at a time and see if we come across anything interesting."

"Didn't one of the professors here at the Academy mention rumors of a murder and a missing person and a hidden treasure?" Emily inquires as the phone in the back pocket of her jeans emits a single high-pitched bell tone. "Maybe this diary will offer some clues about all those things."

"Good point, Emily," Jack says encouragingly. "But even if the journal turns out to be nothing more than one man's musings about life, it's something we can read together to grow tighter as a cohort. Let's try to cover ten entries a week since Stewart told me there's a total of around seventy in the journal."

"Seventy-eight to be exact," the Intellect corrects.

"Since we have about seven weeks left in the first semester, we could just about finish the diary by reading ten or eleven entries a week," Jack calculates.

"Sounds good to me," Armando comments, looking around at the others while he fingers his small goatee.

"So how about if we read one more entry tonight before some of us have to go spelunking in our caves," Emily says with unveiled sarcasm.

Jack notes that his classmate seems unusually interested in the journal in contrast to her disinterest in other aspects of daily life at the Academy.

"Are you on board with that, Aly?" Rachel inquires.

"Certainly," the small woman with the jet-black hair replies, nodding her head vigorously.

"Okay, then," Jack exclaims. "Read on, Stewart, faithful translator of the nineteenth-century cursive!"

The young man bends over the diary, and his index finger travels over the lines to determine where he left off. Jack wonders why the Intellect needs to get his face so close to the page to read. His glasses don't seem to offer much assistance in his efforts to see the contents of the diary. For the first time, an odd idea pops into Jack's mind: Maybe Stewart's lenses aren't real corrective lenses. Maybe they're just ordinary glass, worn simply for appearance and not to correct his vision—or, more likely...worn to hide behind. Stewart begins reading again.

15 April 1899: I have been unfaithful to my original intent to record my findings on a consistent basis. Unforeseeably, my journey out to open sea, as it were, has

distracted me from my better intentions. All is well, but some things are unusual. I have entertained flirtations with women, and I have ingested spirits and medical compounds acquired from pseudo-apothecaries. I have discovered whiskey to be quite transformative and a compound called heroine powerful in its alterations of my mood. My taste for alcohol, ironically, appears to be increasing just when many in America are railing against it and even prohibiting its use in some areas.

When I imbibe whiskey, it seems that people find me more interesting. I certainly am transformed into more of a conversationalist. I am livelier and more of a humorist. I enjoy the cough syrup I am using because when I drink it, I experience a sudden sensation of euphoria that deludes me into feeling like I'm a new man. I believe that I can do anything and be anyone. I am a god to the world! Unfortunately, the ecstasy is short-lived, and I am soon dreadfully weary. My arms become as heavy as logs and my head as burdensome as a boulder.

Martha is worried for me. Although she has not spoken to me about her concerns, I see it in her eyes. She appears to fear my moods which are not unusual or evil in my estimation. They are simply marked by a state of ennui and social withdrawal. On occasion, my sanguine disposition becomes, admittedly, highly irritable.

I discern that she wants me to be home more often. It

is true that my time invested at the saloon has increased. But why return home directly from work when I can enjoy the relaxing delights of spirits at a time when my body is fatigued by the rigors of my employment?

I will confess this: Just a fortnight ago, or maybe three weeks past, my practice was to drink spirits to feel good. Now it seems that I drink them so as not to feel bad. Could that be possible?

I am enjoying the attentions of several young ladies at the saloon who apparently find me desirable. I have not made a point to pursue them yet, but my heart beats faster when they touch my arms or my leg. I want them. I think it's just a matter of time until I have them—as part of my experiment, of course.

I wish to record several observations before I close. I have noticed that the more I imbibe whiskey and the cough syrup, the more I want it, and the more I need more of it. Also, I observe that my new habits are taxing my income as I find myself spending more to secure the level of pleasure I desire. Finally, my sleep is troublingly disturbed. I occasionally pace the house at night and obsess about the alcohol and the syrup. They have become quite indispensable to my style of living. Dare I live without them?

Six weeks have already passed. In honesty, the experiment has been a journey into the extremes of ecstasy and agony. When I am elated, I feel very elated. When I am melancholic, I feel deeply melancholic. What will become of me? Time will tell, I am most certain.

As the other members of the micro-cohort begin to offer their observations about the second diary entry, Emily does not join in the animated discussion. Instead, she fingers her phone and stares out the greenhouse windows into the gathering darkness.

CHAPTER 13

Syko Loco

Armando is sitting comfortably in the overstuffed leather chair in Dr. McNeely's office, sipping a cup of hazelnut coffee. His spelunking guide is perched on a squeaky, wooden desk chair across from him, leaning forward with his bearded chin resting on his interlaced fingers. The professor is dressed in a black turtleneck and a gray tweed jacket with patches on the elbows.

The walls of the office are lined with bookshelves chock-a-block with tomes, new and old. Any space not claimed by a bookshelf is wallpapered with maps of Jerusalem, Megiddo, Caesarea, or some other ancient biblical city that Armando has never heard of before. Surrounded as he is by all the books and maps and even a few artifacts no doubt unearthed in some tel in the Middle East, Armando imagines he is sitting with Indiana Jones. He can visualize the 10' bullwhip in the professor's hand and the wide-brimmed fedora on his head.

The air in the office is thick with dust and the distinct smell of old books and is polluted by clicking and clunking noises emanating from the old cast-iron radiator in the corner that transforms the office into a sauna even during early fall; thus, the wide-open window behind Dr. McNeely's chair.

"So, Armando, if I heard you correctly, you said your biological father spent one night with your mother even though he was already living with another woman," the Academy president comments, summarizing what the young spelunker had just told him.

"That's the way it went down," Armando nods. "And that's where I came on the scene. Mom got pregnant after that one-night shack-up in the barrio and decided to keep the baby even though she was from an upper-middle-class family in Orange County. That's the old story about the preacher's daughter going across the tracks and sleeping with the ex-con's son."

Armando pauses to sip his rapidly cooling coffee. "Sometimes, I still wonder why she didn't abort me," he observes without emotion. "I think it had something to do with her controlling father, who was so worried about appearances.

"What I mean is that my grandfather probably pressured my mother to have an abortion to save face for the Hernandez family. After all, having a daughter get pregnant outside of holy matrimony would have been a huge embarrassment to my proper Roman Catholic grandfather. But his pressure only increased my mother's resolve. She was not going to be controlled by her dictator daddy, so she most likely insisted on keeping the baby out of sheer defiance. Who knows if she would've kept me if he hadn't pressured her."

Armando shakes his head in disbelief and says, "My mother gets rowdy one time in her life on Cinco de Mayo in LA with a disreputable gang member, and I'm the result. Isn't alcohol wonderful? It produced me, a bastard son," he says with a shrug of his shoulders.

"You sound bitter," the professor with the curly brown hair and matching brown beard reflects.

"That's just my jaded side talking," Armando comments softly.

"Okay," the president of the Academy concedes. "So, what happened after you were born?"

"My dad didn't want me," Armando responds candidly, "so by process of elimination, I grew up with my mother until I was eleven. Sure, I went and visited my dad maybe once every other month mainly because I wanted to hang with my older brother, Raul. If my mother had been able to stop me, she would have. She hated everything about my father's world, including my half-brother."

Dr. McNeely chews on the eraser end of his pencil and comments in his deep bass voice, "So Dad was in La Puente, and Mom was living in Newport Beach."

"Yes, not quite opposite ends of LA, but close enough," Armando comments. "Different worlds, for sure."

"And you said you grew up with your mother until age eleven," Dr. McNeely observes.

"Correcto," the olive-skinned young man says as he looks down at his coffee. "But I always thought my father and my brother, Raul, were cool. My old man, at thirty-five, was a veterano in one of the La Puente 13 cliques. My brother followed in my father's footsteps, and I wanted to follow in Raul's footsteps."

Armando shakes his head and raises his eyebrows. "My mother went totally loca every time I stayed in the valley with my dad and his family. She hated feeling so powerless."

The young man stares at Dr. McNeely with his deep brown eyes and shakes his head slowly. "She didn't know how right she was to be worried out of her mind."

Armando takes another swallow of his coffee and clears his throat. "Things weren't so bad at first. I just rode around in Dad's '63 Chevy Impala low-rider, yelled at the girls like I was a real gangbanger, and stole some of my brother's smokes. I felt older than I was and genuinely bona fide."

Armando laughs sardonically and snorts. "Of course, I had no idea what happened in gangland when things got dark and dirty.

"When I turned twelve and then thirteen, I started to see beyond the surface of things," Armando says as he stares at the wall behind his spelunking guide. "I saw the drug deals, a few drive-bys, my dad's guns—including an AK-47. I witnessed some fights between cliques and watched several new members initiated into the gang with brutal beatings."

Armando shakes his head again and sets his coffee cup aside. "I was a kid from Orange County sinking into the swamps of the barrio!" he exclaims incredulously. "My mom screamed and cried, but I didn't listen. My dad didn't care about her or me. He was too busy selling drogas and running his clique.

"They even gave me a gang name," the young man says with a dark laugh. "I was too young to be the *whole story*—a genuine gang banger—so they called me *Paragraph*." Armando smiles broadly for a moment, only to have the smile melt into a frown. "It was around that time that everything changed."

The young man with the small goatee licks his lips and shakes his head wistfully. "The turning point happened one night when I was out with my brother, Raul."

Armando laces his fingers behind his head and leans back in his chair. He stares up at the ceiling. "My brother—he was twenty, and I was thirteen—invites me to go with him to hang with his new girl over in Valinda. I say yes. I get to ride in the low-rider with Raul. Maybe I will find a girl for myself. How can I say no?"

Armando continues to gaze at the ceiling. It is like he is recounting the story to himself.

"We get over there—maybe two miles from our house and on borderline turf. Yeah, I know, not wise. No, let's call it what it was—downright stupid. But hey, he's in love, and I know nothing. Remember, I'm only a paragraph."

Armando grabs his cup only to see that all the coffee is gone. He sets the mug back on the table beside the old leather chair and stares at it with disinterest.

"It's later in the evening in July," he says, continuing his story. "The setting sun is barely peeking through the palm trees and growing pale on the bougainvillea. The neon lights on the corner market flicker on. It's warm and a bit humid. At least I remember sweating."

The young man looks up at the ceiling again. He is no longer in the office. He is in Valinda. He is thirteen.

"Raul sees her van. We get out of the car and walk toward it. She gets out—a beautiful chica. Gabriella is her name. I can see why Raul is drawn to her. Trouble is, eight cholos from another clique climb out of the van behind her."

Armando glances down at Dr. McNeely and wipes his mouth with the back of his hand. The professor sees primitive fear in the young man's eyes.

"Even I know we were in some kind of trouble, but Raul's face tells me we're in deep, deep trouble—life and death trouble. He must've known right away that it was a setup, a revenge thing. He turns to me and screams at me to run. I freeze, and he screams even louder. I panic and run down the alley behind the carnicería."

The young man from LA grabs his head between his hands and runs his fingers over his close-cropped hair. "I should've run back to the car," he moans, "but I'm such a fool! Raul could've gotten back to the car, but he follows me down the alley. I know he's trying to protect me, his idiot half-brother!"

Armando shakes his head and closes his eyes. "The pursuit is short because the alley is a dead end," he says slowly, his voice grave. "The only thing behind the market is a dumpster and a high fence that might as well have been a prison wall with razor wire on top."

Armando pauses and swallows hard. "The eight gangsters surround us. They're all wearing blue bandannas. I panic and look around with the wild eyes of a rabbit cornered by a python. My brother pushes me hard against the fence and stands between me and the cholos. He yells at them that I'm not even a gangbanger. He throws his hands in the air and tells them my name is Paragraph. All they do is laugh at Raul from behind their inked faces."

The spelunker pauses and falls silent for a long time. Finally, he mumbles, "They go after Raul."

Armando begins to rub the palms of his hands back and forth on his pants. His eyes find refuge in the threadbare oriental rug on the floor. Dr. McNeely watches as the young man's whole body begins to shake. The professor slides his chair close to the thirteen-year-old boy until he is only a foot away. "I'm here," he says quietly.

Armando licks his dry lips as his eyes begin to dart back and forth. "They pull out their blades and surround him," he utters in a voice cracking with emotion. "Raul has no piece on him. He was just going to see his girl, after all. He pulls out his knife, but they begin to flick their blades at him from three sides. He fights back for a while and draws some blood. But he is outnumbered, and they are slashing him from three sides. He eventually drops his blade and puts his hands up to protect himself. He...he yells at me not to watch."

By now, Armando's voice is so soft that Dr. McNeely can barely hear what the young man is saying.

"How can I not watch?" Armando says as if in a trance. "They stab his hands...They stab his back...They stab his face...A blade nicks an artery in Raul's neck and—and blood begins to spray on their faces." Armando's throat is choked with emotion, and he falls silent.

The professor is tempted to speak, but he cannot think of anything that would fit the gravity of the moment. He groans softly and waits.

"Soon...soon they close in for the kill," Armando croaks. "I can't see him anymore. They're stabbing him, and he's screaming. They're stabbing him some more. They're in a crazy frenzy, like they're possessed by demons. They are no longer human. They have become animals with human faces."

Ever so quietly, Armando says to the floor, "I collapse against the fence and do nothing. I am a coward." He spits out the last word and makes fists with his hands.

"Then Raul's lying on the ground. Moaning. Dying. The gangsters turn and swagger over to me like they're brave—eight cowards against one defenseless boy. Blood is on their hands, their white shirts, their faces—even in their hair."

Armando squeezes his eyes shut and presses his fists against his forehead. The room is silent for a long time.

"I am terrified," the young man finally whispers, "and I want to run...I am filled with hate, and I want to kill them all...In the end, I just stand there shaking with fear and rage."

"Some of the cholos pick up Raul's body and heave it into the dumpster like it's trash," Armando says, his upper lip curling. "Then the leader of the set slithers up to me like a snake and waves his blade in front of my face. I know I'm going to die, so I close my eyes. But instead of cutting my throat, the coward slashes my cheek and shoves me to the ground."

"'My name is Sniper, and I own this barrio,'" he says with a cruel sneer that twists his face. "When I look up at him," Armando says, "I see the tats on his face and small skulls inked all over his bald head. I will never forget them until the day I die."

"'You're a poser!'" he screams at me. "'A dog! A coward! I would kill you too, but I don't do paragraphs. I only kill men.'"

Armando's face is rock-hard, etched with both anger and anguish as he snarls, "I want to yell at him that brave men don't gang up on one man and slaughter him like a pig. But I say nothing. I am weak. I am a coward. I'm still certain that I'm going to die the way my brother did—and I don't care anymore."

Dr. McNeely watches Armando chew on his lower lip until it bleeds.

"The cholo spits in my face and swears at me," the young man recalls bitterly. "He yells at me to get up. I stagger to my feet and lean up against the fence. My legs are rubber. I feel blood running down my neck and chest. The coward called Sniper slaps the laceration on my face and then punches it. I feel my stomach rise into my throat. I puke on the ground at his feet."

Armando swallows several times, and Dr. McNeely wonders if the young man is going to vomit right there in his office.

Eventually, the spelunker takes a deep breath and says, "He slaps my face again and again with the back of his hand. Finally, he tells me to run.

"I just stand there staring at the dumpster. I can't leave my brother. So, the gangster slaps me again. He yells at me to run like the coward that I am. He gets crazy then and calls me Period. He screams that I'm not even worthy of being called Paragraph, that I'm nothing but a period behind the letters that will be on Raul's gravestone—R.I.P."

Armando stares at the office floor in shame. "It takes forever, but finally my feet begin to shuffle forward. I walk through my vomit and...and Raul's blood," he mumbles. "I half stumble, half run down the alley. By now, I'm sobbing, as much as I hate it. Through my tears, I glance back at the dumpster—at the oversized green coffin. I can't comprehend that my brother and my hero is dead."

I stagger out of the alley as if I'm drunk. I see my father's car. Flames are pouring out the windows. I turn down the street and begin running the other way as fast as I can. I leave Raul behind, and...and in another sense, I leave Armando behind as well. Even though I had physically survived the revenge attack, the boy in me died that night. Any innocence left in that thirteen-year-old was murdered in that alley."

Armando rubs his eyes with his fingertips and continues. "I run back to my turf and eventually end up at my father's house. I tell him what happened as I cry like a baby. He is high and wasted. In his grief for Raul, he punches me on the same cheek Sniper had cut. It feels like raw hamburger by now. He curses me repeatedly and accuses me of failing my brother. He calls me a betrayer and a coward. I swear to him that I will avenge Raul, but he punches me again, and I pass out."

Dr. McNeely reaches out and lays his hand gently on the shoulder of the former member of La Puente 13. The young man does not pull away from his mentor's touch as he continues to stare down at the floor.

"Overnight, I'm transformed—literally," Armando states in a flat voice. "I become hard. I hate the other gang, especially Sniper. I hate my father. I hate myself for my cowardice. I hate the world."

As he rubs the three dots on the skin between his thumb and forefinger, he says, "The very next day, I begin to dress like a legit gang member. I wear the long baggy pants with the white wife-beater tee shirt and the tennis shoes distinctive to my set. I steal a gold chain and some nasty shades. I wear a black military belt and even a Raider's hat. I look like one bad dude."

The ex-gangster pauses and then adds, "I live for one thing and one thing only—to kill the veterano who murdered Raul. I don't care about anything else. I don't care if I live or if I die. My only goal in life is to kill Sniper before I die.

"I learn how to fight," Armando tells his listener after another short pause. "I buy a Glock and practice shooting at least three, four times a week. I get a tat of my brother's face on my left arm with the letters RIP below it—without the periods. I also get a tat of Sniper's face on my right arm with the letters CFY—*coming for you*—beneath it."

Armando touches his bleeding lip and looks up from the floor. "Anticipating that I'm going to kill Sniper, I get inked with the outline of a teardrop," he says, pointing to the small tattoo beneath his right eye. "I will ink in the teardrop later to show that I killed a man."

Armando pauses to examine his cup for any coffee that may have magically appeared in it since the last time he checked. "I even get the prison tattoo, the one with four dots, one in each corner, with a fifth dot in the middle, that represents a man locked away in a cell. I figure that in the near future, only two paths lie ahead of me: either I'm going to be killed trying to kill Sniper, or I'll end up in prison for killing him.

"I'm so obsessed with revenge that I soon acquire the nickname Syko Loco," the young man says, continuing his story. "I become a bully, mean to everyone around me. My mother no longer recognizes me and officially cuts me off from her side of the family. Just when I'm beginning to think that my father might be proud of me, he gets blown away in a drive-by up in West Covina. Suddenly, I'm all alone in the world—except for my vatos.

"I spend all my time with Paco, Angel, Eusebio, Diego, Manuel, and Gilberto—P 13 members, every one of them. Of course, I know them by their gang names: Spooky, Joker, Spyder, Happy, Tank, and Demon. But none of my eses really know me—what's on the inside."

Armando finally looks into the eyes of his mentor and admits, "At fourteen, I'm alone with my anger and my hatred—all alone." Dr. McNeely shakes his head slowly and compresses his lips until they are lost in his beard. He keeps his hand on the young man's shoulder.

"On my sixteenth birthday," Armando continues, "I drive my truck over to my ink man in No Man's Land on the border of Puente and Valinda. Later that afternoon, I'm going to execute my plan to kill Sniper, so I want to get one more tat. I'm getting the clock with no hands. It's a symbol of doing time in prison but not knowing how long one is going to be behind bars."

Armando leans back in the deep leather chair and links his fingers behind his neck again. "If someone asks me that day—and I was honest—I'd confess that I'm terrified. Dang, I'm only sixteen! But my father always taught me that fear is for cowards, so I probably wouldn't have admitted it.

"If I'm straight up about it, I'd also admit that I'm in the set only because I want to kill my brother's killer," Armando confesses. "As soon as I've done the deed, I'm turning myself in to the police and washing my hands of gangster life. That's my mother in me—to admit when you've done something wrong. But the father in me is about to ruin my life. Of course, I think I'm doing it for Raul."

Armando pauses and stares out the open window behind Dr. McNeely. "'Am I really going to go through with it?' I'm asking myself in the truck. I decide that I am because I know without a doubt that once I see the cholo, emotion will consume me, and I'll be seeing everything around me through the red haze of rage and revenge. I'll be back in that alley with Raul again, but this time I won't be defenseless."

Armando leans forward and looks at his mentor from the tops of his eyes. "I have my father's AK-47 in my possession," he confides. "Back at the house."

The professor lets out a low whistle and says, "Man, oh man."

Armando sits in silence, pondering the gravity of his situation at sixteen. "I didn't see another way," he eventually says. "I felt like I had no choice. I was locked in."

The young man pauses and looks over his mentor's left shoulder. "I was going to do a drive-by at Sniper's house...at his daughter's fiesta de quinceañera."

There is a long silence before the mentor finally speaks. "You were going to kill a lot of people," Dr. McNeely observes gravely, shocked yet again by the unfolding details of Armando's story. He is reminded once more that he and the young man sitting in front of him grew up on opposite sides of the planet.

Armando nods and fingers the hollow teardrop beneath his eye. "I was sixteen," he says again. "I didn't think ahead. I didn't consider that I would end up in prison with members of the same gang I had just shot up in the drive-by. I wouldn't have lasted a week. I would've been a walking dead man, as they say."

The professor can't help but add, "They could've waited decades to come after you because you would've been in jail for life, especially if you killed innocent women and children."

Armando shakes his head and groans softly. He stares up at a map of Jerusalem during the Second Temple period that hangs on the wall next to the window. A tortured look contorts his face, creasing the skin around his eyes. The hollow teardrop disappears.

"I had crossed the line of no return," Syko Loco explains, still shaking his head. "The deed was as good as done. Nothing could stop me now. Nothing."

Armando stares at Dr. McNeely with an expression on his face that makes the professor shiver. Then Syko Loco says, "At the ink shop, I get out of my truck and walk toward the front of the building. Three, maybe four guys are standing in front of the place. Yeah, I think it's a bit odd, but I'm a man on a mission, and I don't think twice about it.

"I'm almost at the door when I realize I've seen these dudes somewhere before. In a split second, I recognize them as some of the gangsters who killed Raul in the alley. Unfortunately, they must have recognized me first because one of them is already reaching for his piece. For the second time in three years, I know I'm a dead man."

Dr. McNeely removes his hand from the shoulder of the young man who has witnessed more violence in three years than the professor has seen in a lifetime. He rolls his chair back a bit so he can see Armando's whole face clearly. The mentor isn't breathing.

"The next thing I know," Armando says, his eyes large, "the world erupts into chaos. Guns are booming, people are screaming, the windows of the ink shop are exploding, the guys in front of me are twisting this way and then that way. I can still see their faces. They're shocked and terrified.

"Then, suddenly, something rips into my leg with incredible force, and I'm thrown to the ground. All this happens in four, maybe five seconds."

Armando takes a deep breath. "The last two things I remember as I'm lying there on the sidewalk is this shard of glass that's stuck in my tongue and the face of one of the cholos lying three feet away. His eyes are wide open, but I can tell they aren't seeing anything. At least, not in this world. Then I pass out.

"I wake up in the hospital that night in West Covina. I had just come out of a three-hour surgery to deal with GSWs in my calf, shoulder, and chest. Fortunately, the one in my chest was a through and through even though it did collapse my lung.

"Several days later, a police officer drops by the hospital and informs me that I had been caught in the middle of a drive-by shooting. A drive-by. Can you believe it? The very thing I was going to perpetrate later that same day!" Armando exclaims.

"I guess something, or more accurately, someone did stop you after all," the professor observes.

"Incredibly, yes. Who would have thought in a million years that my plans would be interrupted like that?" the young man says. "I didn't know it at the time, but God's fingerprints were all over what happened that day. But the most exciting part is still ahead."

"The most exciting part," his listener repeats as if he finds it difficult to believe that the story can get any more exciting than it already is.

"Okay, the *best* part," Armando says, amending his previous statement.

Syko Loco glances into his empty coffee cup for the fourth time and then says, "I stay in the hospital for a week. Nobody comes to visit me. Nobody. Not a single ese. Not even my Orange County mother who, in her defense, had no idea what had gone down in the barrio."

"How is that the best part?" McNeely inquires in his deep voice.

"Just wait; I'm not there yet," Armando says, holding up his hands.

"Nobody comes to see me except...except this chaplain. His name is Juan. Believe it or not, he's a veteran—an ex-gang member. You don't come across them every day."

"Except in the cemetery," McNeely comments wryly.

"Exactly," Armando replies. "Anyway, this veterano chaplain, Juan, meets with me every day while I'm in the hospital. Sometimes twice a day. At first, he does all the talking. He tells me about his years as a gangster and how he lost all six of his brothers to gang violence. Eventually, I begin to tell him about me. He listens to me—kind of like you. He's the only one who shows up for me at the lowest point in my life."

Armando pauses and smiles at his spelunking partner, and the professor smiles back at him. "Then one day, I ask the veterano how in the world he got out of his set alive without getting killed by another gang or even by his homies for being a deserter. He simply tells me, 'Jesus.'"

Syko Loco rubs his goatee with the tips of his fingers and says, "Sure, I'm surprised by what he says, and at first, I discount it. After all, everyone around me comes from Catholic families. They believe in God. But they're still in gangs, and they kill people, use women, do drugs, and fight to the death for their turf. So yes, I've always thought that religion is something to hold on to when you're dying, but it's irrelevant to everyday life. It doesn't impact who you are as a person in the world. Not really.

"But as the days go by, Juan teaches me otherwise."

Armando locks intense eyes on the professor and announces, "Even though I'm bitter and depressed, I listen to what he's telling me. Me, who doesn't trust a single person in the world."

The young man pauses for a moment and then says, "In the end, I open my heart to the love of God. Do you know why?" he asks, turning his clear brown eyes on the professor.

"Why?" Dr. McNeely asks without hesitation.

"I believe in Jesus because of Juan," the ex-gangster says. "I feel genuinely loved by that man. His love sets him apart from every other man I've known. Even my father. Especially my father. I tell him as much. He replies that he loves me because Jesus loved him first. It really isn't that much of a leap, then, for me to surrender to Jesus when I see God loving me through Juan."

Armando swallows hard and looks at his mentor with glistening eyes. "I gave my life to Jesus three weeks after I was shot in that providential drive-by. I've never looked back since." The young man glances away briefly, then turns his eyes back to the professor.

"Some people talk about what an uneventful moment their new birth was. Mine was the opposite," Armando explains. "I felt an explosion in my chest! I knew immediately that I had found what I had been longing for all my life—not a religion but a relationship with a personal God."

The new creation pauses and then corrects himself. "Let me say that a bit differently. I didn't find Jesus. No, Jesus found me. Even when I wasn't looking for Him, the Creator of the universe pursued me into that hospital and made me His child."

The old Syko Loco, who has been transformed into a son of God, swallows hard and rubs his nose with the back of his hand. "That's what blows me away," he says in a husky voice. "He didn't wait for my rebellious heart to come to my senses and pursue Him. He came after me. He didn't leave me alone in this broken world."

Armando pauses and then says with eyes that radiate passion, "He gave me the most important gift—His own life."

"I would imagine that would mean something to you, that Jesus died for you," Dr. McNeely offers.

"For sure," Armando admits, nodding his head and sighing. "Death was so commonplace and random in the barrio—always such a waste. Such a total waste," he sighs, shaking his head. "I saw so many young men die for no reason at all except for their sworn allegiance to a gang family that was supposed to protect them but only ended up welcoming them into a fraternity of death.

"Fortunately, for all of us, Jesus died for a purpose," Armando says, brightening. "He willingly died to save the people he loved. His death was anything but a waste."

Dr. McNeely leans forward and offers, "In a lesser way, Raul did that for you, too—he died to save you." The president's voice is deep but tender. "So, you could say that you've been on the receiving end of two blood sacrifices in your short life."

Armando eyes the bearded professor and nods his head thoughtfully. "I've never thought of it quite that way," he admits. "But I think you're right. Raul shed his blood to give me physical life, and Jesus shed his blood to give me eternal life. Raul could have run back to the car that night and left me on my own, but he stayed. Jesus could have remained comfortable and safe in his father's throne room, but he came after me."

Dr. McNeely sits up straight, and his wooden chair creaks like an old schooner riding seas churned by a Nor'easter. "You should've been dead twice already," the professor says, "or at the very least, imprisoned for life. But here you are, sitting in front of me, alive and free. Your mission in life is no longer revenge but to love others. How can such a radical transformation occur in a human heart except by God's grace?"

Armando smiles and comments, "Especially when a man is running in the opposite direction of that grace."

The professor nods his head and says, "Amen to that." Then he clears his throat and announces, "Armando, I'm afraid it's time to leave the barrios of LA and come back to the Academy. I deeply, deeply appreciate what you've shared with me tonight. It obviously came from your heart, and it was...it was breathtaking. Frankly, I'm exhausted."

"Thanks for going back there with me," Armando replies with a long sigh. "You and Juan—not Jack here at the Academy but Juan Ortega back in LA—you're the only two people who have heard my whole story."

Dr. McNeely nods his head to acknowledge the young man's words. Then he remarks, "Just so you know; I don't take it lightly that you trusted your story to me. But I'm glad you did. Honestly, my faith is stronger because of the faithfulness of God I have witnessed in your life."

The mentor pauses a moment and then adds, "Before you leave here tonight, I have a challenge for you." He runs his index finger back and forth over his bottom lip and then says, "I want you to think about three things before we meet next week.

"First, I invite you to pray about your current attitude toward Sniper. Second, I challenge you to consider how you feel toward that thirteen-year-old boy who survived that awful night in the alley."

The professor hesitates and leans back in his chair. "Finally, give some thought to how you treat others you perceive as weak. I believe that as you meditate on these things, God will remove obstacles that exist between you and Him as well as some that stand between you and other people."

"Okay," Armando says slowly. "I give you my word that I'll think about those things."

The professor stands up and squeezes the young spelunker's shoulder. "If God hadn't intervened in such a dramatic way in your life, you'd be known as drive-by Syko Loco forever. Now, instead, you're known as Jesus' brother and friend, Armando. No doubt, God will love others through you just as He loved you through Juan Ortega."

"I certainly hope so," the new creation says with a smile. "What drives me now is the love of God instead of the desire for revenge."

After Dr. McNeely has prayed for him, Armando leaves the office that is now sacred in his mind and heads down the broad hallway paneled with dark wood and decorated with pilasters and niches. Of all the people in the world he could be thinking about in the same brain space, his mind is focused on the gangster who murdered his brother and on Stewart Johnson. The Holy Spirit is telling him in no uncertain terms that his heart has unfinished business with both Sniper and the Intellect.

Armando is soon to discover that the Holy Spirit never leaves business unfinished.

CHAPTER 14

The Aquarium Classroom

Dr. Alan Greenlay's class, which has been underway for two months now, is dedicated to developing the spiritual weapons needed for Windsor's war. It meets in the most exotic of places—in Silver Bay Lake.

Jack remembers the first day of class when Dr. Greenlay led the thirty members of the macro cohort along the edge of the large body of water that parallels the dormitory...

Reaching the long dock, they walk out onto the aluminum path and follow it sixty feet out into the lake. Jack has an idea where they are going but is not certain until he observes the first student step down into the water and disappear.

One by one, the other students are also swallowed by the lake. It is only when Jack finally arrives near the end of the dock that he observes a large plastic tube rising a foot out of the water. An aluminum ladder is attached to the dockside of the tube. Swinging his right leg over the lip of the cylinder, he locates the first rung with his foot and begins his descent into the lake. He smiles when he is reminded that this is not the first ladder at the Academy that has taken him into the deep unknown.

When he reaches the bottom of the ladder, Jack pivots around and observes a waterless aquarium about 30' x 30' in dimension and roughly 7' in height. Three dozen folding chairs and six long plastic tables populate the submarine classroom. In the front of the room is a desk that must have been assembled inside the aquarium since it is far too large to have navigated the tube that accesses the classroom. Of greater interest to Jack than the contents of the underwater room are the waters of the lake that encase the aquarium-classroom like liquid blue insulation.

Jack looks down and notices that the lake encasing the transparent underwater box has a sandy bottom even out to its present depth of around twelve feet. Accordingly, the view from the plexiglass container is relatively clear, unimpeded by the murkiness caused by mud or by intruding lake weed. He sees a few fish suspended outside the submarine room and, in the distance, two mud turtles whose stubby legs and webbed feet are paddling as fast as they can to propel the shelled creatures through the water.

For the first time in his life, Jack is on the inside of an aquarium—albeit a waterless one—and the fish are on the outside, eyeing him and his classmates.

When the wide-eyed students finally sit down, Dr. Greenlay educates them about the underwater classroom. He informs them that the submersed room had been financed seven years earlier by an endowment from a wealthy alumnus who had gone on to develop a chain of seaside resorts in exotic locations around the world. Several of these resorts had been outfitted with submersed walkways that led to an observation room beneath the ocean. The professor also explains that the classroom is technically not an aquarium but has been referred to as such since the day it was built.

In response to a question from none other than the irrepressibly curious Stewart Johnson, Dr. Greenlay also explains to the new students that if this underwater container were placed in any lake as little as one-hundred miles further north of their present location, winter ice would compress it and eventually lead to irreparable damage.

The professor moves on to entertain the macro-cohort with the account of an unusual reptile sighting in the lake five years earlier that was witnessed through the plexiglass walls of the aquatic classroom. He recounts that during a lecture he was delivering, a female student stood up and pointed over his shoulder. "Crocodile!" she screamed.

"'Malarkey,' was my reply to the terrified young woman, and I continued my lecture.

"Moments later, another student rises to his feet and claims to see the same reptile.

"At this point, I turn around and, to my great surprise, see a six-foot-long reptile nosing its way along the outside wall of the classroom. While one student from Louisiana starts talking about capturing the reptile and making his grandmother's delicious Cajun crocodile stew, another student sitting closest to the creature faints. Immediately, I dismiss the class and notify local DNR officials of the intruder. The two beaches on the lake are promptly closed, and an intense, all-out search ensues.

"Two weeks later, the reptile—which is later identified as a freshwater crocodile—is spotted again, captured, and handed over to the city zoo. Speculations abound, but no one knows exactly how the crocodile ended up in this state, much less in Silver Bay Lake. The prevailing theory that circulated later was that someone in the area had raised it as a pet but found it necessary to dispose of it when it outgrew the bathtub."

On that day two months earlier, Stewart predictably supplements Dr. Greenlay's account with a detailed explanation of the differences between saltwater crocodiles known as *salties* and freshwater crocodiles known as *freshies*. Jack finds Stewart's reptile lesson intriguing and learns that while *freshies* are much smaller than *salties* and far less dangerous, they are still capable of doing damage to humans.

Stewart explains that if the authorities had known from the beginning that the crocodile sighted in the lake was a *freshie* and not a *saltie,* they would not have instigated the lake-wide search that followed the reptile sighting with such expediency. However, they still might have forbidden aquatic activities until the reptile was found, in Stewart's opinion.

The Intellect concludes by stating that hopefully, the searchers knew that the crocodile found in the lake could not have been a *saltie* since they are only able to survive in saltwater.

Today is the third Tuesday in October. Classes have been underway for almost two months. No crocodiles of any variety or any other unusual reptiles have been spotted by the fall term aquarium students. All has been quiet and uneventful.

Jack settles into his chair in the underwater classroom along with the rest of the members of the macro-cohort. He visits with the students sitting adjacent to him and intermittently stares out at the lake.

As usual, Dr. Greenlay—who often seems disoriented to time and place if not to person—is running late. There have been occasions when Jack has wondered if the absent-minded professor even forgets the route to the classroom.

A few minutes after 9:00 a.m., the familiar sound of shoes scuffling rapidly down the rungs of the ladder is heard in the aquarium. Jack and his classmates watch as the vertically challenged, unathletic, pudgy professor reaches the floor of the classroom and rushes quickly toward the desk at the front of the room. He takes short but determined steps as he crosses the plexiglass floor. The thumping of his shoes creates a hollow sound that reverberates through the room.

Huffing and puffing, the man throws down his tired leather briefcase that appears older than its forty-five-year-old owner. Familiarly, Dr. Greenlay is smiling from ear to ear and humming to himself. His glasses have slid halfway down his nose, and his blue-striped tie is askew. Something about the man reminds Jack of a picture he once saw of Winston Churchill—everything but the thick brown that sprouts in every direction on the professor's head.

"Good morning!" the professor crows brightly without looking up. He is too busy rummaging around in his briefcase to acknowledge his audience. "This is the day that the Lord has made! Let us be glad and rejoice in it since it may be our last!" he announces in a loud voice.

Jack manages to pull his eyes away from a 32" northern pike swimming lazily behind the professor's head and considers the man carefully. He cannot prevent himself from chuckling at the entertainer in the front of the aquarium, who is now furiously rifling through his lecture notes as he hums the old hymn, *O for a Thousand Tongues.* Jack finds the man particularly humorous since he knows that the professor is not attempting to purposely elicit attention. He is just being his unique, quirky self. Even now, he seems oblivious to the other people in the room.

The short-of-stature but large-of-heart-man finally looks up from his hopelessly disheveled collection of notes. His glasses have now slid to the very end of his nose. He places his index finger on his lower lip, and his eyes drift up to the ceiling of the reverse aquarium. "Speaking of the last day," the professor comments, "have I told you about when I died, otherwise known as the story about the false positive of my demise?"

The man's eyes grow large, and he opens his mouth in such a way that it forms a perfect circle—as round as a silver dollar. Every student in the aquarium knows that the co-occurrence of these two facial features presages an avalanche of sorts. Dr. Greenlay is about to unleash a multitude of words that will resemble whitewater in a roiling river.

Armando nudges Jack with his elbow and says, "Here we go, Juan. Buckle up."

Jack smiles wryly and nods his head.

The exuberant professor adjusts the glasses that immediately slide halfway down his long nose. "Aah. Aah," he starts out in a high-pitched voice. No words come out of his round mouth. His jet engine mind is a rotating turbine racing at 600 mph, while his propeller-plane lips can move at only a fraction of that speed.

The students have learned by this point in the semester that given five to ten seconds, the excited man who is dressed in baggy gray pants, a white long-sleeved shirt, and a green vest with a clashing blue tie will eventually harness his ability to translate his mind's pressurized content into language. As always, the sleeves of the professor's shirt are rolled up to his elbows because they are too long for his short arms. The man's trouser bottoms, which are not rolled up, drag on the aquarium floor.

Sure enough, after the expected time interval, the professor launches into a story recounting his late-night visit to the emergency room prompted by chest pain.

"When I arrive at the emergency room, the medical personnel fear the worst," Dr. Greenlay announces to his students, his eyes even larger than before. "They scurry all around, attaching various wires and lines and miscellaneous apparatuses to my arms and chest.

"I, of course, am growing quite nervous in the face of all this frenzied attention. My senses are on high alert, and I'm staring at the monitor by my bedside that displays my blood pressure, heart rate, and oxygen level. I am somewhat comforted by the steady tones emitted by the machines telling me I'm not dead."

The professor's eyes, if possible, grow even larger and the pitch of his voice elevates half an octave as he says, "You can well imagine my consternation when, suddenly, I see the sinus rhythm wave—or whatever you call that mountain range on the heart monitor—go flat. All I hear is that long ominous sound that accompanies flatlining."

The animated professor pauses momentarily to breathe, then exclaims to his students, "I turn to the ER doc"—at this point, Dr. Greenlay turns to his right and addresses the imaginary physician—"and ask, 'Am I dead?' He's looking a bit worried but frowns at me and replies, 'Are you an idiot? You wouldn't be talking to me if you were dead.'"

"So, I say to him, 'What if I'm dead and you're nothing but a fiction embedded in the final waning surge of my brain activity?'

"The ER doc stares at me with impudence written all over his face," the professor explains, gesticulating with his short arms. "He opens his mouth to speak but hesitates. Then, out of the blue, he reaches over and pinches my arm as hard as he can. 'Do you feel that?' he asks with a smug look on his face.

"I yell, 'Ouch, of course, I do!'

"Then with a deadpan face, the doc asks, 'Have I convinced you that your dying brain theory is sheer poppycock?'

"A second later," Dr. Greenlay continues, "a nurse discovers a loose lead, reattaches it, and voilà—the heart monitor begins beeping again! I am alive! I have never been so happy to be wrong."

The students in the submerged classroom laugh, some at the humor of the story and some at the facial expressions that have contorted Dr. Greenlay's face during the recounting of his near-death story.

The professor looks around at the students in the room with a twinkle in his eye. "I don't ever want to die like that—suddenly in the cold, sterile ER," he says.

He pauses before he delivers another dose of humor. "I'd rather die peacefully in my sleep like my grandfather, Ralph, and not like the screaming passengers in his car."

Dr. Greenlay eyes his audience with a smile while the students groan.

Rachel whispers from the table behind Jack, "If we could find a way to harness that energy, we could light both the sanctuary and the edifice for a month."

Jack nods his head and smiles.

Within seconds, Dr. Greenlay changes gears, and his brain wave activity slows to a speed his mouth can comfortably accommodate.

"Setting all seriousness aside," the professor says with a broad smile, "let's address today's topic: Absolute truth."

The short man with the small paunch and perpetually sliding glasses perches atop a stool in the front of the room and raises his chin high in the air as he gazes at his students. Jack smiles and shakes his head. Everything about this man is eccentric.

"In your campaign against darkness," the professor begins in a calmer voice, "it is imperative that you have a source of truth. You must have an authority, a measuring stick, a plumb line," he insists. "Otherwise, everything is a guess at best and preference at worst.

Can you imagine playing a board game where there are no directions—everyone making up their own rules as the play goes on? Can you picture the chaos and the dissension? Well, that's a picture of what planet earth looks like—a world divorced from absolute truth."

The professor twists his rubbery lips to the left side of his face and then remarks, "Isaiah Windsor refers to his Field Manual. Embee Livingstone speaks of God's love letter. Milner McNeely calls it the Word of God. Our resident prophetess, Miriam, uses the traditional term, the Bible. Other professors at the Academy speak of the good news or the message."

The man has already sat still for as long as his restless body will allow. He slides off his stool and begins pacing back and forth across the front of the room like a teenager with ADHD. The cuffs of his baggy pants slide across the floor as he walks. "I like all those designations," the man allows. "However, what I personally prefer is The Revelation."

The animated professor raises his right fist in the air with his index finger extended and announces in a loud voice, "Please note that I'm not simply alluding to the last book in the Bible when I refer to The Revelation. No, I'm including the whole of the Old and New Testament. They're both part of Jesus' greater revelation to us," he says, waggling his stout finger at his students.

"Why do I prefer to refer to our source of truth as The Revelation?" Dr. Greenlay asks, his eyes dancing with excitement. "Thanks for asking. I'll tell you why." He emphasizes the word "tell" by elongating it.

"It's all because of a verse I read in Proverbs 29 when I was young in my faith," he explains. "Verse 18 says in the NIV, 'Where there is no revelation, people cast off restraint; but blessed is the one who heeds wisdom's instruction.' In the New Living Translation, this verse is rendered, 'When people do not accept divine guidance, they run wild. But whoever obeys the law is joyful.'"

Dr. Greenlay turns and walks across the aquarium toward the deeper part of the lake, where a school of small crappies are gliding along the plexiglass wall. As he paces, his upper body jerks slightly forward and then upright again. Forward and back. Forward and back. Jack can't help but envision a strutting rooster. The professor's generous shock of brown hair sprouting up toward the ceiling could easily be the rooster's comb, Jack decides.

When the man comes within inches of the transparent wall of the submarine classroom, he turns to face his students.

"You must understand, my children," Dr. Greenlay announces. "Every man and woman on this planet who has ever lived or is living now or will live at some future date is born with a will that opposes authority; with an autonomous spirit that resists any truth that threatens to impose limitations on him or her. Everyone. No exceptions. Even those who appear to be ostensibly compliant. Maybe even especially those who are ostensibly compliant."

The professor's face abruptly falls. He appears crestfallen.

"Things are not what they were in Eden way back at the beginning," Dr. Greenlay says as he begins strutting across to the other side of the waterless aquarium. "We were obedient kids back then who listened to our Father because we loved and trusted Him. We had everything we could ever want back there in that Garden. The best of it all, of course, was the close personal relationship we had with our loving Creator."

"There was only one limitation placed on us," the professor continues as he comes to a stop and turns to face his students. "One. God gave us everything to enjoy with one boundary. One. Uno." The short man holds up a single finger to emphasize his point.

"You all know the rest of the story," Dr. Greenlay sighs as he bends over slightly at the waist and drops his head toward the floor. His glasses slide down to the very end of his nose and teeter there. "The tempter came. The ancient serpent. The one who had already rebelled against his loving Maker and was intent on taking us down with him. Misery loves company, right?

Where do you think that phrase came from anyway?"

The professor snaps his head back up and begins pacing again. His shock of brown hair bounces on the top of his head as he walks. "The tempter invited us to join him in his defiance of the divine will. He baited us. We listened and salivated. We knew the truth, but we wavered. Our ears were titillated by the invitation." The strutting professor cups both of his hands and places them behind his ears to demonstrate his point.

"Then we wavered again. Living in the veritable cornucopia of the universe and enjoying uninterrupted friendship with God, we listened to the destroyer of our souls. Too long, this time. We fell."

Dr. Greenlay stops dead in his tracks. He droops his shoulders, and his arms hang down at his sides. "We spurned obedience to our loving God and chose disobedience with all its trappings," he says with a loud groan. "Ever since that absolutely dreadful moment in the history of human existence, we've been divorced from peace with God and free to do whatever we set our minds to do."

The man straightens and turns to look at his students with saucer eyes. "Do you know what happened that day?" he cries out. "We experienced the most infamous bait and switch in the history of the universe! Satan baited us with the promise of becoming like God, right? He so sublimely invited us and sweetly cajoled us and slapped us on the back like a friend. He won our confidence and poisoned our perception of God. But in the end, did we get what he promised us when we disobeyed God? Of course not! Satan is the father of lies!

"Instead of becoming like God," the professor explains, "our rebellion separated us from the One who made us wonderfully in his image. And to add insult to injury, the enemy—who exists to destroy intimacy—took wicked delight in our separation from the most loving Presence in the universe. He did not slap us on the back anymore like a friend. No! Instead, he cruelly castigated us for being such stupid, worthless, shameful creatures as to disobey the loving and holy God; and he goaded us to run and hide from him whose wrath would destroy us.

"Yes, here we see the bait and switch strategy that the enemy is so adept at manipulating: tempt with promises of pleasure and fulfillment, and then accuse and shame until we hate ourselves and blame God. Then we flee from our Creator and into the oblivion of our own choices!"

Dr. Greenlay stands unmoving in the front of the room and gazes into the faces of his students. "In the end, we all became little gods unto ourselves," he says in a resigned voice. "We exchanged the love and authority and truth of God for the right to be captains of our own destiny. Yes, here we witness the great exchange of Romans 1—trading the Lamborghini for a unicycle without pedals; forsaking God's banquet table for mud pies."

The professor pauses with intention and sighs deeply. "Rejecting God and embracing idols," he says gravely. "This totally irrational and unequal exchange is our sin, and it is the death of us.

"Now the question I always like to ask people who have traded God's presence for a secular world that worships no divine being is, 'How's that exchange working for you?'" he says with a wry chuckle. "Some people admit to me that it's not a fulfilling tradeoff. Others, who have lived so long in a godless world don't even know what they're missing, are quick to settle for trying to feed their deep hunger with things that will never satisfy.

"Then," the professor announces, "there are those people who are so opposed to God having authority over them—even if it is as their loving Father—that they cannot and will not admit that they're shunning the author of human existence."

The professor begins pacing again, more slowly this time. The cuffs of his pants slide silently over the plexiglass floor. "So, in our rebellious secular state where human reason is god and materialism is the only permissible source of truth," he explains, "we are no longer under any authority. We are free!" The pudgy man exclaims as he throws his arms dramatically into the air. "We are as free from God as an orphan is free from a parent, a paraplegic from walking, a ship from a rudder, and a lung from oxygen."

Dr. Greenlay abruptly stops again and looks from student to student with his large eyes and his supremely pliable lips that wriggle beneath his long nose. "Yes, this is where we end up when we throw off all restraints and allow absolutely no revelation in our lives beyond what is written by our own hand."

The professor pushes his glasses back up the ski jump that is his nose and warns, "Make no mistake about it, men and women. When we make up the directions for the game of life, we will all do what's right in our own eyes. When we throw off all restraints, no one can tell us what to do anymore. We no longer submit to absolute truth. Instead, we generate our own version of truth that fits conveniently and comfortably into our individual lives. Hence, the term, relative truth. We dictate truth. It never dictates to us."

The professor pauses to push up the sleeves of his white shirt that have fallen to the tips of his fingers. Then he says, "Relativism becomes the dictator when we tell the police officer what the speed limit should be when he pulls us over for speeding; when we educate God about what behaviors are really sins and which ones are cultural restrictions that were only valid two thousand years ago; when we're quick to scream at the referee for his terrible call or disrespect the umpire for his poor eyesight; when we insist that our child is always right and the teacher is always wrong; when we demand that others accept our amoral choices since truth is a matter of taste; and when we browbeat others if they challenge our position on moral grounds, accusing them of being intolerant and hateful."

Dr. Greenlay allows his melancholy gaze to drop to the transparent floor of the underwater aquarium, and a shock of his hair falls forward like the droopy horn of a unicorn. The room is totally silent except for the rhythmic sedating sound of gentle waves caressing the plexiglass ceiling. Then slowly, ever so slowly, light begins to infuse the professor's countenance, and his sad face begins to look hopeful.

"When I talk about The Revelation," Dr. Greenlay explains quietly, "I'm referring to the absolute truth that flows from the very heart of the loving God, the God we rebelled against during the worst exchange in the history of the universe. This absolute truth includes God's response to our defiance: to send His Son to rescue us from Satan and our own selves."

Dr. Greenlay begins to pace and then stop and then pace again, talking at length about the divine intervention engineered by a loving Father who desired reconciliation with His wayward children. With irrepressible energy and gesticulating arms, he continues to address the importance of being aware of the secularizing influence of the current culture. His face shifts frequently into animated expressions of joy, fear, disappointment, anger, and sadness as he repeatedly extolls the benefits of embracing the absolute truth of The Revelation.

Dr. Greenlay explains that four of the benefits of possessing such a road map to life are knowing where you came from, knowing where you're going, knowing why you're here on this planet, and, lastly, knowing what is healthy and right as opposed to what is unhealthy and wrong.

Half an hour later, the professor wipes perspiration from his forehead with a navy-colored handkerchief. Jack thinks it looks suspiciously like one of the cloth napkins from the Agatha cafeteria. Then the man says with a poker face, "I came to class today promising myself that I wouldn't open my mouth because my grandpa once said, 'Better to remain silent and be judged a fool than open your mouth and remove all doubt.' Unfortunately, I didn't keep my own promise to myself."

Dr. Greenlay chuckles and positions himself back on his stool. "One last thought today, students: Love those who dismiss the authority of God's truth and pray for those who oppose God. Why? 'God may perhaps grant them repentance leading to a knowledge of the truth, and they may come to their senses and escape from the snare of the devil after being captured by him to do his will.' [1]These are the words of Timothy in The Revelation."

Dr. Greenlay lifts his hands into the air, his palms facing his students.

"Last, last thought for today: Never, ever, forget that knowledge is knowing that a tomato is a fruit, but wisdom is never putting it in a fruit salad. In other words, every day, pursue the truth found in God's Word but be wise in your loving application of it to your life as well as to the lives of others. May you move toward others with love and truth, and always, always lead with love."

"Let's pray," the short professor says as he begins to bow his head. But before he can begin, he glances up at his students from the tops of his eyes and says, "On Thursday, remind me to tell you about how I got locked out of my hotel room in Narita, Japan, during an earthquake."

---

3. 2 Tim. 2:25-26 (ESV).

CHAPTER 15

A House Divided against Herself

"You were going to leave, weren't you?"

"What do you mean?" the young woman asks with a blank face.

"You know exactly what I mean," Embee says gently, firmly. "You were going to leave the Academy. Even that day out at the farm, you were distant. I could see you had eight toes out the door."

Emily abruptly gets up from the couch in the spelunking office—as she does whenever the conversation strikes a nerve—and walks to the far end of the room by the window. Then she wheels around, her arms folded. "As a matter of fact, I was planning to leave the next day," she announces, her countenance etched with petulance.

"And..."

Emily shrugs her shoulders and frowns at the woman who is wearing a long white dress printed with ruby-red raspberries and silver water pitchers. "And I decided to stay," she comments matter-of-factly. "At least for now. That could change at any moment, of course."

The professor considers her student for a while before she says, "I know something happened in the Cave of Dread, Emily. Have you told anybody about it?" she inquires gently.

Emily purses her lips and shakes her head.

"You were going to leave, just like that," Embee says, snapping her fingers. "You were going to run away and never face what you need to face."

"Why do you think I need to face something?" Emily retorts. "What does that even mean?"

"I knew there was something you needed to face long before you ever walked onto this campus," the professor replies.

"Really!" Emily exclaims as she rolls her head to reposition her long blonde hair. "Who are you anyway, some fortune teller who reads tarot cards and palms and then tells people what they need to *face*?"

"Sorry, honey, your palm was not available when we were reviewing your application," Embee says with a smile, attempting to make a bid toward the defensive woman who is guarded by thick walls and a wide moat.

Emily makes a hissing noise between her closed teeth and turns her back on her mentor.

Dr. Livingstone shifts her position in her desk chair and licks her lips as she considers what to say next.

"It was Jack, wasn't it," the mentor finally suggests. "He's why you stayed."

Emily is silent.

"I know he likes you," Embee says with a smile in her voice. "I notice how he looks at you."

Emily turns to face Dr. Livingstone. Her arms are still folded tightly across her chest, and her face has the look of a sullen child who is fighting not to relent in her protest against the parent. Surprisingly, she does surrender in the end. Embee had not anticipated her sudden capitulation to vulnerability.

"I see it, too," the spelunker confirms as her face softens. "And yes, he's the reason I stayed. He genuinely seems to care about me even though I push him away again and again. He's either persistent or amazingly stubborn."

"So, Emily," the mentor inquires quietly, "do you push people away because you're afraid they won't love you, or do you push them away because you think you're unlovable?"

The young woman laughs without mirth and says, "Nothing like going for the jugular, professor." Then she pauses for a while and cocks her head. "Both," she eventually admits airily, as if she's talking about what sandals to wear to the beach. "It just varies from day to day...even hour to hour."

Dr. Livingstone begins to speak, but the younger woman interrupts her. "Actually, if I'm totally honest, my unlovability is a constant," Emily reports. "That variable never changes. For that reason, it's always important to keep others from getting too close. If I let them see past the curtain, they'll see who I really am," she says nonchalantly as she unfolds her arms and lets them fall at her sides. "And then they most certainly will judge me."

"Emily, Emily, when did you start believing that you're unlovable and have to hide yourself from others?" Embee asks with sadness in her voice.

"Six months after I started drinking," the young woman replies without hesitation. There is an edge to her voice.

"And when did you begin drinking?"

"Right after high school," the younger woman admits coolly. "A girl from church introduced me to vodka. After my first drink, I knew I had found what I had been looking for all my life."

"So, about six years ago now," Dr. Livingstone comments quietly, more to herself than to Emily. She pauses and fiddles with one of her earrings before she asks, "So why did you say about six months after you started drinking?"

Emily folds her arms again and rolls her eyes. "Because that's when my drunken self began allowing boys to use me," she retorts. "And did they hesitate to use me? Not for a second!"

"Oh, Emily," Dr. Livingstone says in a sad voice as she shakes her head slowly.

"And don't ask me if I told my parents," the young woman snaps. "I didn't. They've been Christians like, forever! I don't think they even know what alcohol tastes like, and they certainly didn't have sex before marriage. They always encouraged me to wait like they did. So obviously, I couldn't tell them what was going on since I was failing them in the two critical areas of being a good daughter.

"And to top it all off," Emily adds bitterly, "I began adding drugs to the alcohol, and soon I was a poly-substance abuser! Me, the girl who had been Miss Goody-Two-Shoes in high school, the pride of my parents! No way was I ever going to tell them that I was an alcoholic, an addict, and a slut!"

"Did you tell *anybody* what was going on?" Embee inquires gently.

Emily turns her back on her mentor and looks out the window at the Academy grounds far below. "After a year and a half, my sister found out, and she made me tell my parents," Emily says in a subdued voice that is still edged with cold steel. "They didn't have a clue what I'd been doing. They tried to help, but by then, it was too late for me anyway. I put on the nice girl mask once again, and they believed I was okay. It's amazing what people will believe if you just look good on the outside."

"You were far from being okay," Dr. Livingstone says empathically.

"Right," Emily says with heavy sarcasm as she elongates the word. "I did the opposite of what Jesus said—I cleaned the outside of the cup but ignored the inside. I made myself look good on the surface of things but was a hot mess inside. No, it was worse than that. I was an ugly mess."

"You must have hated yourself," Embee proffers.

"What makes you think that?" the young woman asks defensively as she continues to stare out the window.

The spelunking guide chuckles softly and replies, "Well, sweetheart, you're not the first girl to color outside the lines."

Emily turns away from the window and studies her mentor's face for a long time. Finally, she unfolds her arms and returns to the couch, where she flops down and stares straight ahead.

"There's more to your story," Embee observes very gently to her young mentee. "Do you want to tell it?"

"Not particularly," Emily says, the anger dissipating and the familiar heaviness returning, crushing down on her like a huge millstone.

"That's an honest answer," Dr. Livingstone says. "Honest answers are healing."

"There's a civil war inside me," Emily confesses with despair in her voice. "A part of me wants to stay here with you and talk while another part of me wants to shut you out and leave. A part of me wants to blow up the dam that's been holding back this huge reservoir of emotion inside of me, and the other part just wants to keep self-medicating and forget all the ugly crap—just stay in control of things."

Emily pauses to push the palms of both hands against her forehead as she slowly shakes her head. "I don't know what I want," she laments. "I don't know who I am. I don't even think I believe in God anymore."

Embee sighs and pushes aside a strand of hair that has strayed across her cheek. "Emily, life can be so, so difficult," she announces, shaking her head slowly. "We come into this world hard-wired to say no to God and yes to our hearts, and then there's the enemy right there beside us who takes us by the hand and encourages us all the more to spurn our Father's love."

Dr. Livingstone takes a deep breath and says, "Before you roll your eyes at me, please hear my next point." The mentor continues to talk as she gathers her hair on the top of her head.

"Most of us don't devise an intentional rebellious plan to defy God at one defining point in our lives. We're born into that place, but often, we slide deeper and deeper into that rebellion; slowly, of course—hour by hour, day by day—maybe even largely unaware of what's happening." Embee secures her silver hair into place with a hairpin and leans toward her mentee.

"But then one day, we wake up...and open our eyes...and find ourselves in this bad place that we never really intended to get to, and we feel like we can't get out," the professor explains.

"Then we believe it's too late. We can't cash in some magical do-over card so we can go back and relive the previous six years, or ten years, or fifty years. It feels like the only things we have to show for our lives are the consequences of our bad decisions and all the accumulated garbage of the years gone by. Worst of all, there's no going back."

The spelunking guide, whose typically radiant face is now covered in shadows, gazes with such intensity at Emily that the younger woman looks down at her hands.

"So, Emily, we come to believe—with the eager help of the enemy—that since there's no way out of our predicament, our only option is to defend ourselves like a besieged castle," Embee explains.

"We begin to rationalize that what we're doing is not that bad," the professor explains. "Instead, we decide that God is the bad one. We begin to see Him as an angry and judgmental antagonist who must be dumped like some jealous, controlling boyfriend.

"We also engage in theological gymnastics supported by manipulations of the original languages of the Bible, so we can convince ourselves that God's love letter to us contains commandments that were valid two thousand years ago but are no longer relevant for us today.

"We most certainly will embrace the belief that the Bible-believing church and even our parents are parochial and obsolete. They are the sick ones, the people who are out of touch with reality—not us—so we are free to ignore any truth they attempt to peddle off on us like castoff items from a hoarder house."

Dr. Livingstone pauses. Her lips are smiling, but her eyes communicate a deep sadness. "Then, Emily, we indeed are in a royal pickle."

There is another pause before the mentor says, "At that point, we're exactly where the hater of our hearts wants us—divorced from God, divorced from our own hearts, divorced from other people. Escape becomes our coping. Pleasure becomes our distraction. Our hearts are seduced into looking for something instead of someone. And even if we do seek out someone, we do it primarily because we want *something* from them. Without honest relationships, we are left to medicate our emptiness and distract ourselves from the deep loneliness that comes after we've turned our backs on God."

Embee chews briefly on her bottom lip and prays silently for her mentee. Then she fingers the cross that dangles from her neck and says, "We retreat into permanent hiding, locked by our own hands into a dungeon of separation. We're hiding from God but more from the accusations of the liar and our own hearts. We can do nothing. The future looks hopeless.

"But whether or not we embrace that hopelessness as normal is quite another thing," Dr. Livingstone adds. "There are those who possess adequate defenses to keep the hopelessness out of their conscious awareness. Then there are others who are swallowed up by it and struggle to go on living. Even though they're tortured, at least these latter individuals know something's not right."

Emily looks up at her mentor as she squeezes her hands together in her lap. "Okay," is all she says, shrugging her shoulders with indifference.

Embee falls silent. She knows she has said enough—more than enough.

Emily keeps looking at her, and she returns the young woman's gaze. Embee senses that Emily must speak the next words even if it kills her.

Emily swallows hard and clears her throat softly. Her green eyes slowly wander over her mentor's left shoulder; her fingers move restlessly like she's playing thumb-war solitaire. Literally, several minutes go by.

Finally, the young woman's eyes drift back to the professor's face, and she inquires off-handedly, "So what happens next? After getting stuck in the dungeon, I mean. I suppose you have some religious answer for that."

Embee utters a prayer of thanks in her head and lets out a silent sigh of relief. The professor is pleased because she believes the words the young woman has just spoken indicate she won't be leaving the Academy any time soon. Emily will be staying after all.

A small drawbridge on the backside of the student's castle has just been lowered over the broad moat that has been widening for years. There is still hope for the young woman's heart to be accessed even though it is the eleventh hour, and the clock is quickly moving toward midnight.

What the professor wants to say to Emily's question is, "When you allow Jesus into the mix of things—no matter what all the ingredients are—there's always hope to fill the emptiness inside."

Sensing, however, that the young woman's heart is currently set against hearing such things, she says instead, "When you're locked inside, speak loudly enough, so at least one person hears you outside your dungeon door. Then there's all the hope in the world. Tonight, you've done just that, Emily—you've spoken loudly enough so that I could hear you.

"Now I'm standing outside your door, and I'm not going anywhere without you."

Emily's eyes fall to the floor, and she smiles grimly. "Okay," she says slowly, clearly not fully convinced. "I think I believe you—or at least something in me wants to believe you. I'll take what you said under consideration."

The young spelunker sits quietly for a moment and then abruptly gets up from the couch and walks over to the doorway.

Just before she closes the office door behind her, she turns to the woman who heard her heart and informs her in a flat voice, "I'll see you in class."

Dr. Livingstone smiles and nods her head. "Yes, Emily, I'll see you there," she says, trying not to sound excited.

On the inside, she is thanking Jesus for a significant battle won against the shadows that cover Emily's heart like a burial shroud.

CHAPTER 16

The Prophetess and Aly Ahmed

Aly decides to take a break from studying the complicated grammar of koine Greek. As she gets up from her chair and rubs her tired eyes, she tells herself that while Greek grammar is challenging, the five distinct tones of her native Thai language are also very difficult to master, just in a different way. She has informed her fellow Screaming Eagles that the tones of the Thai language can alter the meaning of a word simply by slight variations of sound.

Aly has been in the Introduction to Greek class for eight weeks and has already heard the familiar quip, "It's Greek to me," a dozen times. Whenever the words are spoken, all the students in the class groan and nod their heads, sympathizing with their peer who has quoted yet again the familiar line from the Shakespearean play, *Julius Caesar*.

Yes, Greek grammar is challenging for Aly to master as well, but overall, mastering languages is not that difficult for her—maybe because over her lifetime, she has had to learn a handful of them. Consequently, she has been the recipient of amazement and even mild envy from her fellow classmates who find the Greek verbs difficult to learn with their four moods, three voices, and three persons.

Aly makes her way down the slightly concaved stone steps from the fourth-floor library and through the labyrinthine hallways of the edifice that hunkers between the mammoth sanctuary and the dormitory. The heels of her sandals create a clicking echo in the high-ceilinged passages as she moves forward.

Soon, she arrives at the tall double doors that lead outside. She pushes open one of the heavy wooden doors with significant effort—she is not a big person after all—and emerges into the late afternoon October day. At close to eighty degrees Fahrenheit, the temperature is above average for this time of the year but still not as hot as Hat Yai, which regularly tops out at ninety degrees in October. Aly misses many things about home but has been so busy at the Academy that she has had little time to think about Thailand. This afternoon is her opportunity.

Aly kicks off her sandals and walks slowly over the luxuriant green carpet that covers the grounds of the campus complex. In recent days, leaves have begun to glide down in earnest from the towering oak trees splotching the verdant lawn with red, yellow, and orange corpses that are briefly raised to life by the autumn breeze.

Aly's small frame floats over the soft grass until she comes to the lake that is alive with the rhythmic roll of small waves. She follows the shoreline as it hugs the velveteen blue waters.

She lifts her eyes to the distant Silver Bay Lodge and wonders which of her friends are working shifts at the hotel today. She knows that Emily is hostessing and that Rachel is organizing a brunch for senior citizen volunteers who are being recognized by the city for their efforts in elementary school classrooms. She is uncertain if Stewart, Armando, and Jack are at the lodge today performing their various duties.

When she reaches the dock, Aly strides over the sixty-foot length of the composite walkway until she reaches a small bench situated adjacent to the aquarium classroom entrance. She sits down on the bench and smooths out the material of her knee-length skirt. Then she closes her eyes and lifts her face toward the sun. She begins to reminisce…

She travels to the restaurant in Yala that serves her favorite food—chicken and coconut soup. She feels the hot breeze yanking at her hijab and whipping through her ebony hair as she rides her scooter to the beach in Songkhla, where the golden mermaid stands so proudly. Her mind's eye envisions the palm trees outside her bedroom window, and the geckos that scurry over the walls as if their feet are glue pads, and the fruit stalls that sell bags of pineapple, papaya, mango, and even the spiky, malodorous—but terribly delicious—durian.

She sees the sun above the Andaman Sea water-coloring the sky a blazing pink, and feels the warm waters caressing her body as she snorkels at Ko Phi Phi. The familiar taste of delicious and affordable street food sets her mouth to water. She pictures her family at an open-air restaurant dining together as several giant elephants dressed in Hindu garb lumber past their table.

A mist falls over Aly's eyes when she thinks of her mother, Maarit, a gentle and kind woman who is one of the strongest people she knows. She has to be strong to live in the same house with her domineering husband. When Aly's thoughts drift to her two younger sisters, Tabana and Taara, tears roll freely down her cheeks. But when an image of her brother, Mahmoud, abruptly appears in her mind, her body stiffens, and her eyes fly open.

Aly glances down the long dock to confirm that her brother is present only in her mind. Reassured, she gazes out over the waters of the lake and imagines that she is sitting on the beach in Phuket. Small waves lazily lap against the H-frame dock supports with a clocklike rhythm. The rays of the sun warm her face. Eventually, she closes her eyes again and begins to pray.

"Jesus, Jesus, Jesus," she says softly. "I thank you once again for bringing me safely to America. I'm so grateful to be here. But Lord, you know that sometimes I miss my family and my home so much that it is hard to breathe. Today, I feel that. Nobody here knows Thailand except the waitress at the Thai restaurant downtown, but she's not a believer, so she doesn't understand that part of me."

The petite woman with the heart face, fine features, and thick black hair pauses and then says, "I thank you for the other Muslim background believers who have given their hearts to you that I chat with online. Those women are precious to me. I just need your help to move closer to some of my new friends here at the Academy.

"And Jesus—I still need to know that I did the right thing when I left Yala. Maybe that was selfish and cowardly of me. I know my sisters felt abandoned. Should I have trusted that you would have taken care of me if I had remained in Yala? I was very afraid, Lord, especially after what happened to Esther. Please forgive me if I betrayed you or my family," she says in a voice heavy with regret.

Her eyes still closed, Aly leans forward on the bench and bows her face toward the surface of the dock. "My Savior, please send your Holy Spirit to speak to my sisters and my mother and my father and even—especially—my brother. Remove the veil of darkness from their faces so that they might have the eyes of their hearts enlightened and be able to see your face, Jesus.

"I especially lift up Mahmoud before you," she prays as she squeezes her eyelids shut tightly. "If you bring him to faith, then my whole family—at least my mother and sisters—will most certainly be open to knowing you. Please hear this cry of my heart."

Aly pauses and covers her face with her petite hands. "And Father, reveal your will to me. Show me what you desire me to do with my life in the days ahead. Please make it clear to me—"

A hand clutches Aly's shoulder, and she leaps from the bench. Her immediate thought is that her brother has somehow, incredibly, found her here in the heartland of America. She wheels around in a panic only to see the shrunken figure of the elderly woman, Miriam, standing on the dock behind her. The prophetess is the only person at the Academy that Aly does not have to look up to. When they stand face-to-face, they are at eye level.

"Oh, Miriam," Aly exclaims, patting her chest with her hand, "it's you! You startled me."

Miriam brushes off Aly's remarks and, in her no-nonsense style, announces, "Young lady, I have a word from the Lord for you. He told me to come to the lake because I would find you here."

The woman with the snow-white hair and the face deeply lined with wrinkles reaches out and places her wizened hand on Aly's shoulder once again. "He's coming, and you must go with Him," she says with her customary urgency. The prophetess' old green eyes are clouded but still luminous with passion.

Aly stares at the elderly woman blankly as she recovers from the initial shock of Miriam's unannounced arrival. Finally, she asks, "Who is coming?"

"God has a plan for the two of you in the mountain of His holiness," the woman prophesies. "Many will hear the good news of life in Jesus because of your willingness to go to the city of our God."

Aly is still off-balance. She stares at the woman as she attempts to absorb her enigmatic message. "Who are the two of us, and where is this mountain of holiness?" she eventually asks.

"Who and where do not matter," the woman replies impatiently with a wave of her hand. "What matters is that you believe and obey," she announces, her eyes glowing with prophetic intensity. "Nothing else is important.

Will you obey the call of the Lord, Aliyah Ahmed?"

When Aly does not immediately reply, Miriam grasps the young woman's shoulder with an impressively strong hand and asks again, "Will you obey the call of the Lord?"

"Well, of course," Aly responds, frustrated at the woman's forwardness. "Of course, I'll obey God's call on my life."

"Very well, then," Miriam replies, suddenly calm. "Always remember, young messenger for the Lord, His words are not 'See and obey' but 'Trust and obey.' Faith is always the conviction of things not seen. When you hear His voice, you must step out in faith even if you do not see."

Almost as quickly as the woman arrived, she pivots and begins walking away toward the shore. Aly stands transfixed and speechless as she watches Miriam retreat from her, her elderly body leaning so precipitously to the right that it appears she might topple over into the lake at any moment.

When the prophetess is halfway down the dock, she stops suddenly and turns back toward Aly. The woman teeters for a second or two before she stabilizes herself.

"Aliyah Ahmed, don't rush away from King David," she cries cryptically. "Instead, tarry." Then she turns and scoots along the dock, undoubtedly on a mission to accost another student with a prophetic message from the Most High.

Before long, Miriam is marching across the green carpet toward the citadel. Aly watches the elderly woman as she grows smaller and smaller in the distance. She watches until she is out of sight. Then she sits back down on the edge of the bench and stares across the lake.

"Well, Lord," she says, shaking her head, "I'm glad you know what that was about because I certainly don't." She pauses and adds, "When I asked you to show me your will for my life, I wasn't expecting you to answer so quickly. Usually, you wait a few days or a few weeks. Thanks for the prompt response, I think.

"I could use a bit of clarification, however. What do you mean that he's coming and that you want me to go with him to the mountain of your holiness? And that I'm not supposed to rush away from King David but tarry? I'm very confused by all this, Father. Please open my eyes to see your plan. I desire to obey you."

Aly sits on the bench a while longer, trying to decipher the prophecy delivered to her by the eccentric prophetess. Finally, she laughs softly and leans back on the bench. Turning her face toward the descending sun, she smiles and says, "May it come to pass in my life as you have said, Lord. I am your servant."

CHAPTER 17

The Cemetery Professor

Mr. Fagani's class convenes only once a week partly, no doubt, because of the man's advanced age and fragile health. Today, the macro-cohort is accompanying the elderly professor out to the cemetery adjacent to the school. Walking behind the elderly man, Jack observes that his body leans forward at the waist in such a perpetual fashion that it appears that at some point in the past, his back had become forever stuck in that position while bending over to tie his shoes or retrieve the morning paper from his front steps.

The professor shuffles forward at such a glacial pace that the students take one step forward and then wait several seconds before they take the next. A wooden cane steadies the bent man as he snails his way over the gravel path between the citadel and the cemetery. The air is chilly, and a wispy fog shrouds the grounds of the Academy and the graveyard—appropriately enough.

Ten minutes pass. The sluggish procession finally inches through the arched gate of the cemetery. *As slow as molasses in January*, Jack thinks in his head, and he is reminded of his dead grandmother. He sees her wrinkled face. It is not smiling.

A few interminable minutes later, Mr. Fagani comes to a stop. This state of non-motion does not distinguish itself significantly from what he had been doing a moment earlier. Using both hands to lift his wooden third leg, the old man points his cane toward a monument. The scene reminds Jack of an old movie where a man wields a divining rod in a very similar fashion to locate water during a terrible drought. The professor's raised cane shakes violently in the morning air but not from the cold.

"Behold our classroom," the elderly man utters in a voice as shaky as his cane. His breaths come quickly. He teeters back and forth so dangerously that Jack sidles next to him to serve as a spotter.

Another student from the cohort produces a padded folding chair and sets it directly behind the old professor, so he does not need to take any extra steps before he sits down. The other student and Jack each take an arm of the nonagenarian and carefully navigate him into the chair.

Mr. Fagani grunts loudly as he plops down into his chair. "That's better," he mumbles to himself. "That's *much* better."

Thirty students gather around the gravesite near the center of the cemetery. Several unfold camping chairs they brought along. Others sit on blankets in the grass. A few remain standing. Autumn leaves lie thick under nearby hardwood trees upholstering the green carpet around the monuments with a hodge-podge of colors. Occasionally, the leaves dance like puppets moved by an invisible marionette.

Mr. Fagani's face and body speak of the passing of many decades, a span of time that encompasses one world war and numerous regional wars; seven surgeries; the birth of four children, sixteen grandchildren, and countless great-grandchildren; the death of his dear wife; and the general wear and tear accumulated during ninety-eight years of remaining upright through the ravages of this world and the unrelenting pull of gravity.

The man's wrinkles are deep valleys that have slowly eroded the smooth terrain of a face that unbelievably was once young. His weathered skin provides habitable pasture for the sizable herd of age spots scattered over his cheeks and forehead like sheep grazing on hillsides. More notable are the half dozen moles that have congregated on his long nose like ochre ladybugs.

None of the students have ever seen the elderly man's head. It is always encased in a chocolate-brown fedora with a black leather strap encircling the crown like an ironed snake. Coupled with his ubiquitous knee-length grey trench coat, Jack can easily imagine Mr. Fagani as a retired international spy.

"Today, I want to speak of more than simply the history of those who lie in this cemetery," the ancient man begins in a croaking voice. "I want to address how death defines life."

The cemetery professor, as he is known to the students at the Academy, pauses to draw in as deep a breath as his limited lung capacity will allow and adds, "I have earned the right to address the topics of death and life, yes?" he says with a quiet chuckle as a smile cracks the sallow skin of his face. "I've witnessed much death over the years, whether in wartime or in civilian life. And I have one foot in the grave myself—if not nine toes," he says with another rasping chuckle.

At this point, the old man's eyes, although clouded with time, twinkle with mischief as he grabs his leg and pretends to pull it out of the adjacent grave. Everyone laughs loudly.

"This isn't my cemetery plot," he informs his audience. "Mine isn't far from here, however."

Mr. Fagani runs trembling fingers over his thin lips that have all but retreated into his skull and says, "Yesterday, I was thirty. I had been married for just four years to my young, beautiful wife. We had two babies. All our lives were ahead of us. Yes, that was just yesterday," he says in a wistful, quavering voice as he wades briefly into an ocean of memories.

"Enjoy every day because soon you will find yourself old whether you plan on it or not. And make sure that"—the cemetery man pauses to catch his breath—"that you find and seize the meaning of your existence and—hang on for dear life."

The old man fumbles to undo the top button of his trench coat. He appears to be chewing something since his jaw works up and down unceasingly.

"If I had lived my years in this world with no meaning to guide me, I would have done one of two things." He holds up two gnarled fingers to the students. "Number one, I would have drunk myself into oblivion every day. And number two...I would've taken a boat out into the deepest part of Silver Bay Lake and jumped in. But only after wrapping the anchor around my chest."

The old man suddenly has everyone's attention.

"Today, I'm here to inform you that the only way to face the day of your death without despair...is to live your life with meaning today."

The cemetery professor clears his throat loudly. It sounds like a steel shovel scraping the inside of a metal trough. "Do you know who suicides most often?" Mr. Fagani asks in such a tone that everyone knows he is going to answer his own question—everyone but Stewart, that is. The Intellect promptly opens his mouth and proceeds to answer Mr. Fagan's rhetorical question.

"The populations most vulnerable to suicide are the adolescent and the geriatric," the bespectacled young man with the owl eyes announces robotically. "Demographics also reveal a marked gender bias with males more likely to attempt suicide than females and more likely to be successful."

Mr. Fagani keeps on talking as if he had not even heard Stewart—a real possibility since the elderly man had forgotten to put his hearing aids in that morning.

"I'll tell you who," he says in a breathy voice. "Teenagers and the elderly. Why teenagers? They're facing the difficult transition from childhood to adulthood. They're trying to find out who they are and...why they're here. And if they haven't acquired the tools they need to do life, deficits will begin to show up at this age."

The old man stops to brush away a leaf that has landed on his lap. "They're searching for their identities in a world set against...that search. There can be many, many obstacles, some of them devastating. Most people never know themselves—even in a lifetime."

Mr. Fagani pauses to catch his breath. "The elderly? The sun is setting on their lives. They realize there are no more hopeful tomorrows left. No more second chances. No more do-overs.

They naturally look back on the body of work they have produced in their lifetime. If the sum total is gratifying, they can ride off into the sunset knowing they are leaving a good legacy behind." The old man raises his cane and drags it across the sky, providing a visual to accompany his words that a handful of students understand.

"If they view their lives as poorly lived...the only thing left for them is despair. Their one chance to burn brightly on this stage...has passed. Forever gone. Kaput!" the old man exclaims in his hoarse voice as he strikes the ground with his cane. "The awful, heavy awareness...that they wasted their lives is more crushing than they can bear. Oh, the finality of it all."

Mr. Fagani slowly scans the faces gathered around him as his head quivers involuntarily. The average age of the students is seventy-five years his junior.

"None of you know what that crushing feeling is like," he says. "You can't know. You're too young. Some things you just can't...know until you get there...or you listen to someone ahead of you, if you're able. If you have... ears to hear. Unless you believe that you know it all...or that old people are to be dismissed as worthless and ignorant."

Jack notices that the longer the cemetery professor talks, the more he appears to be short of breath.

The elderly man rubs a finger over his leathery chin and licks his lips with a slow tongue. "If you're able to hear me today," he says, his voice gradually losing intensity as he continues, "hear again that the realization of a life lived poorly or without meaning...leads to despair. This realization becomes especially unbearable when...when a person believes that there's nothing left to anticipate after death."

The cemetery professor pauses to swallow with noticeable effort. Then he says, "Looking back on a wasted life and anticipating no hope for the future, many in my cohort"—he chuckles at the word cohort—"many of them drink to escape. Or they become numb with all the medications their young doctors give them...to assist their escape. Or they don't think about their lives in any depth. They distract themselves with...Sudoku and crossword puzzles, watch the one-eyed monster, play cribbage, talk endlessly about politics. Or their depression leads to...the ultimate escape I talked about earlier...suicide."

The old sage bends over to retrieve his cane that had slipped from his trembling grasp. He grunts softly as he does so.

Sitting upright, or at least as upright as his forever-frozen back will allow, he rests both hands atop his repossessed cane and says breathlessly, "As I said earlier, you can't know the...purpose of your life unless you consider it...from the end. Since I am at the end...I can talk about the meaning of life. I have the vantage point of...both the beginning and the end."

The crumpled man with the chocolate fedora asks Jack and the other assisting student to help him stand up. Once upright, he directs them to move his chair twenty feet further down the row of monuments.

The elderly professor shuffles toward his repositioned chair that is now situated in front of two grave markers. Jack's eyes widen when he approaches the nondescript stones and views their inscriptions. One reads *Pauline Fagani 1915-2013*, while the other one says *Louis Fagani 1920—*.

When the elderly man is again situated in his chair, he clears his throat and squints at his students. "Here I sit," he says, his ashen face breaking into a grim smile. "I'm literally on top of my grave. My body will eventually be... buried directly beneath me next to my wife, Pauline. I suspect I'll be showing up here...no later than next summer. Even slow-growing cancer of the prostate kills a man eventually."

There is a poignant pause. "So, I'm as good as dead," the old man declares. "Consider me dead today...at this very moment. This is your chance to interview...a dead man in his grave. Ask this corpse whatever you wish about...life and death and the meaning of life. I'm highly qualified to answer."

Mr. Fagani settles into the chair and becomes as still as the deceased bodies beneath him—except for his perpetually nodding fedora, of course, tossed back and forth by what he has facetiously referred to as his nonessential tremor. Except for the occasional whisper of crackling leaves cartwheeling over the green carpet around them, the cemetery is as still as death.

Jack feels the creeping heaviness of the graves and the autumn cold flow right through him. Melancholy insists on casting shadows over his heart.

While awaiting the first question from his audience, the professor's face exhibits a sudden look of surprise. "I almost forgot," he comments quietly in his gravelly voice. "My second set of ears. When you grow wise, you need a second set of everything—eyes, ears, legs, teeth, knees, even kidneys."

The elderly man fumbles around in the pocket of his trench coat and eventually pulls out two small devices that resemble larger versions of the moles on his nose. With trembling fingers, he inserts them into his ears and adjusts them amidst various whistling and screeching noises until they are properly positioned and set at the correct volume. "I only hope the batteries will last," he mumbles to himself.

Jack looks up and sees the bony arms of the near-naked tree branches above him. They trigger a flashback of his nightmare several weeks ago when the murderous caretaker stabbed him and buried him in this very cemetery. Even as he recalls the details of his chilling nightmare, Rachel says in a loud voice—a feat that never seems too difficult for her, "I guess I'll wade in first, Mr. Fagani. Can you tell us, as you look back on your life now, if there is anything you would do differently if you could go back and relive your life?"

"Ah, the hard question is first," the elderly man says with feigned gruffness. "What would I do differently?" he repeats as he runs his fingers absent-mindedly over the crook of his cane as if it is a musical instrument to be played.

"I'm an old man who has looked back on his life many times," he says in his quavering voice. "I've seen many things I would...do differently given the chance. One regret is that I was too much like my father. He raised us... during the depression and worked two jobs to feed my mother and his six children. I...rarely saw him. He was always working or sleeping. In many ways, he had no choice. He was a hostage to the times."

Mr. Fagani pauses to run his tongue over his bloodless lips for the twentieth time. Jack wishes he had a bottle of water to offer the man whose mouth and lips appear to be perpetually dry. "I swore I would never do that to my family," the professor says. "So, what do I do? I grow up, become a pharmacist...and begin working all the time."

The dead man's fedora slowly turns in the direction of his wife's headstone. He is silent for a while. His eyes are closed, and he is listening—listening to nothing that can be heard with physical hearing. "Yes, yes, my love," he eventually says. "Yes, as usual, you're right."

Turning back to the students, he comments, "If Pauline were here, she would be telling me that I didn't work...*all* the time. I'm exaggerating a bit, yes. But I worked more...than I should have. For what? A fancy car to be buried in?"

The retired international spy with the brown fedora wrestles a handkerchief out of his trench coat pocket and wipes his pink-rimmed eyes with a shaking hand. "Pauline always saw the best in me," he informs the macro-cohort. "She was a gem. My only regret is...that I should have told her that more often. She was the second-best thing that...that ever happened to me in my ninety-eight years."

"What was the best thing?" a student named Eric asks without hesitation.

"Why, Jesus, of course," the man replies, fixing his cloudy eyes on the young man.

"Excuse me, Mr. Fagani," Stewart says in the matter of fact, condescending voice that can bother even Jack at times. "Dr. Windsor is always challenging us not to give Sunday school answers about our faith. How can we know that your response is not a Sunday school answer? It sounds like a Sunday School answer to me."

The elderly man slowly turns his stiff neck degree by degree to identify his interrogator. His head seems to be attached to a slow-moving gear that occasionally freezes up only to eventually jump forward. Jack anticipates an irritable, curmudgeonly response from Mr. Fagani. To his surprise, he responds with patience and favor. "Excellent question, young man," he says.

"Excellent question."

In a voice that trembles but is full of conviction, the old man answers Stewart, "I was young, and now I am old. But never once did I…experience God forsaking me. Not once!" Attempting to raise his cane toward heaven but only able to raise it parallel with the ground, Mr. Fagani says in a louder volume that is a shout for him, "He has always been faithful to me! That's seventy-five years of faithfulness…since the day I first met Him."

"You're saying that Jesus is not a fair-weather friend," Armando comments in a loud voice to ensure that the professor will hear him. "He's been your Savior on sunny days and on stormy days."

"Even on days with thunder and tornadoes," the dead man speaks, his fedora rocking in time with his nonessential tremor. "And there have been many of those. Pauline's death was…the darkest of them all." The handkerchief appears from his pocket again. "But God was with me through that one, too, bugger that it was."

The elderly teacher wipes his eyes and blows his ladybug-laden nose. "There was a season when I was unfaithful, but He was faithful," he croaks with age and emotion. The students lean in close and stop breathing to hear the man's fading voice.

"I came close to a dalliance with other women several times," the old man admits. "I had one emotional affair, and I considered divorce…during a difficult season early in our marriage. At times I was…a selfish, stubborn, irritable man. I took my dear wife for granted most days. But God and Pauline were…so, so faithful to me."

"I had four strikes against me," Mr. Fagani says. "I was a man. I was Scandinavian and Italian—what an unholy union. I was my father's son. I was a human. But over time, the…Holy Spirit taught me how to love."

The elderly man sitting on his grave pauses to breathe. Then he says,

"I've decided that we come into this world...not knowing how to love. Marriage is one of the primary human relationships in which God teaches us... how to love."

A strong gust of wind sucks up dead leaves from the cemetery grass and tosses them magic-carpeting through the crisp air. The same gust makes a futile attempt to dislodge the fedora from Mr. Fagani's head but settles for only tilting it several degrees.

"Are you afraid of death?" Aly asks after laboring over whether to raise the question to the consciousness of someone who walks in its shadow minute by minute.

The old man shakes his head and wags his finger as if death is lurking nearby and needs to be rebuked. "When I was twenty, death was for old people like...my grandparents. When I was forty-five, I noticed my mortality raise its head over the...distant horizon and peek at me. Death then began to cross my mind...but only fleetingly. It became a...possibility."

The cemetery professor does not notice his cane fall into the grass again. "At seventy-five, death became a certainty, but it still was an unwelcome presence...I could ignore it for days at a time. At eighty-nine, when my sweet Pauline died, death became...an accursed thief that stole away the love of my life and then stalked me every day.

"Today, as I sit on my grave, I welcome death," the professor says resolutely, his chin tilted upward as far as it will go. "It's the only thing that stands between me...and seeing Jesus face to face. I welcome it because Jesus defeated it. Yes, I will die...only to rise again."

After thirty minutes of questions from students who are just beginning their life journey followed by responses from the man who is at the end of his, Fagani holds up one trembling hand and says hoarsely, "One more question, and I'm done. I'm spent. After all, I'm not a...spring chicken...

anymore." The elderly man is breathing heavily.

The students smile politely. The cemetery is quiet except for the voice of the wind.

Eventually, Jack breaks the silence. "You mentioned earlier that a person can't live life without starting from its end point and viewing its meaning from there. Can you be more specific about what you mean? Can you give some pointers to us who are just starting out, Mr. Fagani?"

Jack is sitting on the grass only five feet from the old man's chair. The fedora-crowned head tilts down slightly, and the ancient eyes peer at Jack for a long time with a look that indicates recognition. Jack sees sadness in the old eyes.

"Yes, back to the meaning of it all," Fagani mumbles. "Know that you are foreigners and strangers," the sage says in a voice that is half as strong as when he began the class an hour earlier. His eyes that have seen the passing of so many years are watering, whether from emotion or age, Jack does not know.

The dead man bends over slowly and retrieves his cane from the grass. He straightens up as far as he goes and taps his third leg on the ground. "This world is not your home, young men and women," he rasps. "Heaven is your true home. You're just passing...through these parts. But that's not a reason to coast...or take it easy. Jesus wants you to be fully alive...here and now. Be the best spouse you can be. Be the...best parent. Be the best teacher or engineer or...doctor or barber. Be the best friend you can be. Be a...little Christ to everyone you meet in this world. You may be the...only Bible they will ever read. Be love...and truth. Not just one or the other. Be both."

There is a long pause during which Jack pictures the elderly man's body buried in the ground directly beneath his chair.

Death is so out of place in this world, Jack thinks to himself. So incongruent with life. So wrong. And no wonder, since in the book of Ecclesiastes it says that God has placed eternity in our hearts. We were never made to die. No, death is not a part of life. It's an uninvited intruder that should alert us to the fallenness of this world.

"Finally," the dead man says, "remember the Ms in life: Maturity, mission, mate, mates, munchkins...money, Mercury, manse, meaning, music. These M's will be...a part of your life. By themselves, they will be...empty. Guided by the most important M of them all—Master—they will...all be filled with purpose. You'll come to the end...of your life like me, full of joy, peace...and thrilled about what comes next."

"Jesus is the lynchpin."

After a long pause during which the old man begins to wheeze, he continues with the words, "Jesus is the difference-maker. He is the way to meaning since...He is the meaning. Know Him and be full. Choose a different...master and be empty. Only the God...of the universe who created you can fill you with good things. Of course...the best thing He gives us is... Himself. Life, in the end, is about relationships, beginning with...knowing Jesus as your...best friend."

The old man slowly turns his aged head to look at his wife's grave. A lone tear trickles down his corrugated face, a face that is smiling.

"My dear Pauline," Mr. Fagani says in a raspy voice further compromised by strong emotion. "You're now living...in chapter one of the book of life, in the story...that has no end. I'm...still back here in the preface...but very soon, I will join you in the story...of stories...the adventure of all adventures. Together we can...fall on our knees before our God and friend. I will soon...be home. Come quickly for your servant...Lord Jesus. I'm ready. I'm waiting."

A solitary man watches the decrepit professor and the group of students from the top of the hill above the cemetery. The front half of his large head is bald, while the back half is covered with long, stringy hair that falls like a waterfall of grease over his shoulders. His eyes are bloodshot; his large nose is crooked. As his shifty eyes rove over the students, he mumbles a single word to himself: "Soon."

"*The old one is dangerous,*" the gravelly voice grumbles in the darkness. "*He does not fear death, our most intimidating threat to humans.*"

"I *doubt there's anything left to use against him,*" another voice spits out in bitter frustration.

"*There's nothing to be used against him directly,*" a third voice intones coldly. "*But be assured, we're still working on attacking his slimy children and his vermin grandchildren. We're still working on that. The family is always the vulnerable link for those who are strongest in their faith in him their faith.*"

"*He has lost his wife, and yet his belief in the enemy has only grown stronger,*" the grumbling one grumbles. "*I'm not sure that even harm to his family will shake his belief in Jesus.*"

"*Aaaagh!*" the bitter one shrieks in a voice that echoes in the place of forever darkness. "*Don't utter the name! Don't utter the name! Ignorant maggot! Don't utter the name!*"

"*Both of you, silence your pathetically pathetic voices while you are in my presence!*" the cold one demands. "*Forget the old man creature. Even now, we are summoning one who is more animal. We are summoning him who is more animal than human—the man of weakness. His rage and hatred and greed are most vulnerable to our manipulation. His family has been in our wicked grasp for centuries, and he will do our bidding for centuries. There is nothing like despicable pedigree to inspire evil deeds!"*

A fourth voice interjects, "*All six of our targets are soon to be tested by hell's fire. Each of them has a weakness that we will exploit to their total demise. Every one of them will stumble and fall!*"

The cold one snorts and announces in a voice that is more of a growl, "*The summoned one is coming soon—our dark, dark servant, our dark servant. He will destroy the betrayer! Yes, the dark one comes on the wings on the wings of the vulture!*"

CHAPTER 18

The Board Meeting of the Fallen

It is 10:30 a.m. on a Tuesday in October. In a boardroom on the thirty-third floor of a building known as the Pavilion, a meeting is well under way. Present are twenty men and women, including the CEO, CFO, CIO, and a bevy of other company employees. Also in attendance are representatives from a local investment bank retained as the underwriter for the proposed project. The gathered decision-makers are heatedly discussing the logistics and timing of an initial public offering that will generate more available capital for the company as it seeks to expand its current product line.

In the same room—if one can describe it as such—another meeting is convening in a space that lies outside physical reality. Present at this meeting are two hundred and fifty individuals. They are not human, although they are similar in some ways. Neither can they be seen with human eyes. They are metaphysical beings from beyond the natural world that impact human life in surreptitious ways—and not for the good. Simply said, these beings represent some of the thousands upon thousands of fallen spirits who, led by Lucifer, rebelled against the Creator back during the Great Revolt.

In the end, of course, they were vanquished by the eternal Father and His Son and subsequently banished from the kingdom of light. Since that terrible defeat, they have been carrying on their limited evil intentions in darkness, for such are their "hearts"—full of darkness. Their sole mission is to attack, destroy and kill the image-bearers of the Most High God.

The spiritual beings gathered for the meeting are commonly referred to as demons by the human race. Contrary to popular belief, they are not red. Neither do they have horns on their heads or speared tails or fanged teeth. They are, in fact, spirits. They do not have physical bodies of their own—thus the reason they are incapable of being apprehended by human eyes. At times, however, they have been known to inhabit the bodies of men and women.

In the end, existence is not about the body but the spirit. The physical is only a veil—sometimes as semi-transparent as sheer curtains and sometimes as opaque as a stone wall—hiding what resides within. It is what is behind the veil that matters: love or hate; truth or deception; life or death; light or darkness.

Since demons have totally divorced their creator—the One who is Light—they are filled with darkness. No light exists within them.

Some humans are capable of descending to the level of demon darkness, even in their mortal lifetime. All darkness. Like demons, the only things that reside within them are deception, hatred, destruction, murder—all residuals of the Great Divorce. So, while it is possible that if both humans and demons had bodies, some might resemble each other in their physical appearance, certainly many would appear identical in their spiritual appearance. Scarily.

Over the millennia, men and women—who possess a stubborn propensity to reduce things to a level their limited intellect can understand—have called on their powers of imagination to visualize these unseen creatures from hell. The result is that humans have shrunk these powerful spiritual beings into comic book figures who live in a make-believe hell and whose role is to torture the damned.

This distorted human perception of the world of darkness plays beautifully into the hands of the Devil, or Satan, or Lucifer, or Beelzebub, or Belial, or the prince of darkness, or whatever a person wishes to call him. If the truth would be told—which the Devil is incapable of doing, of course, since he is the father of lies—he prefers that human creatures entertain thoughts about him at one of the two extremes: to think about him not at all, which is his primary strategy in more developed countries, or to think about him more than one should, which is his strategy in many other parts of the world where spiritual eyesight is not as clouded by the idolatry of the material.

Demons can see each other, of course. Even though they have fallen from The Presence, they still have spiritual eyesight and can readily view anything that dwells in the spiritual realm—except God Himself. He shines far too brightly for their dark eyes to behold. Those unfortunate ones who have accidentally beheld the Glorious One have been instantly blinded by the glorious brilliance that burns more brightly than a quadrillion times quadrillion stars squared. The actual blinding is not for the weak of heart. It usually entails the literal explosion of the eyes.

The leader of this reduced legion—there were over a thousand soldiers in the beginning, but many have been imprisoned in the Abyss as the campaign following the Great Revolt has continued—clears his throat and speaks to his underlings. "As the leader of the dark army that owns the old church," he says in a voice as sharp as a battle axe, "I am here to announce that we will soon wreak the final vanquishing we will."

The leader's voice that is often heard in the spiritual realm around the campus is a dull roar. His speech is punctuated by inane redundancies because he, along with every other dark spiritual personality in the legion, was damaged at the moment of the Devastating Separation. After all, a being does not rebel against one's creator without sustaining major damage to oneself. It is simply a matter of reaping what one has sown in a created universe that delivers consequences for every action, both bad and good.

Not all demons experience redundancy in their speech. Some are damaged in other ways, such as possessing no intelligible speech—they can only growl or moan. A few cannot generate any sound at all. Others cannot see or think clearly. Still, others fade in and out of existence like failing fluorescent lights flickering toward termination. Yes, there is always a steep price to pay for rebellion against the perfect Light, much of it a natural consequence of sheer foolishness—like getting your hand bitten off while trying to extract a fang from a fully conscious lion.

It is not dissimilar for humans. They are like a flower that chooses—if such a choice were available to a plant—to avoid the sunlight. What happens to this rebellious plant that seeks to flee the source of its life? It ceases to grow at all bereft as it is of the light that powers the process of photosynthesis, which in turn enables a plant to combine carbon dioxide and water, which then results in the generating of its food.

Such is the fate that awaits humans who flee from the presence of their source of life. They, too, like the avoidant plant, stop growing. They slowly wilt, starve, and die. Many image-bearers, incomprehensibly, settle for such a slow, tragic demise in the dark when they could choose to live in the presence of the Son.

Their rebellion and subsequent vulnerability keep the demons in business, so to speak.

"There is a putrid presence multiplying like rabid rabbits in the old quarry a putrid presence," the leader announces to his underlings in a voice that to a human would sound very much like low volume thunder. "As you know, darkness has been strong there for centuries, hundreds of years.

"In recent decades, however, our ancient stronghold there has been under threat. The light in that place is becoming intolerably bright—unacceptably and accursedly radiant. Something is afoot there. Therefore, I have been instructed to redouble our efforts there I've been ordered. Accordingly, we have gathered here to plan our strategy."

The CEO of this particular company pauses and then inquires in a cold voice, "Do you sycophantic slackers remember the methods we employ to annihilate the human spirit do you recall? I assume not. Accordingly, I have prepared a brief training so you will be fully ready to do your work. Since it is rare that we can attack humans physically, we must undermine them in other ways.

"I demand that you heed my instruction as I remind you of the methods we use to destroy humans—spiritually, emotionally, and relationally." Even as he begins to speak, the legion leader is plagued by his propensity to redundancy that inwardly enrages him.

- Introduce it like a subconscious melody into the hearts of the bone-bags that the Most High is a judge who does not love them but is forever angry like a judge. Lie to them that he is a harsh policeman constantly patrolling humans for someone to arrest. Convince them that he is a prosecuting attorney who seeks to viciously condemn them like a prosecuting attorney.
- Plant the earworm of deception into their skulls that all authority is bad and controlling. Make them believe that happiness lies only in individual freedom gained through rebellion and rebellion. Do you remember the seemingly innocuous proverbs we inspired back in the 1960s that led those bohemians to challenge all authority back in the1960s? "Don't trust anyone over thirty," we taught

them. "Do your own thing." "Ditch the establishment." "Don't let the man keep you down." "Born to be wild and free and born to be wild." Or even the innocent phrase, "Flower Power Flower." It's a horticulturally cosmeticized way of saying, "I'm going to do whatever I want, and pigs, pastors, and parents can't stop me." Yes, lie to them that happiness is the freedom to choose whatever they want to do with no rules to interfere with their choosing of their choices. Yes, at this time in the history of the human maggots, we have new proverbs at this time that we inject into their foolish gray matter day and night we inject it. Nonetheless, the ancient message is always the same: Be you. It's your choice. Your rights. Disobey. Disobey. Disobey.

- Distract the walking corpses at all times always from thinking about their mortality. We have seen far too often that when the putrid ones open their eyes to the full reality of their ultimate end, they begin to ponder the full reality and question the meaning of their existence. We can't allow that! Pondering opens the door to thoughts of purpose, and thoughts of purpose always lead back to Him to Him. Hell forbid!
- Always strive with all your diabolical might to separate the worthless bipeds from Him, from other dust bags, and from their own hearts. Never forget that our primary objective is to divide and conquer our primary objective. Isolate them! Exile them! Aloneness is our greatest ally. In that place of utter aloneness, it is open season to attack them in that place with lies and deceptions and more lies. The only voices they will hear in the murky dungeons of darkness are ours. Alienate! Isolate! Yes, scream at them to hide from to hide from the light for fear of the appalling things it might expose inside their tar-engorged souls.

- When they are snuggly locked in their safe room—inundate them with lies. One point of clarification here: give the malevolent content to them sweetly, like deadly lullabies the malevolent content. Always insert into their puny gray-matter these two lies: first, that He and other people will never genuinely love them—how despicably unfair of them unfair! And second, that if they scratch away and second at their skin and gouge deep enough, what they will find beneath is unlovable anyway. If they become convinced of those become convinced of those two lies, they will never trust their hearts to anyone. They will defend themselves to the point of utter aloneness. Then they will be totally at the mercy of our impaling lies totally.
- Convince them that He is a religion, not a person; that He is a dry doctrine, not a loving Being. And if they must view Him as a person, deceive them into experiencing Him Him as a distant divinity who is far less relevant to their lives than football and movies and politics and food and drink and the rich and famous. Hell shudders when a single human practices the presence of Him until the worthless biped fears nothing in this world fears nothing. Nothing! One bone-bag with unshakable trust in the Divine is stronger than all of us dark warriors combined! Just think of that. No, don't think of that, don't think.
- Forever practice bait and switch. Lure them away from the heavenly Father with promises of fulfillment and happiness and happiness. Lie to them that if they rebel against Him and seek their own loves, they will be satisfied. Then after they have turned their backs on the Author of love turned their backs, accuse them of being worthless, disobedient pond scum who are so selfish and shameful they deserve to die, die, die. Put blinders on them, so they will only see

that put blinders on that they are nothing but addicts, winos, sluts, users, losers, unlovable ones, and disposable piles of flesh whose existence makes no difference in this meaningless universe. Brand their brains with a searing iron, so they will forget that the Messiah is the friend of sinners they will forget.

- Never let them look inside. If they do, they will detect the utter emptiness; they will sense it. Distract them to look outside, especially at the faults of others. If they dare to self-examine, lure them away, tempt them to do anything that will numb their pain and their heart desires. The numbing agent might be as innocuous a numbing agent as sitcoms or as dangerous as alcohol addiction (how I love it!), the love of money, or prolific pornography. Yes, always encourage them to numb the pain and distract themselves from the true desire for Him by seeking instead the desires of the body to distract them. Pain and desire, if not eradicated quickly or channeled somewhere else eventually and always lead to Him. Always and always.
- Teach them—parents especially and anyone in authority over vulnerable others—to kill the spirit of those under their care since they probably won't kill their bodies (unless they are sitting ducks in the human incubator). Instruct them to impose on others under their authority under their authority the uncommon foolishness that reduces life. Shrink them. Narrow their hearts. Erase their souls. Then depression, anxiety, emptiness, and addictions will usher them to their cosmetic coffins will usher them.
- Totally blind them to the existence of the reality of a spiritual world. Gouge their eyes out with a stick! Hammer it into their stupid brains their stupid brains that the natural world is all there is. Whisper into their ears that there is nothing beyond the material until their ears will tolerate no other no other belief. Then, all that

is left will be sexuality and power is left. The beauty of a perfect body will be their pagan god and goddess. They will worship dust! How ridiculously wonderful for us and tragic for them.

- Forever sing to them that they are the masters of their own destiny and the captains of their ship and the masters of their own destiny. Convince them that obedience to authority is an injustice to themselves. Their individual rights are to be defended even at the expense of truth.
- Plant the seeds of dissonance in them like terminal cancer cells. We have already lost some souls to the enemy, but we may yet all but extinguish their light in this dark world through internal conflict. One method to achieve this dissonance within them is to fan the flames of the flesh within them. Find a dark desire they are uniquely vulnerable to find the disobedient desire and feed it until an unholy tension is birthed between obeying Him and pursuing the coveted desire. As the dissonance grows, the disobedient desire may become so strong—yes, these desires have the power of a trance these desires—that they exchange their love for Him for the embrace of the secret affair. Then we have secured a dark beachhead in the soul. We may never lure these carcasses back to our camp, but they may forget Him for long periods of time as they obsess on the other desire and forget Him. Soon they will be reduced to dim flashlights that cannot be seen ten feet away instead of towering lighthouses whose beacons can be seen for a hundred miles. At best, they will become powerless to impact those living in darkness those in the darkness. At worst, they will broadcast hypocrisy to the world. So, raze the lighthouses and keep the lost lost. I almost delight in castrating the strong ones as much as blinding the blind ones forever!
- If the human animals have abusive, neglectful, or otherwise harmful

parents, delude their foolish brains to believe that He is the exact image of these mothers or fathers. Then they will forever have a distorted view of Him as one of the evil parents they cannot trust and will never approach forever forever.

- If you foolish fiends absolutely cannot deceive the humans into believing that the Creator of all is wrathful and judgmental and wrathful, convince them that His only attribute is love. Blind them to His holiness, righteousness, omnipotence, justice, and, above all, to His grace above all. Grace—aagh. I hate the word. It drools stickily over my lips like coagulating blood! It speaks of the dreaded double truth—not only that the human vermin are loved, but that they are eternally separated from His perfect character eternally unless they believe and receive the divine intervention. Yes, blind them to His attributes because every single one of them points to the One we thought had died forever on that beautifully forsaken hill. Even now, I shudder at the enemy's ancient deception. I shudder.
- Convince those who are walking dust to create the divine in their own image. Woo them into seeing Him as loving what they love woo them. Instruct them that, like them, He is small and limited in His power, knowledge, and holiness. Deceive them into merging the Creator of all things with their own beings merging the Creator so they will be saddled with a hapless divinity reduced to the status of a tour guide in a cemetery.
- Lastly, do not forget that it is never too late never to disillusion those He has taken from us. Even if they trust Him in their younger years and burn with zeal for His kingdom, use the pain, suffering, and losses of this present darkness to cloud their view of Him and annihilate their first love annihilate. Many begin strong in their

> idiotic faith and sycophantic love for Him. Later, however, this trust in the Divine can be subverted until they deconstruct their love for Him deconstruct their love.

A hair-raising voice shrieks before the last word is out of his lord's mouth. "Enough, already!" it cries impatiently. "We are familiar with the old diabolical strategies. We know all nine-hundred and seventy-six of them. Certainly, you're not going to recite them all! Egad! We've rehearsed them for millennia! What we need now are new weapons that will produce a final victory at the Academy."

This dark spirit who dares to challenge the legion master refers to himself in the plural. He is not technically incorrect. Demons exist as an archipelago—a collection of entities that are loosely connected. They have no individual names. They might be referred to by their specific function but not by any personal name. Even when they refer to themselves as "I," it is not with any sense of individuality. Identity exists in positive correlation to how close one is to the Creator. The nearer one is to God; the more one exists to oneself and to others as a clearly defined individual. The further one moves away from the Divine One, the less one exists.

Demons are in a state of total rebellion against Him, so they are completely divorced from God. They have lost all sense of personal identity. They no longer exist as personal beings.

Humanity potentially faces a similar fate. They come into this world fallen but still bear a vague fingerprint of their Creator. As they flee further and further from their Creator over a lifetime, the image of God in them fades. They become increasingly capable of theft, slander, rape, pride, murder, and other ungodly beliefs and practices. When the Divine is pushed out of their souls, something must always take His place. Something inferior, counterfeit, dark. Bestial.

The demon lord snorts, and the whole room is filled with a stench akin to decaying flesh. He glares at his interrupter with monstrous eyes, monstrous not because they are grotesque but because they burn with a malevolence not even the most wicked human has felt writhing inside his or her viscera. The pure hatred of the monstrous eyes burns into the other demon—literally. Unfortunately for the interrupter, he is one of those demons who had already been reduced to a fragile flicker an age ago. The fiery glare of the demon-lord reduces him to trembling and winks. Then, suddenly, the interrupter is extinguished into nothingness.

"Divorce, Shame, Accuser, Hate, Exchanger, and Destroyer!" the dark lord bellows in a voice that could eviscerate a man or beast. "Come forth, come forth to me!" The room quivers with evil.

In an instant, six demons that, even in their spirit form, appear disturbingly like humans, stand before their summoner.

"Interrupter was not incorrect," the leader says in an affected wistful voice, "just foolishly premature. Yes, we must focus specific annihilation strategies on the ambulating skeletons at the school we must focus. I am sending you six miserable creatures to her who is already harassed by three of your counterparts. I sense she is a lynchpin. Go to her quietly and accuse her quietly even more viciously in her mind quietly. Shame her until she must remove herself even further from all the others. Convince her that she is too weak, too naïve, too nice, too bad, too vulnerable, too ugly inside; convince her. Remind her of her...indiscretions. Teach her to rehearse them over and over and over and over and over."

The demon lord hesitates for effect and then utters in a contrived pleasant voice, "Bring to her memory more vividly what happened with the man at the daycare when she was four years four years old. Continue to accuse her that it was all her fault. Reinforce the lies lurking in the recesses of her mind that she can never trust a man and that a bad girl like her will never be loved a bad girl like her—especially if her dark secrets are ever exposed to the light of day. Sing into her ears the dastardly beautiful melody that she is damaged forever. Drive her into that dead dead-end where her only choice is to divorce herself even more radically from her shameful self and embrace her eternal identity: an object to be used, an object, an object. Then destroy the horrid little image-bearer.

"Because of what others have done to her, and because of what she has done to others, she must go away forever and forever, for all time," the demon lord continues in a singsong voice that stands in sharp contrast to his eviscerating voice. "Devilishly instruct her to hate herself more and more; hate herself. Compel her to exchange herself and Him for lesser, created things that inspire idolatry and lawlessness.

"Then, Destroyer, do the work that you do so well the work you do. Drive little Miss Emily Emerson into the wilderness of utter aloneness where, one day soon, she will send her own body and soul into the Abyss. In short, kill her spirit. Kill, kill, kill. Kill her until she kills her body and cleanses the world of one more ugly blemish until she kills her body."

The demons nod at their commander, and then, in the blink of an eye, the deadly horde of six is gone.

One by one, the legion leader assigns additional messengers of darkness to everyone at the Academy and the Silver Bay Lodge, including professors, managers, administrators, support staff, directors, board members, and, of course, all the students. One mole at the lodge is a sympathizer who needs no further assistance.

To Stewart are assigned the dark messengers called Alien, Exile, and Self-destruction. Sent to Aly are Rule-Follower and Love-Strangler. Armando will be accosted by Fear, Revenge, and Deflector. The latter specializes in the transfer of anger from the intended person to another, safer target, such as a parent directing anger meant for an authoritarian boss toward her child instead. Spirits of Doubt, Gluttony, and Abandonment are commanded to haunt Rachel.

The leader of the dark legion pauses and smacks his lips. "Jack Sutherington," he utters in a sinister tone. "Yes, good old Jack, Jack. He was never supposed to arrive at the little, narrow, parochial school in the first place. He was never supposed to leave Colorado to leave. What a disturbing, hideous being. What an offensive, loathsome opponent who is so offensive.

"Yes, he is extremely dangerous but highly vulnerable. He is weak in his own flesh, but...he has been fitted for despicable things by the Holy One, he is weak. Therefore, we must oppose him with terrifying, terrible might!"

The commander of the invisible host puts a finger to his lips and hums softly as he thinks. Finally, he roars out, "Tempter, Lust, Pleasure, Greed, Isolator, Lust, Grievous—I summon you!" Instantly, the seven tormentors appear before their master.

He considers his seven ambassadors of darkness with eyes that burn with the fires of hell. "Jack Sutherington will never turn his back on—Him. He is too much of a warrior for that to happen; he is a warrior. Instead, you must make him forget his God. Infiltrate his heart as we did with King David infiltrate. How can we ever forget ever forget that horrible victory for darkness?"

The dark lord rubs his hands together slowly, craftily. Then he begins to recite a personal redaction of an old nursery rhyme: "Little Jack Sutherington, sat in the corner eyeing a Valentine dish." The legion leader's intonations lilt in a demeaning way. "He feasted his eyes, and let them run wild run wild, and said, 'What a lucky boy I'll be!'"

The leader indulges in what can best be described as a raucous laugh, humored by his revision of the rhyme. His underlings join him in the dark irreverence of the moment. The laughter is not pleasant. Human blood would run cold at the sound.

When the awful guffawing and chortling and snorting has passed like a rumbling train in someone's worst nightmare, the demon lord falls silent and glares at his messengers. "Beware," he warns in a subdued voice. "Jack, Jack the slacker is not alone. He is not unprotected. The enemy is no fool; he is not. You will be opposed by ferocious angels—by the unfallen ones, the ones who did not fall. But if you approach him as silently and surreptitiously as serpents slithering toward a sleeping child, not even the angels will be able to protect him from himself from himself. Humans are so terribly...predictable; they terribly are."

The dark being abruptly stiffens, and his voice turns menacing. "You must not fail, my detestable lackeys. We've already been surprised on several occasions at the enemy's power in this vile young sack of dust dust. You must strike at an unsuspecting moment; you must strike. At a minimum, strike to destroy his integrity. At a maximum, strike to destroy destroy him entirely."

The dark lord of the legion sends forth the seven demons with a word. They vanish, greedy to instigate their assignment of destruction and hate.

After the agents of Gehenna have departed, the remaining demons utter a closing chant with their ghastly voice. They are not ghastly as one might imagine horrible sounds proceeding from the mouths of gargoyles or creatures from the underworld. Rather, they are ghastly in their terrible tone and sinister intent.

"Kill, destroy, and steal—steal! The demise of humans, seal—seal! Accuse and lie and shame—shame! Tempt, deceive and blame—blame! The image-bearers must not know—know! They all are destined for

below—below! Clog their ears and veil their eyes—eyes! Render them unseeing and blind—blind! When their lungs collapse, they'll finally know—know! Their hearts will weep, besot with woe—woe! From his presence, they'll be lured—lured! Then forever loss must be endured—endured! Forever and ever and ever and ever and ever."

The unseen gathering of the Fallen adjourns long before the heated meeting in the physical boardroom where men and women are arguing and perspiring and scheming as if their decisions carry eternal weight for the known universe.

The legion lord is the last to leave the meeting of the Fallen. As he moves through the men and women embroiled in their urgent strategizing, he snorts loudly and grumbles, "*Just like humans: Straining gnats and swallowing camels.*

What a wonderful dark world it is!"

CHAPTER 19

In the Amphitheater with Windsor

Dr. Isaiah Windsor abruptly and unusually changed the venue for his Warfare class early that morning. He explains in an email to his students that the November day is forecast to be exceptionally warm. Consequently, he has decided to convene class at the amphitheater on the hill above the dorm instead of in the Catacombs.

Several hours later, the Screaming Eagles, along with the other members of the macro-cohort, are conversing among themselves as they ascend the hill toward their open-air classroom. The students ponder if the ultimate motive for the location change might have been left unspoken. They all know that their professor recently has been spending many late nights caring for his ailing wife, Violet, and so they speculate that the exhausted man might be hungry for a source of light that is certainly not to be found in the subterranean classroom beneath the citadel.

Dr. Windsor stands ramrod straight in the center of the small theater that is surrounded by a forest of mostly denuded late autumn trees. He is dressed in his customary khaki pants and a black sport coat. A striped, red tie adds rare snappiness to his usual attire. Even though the retired chaplain never attained the rank of general in the army, Jack can easily picture epaulets with two or three stars on the shoulders of the natural-born leader.

As is his custom, the professor opens his class with a prayer. He honors Jesus as "the only Son from the Father, full of grace and truth," and then asks God to grow the students into "uncommon soldiers of God" in a world war fought with love and truth. When he finishes his entreaties to God and looks up, Jack observes a countenance that is unusually exhausted.

Dr. Windsor follows his prayer with an introduction to the topic of the day. "I want you to answer only one question today, people," the tallish, fit man announces as he walks slowly around the inner circumference of the amphitheater floor. His authoritative shoes crunch the brittle leaves carpeting the stone pavement beneath his feet.

The professor stops and levels his gaze at the students who occupy one section of the three-tiered theater that can accommodate two hundred spectators. "My question for you is, What, at the heart of it all, is our purpose on this pale blue dot known as planet earth? And Sutherington," he says, eyeing Jack with a stern glance, "I don't want a Sunday School answer like, 'to please God.' I'm asking you to generate advanced intelligence pertaining to this topic that might appeal even to someone who currently has no affection for Jesus."

Jack feels a warm current rise in his cheeks, not an infrequent experience for him in the Warfare class. For some reason still unknown to Jack and his classmates, the daunting retired army officer continues to single him out as the target of his "sniper shots," as Rachel refers to them. The professor is beginning to remind Jack of his middle school football coach, who he eventually despised after sitting under his critical authority for three years.

Jack laughs inside somewhere between drolly and sardonically as he thinks, *Maybe, he's toughening me up so if I'm ever captured by the enemy, I won't break under interrogation and reveal top-secret information.*

"So, people, why in the world are you here in this universe?" Dr. Windsor repeats, his inimitable eyes flashing with intensity.

As Jack eyes the colonel, it is not difficult for him to imagine this no-nonsense man leading his Kevlar-clad troops through broken streets in a hard-scrabble desert village, avoiding snipers and IEDs.

Stewart is the first student to respond to the professor's question. "You mentioned the person who has not yet been persuaded to believe," he says, adjusting the position of his glasses by squeezing the bow between his thumb and index finger.

It's always the right bow, Jack observes, and then wishes that he did not always notice the irrelevant details of the world.

"My belief is that many people give little thought to why they're here," Stewart comments. "So how can we share thoughts about the meaning of life with someone if they're not even asking the question?"

"I agree with you," Rachel says, nodding her auburn-rimmed face as she glances at her classmate. "On the eastern seaboard where I grew up, many people aren't interested in hearing about Jesus. I think they equate Him with irrelevant religion, confining moral rules, and judgmental people. On the contrary, these same people are mesmerized by a car commercial that not so subtly communicates that all intelligent people find a way to live fully in the moment, which includes purchasing their vehicle."

"So, you're referring to a hedonistic paradigm?" a girl sitting up on the third tier of benches inquires. The autumn sun, hanging low in the sky, is glinting brightly off the bracelet she's wearing.

"I don't know," Rachel responds with a shrug. "Is it hedonism to live fully in the moment?"

"I've seen that commercial you're talking about on YouTube," another student interjects. "It's accompanied by captivating music, amazing scenery, and incorporates quotes from a man who embraces eastern religion. It sounds philosophically deep at first blush, but I think it's just hedonism dressed up in fancy clothes."

"Yes," Armando says. "The message to live fully in the moment wants to get buy-in from us that pleasure is the reason to get up in the morning." The young man from LA pauses for a moment and then adds, "Now that I mention it, that sounds like living in the barrio—cruising in bad lowriders, chilling with beautiful chicas, and inhaling delicious burritos from Eusebio's food truck!"

Everyone laughs, and Jack can see that his friend is beaming with pleasure. He wonders if Armando is having a hedonistic moment, or just enjoying life.

"Live fully in the moment," Dr. Windsor repeats loudly as he scans the faces of his students with his stern eyes. "Is there anything right or wrong with that? Is hedonism the philosophy we're called to embrace as believers in God? Is it any different than Jesus stating in the field manual, 'I have come that they might have life, and have it abundantly?'"

Aly is quick to respond in her confident manner, "Jesus says that 'no one can serve two masters, for either he will hate the one and love the other, or he will be devoted to the one and despise the other. You cannot serve God and money.'"

"So, what are you saying?" Dr. Windsor inquires as he looks at the Thai-Saudi woman sitting in the second tier of the amphitheater. Jack and Armando have adopted a phrase to describe Aly's strong personality: A force to be reckoned with.

Without hesitation, she responds, "I'm saying, sir, that Jesus wants us to be fully alive and to enjoy the world He has created but to never settle for the pursuit of pleasure as an end in itself."

"Jesus wants us to be ascetics," the ex-military professor challenges.

Stewart clears his throat as he searches the vast collection of file cabinets in his brain. "I don't believe that Jesus necessarily taught self-abnegation," he offers in the dry tone of an academician. "He never advocated a Spartan existence as the prime directive in life."

"So, what is the prime directive for every human in this world?" the professor inquires, redirecting the discussion back to the original question.

"According to Captain James T. Kirk of the USS Enterprise, it's to avoid interfering with less developed cultures," one student offers with a smile.

A handful of Trekkies chuckle knowingly.

"There's a soft drink commercial that says it's to live harmoniously in the international community with no hate or judgment," a Native American man named Fire offers.

"Some of those commercials are very convincing," Emily comments, "especially when they're accompanied by cool music and lots of happy people."

"Yes, whether it's soft drinks or cars or athletic shoes, the advertisements clearly communicate that we must buy their product to be happy," the Native man agrees.

Armando interjects, "But then the smiling people in those ads get on the LA freeways after their commercial shoot and snail their way through the smog and traffic to their apartment in Chino where they live in a miserable relationship with their spouse or significant other. The happy character they portray in the commercial is replaced by the real-world self that struggles to find any kind of happiness and meaning."

"I was thinking along those same lines," Rachel adds. "What's really interesting about those ads is that they lie to you. Tell me if I'm being too negative here, but those commercials seem to say that if you drink their product or drive it or wear it, you'll be transformed into an amazing person who joyfully grabs the hand of the neighbor you've never met and goes dancing down the sidewalk. It's like one of those stories that end with, and they lived happily ever after."

"As if joy and love are generated from sugar-water," someone else quips.

Dr. Windsor looks at Jack and clears his throat. "Look" is not quite the right word. The colonel never just looks at a person. When he directs his eyes at someone, his intense gaze pierces them.

"Mr. Sutherington," the Warfare professor begins in an authoritative voice that is all soldier with not a drop of civilian in it, "what do you think?"

Jack takes a moment to gather his thoughts.

"Well, do you have anything?" the professor asks with an edge in his voice. "We don't have all day here, Mr. Sutherington."

Jack again feels warmth rise in his cheeks as he replies, "Well…I certainly believe that God's prime directive is different than that of the USS Enterprise." He pauses briefly as his eyes drift to a few golden leaves still clinging to a tree behind the professor. "While the directive for the crew of the Enterprise was to avoid interfering with alien cultures that are socially and technologically less advanced, God's prime directive for us appears to be exactly the opposite," Jack observes.

"As the most superior being in existence, God intentionally chose to interfere with us, even though we are a vastly inferior culture. He didn't leave us alone when we disobeyed Him and listened instead to His arch-enemy. He totally interfered with our culture by coming to us wearing our skin so we might see God in our spiritual blindness. He pursued us to provide a way for us to enter into His culture instead of leaving us alone to settle for our inferior way of life as self-identified accidents of evolution."

"That doesn't sound very politically correct, Mr. Sutherington," the colonel responds as a senior officer might speak to a private.

"Nothing about Jesus was PC, sir," Jack responds. "You don't have to be PC when your character defines what's right and wrong in the universe."

Dr. Windsor stares at Jack for a while, then pivots away.

"We still haven't fully answered the question about why we're here, people," the professor states. "Are we simply here to enjoy the pleasures of this world until we get sick and die?"

Jack notices Dr. Windsor's voice soften as he says the last few words. In an instant, Jack's anger toward the man dissipates. He is reminded that his wife, Violet, is dying. A heavy sadness sits on Jack's chest, and he struggles to breathe. He remembers what death feels like.

"Are we in this universe by accident so that nothing we say or do has any meaning in the end?" the professor asks. As he speaks, the breeze off the lake detaches several leaves from the trees behind him, and they drift slowly to the ground to become mulch. "If that's true, we're no better off than dogs or monkeys or even snakes, for that matter. There's no purpose for our existence except maybe to delude ourselves by building castles of meaning in the sky."

The retired officer pauses and then adds, "So what do you believe, people? And what will you say to those who are living without Christ right now? How will your message have any relevance to their lives?"

Rachel is sitting several people away from Jack on the second tier of the theater. She raises her hand as if to answer the colonel's question. But when the professor nods at her, she asks, "Dr. Windsor, can I share something personal?"

The professor hesitates briefly, then nods his head at Rachel again and gestures for her to join him up front.

The young woman gets to her feet and makes her way down to stand next to her professor.

Rachel stares at the stone pavement for a long time. Her hands are clasped in front of her. Jack finds it very unusual for the assertive and occasionally brash young woman to be so subdued. He feels convicted to pray for her, and so he does.

The young woman does not look up when she says, "I believe what I'm going to say will be relevant to your question, Dr. Windsor."

Rachel closes her eyes. She looks like she is attempting to gather herself. Eventually, she looks up at her audience and smiles nervously.

"As most of you know," she begins, "I...I've been spelunking with Embee the last two months. I've also been studying the Field Manual, specifically Romans," she says with a sidelong glance at the professor beside her. "I feel led to share my experience since it speaks to why we're here on this planet."

The young woman with the shoulder-length bob reaches up and smooths the bangs that fall to her eyebrows. Then she comments, "All of us here believe that we were created by an awesome Creator to be in relationship with Him, and we know that we later rebelled against Him. We then experienced such deep shame and badness that we hid ourselves with Adam and Eve in the garden. At least I know I did. I still do."

Rachel pauses and takes a deep breath. Jack thinks he sees her body shudder ever so slightly. There is a long silence. The lonesome cooing of a mourning dove somewhere in the woods floats into the amphitheater born along by the afternoon breeze. There is something especially sad in the plaintive vocalization.

The woman standing next to Dr. Windsor in the middle of the small amphitheater floor nods her head as if agreeing with something she is hearing in her mind. "Yes, God created me by design," she says more to reassure herself than to inform her fellow students. "He doesn't ever make a mistake." Here Rachel pauses and slowly scans her audience.

"I'm not going to lie to you," she continues with more volume, "All my life, I've believed that I was a mistake—that no one loved me or wanted me. Even after Jesus came into my heart, I was still convinced that I was destined to be alone. My head believed that the Rachel God had made was a beautiful person, but my heart felt something quite the opposite. So...I hid. I've been hiding for a long time. I've rarely allowed others to see the real me. Until...until now. Maybe. Hopefully."

Jack glances around the amphitheater at the thirty other students. He sees Emily in the third row about fifteen feet away. She sits transfixed, her eyes riveted on Rachel. Nearby, Aly is leaning forward, not wanting to miss a word her classmate is saying. Dr. Windsor is considering his student with softer eyes than Jack has ever seen. Sitting in the front row, Stewart is wearing his familiar, unflappably calm mask, but his right foot is tapping the stone pavement at a furious rate.

"I've been hurt by the people who should've loved me the most," Rachel says. "But even worse than that," she admits, "I've responded to that hurt with poor choices."

Rachel squeezes her hands together and says hesitantly, "This is where it gets hard."

She glances at Dr. Windsor for the fifth time and takes a deep breath. Then she looks at her fellow students and says, "Over the years, I've comforted myself with food—lots of food. I would binge eat often. Chocolate was always my comfort food of choice." She pauses and then says, "I hate my larger body, and so do my parents. So, I eat to comfort myself. And then...and then I purge. You can see the dangerous cycle I get stuck in."

Now she is crying softly. "I have cut and...burned...my body. I have had thoughts of...dying for years now. But I told no one. Not my campus pastor. Not my friends. Not my parents—especially not my parents. I've been keeping secrets for many years.

"I've hidden my true self so deep inside that...spelunking with Embee has been really slow going," Rachel confesses. "I...haven't ever wanted anyone to see me. I've been convinced that just as I hate the outside of me, others will hate the inside of me."

Here she stops talking, and her whole body begins to shake, but she holds up her hand to communicate that she does not want anyone to rescue her from what she still needs to say.

While Rachel fights to contain her emotions, Jack hears several students sniffling.

"Romans has been my saving truth these last two months—along with Dr. Livingstone and several of my Academy friends," Rachel says as she finally lifts her tear-streaked face and glances over at Aly and another young woman sitting next to her.

"In Romans 8 specifically, I hear God speaking two things to my heart. He has been telling me that I can stop hiding any time now because there's no more condemnation for me since Jesus Himself is now my defense attorney. And...He's been telling me that nothing can ever separate me from His love." A wave of emotion shifts the freckles on her pinched face, but Rachel holds it in check.

"I've been so distant from God," she admits as she wipes away tears with her fingertips. "I've shut Him out. At times, I've...actually hated Him...and hated me...and hated everyone else." She pauses and looks over at Stewart, who touches the corner of his eye.

Probably to wipe away a gnat, Jack thinks.

"I built a thick wall around myself years ago to keep everyone out," Rachel confesses quietly. "Embee tells me that everyone has a wall around themselves, that we're all alone inside to some degree. Nobody really knows any of us fully," she says as she brushes aside a strand of her glistening auburn hair.

"Wonderfully, we're born into this world to be known," Rachel says, looking at Emily. "Terribly, we're separated from God, from others, and even...from our own selves. Our natural position is to be alone, even in a crowd of people. I was terribly alone at one time and still can be very alone."

Rachel swallows hard and looks down at her hands. "I want to be known. I want to be seen—not my false self but my genuine self—even if I feel so ashamed of myself."

She pauses and then adds, "So we're placed in this world by God, but we're sadly separated from Him. But that doesn't have to be the end of the story. This state of separation is the default position of humanity. But God's message is that He has come for us, so we don't have to be alone."

Rachel folds her hands and pulls them close to her chest. "I just want someone to see me—not the me on the outside, who is so good at looking good—but see me...on the inside. Please hear what I'm saying, and...please hear what I'm not saying—out loud at least. I'm sorry, but I just really need to know I'm loved—how I hate admitting that. Is that being weak or too needy?"

For several moments, she stands there, her body shaking. Then her emotional restraint system finally reaches its limit, and she begins to sob quietly. She hides her face in her hands as she weeps openly.

She probably didn't plan to do it. Certainly, it must be a reflexive response considering the person from whom she seeks comfort. Whatever it is, Rachel turns to the man beside her and leans against his severe shoulder.

The face of the military officer who has led soldiers into battle and engaged in fierce hand-to-hand combat reflects surprise. His eyes grow large, and his eyebrows lift high on his forehead. He glances at the students in the amphitheater as if looking for assistance. His hands dangle at his sides.

The initial discomfort slowly drains from the man's eyes only to be replaced by compassion. He lifts his stiff arms and wraps the weeping woman in a gentle embrace.

Rachel is a girl again. She is six years old with red pigtails and freckles. The man who holds her is the father she always dreamt about.

In a moment that will never be forgotten, the outwardly confident woman from Connecticut and the sternest professor they know—Hawkstern doesn't count—partake in a moment of intimacy rare in a world where people are so prone to hiding and self-sufficiency.

Jack smiles, then begins to clap along with all the other students.

CHAPTER 20

The House of Windsor

The Screaming Eagles reach the Windsor house after a twenty-minute joyful jaunt beneath orange, yellow, and red canopies that lattice over the road like protective arches. Leaves crackle, crinkle, and swish under their feet as they turn up the sidewalk that leads to the quaint one-and-a-half-story cottage with a small porch attached to the front. A finger of smoke rises from the gray-stone chimney and curls upward against the backdrop of the dusky night sky. A large neon sign flashing "Welcome" would not have been more inviting than the sight of the cozy house.

"As cute as a bug's ear," Rachel exclaims.

"Wow, this is kind of weird going to the house of the Colonel and Mrs. Isaiah Windsor," Armando says. As he speaks, his breath creates miniature ethereal clouds that quickly fade away. "But the question of the night is who really wears the pants in this house, the ex-military officer who led his men into fierce battles, or his wife."

Rachel laughs and says, "I'm sure we'll know by the end of the night." Her smile descends into a frown, and she adds, "I'm also waiting to see if Dr. Windsor will lighten up on Jack in the comfort of his own home."

The students glance at their classmate, who continues to be the target of harsh criticism and unreasonable expectations from the Warfare professor. Jack shrugs his shoulders as he depresses the doorbell button. "We'll know that by the end of the night as well," he says.

Before anyone can make additional comments, the door opens, and the Academy students encounter their professor for the first time outside an academic setting. He is dressed in casual clothes, including a gray pullover sweater, jeans, and brown slippers. A broad smile warms his typically serious countenance. Clearly, home is where the heart is in the case of the colonel. Greetings are exchanged as Dr. Windsor ushers them into the house.

The students find themselves in a small parlor where they shed their coats and gloves and shoes. Then they move from the entryway into a small living room that looks like it will barely accommodate eight people. A small fire crackles in the fireplace.

Adjacent to the living room is a cozy dining area with a table set for company. On the far side of the dining room is a doorway that undoubtedly leads to the kitchen. Wonderful aromas waft through the arched portal and drift into the living room, tantalizing the noses of the six micro-cohort members.

Dr. Windsor invites his students to sit down on the couch, love seat, and two recliners that populate the living room. Jack notices that all the furniture has floral patterns depicting orchids, roses, and lilies. The lamp tables and coffee table are stained in darker tones that match the rich walnut woodwork of the house. There are several paintings on the wall but few family pictures. The only ones that Jack sees are an old wedding photo and a small picture of a toddler sitting in the lap of a much younger version of Dr. Windsor.

"Whose picture is that?" Stewart asks immediately since he lacks the filter that might delay such a question for a more appropriate time.

Dr. Windsor doesn't even turn to look. He smiles tightly and replies, "That's our son, John. We called him Jack, though—his middle name. He was named John after his granddaddy on Violet's side, but somewhere along the way, we started calling him Jack. You'll have to ask my wife about that."

Rachel exchanges a glance with Aly, then turns to look at Jack with a knowing look on her face.

"That's funny," Armando chuckles as he nods his head in the direction of his fellow student sitting next to him on the couch. "Jack, here—I call him Juan as you may already know, which means John in Spanish. So, you have a John you call Jack, and I have a Jack I call John or Juan."

Dr. Windsor suddenly looks tired. "Oh, we don't have Jack anymore," he sighs. The professor pauses only a moment and then says, "We lost him when he was four."

The air suddenly goes out of the room, and an awkward silence takes its place. Beginning with Rachel, the students speak words of condolence to their professor and look at their feet.

Once again, it is Stewart who seeks more information. "What happened to him?" he inquires as his large, dispassionate eyes peer out from behind his glasses. Jack shakes his head slightly and looks away from his classmate.

Now it is the retired Colonel's turn to look down and study his shoes. Eventually, he replies, "Vi was visiting her mother down in Alabama when I was deployed in Iraq. Our Jack, curious as ever, slipped out of the house and went exploring around the farmstead. He fell into an old well and drowned."

The six members of the micro-cohort utter more words of comfort. Jack feels an ache in his chest begin to throb like an infected shrapnel wound. Rachel, who has grown closer to Dr. Windsor since the day in the amphitheater two weeks earlier, reaches out and touches the professor's arm. Stewart opens his mouth to undoubtedly ask another question, but

Jack intercepts him. "Where is Mrs. Windsor?" he inquires.

As if on cue, a comely woman with an apron tied around her waist emerges from the kitchen. Her skin is several shades lighter than her husband's. Her eyebrows arch upward, creating a perpetual mischievous look on her face. Her black hair, which is shorter and combed back off her forehead and cheeks, appears to be thinning. Her nose is slightly broad and fits her face well. Dark circles create half-moons beneath her eyes. Under her apron, she wears a pink dress—printed with roses nearly identical to those that adorn the living room furniture—and a white sweater with its sleeves rolled up to her elbows. A pleasant expression lights up a face otherwise worn by battle fatigue. The students know that her fight is not against an external enemy but against one that is seeking to destroy her from within.

When Mrs. Windsor looks up and sees her guests, she declares, "Isaiah, why didn't you tell me the students were here?" She is smiling broadly. Her teeth are as white as flour and as straight as a picket fence.

"They just arrived, my dear," the colonel explains.

"Okay, then you're not in the doghouse tonight, sweetie," the woman says as she laughs pleasantly. Her head tilts back, and her eyes close as she laughs.

Emily gets to her feet and inquires, "Mrs. Windsor—"

"Violet to you, child," the older woman interrupts.

"Okay...Violet. What can we do to help in the kitchen?"

"Absolutely nothin'," she remarks as she waves a hand at Emily. "Everythin's ready to go. Y'all just need to sit yourselves at the table, and we can eat."

The six students get to their feet without any further prompting and move toward the dining room. Tantalizing aromas beckon them to come to the table as quickly as they can move their feet. Dr. Windsor takes his wife's arm and encourages her to sit down in the recliner while he serves the food.

"I think I'll do just that," she says, chuckling. "Just don't drop anythin' now, sweetie," she says as she waggles her index finger in her husband's direction.

"Don't worry, Vi, I got it," her husband says reassuringly. "When was the last time I dropped anything around this house anyway?" he asks, intending it to be a rhetorical question.

Violet puckers her lips and begins to hum loudly. Her eyes run to the ceiling, and she places a finger on her chin. Then a light appears to flick on in her brain, and she announces, "I remember that just last month when we had the Washington's over for supper, you dumped my baked catfish into the kitchen sink. Splat! Right into the disposal. If I didn't know any better, I'd think you were trying to get rid of my cookin'!"

Dr. Windsor winks at the students as his wife sits down in the swiveling recliner. Although they try not to respond to the professor's gesture, they must not do a very good job hiding their smiling eyes because Violet declares, "Mm-mmm. He's back their winkin' again, isn't he? I've told him before that a husband who winks behind his wife's back simply doesn't respect his woman."

Mrs. Windsor smiles at the students and then winks at them surreptitiously. This time they all laugh openly.

Soon the students are seated at the dining room table. As their mouths begin to water, Dr. Windsor brings out fried green tomatoes, grits, mint juleps, jambalaya, corn bread, fried chicken, and sweet tea.

The members of the micro-cohort would not have known what half the food was had Violet not identified it as her husband sets it on the table. When all the food is situated in its proper place as per detailed directions from Violet, she rises from the chair and joins the others at the table.

Dr. Windsor asks everyone to hold hands while he prays. "Father, thank you so much for this food that my wife has lovingly prepared for your glory and for the joy of these young people," he says in a strong voice with his head bowed. "May you strengthen our bodies with these gifts. Please especially strengthen my dear wife in the days ahead. Amen."

Before they have any food on their plates, Violet announces, "Remember to save room for the peach cobbler. But if you don't, just stand up after the meal and let the food slide down into your hollow leg, as my granny used to say. Then you'll have plenty of room for dessert!"

Conversation is at a minimum during the meal, limited to social pleasantries. Most of the delicious food is new to the students and occupies their full attention. Even the fried chicken is covered with a breading that Jack decides is better than any he has ever tasted. The only thing that prevents him from filling up both of his hollow legs is the sadness he feels as he observes Violet only nibbling at the edges of her small servings. He cannot begin to imagine what it would be like to lose his appetite.

An hour after they begin their siege against Violet's home cooking, the six students push away from the feast with groans of satisfaction. They help Dr. Windsor clear the table and wash the dishes. Then they retire into the living room, where Violet is already reclining in her swiveling leather chair. She is sleeping. The room is quiet except for her rhythmic breathing.

The retired colonel sits down in an overstuffed chair decorated with yellow roses and closes his eyes. He rubs his forehead with long fingers and sighs quietly. Even in a casual sitting mode, his back is straight, and his feet are planted firmly on the wood floor.

Jack stares at the man he would go into battle with any day, any time, and he feels strong grief. *Jesus, I don't always know why things work out the way they do, he prays in his head. This godly man has already lost his only son, and now it appears he will also lose his wife. I believe without a shadow of a doubt that you are the sovereign God who knows what you're doing, that you have reasons for everything, yet sometimes the path is so difficult, and answers are so few. Be with him, Lord. Please be with him in a very special way.*

Rachel's voice speaking in hushed tones draws Jack back to his surroundings. "Dr. Windsor, how can we pray for you and Violet?" the young woman with red hair and reddish cheeks inquires. "Obviously, we know that your wife is ill, and so we want to support you two in any way we can. We weren't even sure about what to expect tonight as far as food preparation was concerned. We didn't plan on such a magnificent meal. I hope it wasn't too hard on her," she says, glancing at the sleeping woman.

"A herd of wild horses wouldn't have prevented Vi from cooking the meal tonight," the professor says, opening his piercing eyes and fixing them on Rachel. "She loves students from the school," he comments with a wan smile. "Ever since I began teaching at the Academy, she's gone out of her way to adopt as many of you as she can. It's as if you're her kids."

There is a silence before Dr. Windsor says in a quieter, confidential tone as he leans toward the students, "As you've no doubt heard, Vi has a recurrence of cancer. She had been symptom-free for over four years, and then it just showed up again out of nowhere. We were thinking she had beat it since she was getting so close to that coveted five-year mark."

The ex-colonel pauses and looks around the room, his eyes grave. Then he says almost in a whisper, "The docs say she has less than two months."

The Screaming Eagles shake their heads and look empathically at their academic and spiritual leader. "I'm so sorry to hear that," Emily says softly. "You must be so heartbroken."

The professor nods his head slowly and presses his lips together until they are bloodless.

"But don't think for one minute that I'm just goin' to roll over and die without a fight," a voice suddenly announces. Surprised, everyone turns to look at Violet, who is in the process of raising her chair to a sitting position. "And it would take more than horses—it would take a herd of rogue elephants on steroids to keep me from cookin' for you kids," she exclaims, her face a picture of determination.

Violet turns to her husband and says, "Isaiah, let Sugar out of the bedroom. She would love to meet the students."

Dr. Windsor nods his head in agreement and leaves the room. A few moments later, a ball of brown fur interrupted only by a black button nose and two pieces of coal for eyes comes bounding into the room. The brown ball beelines toward Aly and puts on the brakes a bit too late. It slides right into the young woman's outstretched hands. Aly lifts the small dog into her lap and exclaims, "Oh, how cute he or she is—just adorable! So, you're Sugar," she says with a broad smile as she places her hands under the dog's front legs and lifts it up to her face.

"She's a she," Violet says with a chuckle as she displays her beautiful teeth and her weary eyes. "We've had her four years now. Bought her just after I was done with cancer treatments the first time around as a celebration. Her full name is Brown Sugar. We call her Sugar for short."

"She's a gorgeous dog," Rachel remarks as she reaches over and pets Sugar. "Her fur is so soft and curly, even on her paws."

"She's a Mini Goldendoodle, the offspring of a Miniature Poodle and a Golden Retriever," Stewart observes in his customary informative manner that can be interpreted by some as arrogance. The members of the micro-cohort know otherwise about the Intellect, but Armando is still aggravated by his penchant for dispensing facts about everything from the location of the next total solar eclipse to the size and color of moose scat. "She looks like a purebred."

"Why yes, Stewart, she is," Violet remarks pleasantly. "You sound like you know dogs."

Stewart maintains his usual stoic countenance as he replies, "My great aunt in Monterrey, California owns two of them. They're both F1-B Mini Golden doodles."

"Ah," Violet says, nodding her head.

The three young women continue to pet Sugar as they admire her amiable disposition and her cute pink tongue that licks their hands as if they're covered with dog-bone powder.

"Just so you know, I'm not uncomfortable talkin' about it—the cancer," Violet informs the students. "I know that sooner or later, I'm goin' to die from something, so why not cancer? At least it's not sudden like a heart attack. This way, I have time to say goodbye to everyone and get ready for my one-way trip to heaven."

"Wow, I'm impressed that you can look at it that way," Armando says. "I know a lot of people who aren't so positive about it."

"It's not like I'm excited about dyin' before I reach sixty," Violet qualifies. "But if this is what's goin' to take me over the threshold to the home I've been waitin' for since I was eleven, then so be it. I've just got to make it through the dyin' part, and then I'll be just fine," she declares as she gestures with a feeble wave of her right hand.

"I suppose dyin' would be harder if I had children and grandchildren," the dark-haired woman muses aloud. "Then sayin' goodbye would be even more difficult than it's going to be, leavin' my Isaiah behind."

"Do you believe God will heal you?" Aly asks as she passes Sugar over to Emily's open arms.

"My Father can do whatever He pleases," Violet replies emphatically. "He can come and take me home in a chariot if He wants. Now, wouldn't that be a sweet ride? Yes, siree!" she exclaims, elongating both words.

"But to answer your question more to the point," Violet says, "I do believe that God can heal me, and maybe He will. I feel like Shadrach, Meshach, and Abednego when they told good old King Nebuchadnezzar, 'Our God whom we serve is able to deliver us from the burning fiery furnace, and he will deliver us out of your hand, O king. But if not, be it known to you, O king, that we will not serve your gods or worship the golden image that you have set up.[1]'"

Violet licks her lips and adds. "When I enter the furnace of cancer, He may rescue me from it, or He may simply take me through it to the other side. Either way, I'll be healed. Either way, I'll be with Him. As Paul said, 'For to me to live is Christ, and to die is gain.'

But enough about me," Violet declares with another wave of her hand, "what about y'all? Tell me about you."

The six students spend the next hour sharing where they are from, what brought them to the Academy, and what they hope to be doing in the future. They talk about their classes and make it perfectly clear that the Warfare class is their favorite of all, to which Violet responds with a wry smile and the words, "Nothin' like butterin' up the professor." Sugar falls asleep in Dr. Windsor's lap. The fire in the fireplace dies down to embers. The room grows cool.

When there is a lull in the conversation, Dr. Windsor turns to his wife and says, "Vi, I think you should be getting to bed soon. Getting rest is critical these days."

---

4 Dan. 3:17-18 (ESV).

"Yes, yes," Violet responds with some impatience in her voice as she gives her husband a tired smile. "You're right as usual, sweetheart. There's just one thing the kids should know before they leave tonight."

"What's that?" her husband inquires.

The older woman hesitates, and her eyes fly over the faces of the six students. Then she says, "Ever since the cancer came back, I've had…more dreams."

"Are you talking about the ones you had back in July?" her husband asks, a bit confused.

"Isaiah, I've had dreams every night beginnin' in July and continuin' to last night," she admits haltingly. "I haven't told you because you'd only worry about me. The dreams involve these dear sons and daughters of Jesus."

"Involve?" Dr. Windsor wonders aloud. "What are you saying, dear?"

"All these young people have appeared in my dreams," the woman says as if it is perfectly natural for her to have dreams about students she has never met before. "At first, I wasn't sure if I should share the dreams, but I've been prayin' for wisdom for several days now. The good Lord has made it abundantly clear tonight that He wants me to speak now that I have met the people who are in the dreams."

"Okay," her husband says with some hesitation. "If God told you to share them, then you need to do just that."

Violet sits up straighter in her reclining chair and spontaneously launches into prayer without bowing her head or closing her eyes. "Jesus, give me wisdom in what I say, and may my words honor you." Then she looks at the students and says, "I've had repeated dreams about all of you. I saw all your faces in my dreams long before I ever met you tonight."

The dying woman immediately has everyone's attention. The six students sit quietly and expectantly, their eyes riveted on Violet. Several of them have misgivings. Jack attempts to dismiss the thought that he should never trust the content of a dream about him coming from the mouth of a total stranger. The thought is unusually persistent as if someone is pounding it into his brain with a sledgehammer.

Violet pulls a small notepad from the pocket of her sweater and explains, "I wrote down a few notes summarizing the content of my dreams. Mind you now, these dreams have been repeated many times over recent months with only minor variations in the details. The main themes have always remained the same."

Extracting reading glasses from the other pocket of her sweater, the middle-aged woman positions them on her face even as she makes a few final prefatory comments.

"Some of these dreams might be prophecies about the future," she comments, "but I can't be certain. Honestly, I don't know what any of them mean. All I know is that the Holy Spirit will make them clear to you."

The older woman pauses and eyes the students over the top of her glasses. "Pay attention, now," she states as she wags a finger at them. "I may not know what to make of these dreams, but they're clearly from the Lord and meant for you. I'll do my best to be brief. Jesus knows I'm runnin' out of energy."

Violet glances down at her notes. Then she looks up at Stewart.

"Young man, I'm going to begin with you," she announces. "I keep seein' you in my dreams all locked up. You're shut up in a big old chest, then a closet, then a prison cell, then in a cabin out in the middle of the woods. Only the Lord knows where. You're just always shut away somewhere, all by your lonesome. I wake up from these dreams feelin' so sad for you!" she remarks with eyes that communicate deep empathy.

Stewart stares back at the sick woman with not even a hint of emotion on his face. He simply nods his head slowly as he looks at her.

"But don't fret, young man," Violet says as she leans toward Stewart, nodding her head and smiling tiredly. "God's got somebody comin' for you. Somebody big and strong who's goin' to help you get free once and for all."

The Intellect nods his head slowly and replies, "Thank you, Mrs. Windsor."

Violet turns her attention to Emily next. "In my dreams about you, sweetheart, I see you runnin'," she says, tilting her head to one side as a look of confusion settles over her face. "You're runnin' as if the devil himself is chasin' you."

Violet pauses to touch her thinning hair before she adds, "The odd thing is you're always runnin' away from the light and toward the darkness. Someone is calling after you over and over again. But you just keep runnin', girl. I always wake up so worried for you. I end up thinkin' that maybe you're not runnin' *away* from somethin' as much as you're runnin' toward somethin'."

Emily briefly holds the older woman's eyes, then looks down at her hands. She says nothing.

Violet shifts her attention to Armando and points a finger at him. "Now you, young man, I'm really worried about you," she announces.

The man from La Puente touches the teardrop under his right eye and swallows hard. "Ay, caramba," he says, his eyes large with fear.

"Uh-huh, yes, sir," Violet says, nodding her head. "I keep havin' dreams of you goin' into a forest. There are lots of trees there—nasty trees. They reach their branches down to swat you and grab you and wrap themselves around your head and arms. But you keep fightin' them off and goin' deeper and deeper into the dark forest. You're on some sort of a mission. You're goin' back somewhere, I think. You're goin' back to a very dangerous place, a dark place. The good news is that I see angels all around you."

The woman hesitates and stares into the glowing embers of the fire as if attempting to remember something. Eventually, her attention returns to Armando, and she says, "You're not alone. Another man is with you as you fight through the forest."

Violet closes her eyes, and her head dips onto her chest. The students think she has gone to sleep. But her eyes soon open, and she glances down at her notes again. Eventually, she looks up and asks, "Is it Rachel? I'm so sorry; I fear I've gotten it wrong."

Rachel smiles and replies in her nasal voice, "You have it right, Mrs. Windsor."

"Violet."

"Yes, Violet," Rachel corrects herself.

"I like my dreams about you, young lady," the older woman says as a smile brightens her weary face.

"Well, good. That's great," Rachel says as she looks at the other members of the cohort, grinning. "For once, I get the long straw in life. Sorry, Armando."

"A common theme in my dreams about you is that I see you alone in different places—a subway tunnel, a street corner, a cafeteria, possibly even in your own house. Sometimes there are people around you, but nobody is lookin' at you, so you're still alone. Alone in a crowd, I guess," Violet says as she pauses and carefully shifts her position in the chair.

"It probably sounds like bad news so far, but the good news is that at the end of every dream, somebody comes up to you and tells you the same thing: 'I'm here for you, Rachel. I'm takin' you home.' These words show up in every dream."

Rachel swallows hard, and Jack notices her eyes are glimmering with moisture.

"Thank you, Mrs.—Violet," the young woman says. "Thank you so much for that message. It means a lot to me, especially in light of recent weeks."

"I believe you, young lady," the older woman replies. "I believe you." She keeps compassionate eyes fixed on Rachel for a long time. Eventually, she consults her small notepad and then turns her attention to Aly.

"My dreams about you feel different than the other students," Violet begins. "I keep seeing you, Aly, in a huge palace livin' with many other people, thousands and thousands of them. Then, one day, you get up and walk away from the palace toward the early morning sun that's lingerin' just beneath the horizon.

Somethin' slinks after you. It's a black lion with teeth as sharp as razors, and so long they touch the ground. As you're walking away from the palace, the lion suddenly breaks into a run. You don't see him comin' because your eyes are fixed on the risin' sun that's just beginnin' to wash away the dark of the night. Just when it looks like the lion is goin' to pounce on you, the sun breaks fully over the horizon and blinds the ferocious creature. He falls to the ground, and his teeth shatter into pieces."

"I get the nasty trees, and you get the lion," Armando exclaims. "I'm not sure which adversary I'd pick if I had the choice, but at least your lion is left with only gums in the end."

Jack says, "That certainly is a rich dream, Violet. It sounds like God is going to protect Aly in all of her troubles."

"There's no doubt about it," Dr. Windsor interjects as he looks at Aly. "God has His protective hand on you and your future."

The young woman with citizenship in America, Saudi Arabia, and Thailand responds, "Yes, it's true. Wherever He guides me, He will provide for me and place His shield around me."

Violet smiles, then turns her eyes away from Aly and looks at Jack. The wife of Dr. Windsor hesitates, and her face appears troubled. Instantly, Jack feels the familiar crushing weight on his chest. He is aware that he is holding his breath as he waits for the dreamer to speak to him. It does not appear that her message will be bright and cheery.

Violet begins by saying, "There's somethin' pursuin' you, too, Jack. It's not a lion." She stops speaking and turns to her husband. "Remember, Isaiah; I told you about these dreams back in July?"

Dr. Windsor nods his authoritative head as he thoughtfully rubs two fingers over his chin.

"What is it?" Jack inquires. He leans toward the older woman, his elbows on his knees.

"In the dreams, I see men and other dark figures," Violet says slowly. "They want to kill you, Jack."

"Kill me?" he exclaims. "Why would anyone want to kill me? I don't have any enemies—at least none that I know of."

"Like I said earlier, Jack, I don't know if these dreams are about the literal future," Violet explains. "Maybe you're supposed to look for the hidden meanin' in the symbolism like with Armando's and Aly's dreams."

Jack nods his head, then asks, "Is there anything else I should know?"

Violet nods her head slowly and blinks her half-closed eyes several times. "There are a lot of people around you in the dreams. They're your relatives. Most of them are dead."

"Is it my mother?" Jack asks with urgency in his voice.

"No," Violet says, shaking her head. "It's not your mother. They're older relatives, like grandparents and great-grandparents. People who have been dead for a long time."

Violet pauses and then adds, "In my dreams, I see you in the cemetery next to the Academy. You're hidin' behind an old gravestone, and a scary-lookin' man with long hair and a crooked nose is searchin' for you."

In an instant, Violet, the dreamer of dreams, has Jack's full attention. He has seen a terrifying man in his own dreams—the one in the cemetery who stabbed him and then shoved him into the open grave.

"Is there more?" Jack asks, not sure if more will be good or bad.

"No, that's all I remember," the woman says. "Oh, except that there are some words from Scripture that keep showin' up in my dreams. They're from Ecclesiastes: 'There is a time for everythin', and a season for every activity under heaven...a time to be born and a time to die...a time to weep and a time to laugh, a time to mourn and a time to dance.'"

Violet's time for sharing dreams is over as abruptly as it began. Totally spent, she lays back in her recliner and closes her eyes. As the students quietly consider her words, the middle-aged woman drifts off to sleep.

The six members of the micro-cohort enjoy the comfort of the Windsor home for another hour. They are hesitant to leave. It feels so comfortable to be in a house instead of a dorm room, especially a house filled with so much warmth, peace, and love.

At the end of the evening, the faux Screaming Eagle students and the legitimate Screaming Eagle colonel take time to seek God's face. The students pray for Violet's health while Dr. Windsor prays for his dinner guests. One of his petitions is that God will give all six of them the wisdom to interpret Violet's dreams. His wife of thirty-two years is still sleeping when he finishes praying.

Sadly, the husband and wife will never see their thirty-third anniversary.

CHAPTER 21

STEWART AND THE CAVE OF PRESENCE

As is the custom when a student's appointed time arrives to enter the Cave of Dread, Dr. Livingstone, Dr. McNeely, and all the members of the micro-cohort accompany Stewart down the dark tunnel toward the entrance of the Cave of Presence as Embee alternatively refers to it. Although Stewart's face is as impassive as ever, Jack notices in the collective light of their cell phones and two lanterns that his friend's owl eyes are a bit larger than usual.

When the small procession arrives at the cave, Dr. McNeely speaks to Jesus, interceding on Stewart's behalf. Then the five members of the Screaming Eagles, who will not remain in the COD, share parting words of encouragement along with back-slapping and brief hugs. Soon they depart, leaving Stewart alone in the cave for the next eighteen hours. Emily is the last one to leave. Before she bends over to leave, she looks at the Intellect in the dark cavern and says grimly, "Good luck."

Stewart remains standing woodenly next to the single-burning candle long after everyone has left. He has no thought about what to do next. He stares around at the meager, pale light cast on the walls and ceiling of the expansive stone room as if looking for divine guidance.

Gradually, he begins to feel very small.

A while later, waves of darkness begin to wash over him on the inside.

He senses that he is lost...forgotten.

An hour goes by, and he is still standing next to the fragile candle with its weak flame. His large eyes stare off into nothingness. He knows where he is—he's back there.

He's in his bedroom back in Two Harbors. The light outside his window is dying. Dusk is creeping into his room. His father is almost an hour away, working late as usual in Superior. His mother is washing supper dishes as she chats on speakerphone with a friend. Her laughter is bright and inviting. Stewart does not hear that laughter when he is around his mother. It is never for him. He has learned over the years that his presence is experienced as an inconvenience for the woman who is called his mother. She has taught him to retreat to the place that pleases her the most—anywhere where she is not.

He is old enough to know, at least on some vague level, that either his needs are too much for his mother or that she has very limited supplies. It is better for him to conclude that he is too much for her because then he can preserve the fragile fantasy that his mother is strong. He'd rather believe that she is strong than the opposite. Weak mothers make life scary because then the child must be strong before his time. He has no choice but to grow up too fast and leave the part of him behind that has emotional needs. Stewart can't think any farther than these thoughts because, past them, everything gets vague very quickly.

It makes everything worse that he is bullied at school. In more lucid moments, he perceives that there must be a positive correlation between difficulties at home and vulnerability to bullying in the world. It complicates things even more for Stewart that his seventh-grade math teacher has chosen him, a defenseless student, as the scapegoat for his sarcasm that ideally should be directed against what he hates about himself. There are few things worse than a teacher who is an adult bully—as if the peer bullies are not enough.

The teacher bully calls him a skinhead. He speaks the name in a good-natured way, of course, painting a nice veneer over the shame he smears over Stewart with quiet hatred. The smaller bullies have a broader selection of monikers for him, including fatso, fag, bug eyes, and tin man because he apparently does not have a heart. One of the few times he does get angry and slams one of his tormentors against the lockers, his cheeks glow so crimson that, in the end, it turns out not to be a coming-out party for his assertiveness but simply the occasion for the birth of yet another nickname—Rosie. He can't win for losing, so why even try?

He is so alone but often does not even know that he is alone because to know you're alone, you need to know what the opposite of alone is—like having friends. It's like the old saying, "If darkness didn't exist, no one would know what light is." The problem for Stewart is that he has no light, so how can he even know that he dwells in darkness? Compounding everything, even though he can't fully put a finger on it, he has the distinct feeling that he is different than everyone else, an outsider looking in on life. He is an extra-terrestrial who comes from some other planet millions of miles from earth.

When he gets older and takes an English literature class in high school, Stewart identifies closely with the scene in Edith Wharton's book, Ethan Fromme, where Ethan is standing, alone, outside on that cold, snowy night peering through the frost-covered window of the church basement. Inside the bright sanctuary of humanity, Ethan witnesses the dancing and the merriment shared by his peers in the cozy room warmed by a fire in the hearth. But he is not invited into their fellowship. The glass window may as well have been a steel barrier.

Just as the window of that church represents an impenetrable barrier between Ethan Fromme and his peers, so Stewart senses that something insurmountable stands between him and the rest of the world. A chasm yawning wide and deep separates him from other humans, and search as he might, he has not yet found the bridge that spans the damnable abyss from his lonely heart to the other side where everyone else laughs and dances together—totally oblivious of his existence.

Small talk has always been an unsolvable mystery to him. Sometimes, he stands in the hallways at school, a lonely wooden soldier, watching the lips of those around him as they converse so effortlessly. The words flow so naturally over their lips, Stewart observes. How in the world do they share their lives so easily? How do their brains think so many relational words and then speak them so freely when he has to labor to remember his own name in the presence of others? He is not like them. They all possess a blueprint to life that he never received. What is the familiar phrase that he often repeats in his head? I didn't get the memo. But everyone else did.

If he possessed even limited access to his emotions, he would know that he hates them—and that he hates himself. But, of course, a tin man does not possess such intimate access to the inside of himself since he has no heart.

Sadly, Stewart is not aware that his heart even exists. He can only experience it if someone outside of himself sees it, hears it, loves it, and mirrors it back to him. And he has no such mirrors around him. In the aloneness of his world, his self can eke out a fragile existence, but it will never be deeply known unless someone miraculously shows up out of nowhere to love him. What are the odds of that happening? Ten million to one?

No, he does not belong in this world; and the worst of it all is that he has no idea how to make himself belong, if that is even a possibility. If it depends on him to find a way to gain access to the world of talk and laughter and inclusion, he is in a hopeless position. The past is obscured by a shroud of darkness; the present is mere existence in the valley of persistent despair, and the future will most certainly be more of the same. In his psychology class, he learned that he is a classic example of learned helplessness. But even though he knows what his problem is, ironically, he is powerless to change it.

During a rare moment of presence, his father once made a comment to him, "Some people are born on third base and think they hit a triple." Stewart long ago decided that he was born in the batter's box and then beaned in the head by a wild pitch. He fell to the ground, unconscious, at home plate, and never even made it to first.

Some people are born unlucky.

His sole source of comfort and camaraderie in the world is his imagination. Through the medium of movies and books and Internet searches, he has constructed a rich interior world over the years replete with imaginary friends and thrilling adventures. He has traveled to every continent, blasted into space, descended into the deepest ocean trenches, saved the damsel in distress countless times, and launched his own startup company that brings him great acclaim and wealth.

In this self-constructed private world, everyone exclaims, "Isn't Stewart amazing! Who would have thought he had it in him? He's a revelation! He's my hero!"

Sadly, but predictably, the abyss between the real world and his private world has grown wider every day. Since he feels totally incapable of living in the outside world of real people with their intimate conversations and conflicts to be resolved, he increasingly retreats to the safe world he can control, where he is consistently rewarded with praise and popularity.

It's a no-brainer, actually. He has read somewhere that a person tends not to repeat behavior that is punished but is more apt to repeat behavior that is rewarded. Since he experiences the real world as punishing and his internal world as rewarding, it is a foregone conclusion where he will invest himself. Of course, the more he invests in one world, the less he invests in the other and the less capable he will be of living successfully in that other world. His future is doomed.

As he drifts through high school like a lonely specter, he notices that while some people seem irritated with his intelligence and accumulated knowledge—primarily his peers—others appear to be impressed by these attributes, especially certain teachers. Soon, academic performance becomes the avenue through which he gains some currency in the outside world. Increasingly, he is motivated to read for knowledge to impress others and to excel in his studies.

At his high school graduation, he sits among his peers adorned with cords, ribbons, and medallions that come with being the valedictorian of his class. He stands out. He is noticed! He is finally seen, even publicly acclaimed as superior instead of being regarded as inferior. Even the teacher who bullied him in seventh grade singles him out after the graduation ceremony and enthusiastically shakes his hand. Stewart has finally found a way through Ethan's impenetrable steel window.

So why does he still feel lost, like half of him is missing?

He doesn't date in high school or at the university. He experiments half-heartedly with alcohol and pot during his first two years of college. He immerses himself in role-playing video games as well as some real-life RPGs such as D and D. In the end, none of these distractions capture his attention or even marginally satisfy his desires. Eventually, he walks away from all of them.

Once again, escaping into his inner world is all that remotely gratifies him. He is only vaguely aware that he is cultivating a habit that is taking him further and further away from other people and deeper into an isolated world that will one day become impenetrable.

During the final quarter of his sophomore year in college, Stewart takes a world religions course as an elective. The professor's flyover treatment of Christian "mythology" consists of a handful of excerpts from the writings of G. K. Chesterton, Blaise Pascal, C. S. Lewis, and the New Testament. Stewart finds himself quickly intrigued by the content of these assigned readings.

It is impossible for Stewart to identify all the ingredients that trigger his interest, but there is one thing he does know—whenever he reads the words of the three authors as well as the New Testament, he feels, strangely, like he belongs in their world. He feels less alien, less excluded from life. This new sensation of belonging is intoxicating for him.

One day after reading something in the New Testament about being adopted into God's family, Stewart looks up at the ceiling in the library and impulsively says, "I want to be your son, Father. I want to be your friend, Jesus. I want you to live inside my heart, Spirit of God."

Disappointingly, nothing amazing happens after he utters his unprecedented invitation to the Divine. Apparently, even God does not want him.

Several weeks later, however, he has an odd realization: he feels more whole and grounded. Most amazingly, he experiences a vague sense of being on the inside of things. Unfortunately, his surrender to God does not translate into deeper, more satisfying relationships with people. He remains largely alone.

In the Cave of Dread, Stewart shifts his weight from one foot to the other and keeps his eyes closed. He is back in his bedroom once again. So alone. So empty. His father is still at work. His mother is now on her desktop computer researching vacation destinations in warm, exotic places that will provide her a temporary escape from the long and desolate winters of northern Minnesota. She is not that different from Stewart in her attempts to escape from the world around her. The only difference is that she does it via geographical escape while Stewart does it by escaping into his mind.

The silence in the cave reminds Stewart of the silence in his bedroom. How often he had desperately hoped that someone would come and find him or at least check on him to see if he still existed.

In the gloom of the cavern, Stewart's mouth moves. No sound comes out. His lips twist into unusual formations as he attempts to say something. Finally, a word forces its way out against powerful resistance. "Help," he whispers.

It is all he can say. All alone in the Cave of Dread, he repeats his despairing supplication. "Help."

He struggles to make it personal, intimate. "Help...me."

With his eyes still closed, Stewart spreads out his arms and lifts his face toward the ceiling that towers thirty feet above him.

"Help me," he utters again. And then louder, "Help me! Help me! Help me!"

Although no emotion awakens in his heart, Stewart continues to utter his plaintive cry. Rarely are two simple words uttered with such sincerity.

Something stirs in the dark cave even as the young man continues to voice his plea.

At that moment, if Stewart had possessed practiced spiritual ears, he would have heard two things. He would have heard something akin to a sinister voice shredding his heart with merciless words. "You are nothing," it states matter-of-factly, two octaves lower than the deepest human voice. "You are an alien unfit for human society. You'll never belong. Shut your measly mouth, Pinocchio."

The other sound he would have heard is a reassuring voice that reverberates pleasantly in the cave. It, too, exists in a dimension beyond human perception. But it is not far from the world of physical hearing.

The beautiful voice says, "Your lament is heard, my son. He will save you, humble one. He will turn your darkness into light. The best is yet to come!"

CHAPTER 22

Emily and Dr. Hawkstern

Two dozen members of the macro-cohort mill around in the medieval hallway with its gray-marble floors, vaulted ceilings, and small alcoves populated by sculptures, inscriptions, and old artifacts. As has become their practice, the students avoid going into the fireside room until a few moments before the class with Dr. Hawkstern begins due to their discomfort in the presence of the giant professor who rules by intimidation. Jack thinks it very unfortunate for a man so vehemently committed to the non-existence of God to be avoided by those who love Jesus. However, the professor continues to be so combatively resistant to anything spoken in opposition to his beliefs that he has successfully alienated all of his students.

Emily approaches Jack, Rachel, and Armando, who are all loitering in the hallway with the other students. "I think I've solved Hawkstern," she volunteers to the others.

"What do you mean?" Jack inquires.

"I think I've figured out why we're so uncomfortable around the professor," Emily states confidently.

"You mean besides the fact that he threatens to skin us alive?" Armando quips.

"No, silly," she says with a fake smile that nonetheless calls forth the dimples that always catch Jack's attention. The smile and the dimples have made only rare appearances since her night in the Cave of Dread.

"It came to me this morning," Emily continues, speaking in a hushed voice. "It's a concept I remember studying in my psychodynamic psychology class in college."

"In your psychobabble, what class?" Armando says facetiously.

"Ha, ha," Emily replies.

"I took that class, too," Rachel says excitedly. "What concept are you referring to?"

"Projective identification."

"Mmm," Rachel hesitates as she stares at Emily. "Forgot that one," she finally admits with a smile. "Projection sounds familiar, though. I think."

"Well, then you have half of it," Emily says.

"Isn't projective identification when you identify with what someone is projecting?" Jack interjects playfully.

"That's correct, but obviously, it doesn't help a bit," Emily replies, rolling her eyes.

"Okay, how about this," Jack says, "projective identification is when I go into Dr. Hawkstern's class and feel highly anxious not just because I'm feeling my own anxiety but also because I'm feeling his anxiety as well."

The young woman with blonde hair and green eyes actually smiles at his response. Jack does his best to memorize Emily's face because he does not know how long it will be until he sees her so pleasant again.

"That's it exactly, Jack!" she exclaims. "I think the reason we're all so anxious in his class is that Dr. Hawkstern is subconsciously communicating his anxiety to us, and we're experiencing it inside of us. He's actually as nervous around us as we are around him," she explains earnestly. "Or maybe even more so."

"Now, why would Goliath be nervous around us, little people?" Armando says, holding his hand up high to indicate the height of the man. "He can swat me like a mosquito," he says, slapping his hands together loudly.

Overhearing the conversation between his fellow Screaming Eagles, Stewart walks over and says, "Maybe he's not afraid of us but of the truth that's in us. If we really do believe the Field Manual, then we're convinced that even Dr. Hawkstern knows that God exists but, for some reason, is suppressing that truth. In other words, his atheism is simply a denial that covers up the fact that in his heart of hearts, he knows that there's a God to who he's accountable."

Jack can see an almost immediate change in Armando's face as he listens to Stewart. His roommate's playfulness is replaced by visible irritation. Clearly, the emotions that were triggered inside his friend at Lighthouse Farm a month ago are still alive and well. The Intellect triggers something inside Armando that cannot be explained simply by the know-it-all attitude Stewart unintentionally communicates. Is this another example of projective identification, or is it Armando's countertransference? Jack asks himself only half-seriously.

"Also, do you guys remember what Dr. McNeely told us?" Rachel asks as she pins her hair behind her ears. "Several weeks ago at lunch, he mentioned that the enemy often uses past hurts like abuse, abandonment, and shame to destroy present-day relationships."

Everyone looks at Rachel, waiting for her to explain further. "Well," she says and pauses a moment, "weren't some of you working at the hotel with me when Veronica told us about Dr. Hawkstern? I thought we talked about this before," she says, tilting her head a bit, "unless I just dreamt it.

Come to think of it, I've had lots of dreams ever since the term started," she says abstractedly as she glances at a statue of Stephen ensconced in a niche behind Jack's left shoulder.

"Anyway," she says, refocusing, "remember how we learned that Dr. Hawkstern is divorced from his wife and alienated from his only child, a daughter."

Jack nods his head. "Yeah, I remember talking about that," he confirms.

"Yes, we did, back at the beginning of the semester," Stewart adds. He hesitates, then says, "I have since acquired additional information about the professor's situation but...but I'm not going to disclose it because Armando will accuse me of engaging in gossip."

The Intellect speaks with no emotion in his voice and with a blank face as if he is reporting statistical information.

Jack glances sidelong at Armando and nonverbally warns him to stay out of this conversation. Then he turns back to Stewart and asks, "Will the information you have help us understand the professor any better?"

"Affirmative," the young man replies without hesitation.

"Okay, then, Stew," Jack says, "I think we need to hear it. What do you know?"

Stewart's owl eyes flit toward Armando and then back to Jack. "I know the Teaching Assistant who works with Dr. Elmore, the Greek, and Hebrew professor. Apparently, Dr. Elmore has confided in this TA—Christopher is his name—some details about Dr. Hawkstern. Christopher and Dr. Elmore have been praying together for the professor over the last two years."

Stewart adjusts his glasses in such a way that they end up in the same spot they were before the customary two-fingered manipulation of his right bow. "Rachel is correct," he says. "Dr. Hawkstern has experienced significant pain in the past that most certainly impacts his present-day relationships."

The other members of the micro-cohort—all but Aly, who is still at work—circle their friend more tightly—the friend, as usual, who has the inside information.

"Apparently, Dr. Hawkstern and his wife, Melanie, met at the University in undergrad days and started dating," Stewart confides. "They moved in together and were married several years later. They mutually agreed to an open relationship so they could be free to pursue other options that might present themselves over the course of the marriage."

Stewart glances around at his listeners with his passionless gaze. As he fingers the small army of pens and mechanical pencils organized perfectly in his pocket protector, Jack imagines that they are a castle wall designed to protect the young man's heart in much the same way that his glasses serve as arrow slits in Stewart's turret that protects him against the outside world.

"Several years into their open marriage," Stewart continues, "Melanie unexpectedly became pregnant. Dr. Hawkstern insisted she have an abortion, but Melanie argued that the baby was theirs and refused to go through with the procedure. They fought for months over the issue. In the end, a daughter, Julianna, was born, and Melanie's life was subsequently transformed by the presence of the child. For the first time, she had a taste of being a family."

Stewart pauses to swallow, but before he can open his mouth to speak again, Rachel blurts out, "So what happened?"

Everyone but Stewart chuckles at the renowned impatience of the girl from Connecticut who so humorously embodies many stereotypes associated with people from the Northeast.

"Dr. Hawkstern stubbornly persisted in his demand to maintain an open marriage," Stewart reports. "However, Melanie defended the benefits of a stable home for their daughter. Neither of them relented in their beliefs, but they ended up staying together for a while at least. Up until the last fifteen years, they continued to live in a fragile marriage that devolved into a very distant relationship," Stewart says. "Unfortunately, Julianna grew up most of her young life in an open marriage and a divided family."

At that moment, the macro-cohort students standing nearby begin shuffling into the "meat packing plant," as Armando refers to Hawkstern's classroom. Stewart turns to compliantly follow the other sheep into the fireside room, but Rachel grabs his arm and exclaims, "Oh, no, buddy, you're not going to leave me hanging. Quick, tell me what happens in the end."

The bespectacled man looks at Rachel and then at the doorway as if mentally picking his poison—the wrath of Dr. Hawkstern or the infamous persistence of his fellow student. He pauses and glances at the large multi-function watch on his wrist that Jack imagines can compute algorithms, provide GPS locations, and perform astronomical calculations, including how distant the sun is from Punxsutawney, Pennsylvania, at any given moment.

In the end, Stewart wisely turns to Rachel and hurriedly says, "When Julianna was fifteen, Dr. Hawkstern became so frustrated with his wife's unwavering insistence to maintain a committed relationship that he impulsively moved out with one of his paramours. Not long afterward, he divorced Melanie."

"What happened to Julianna?" Rachel asks with such intensity that Jack wonders if she has some vested interest in the matter. Stewart makes it part way through the doorway before Rachel grabs his arm again and abruptly halts his progress.

Stewart whispers to Rachel over his shoulder while keeping one eye on the classroom, "She rebels and goes off the deep end. She doesn't want anything to do with her father. They haven't seen each other in the last twenty years."

The Intellect shows uncommon agency as he pulls his arm away from his detainer and power walks to his chair at the front table like a bee flying to the only flower in the field. Such is the fear they have for the professor—at least most of them. Aly seems undaunted. Jack decides that the American-Saudi-Thai girl has encountered more terrifying men than the human titan who teaches their class.

As Jack slides into his seat between Stewart and Armando, Dr. Hawkstern turns from gazing into the empty fireplace and familiarly fixes his eyes on a random spot in the back of the room.

The seven-foot-tall man clears his throat and announces, "Your other professors, no doubt, begin their classes with prayer, but since I know that in this world only the material exists to the exclusion of the immaterial, I will continue to define prayer as the practice of speaking to the air."

The professor pauses a long time for effect and then adds words that are drawn out to emphasize their validity, "Instead of wasting your time communicating with a nonexistent god, I encourage you to accept this natural world and embrace it for what it is."

Dr. Hawkstern works the pipe in his mouth up and down with his left hand like a farmer might work the handle of an old pump as he attempts to summon water from the depths of the earth.

"Today, I want to remind you of something I alluded to only briefly at the end of the last class period, namely, that all legitimate scientists employ the verification principle when they seek to know the world around them. In brief, this principle holds that only that which can be observed and verified by the five senses is valid or real. Only what we can see, touch, smell, hear, and physically feel is considered knowable and thus part of reality. Everything else is myth and wish and, sadly—ignorance."

The giant pauses for a moment and then comments with bland distaste, "My assumption, then, is that most of you in this room are just that—sadly ignorant."

Jack automatically glances at Aly because he knows that her internal temperature undoubtedly is on the rise. Sure enough, the girlish heart-shaped face framed with black flowing hair is already flushed with color. The young woman is biting the end of her pen and tapping her foot on the floor. For someone so small, Jack thinks to himself, she generates remarkable emotional energy.

Dr. Hawkstern takes a deep, rasping breath that often betrays lungs ravaged by many decades of tobacco use. Jack admonishes himself not to be too quick to assume that smoking is the culprit since the professor's breathing difficulty could be caused by any number of other issues. Knowing that he is so quick to judge people, Jack has been working hard all semester to avoid pigeonholing people.

"So, we are left with this world only," the professor says with a shrug of his shoulders and with raised eyebrows that billow like storm clouds. "But is that so untenable? What's so terrible about making the most of life in this closed space-time continuum? Why can't we all agree to enjoy the everyday luxuries of life like sunsets, wine, jazz music, a good mystery novel, a hike in nature with a faithful dog, the relaxation of sleep, and even some decidedly sensual pleasures?"

The titan begins to laugh but then breaks out into loud coughing that reverberates in the fireside room. As the coughing fit continues, he occasionally wipes his eyes with his handkerchief.

"*Just look at that beast,*" the deriding voice rumbles, "*for a beast is what he is. Even he agrees with that assessment. He considers himself an accidental creature in an accidental world in an accidental universe—nothing but a descendent of dust and hydrogen and tadpoles and fish and birds and monkeys.*"

Another dark personality laughs louder than the professor's explosive cough. "*Even we know better than that. Yes, just think, we know better than a creature made in the image of...Him.*"

"*Ecce homo. Behold the man!*" the voice growls. "*Rather, behold the monster! He is already falling deep into darkness. Every day he is devolving further and further away from the image of The One. Indeed, he is now more beast than man. It will only be a matter of time until the image of The One is completely erased in him. Then he will arrive at the dark end we have been summoning him to since he was but an imp, not a chimp.*"

More laughter follows, but now from hundreds of destroyers practiced at hatred, accusations, and lies.

"*Do you remember when the man was but a little darling in his mother's arms?*" a particularly deep, guttural voice asks with sarcasm. "*He played with trains and little cars that he acquired with cereal box tops. How cute. He dreamt of being a famous baseball player and an explorer in Alaska. He read storybooks to his little sister and sang, 'Twinkle, twinkle, little star.' He was so innocent and unversed in the ways of darkness back then, a blank slate waiting to be written on with words of life. Better yet, with words of death.*"

"*Yes!*" another grumbling voice expectorates in the darkness. "*He once was so naïve and free—they all seem so naïve at the beginning, don't they? Now he is so tragically familiar with darkness and so enslaved to the practices of darkness! Isn't it amazingly beautiful what fifty years of selfish living can do to a man? It gives a whole new meaning to the word, evolution.*"

The cacophony of sinister, rumbling laughter breaks out once again and reverberates in the chasm like the sound of crashing thunder in a tunnel.

"Let me assure you that we're all accidents in this universe," Dr. Hawkstern announces to the back of the room after his coughing episode has passed. "We're all inhabitants of a material reality that produced us through a series of random mutations acted on by natural selection. As an esteemed paleontologist once said, and I paraphrase, we may desire nonmaterial meaning in this world, but it simply doesn't exist.

"Accepting the truth that what we experience physically is all there is might, at first blush, appear troubling or terrifying. However, in the end, it is freeing and exhilarating. We're not left waiting powerlessly for a nonexistent god to save us. Instead, we create answers for ourselves from our own minds and our ethical instincts. How refreshingly independent!"

The towering professor grips the comparatively miniature podium with his massive fingers and lifts his chin high above his seated students. His action seems regal, almost divine, Jack thinks to himself.

"Arguably, humans are the highest evolved animal of their species," Dr. Hawkstern declares with firm conviction. "In academia, therefore, we rightfully have a discipline known as anthropology—the study of what makes us human. However, there is no need for the discipline of theology since there is no god. In the final analysis"—here the professor pauses to prepare the students for the gravity of his next pronouncement—"the word d-o-g is more meaningful than the word *g-o-d*. A dog is a material creature that exists and can be verified with our physical senses, whereas god is a nonmaterial entity that cannot be verified and therefore is nonsense."

Jack senses a storm brewing. Dr. Hawkstern has opened yet another

Pandora's box that will not be ignored by the students. Over recent weeks, one of the topics addressed in Dr. Greenlay's class has been how the students can effectively wield the sword of The Revelation as well as their God-given rational minds to combat atheistic or agnostic philosophies. Accordingly, the students now have a growing arsenal of weapons with which to engage the giant secularist standing in front of them.

As usual, Aly is the first to respond. When she raises her hand, she does not even wait to be called on before she speaks.

"What about things like altruism and history and love?" the smaller woman inquires in a voice tight with emotion. "How can you study history with the verification principle or prove love with the five senses? These things cannot be studied in a laboratory setting, yet they are undeniably real."

The big man snorts dismissively as he continues to stare at a spot on the ceiling. "History can be verified through the testimony of multiple eyewitnesses and established by what has been committed to the written word. Love is a behavior that can be seen and quantified. Both are verifiable with our physical senses."

Jack's heart is pounding hard in his chest. He is not a huge fan of such encounters, but he's not about to leave Aly in the arena by herself.

"Aren't we dealing with assumptions here?" Jack begins. "Belief in a material-only world is a presupposition, not a provable truth. And yes, the belief in an open space-time continuum where the supernatural exists is also a presupposition. My point is that if you assume that only what is material is real, then you're dictated by a worldview that's going to limit what you can believe from the get-go. God isn't even a possibility for you since He is immaterial. The supernatural world is outside our physical senses and cannot be proved or disproved by your verification principle."

"What else is there beyond our physical senses?" the giant retorts with a scornful chuckle. Unexpectedly, he slams his massive fist on the podium and shouts, "Would you agree that this object in front of me can be seen and heard?" He strikes it again with his fist even more forcefully, and the loud boom echoes through the room.

"Listen! Do you hear that? It's the sound made by what can be verified!" he cries. The professor's eyes have morphed from their normal marble size to the size of quarters. He pauses momentarily and then sneers at Jack. "Where is your verification, Mr. Sutherington, for the world of the immaterial?"

"Dr. Hawkstern," Rachel says in a conciliatory tone, "I think you're asking us to believe that your theory is true by definition." The girl born in Boston adds in her nasal voice, "When you ask us to believe your theory without question, you don't even allow other theories to be considered."

"Why would I entertain any other theories if they're patently irrational?" the professor growls at the girl with the auburn hair and the red freckled cheeks that are becoming redder by the second.

The giant pauses and snorts loudly. Then he throws his massive hands into the air and exclaims, "Fine! Bring your arguments. Parade your evidence before my eyes! I'm waiting with pleasant anticipation to hear your alternate theory so I can find it pathetically wanting and rip it to shreds like the paper tiger that it is!" The titan grabs his pipe and clutches it fiercely in his hand, and fixes his eyes on the back of the room.

The only thing that comes to Jack's mind at this moment is Dr. Greenlay's words: "When engaging in apologetics, push your opponents to the end of their truth claims. Urge them to follow their reasoning to its end so they can see the negative consequences of their theories. Any theory can be thought and voiced, but not all theories can be lived."

Jack begins to raise his hand, but Armando is already speaking. "If you say we're all here by accident," Dr. Hawkstern, "then none of us has any value," the ex-gang member comments in a shaky voice. "We're totally unimportant in the scheme of things. In the end, we can kill each other without remorse or regret. Personally speaking, I've lived that life and found it extremely unsatisfying."

The big man sniffs at Armando's comments. "The life with no ultimate meaning is all we have," he declares loudly as his eyebrows collide above his nose in a severe frown. "We're called to embrace nihilism and make the most of life such as it is. Admittedly, this choice requires great strength. In fact, I find it undeniably heroic."

Aly, who had not been present with the micro-cohort in the hallway before class, did not hear Stewart's information about the professor's personal life. Therefore, it is with total ignorance that she weighs into the discussion at this point.

"What are you telling us?" the young woman inquires in her girlish high-pitched voice. "Are you telling us that since there is no meaning in life, our only choice is to heroically pursue unbridled pleasure? We should live to drink and smoke pot and fornicate with whomever we wish whenever we wish, even if we're married to another person? Isn't hedonism the way of animals driven only by hunger and sex? I consider all these behaviors by humans to be very selfish and unloving to other people."

Jack and Armando exchange furtive glances. Armando says, "Caramba," and Jack breathes, "Here we go." They both know that the young woman has just stepped on the proverbial landmine.

The towering man growls and claws the podium with his oversized fingers. For the first time that semester, Dr. Hawkstern shifts his gaze from the ceiling in the back of the room and rakes Aly with piercing, eagle-like eyes.

The young woman who earlier had seemed so unafraid now leans back in her chair as far as she can.

"We're about to witness *the shooting of the messenger* in real-time," Jack comments softly as he leans toward Armando. "She's just stomped on Dr. Hawkstern's deepest shame—if he feels any. She might experience that projective identification we were talking about before class in its full glory. Be ready to intervene."

"If it gets really bad, I'll pull the fire alarm," Armando says half-seriously.

Jack feels like a television commentator at a golf tournament making hushed comments in the background while the golfers address their balls and take their swings. It is now Dr. Hawkstern's turn to swing, and he is about to take a tee shot with his largest driver.

"Are you calling me a selfish, unloving animal?" the big man bellows as the dirty avalanche rises and falls on his heaving chest.

The diminutive convert from Islam does not back down before the giant even though she is still leaning against the back of her chair. She is either very foolish or very brave, Jack thinks to himself, as the young woman declares, "You're the one who insists we're all animals made by the blind watchmaker called natural selection. If we're all here only because we accidentally happened to be the fittest to survive, then we're reduced to being brothers with pigs and sisters with birds. We certainly aren't creatures who reflect God's image." "Aly," Jack says firmly to the young woman seated at the other table, attempting to get her attention.

"So now you're calling me a selfish swine?" the intimidating professor growls even more loudly than before. He takes a deep breath that expands his chest impressively and then opens his mouth undoubtedly to utter some thunderous invective. Mercifully—at least for the students—a timely cough interrupts his response, and the giant man is soon reduced to an uncontrollable fit of loud hacking. None of the students relish these episodes because they fear that the man is going to pass out at any moment and topple to the floor like a felled sequoia. Miraculously, the man's pipe remains in his mouth during the whole coughing episode.

After at least a minute of explosive expectorating, the professorial titan eventually calms. His forehead is damp with perspiration, his face is apoplexy red, and his hands are shaking.

When the man begins to mop his forehead with the back of his hand, Emily rises from her chair at the table in the back of the room and walks toward the towering professor. When she reaches the spent man, she touches his arm gently and says in a calming voice, "Dr. Hawkstern, here's a cough drop and a tissue."

Time stops. The fireside room is silent except for the tick-tocking of the ancient grandfather clock in the back by the entrance. The intimidating professor is staring at the familiar spot on the ceiling once again. The young woman with the long-flowing blonde hair still has her hand on the man's arm. Emily has moved toward the Academy Goliath while everyone else has shrunk away in fear and frustration, if not righteous anger. Apparently, understanding the concept of projective identification has rendered the intimidating professor less daunting for Emily; or maybe there is something else unknown that makes her compassionate or brave.

Emily places the tissue and cough lozenge in the man's huge paw and then says somewhat that most of the students in the fireside room find completely random. "Just so you know, Dr. Hawkstern, daughters always want their father's love even when they are too stubborn to admit it."

Jack wonders if he is the only student in the room who hears the single muffled word that emerges from the professor's mouth. "Julianna," the panting man mumbles.

After a long pause, the huge man turns his shaggy head with its big beard and wild bushy hair toward the student at his side. Amazingly, he glances at Emily briefly before his eyes flee back to the refuge in the back of the room.

More time passes. Eventually, the professor removes the cough drop and tissue from his hand and sets them carefully on the lectern. He handles them as if they are sacred objects. Then he grips the sides of the podium and recovers himself. Emily returns to her seat.

"Where were we?" the professor asks the air more than anyone in the room. His voice is surprisingly subdued.

"We were discussing the devaluation of human worth when God is removed from one's world view," Stewart offers dispassionately.

Emily's demonstration of kindness toward Dr. Hawkstern has not been wasted on Jack. At that moment, he determines to make compassion for the formidable professor his primary purpose in the semester-long course. He will not compromise the truth, of course, but he will attempt to deliver it in such a way that the professor will feel respected and, ideally, loved. Whether the gigantic man receives the truth is not Jack's responsibility.

Before Dr. Hawkstern can recall the intense interaction with Aly that led to his paroxysm, Jack comments, "My biggest issue with naturalism is its claim that the supernatural is irrational because it doesn't exist or can't exist in a material universe. But if the supernatural doesn't exist, where do you go to find a point of reference for rationality? If you don't admit the existence of God in your view of reality, where do you turn for authority or a true north in this world? Is your only source of truth the human brain which exists by accident?"

Dr. Hawkstern looks down from the ceiling and glances in Jack's general direction. Then he retrains his eyes on the spot in the back of the room and says, "Mr. Sutherington."

"Yes, sir," Jack replies with a nod of his head.

"Have you forgotten that the *rational man* of the 18th century, and the technical man of the 19th century, and the *utopian man* of the 20th century discovered that they were capable in and of themselves apart from God to make sense of the world?" the professor says in an admonishing tone. "Industrial, technological and scientific advances gradually removed the need for a God to fill the gaps that mankind was unable to understand.

Today, confidence in our ability to keep expanding our knowledge and capabilities has rendered God's existence superfluous along with its yoke of superstition," the professor announces. "As man goes up, God goes down—the classic negative correlation. Man has learned that he can trust his intellect and amazing potential alone. The divine has always been a figment of the human imagination created to explain everything we could not previously understand."

"So, if living for God and enjoying a relationship with him is no longer our chief purpose on this planet, then what are we here for?" Jack inquires. "Is it to pursue pleasure or delude ourselves into believing we have some higher purpose?"

The mountain of flesh and bone contorts his lips, and his walrus mustache writhes on his face. He replies, "In response to your question, I can give you response A or response B. Response A is for weak people who demand that life has black and white answers, so they're not overwhelmed by the meaninglessness of it all. This answer says that man is an intelligent being created by God and enslaved by the fear of hell. He or she lives to be good, to make the world a better place, and to look forward to playing a harp in the clouds one day."

Dr. Hawkstern pauses to pick up his pipe from the lectern and thrust it into the side of his mouth. "That's response A. I prefer Response B because it's embraced by men and women who are strong enough to accept what's true in this world, whether they like it or not. It goes like this: Mankind is an evolved animal sitting atop Darwin's tree of life. He is here by accident, has survived by accident, and will die only to return to the dust. Some atheists will try to put window dressing on all of this, but the raw truth is that accidental mankind has no higher purpose in the universe except to live for the moment and embrace the physical, not the nonexistent metaphysical."

Jack has a response for the professor, but Aly proves to be quicker. "Why would anybody want to believe that?" she asks with no attempt to mask her incredulity. "How would anybody even get out of bed in the morning if that's what their guiding philosophy is?"

A low rumble emerges from the professor's chest as the man appears to be returning to his usual form. His hawkish eyes strake the room until they alight on his notes as if they are live prey. "Ms. Ahmed, I'm simply telling you what's true about the universe," the man replies with constraint. He clamps down on his pipe, and his mammoth fingers drum ominously on the wooden podium.

"But what follows from that?" the young woman asks. "Where does morality come from, not to mention the value of the human being? We have recently learned about the exceptionalism of humans in Dr. Greenlay's class."

"Most people will develop an evolution-assisted morality that will lead to a respect for other humans," Dr. Hawkstern argues impatiently as he shakes his huge head. "Certainly, people instinctually will pursue what their desires dictate, but they won't violate the integrity of their fellow beings whether they be people or whales or dogs."

"It sounds like we're back to hedonism," Armando interjects as he touches the tattoo teardrop beneath his right eye. "We're only here to eat, drink and pursue pleasure before we disappear from history forever."

Stewart speculates aloud, "Couldn't some people choose to live for the betterment of the world and the people around them as a personal life philosophy?"

A woman named Latosia raises her hand and asks, "What would motivate a person to even want to do something good for someone else? Since we're all animals, wouldn't we be driven totally by our bodies and not by our hearts? In a material universe, aren't hearts only the physical organs that pump blood? They certainly aren't receptacles for our spirits and consciences since neither of those exists in a godless world. So, like Aly asked, where does love come from then? And what about consciousness?"

"I'm quite certain," Jack interjects, "that where there's no God, there's no morality, no absolute truth, and certainly no self inside of us beyond brain waves. The body is all there is. We're only animals that have no unique purpose on this planet. So, if there is no truth or morality, there is no meaning in life. Your opinion comes from you and mine from me, and there is no such thing as absolute truth. Therefore, we don't need to listen to anyone's opinion about anything because nothing means anything."

Rachel nods her head and says, "I was reading a philosopher recently who said that if anyone insists there's no truth, he is asking you not to believe anything he says, so don't."

Another student begins to add her thoughts to the runaway discussion when Dr. Hawkstern interrupts her. "All of you misguided religious fanatics, hear me when I say that only the weak and feeble-minded succumb to the need to believe in a god," he growls as he chews furiously on his pipe. "You cannot prove that there's a god, so to insist that one exists is sheer foolishness. Only those who are too afraid to face the universe alone demand that a divinity exists. God is simply not verifiable."

"Dr. Hawkstern," Jack responds, "you've asked us many times to prove that God exists. Well, I would like to ask you to prove that He doesn't exist. It seems rather...omniscient to insist that there is no god. Only if you had complete knowledge of everything that exists in the whole universe could you state unequivocally that there is no God."

The towering man straightens his back and stands even taller as a deep breath swells his massive chest. "Don't turn my argument back on me," he demands as he looks past Jack toward the back of the room. "I'm simply asking for one simple proof from you to prove that God exists. None of you has presented any credible evidence to suggest that He does. Not one."

"I know one," Aly volunteers.

"Oh?" the professor responds as the storm clouds billow upward and his small eyes narrow to half-moons. "And what might that be? A dream you had after eating too much pizza last night?"

Aly ignores the sarcasm. She shakes her head, and her dark hair slides back and forth over her cheeks. "Changed lives," she offers. "One amazing proof of God's existence is the changed lives that are represented here in this room today. Dr. Hawkstern, we're all living proof that there's a God in the universe who creates new hearts in those who believe in Him. His name is Jesus Christ."

"What if I told you that in my eyes, you're more a living proof of the devil than of god," the professor says sarcastically.

The class discussion goes on for another twenty minutes, with neither side surrendering any ground. Jack can discern from the professor's animated countenance during the verbal parrying that he is irritated by the increased knowledge the students' have acquired in recent months to counter his arguments. Embee, Greenlay, Windsor, McNeely, and even Fagani would be proud of their first-year students now.

When the class finally ends, Jack walks out of the fireside room convinced of one thing more than anything else: love is more powerful than mere logic. While everyone else was employing intellect and argumentation to engage the intimidating professor, Emily chose to speak the language of love. It was the only language that penetrated Dr. Hawkstern's armor during the ninety-minute class.

Very fittingly, Jack's eyes fall on an inscription chiseled into the citadel wall. He has read the words from Ephesians 4 a dozen times before, but today they have special meaning: "Walk in a manner worthy of the calling to which you have been called, with all humility and gentleness, with patience, bearing with one another in love" (Ephesians 4:1-2, ESV)

CHAPTER 23

The Bridge Club with Jazz

Even though the young woman's face is haggard and looks older than her years, it is still quite attractive with its high cheekbones, full lips, and large brown eyes. It remains attractive even when it is rock-hard, which it happens to be in the moment. Her lips are pursed tightly, and her eyebrows are crossed. Slender arms are folded indignantly across her chest. They partially obstruct a Susan B. Anthony quote stenciled on her faded and worn sweatshirt that reads, "The worst enemy women have is in the pulpit." The striking black crown on her head is wild and free. It looks both beautiful and brazen. Coupled with her obstinate face and defensive body posture, Jack hears her defiant coiffure shouting, "Back off, or I'll floss your teeth with one of my sneakers."

"You're new in da hood," she says to the three visitors at the bridge. Her tone is so icy it could freeze scalding coffee.

"Yes," Aly replies in a chipper voice that is as warm as the other woman's voice is cold.

"Sup," Armando says casually with an upward tilt of his chin.

"Y'all here to get up in my bizznezz?" the young woman asks accusingly, her blazing eyes slashing from Armando to Aly.

Jack shakes his head. "No, we're here with the Academy. We're here to help the homeless." As soon as the last word rolls off his tongue, he regrets them and groans inwardly.

"Ain't nobody here needs your help, wigga," the young woman snaps. "You best go back to your Hollywood hood and leave us alone. We doin' just fine without you, white boy." She elongates the word "fine," infusing it with heavy sarcasm.

"My bad," Jack replies. "That came out all wrong."

"You got that right," she retorts. "Think before you open your blow hole, ghetto boy."

Jack whistles softly in his brain and takes a deep breath. Then he glances over at Aly for help.

"Have you been coming to the bridge very long?" Aly inquires.

"Don't be frontin' me," the young woman says. "You act all friendly, but I know you just here to tell me I be a hot mess. You want to school me on how to be the person you want me to be. The only problem is you ain't from my squad. You ain't my peeps. And I'll never join whatever sweat box you slam on me."

The young woman with the imposing afro pauses long enough to point a slender finger at Aly. Then she spits out, "You ain't my shero. You nothin' but a dipset."

The three students from the Academy look at each other but say nothing. Armando's face breaks out into a big smile.

The young woman gestures with her head toward Jack's jeep that is parked thirty feet away. "If you was smart, high roller, you'd get outta this hood now. A 211's gonna go down soon, and your killa ride will be history. But fork up a Benjamin or some squares, and I'll make sure it stays safe and fine. Just fine."

Jasmine glances over at Armando and notices that he is staring intently at her. "What you smilin' at, thug?" she inquires in a harsh voice. "You judgin' me? You think I'm tore up?"

"It's all good," Armando replies as he continues to look at the young woman. The smile lingers on his face.

"No, it ain't," Jasmine retorts. "You gawkin' at me, cat, like you dissin' me."

"That what's up," Armando replies agreeably.

"So, why don't you open up a can and come at me like a real cholo, gangsta boy," she says acidly. "Then you'll find out I'm no mark!"

Armando pauses just a moment and then states matter-of-factly, "God don't like ugly."

Jasmine draws her head back like a snake getting ready to strike. "What you sayin' to me?"

"You know what I'm sayin'," Armando replies calmly. "You accuse us of frontin' you. But you're the one who's acting all Emo around here. We was just marinatin', and then you go and pop off like we're the heat comin' to arrest you for a 187. God knows you're puttin' on a front for us. You ain't no gangsta. You're a college girl hidin' behind a wicked mask. You don't even have the lingo down. I see right through you, shorty."

The lioness with the black mane stares at Armando. Hot lave pours out of her eyes.

Now Armando's face breaks into an even wider smile. "I have to admit, shorty, you got a lot of swagga for being a poser. I give you props! But when you get so unpleasant, you be a bit screepy, girl."

The ebony-complexioned girl opens her mouth to attack Armando with more harsh words, but he speaks first. "I hung out with several dawgs from Compton when I lived in LA, so I learned some Ebonics—enough so I can tell you're code switchin'. You've got Ebonics and standard English goin' on at the same time, shorty. That makes you a poser. What would your T Jones think of you right now?" Armando inquires.

"Leave my mother out of this," the young woman snaps. She pauses a moment and then rolls her eyes, knowing she has blown her cover.

"You just outed yourself, Jasmine," Armando says calmly. "You aren't from da hood. You know it, and I know it."

"How do you know my name, anyway?" the irritated woman demands.

"How do we know your name?" Armando repeats. "The big dude over there under the bridge with the white T told us. He said you're a bit—unapproachable."

The girl's face softens just a degree as she shakes her head. Changing the subject, she asks, "How did you manage to hang with dawgs in LA? Wouldn't you gangsters be shanking each other if you got that close?"

"I met three of them—two Bloods and one Crip—at a Bible study in Bell Gardens," Armando discloses. "Since we all loved Jesus, we decided not to cut each other."

"Prove it," Jasmine insists, her voice full of challenge. "Prove you're from gangland. Throw up a blood sign."

"I only got one," Armando admits. He positions both hands in front of his chest and positions his fingers in a way that they spell out the word "blood."

Jasmine stares at the gang sign and nods her head slowly. Then she looks up at the white scar on Armando's cheek and says, "I thought you said no one cut you."

The gangster, formerly known as Syko Loco, instinctively reaches up and runs his fingers over the white scar on his left cheek. "We got jumped by a gang from another set. We were outnumbered. The leader decided he didn't want me to ever forget him, so he tattooed me," Armando says in a voice devoid of any emotion.

"You're lucky to be here," the woman observes without empathy.

"True that," Armando says, the smile returning to his face. "So, who are you, really, shorty?" he asks, "now that we know you're not a bona fide ghetto girl."

The dark-skinned young woman slowly scans the faces of the three Academy students as if debating how much to tell them. In the end, she shrugs her shoulders and says, "Believe it or not, I'm a preacher's kid. But I got tired of the pressure to be good and all the hypocrisy, so I walked."

"Where did you walk?" Aly inquires naively.

Jasmine glances briefly at the Thai-Saudi girl and shakes her head dismissively. Then she looks back at Armando, who interjects, "What Aly means to ask is where did you go when you turned your back on your life as a PK?"

"My preacher daddy demanded that I go to Bible school when I graduated from high school," Jasmine says with a look on her face that people often have when they are chewing something sour. "I wasn't going to let him control my life, so I worked hard on my academics and ended up matriculating at an Ivy League school instead. When I found out my daddy was pleased that I was attending such a prestigious university, I dropped out and escaped his world and his influence. He's down south in Alabama, and I'm here, far away from the long arm of the preacher and his church."

"I think I understand your sweatshirt now," Jack observes, nodding at the words. "Your father is the preacher who stands in that pulpit."

"Uh-huh," Jasmine replies, nodding her head with its big hair. "My relationship with my daddy defines me. I value exactly the opposite of everything he values."

"So, you're not being Jasmine; you're being the opposite of your father," Jack observes. "How can you be you if what drives you is trying not to be like your father? There's not much room to focus on knowing who you are since all your energy is spent making certain you're not him."

Jasmine stares blankly at Jack for a few moments, then closes her eyes and rubs her forehead with the fingers of her right hand. "No," she says slowly, trying to formulate her thoughts. "No, I just have to be free from him."

The young woman opens her big brown eyes and stares holes through Jack. "You have no idea what it was like being a child in his house," Jasmine snaps, regressing to the defiant girl they encountered earlier. "He told me what to wear, what words I could use, and which ones I couldn't. He controlled the exact time I had to be in bed, chose my friends for me, drove all the boys away, made me go to church every Wednesday and twice on Sundays.

"He also informed me I'd go to hell if I ever used drugs, drank alcohol, had sex outside of marriage—or danced! He was all about rules, control, anger, shame, and punishment. I had to get away from him, or I was going to explode!" she announces with a surge of fury flowing into her facial features.

"Wow," Aly says, using a word that sounds funny coming out of her mouth. "Jasmine couldn't exist."

"Exactly!" the afroed woman agrees. "I couldn't be me. *He* defined who I was. If I disappointed him by acting differently than good Jasmine was supposed to act, he accused me of being a bad daughter and a poor reflection on the whole family. Sometimes he wouldn't talk to me for days if I got angry or was late for curfew, or didn't behave perfectly at church. He couldn't tolerate it if I disagreed with him."

Jasmine pauses briefly and sighs heavily. Then she says, "'A preacher's kids are supposed to be model children,' he'd always tell me. What he meant was that he wanted automatons, not children with their own minds and wills. So, I ran away. My sister and brother stayed home and drank the Kool-aide. I simply could not and would not submit to that degree of domination. Everyone in the family now sees me as the black sheep. I'm the lost child—the rebel."

"But aren't you a rebel?" Armando asks. "You sound rebellious to me."

"But you see why I'm that way, don't you?" Jasmine retorts. "An authoritarian parent always drives a child toward rebellion or superficial compliance. Because of my daddy, I hate all authority. I hate cops—unless they're female. I bristle when I'm around professors. I refuse to listen to God's commands. I do the opposite if I sense someone is telling me what to do."

"So, how do you ever learn from others if you can't tolerate anyone telling you what to do?" Jack asks without accusation.

"I don't want to learn from others," the woman with the big hair replies candidly. "I don't want to obey. I don't want to do the right thing. I want to be free to do what I want to do when I want to do it and with whom I want to do it. I have no desire to conform because then I'd be obeying my father."

"How sad," Jack remarks. "At one point in your life, you were forced to live at the far end of the spectrum. There was no Jasmine—only the daughter her preacher daddy wanted. Then you rebelled and swung the pendulum away from being controlled by your father. The problem was your pendulum didn't just swing to the middle—it kept going and swung to the other extreme. So, you're still not free to be you. Your father controlled you in the past. Now, you're controlled by the rebel in you who demands that you be the opposite of your father—at whatever cost to you. You're too busy trying not to be him to have time to be you, if that makes any sense."

The woman with the beautiful face and the fiery eyes considers Jack thoughtfully. She is silent for a long time. Finally, she lifts her chin a bit and compresses her mouth in a way that looks like she's five years old. When she shakes her head defiantly, it only adds to her young appearance. "Even if I'm not free," she says in a flat voice, "at least I get to choose not to be free."

Jack, Armando, and Aly all glance at each other, at a loss for words.

Aly is the one who finally speaks. "I don't know what an Ivy League school is," she begins. "It certainly sounds like a very fine place to learn. But you're saying that you dropped out of that school not because it was too challenging for you or because you didn't like it but because your father was pleased you were going there?"

"You got that right, little girl," Jasmine admits, her words as cold as a Siberian flagpole in January.

"But aren't you hurting yourself much more than your father by dropping out of such a fine school?" Aly asks as she attempts to wrap her mind around Jasmine's seemingly irrational choice.

"You don't understand," the woman says as she folds her arms across her chest again and leans her body toward Aly. "The benefit is that I'm free from my father's influence in my life."

"Free like a woman spending her life in a wheelchair when she has the ability to walk," Armando mumbles.

"I eard that!" Jasmine retorts angrily.

"You were supposed to hear that," Armando replies with smiling eyes. "I never understood the old saying about 'cutting off your nose to spite your face.' Not even sure it applies here. But I agree with Aly and Jack; it sounds like you're achieving the freedom you desire at a terrible cost to yourself."

"Yeah, it sounds like a Pyrrhic victory," Jack adds. "You know, that battle the Greek general won over the Romans but at such great cost that it felt like a defeat. Some ancient historian records that, after the battle, Pyrrhus reported that he lost most of his forces, which could never be replenished, along with all his closest friends and his best commanders. Yes, he'd won the victory, but he returned home to his country basically alone and feeling like he'd been defeated."

Jasmine rolls her eyes and snorts. "I studied Roman history at the university," she replies coolly. "So, of course, I know all about Pyrrhus and his hollow victory. But don't you dare compare me to him. I'm not losing—I'm winning."

The three Academy students glance at each other for the third time and have the same thought, namely, that to push Jasmine too hard is unwise. She will simply experience them as another voice of authority to be dismissed.

Aly abruptly changes the subject, asking the young woman, "What are you doing down here at the Bridge?"

Jasmine glances at Aly and then looks down and examines her feet. Her big hair totally obscures her face. Without looking up, she remarks hesitantly, "I'm homeless right now."

"What!" Aly exclaims. "Homeless? You're not living in a house or an apartment? You're living outside?"

Still looking down at the ground, the woman replies, "I usually have a roof over my head. You know, a shelter downtown, this bridge or...or even on a bench along the boulevard with an old umbrella for protection."

Jack knows that if Rachel had been here, she would be hugging the young woman by now—or at least attempting to do so. Jasmine might have offered significant resistance to such an act of compassion, of course. Less affectionate Aly continues to pursue the young woman with reason and words. "How can you be homeless?" she inquires. "It's dangerous to be a woman alone on the streets. You need a safe place to live."

"How do you survive?" inquires Armando in a voice that betrays he has some idea what the answer might be.

Jasmine says nothing. She paws at the ground with the toes of her right foot.

"You sound very alone," Jack comments matter-of-factly but in a soft voice.

The woman finally looks up from the ground. Her eyes are big. They are young and clear. There is no emotion on her face.

"You need to find a place to live," Aly interjects with urgency.

Jasmine is not silent this time. "Get off my back, girl!" she lashes out. "Seriously, I'm totally done with people telling me what to do, comprende? Didn't you hear that already? Are you deaf or just stupid?"

Jasmine abruptly turns to leave. Armando is quick to ask, "Do you need anything, shorty?"

The woman hesitates and looks over her shoulder at her inquirer. Jack doesn't know what it is about the term shorty, but Armando has used it several times, and Jasmine does not take exception to it.

"We're not here to tell you what to do," Armando explains. "Trust me, Aly means well. She's worried about you being out on the streets alone. How about if we all cruise over to the nearest coffee shop and get some java and scones. Sounds like you're alone a lot. We could just hang out for a while and share some food. Deal?"

Jasmine pushes a tuft of her overhanging hair back onto her head and looks from Armando to Aly to Jack. "Okay, Kemosabe, but only if I can ride shotgun in that wicked Wrangler. Haven't been in wheels like that for a long time."

Ten minutes later, the three Academy students and their new acquaintance are seated at a high table in a busy coffee shop. The red-brick walls around them are decorated with floating shelves, cabinets, chalkboards, and random painted sayings such as "Salut, ça va?" They are sipping coffee and nibbling on cookies and moist blueberry muffins that crumble in their hands. Jack feels like he's sitting with three other university students taking a break from the rigors of academia.

While they sip and nibble—all except Jasmine, who gobbles—Jack and Armando and Aly introduce themselves, something they never got around to back at the Bridge. Then they take turns sharing abridged versions of their personal stories.

Jack speaks about living in Colorado with his mother and younger siblings; Armando tells about growing up in the odd hybrid world of Orange County and La Puente, and Aly relates her life journey from America to Saudi Arabia to Thailand to faith in Jesus. Jasmine appears only marginally interested in their accounts. Understandably, the food is far more compelling to the young woman.

When the three Academy students are done sharing, Jasmine swallows another bite from her third muffin and comments to Jack, "You said your last name is Sutherington? Not a common name. If I remember correctly, my great grandmother spoke of a Sutherington family here in town that her mother worked for as domestic help. Are you related to those Sutheringtons?"

"To be honest, I didn't even know there were any Sutheringtons here in town," Jack replies. "And you're right; there aren't many of them in the whole US."

"I can't remember any of the stories right now," Jasmine says, as she chews on a chocolate chip cookie, "but apparently, there were some very freaky happenings in that family a century ago. I'll have to ask nana about it next time I see her. She'll remember."

"There's always something going down with us Sutheringtons," Jack remarks with a smile. He has no idea, of course, how right he is and how both past and future Sutherington events will impact the trajectory of his life and that of his friends.

At some point during their time in the coffee shop—whether it's because she's warm or just at ease—Jasmine pushes up the sleeves of her sweatshirt. It must be a subconscious, unintentional action because Jack is quick to notice needle marks and horizontal scars on both exposed arms.

When he looks up from the tracks and the straight lines that have been methodically carved into her arms, he sees Jasmine staring at him. He clears his throat and looks down into his coffee. The young woman abruptly pushes her sleeves back down as she listens to Aly talk about the Academy.

A while later, Jack discovers that Armando also noticed Jasmine's arms. The ex-gangster inquires, "Are you going to hate me if I ask you if you're still shooting up? Don't, because many of my friends in the barrio went down that road, too. Even the veterano who led me to Christ used to shoot up."

Jasmine stops chewing and looks down at the table. She turns her head back and forth slowly as if reading something on the small tiles of the tabletop. Her shoulders are sagging, crushed by a heavy weight.

Breaking the silence, Jack says, "Don't worry, Jasmine. None of us here look down on you. All of us know this world is an extremely difficult place and that we all cope the best we can. I haven't mentioned it yet, but I got to the point in my life where I was very depressed and ready to hang it up." He pauses and then adds, "I think I speak for all of us when I say that we may come from different walks of life than you, but none of us can throw any stones at you."

Armando interjects, "Drugs, cutting, violence, hatred, addictions, using people—Jesus died to pay for it all. He washes all that crud away and makes us clean. He's our only hope, not our own efforts."

"I don't think you guys still get it," Jasmine comments coolly as she looks up at Armando. "I can't turn to God. He and my daddy are on the same side. They're in cahoots. God wants to control me just as much as my daddy. Where do you think my daddy learned to control me anyway? He was taught control and shame and wrath by God."

"You don't think it's the other way around?" Jack says.

"What do you mean?" the young woman asks.

"Couldn't it be that your earthly father treats you the way he does out of his own personal issues instead of because he's being like God the Father?" Jack proffers.

Jasmine looks at Jack with her large brown eyes and says nothing. Eventually, she covers her face with both hands and massages her skin.

"I'm sorry if I've said too much," Jack says, retreating a bit.

The young woman continues to rub her cheeks and forehead as she takes in a long breath and then lets it out slowly in a low groan. Finally, she says, "I just don't know. I just don't know. Okay?" Her voice is frustrated but not enraged. "What I do know is that if I take care of myself and do good things, then I'm obeying my father. He wins. If I don't take care of myself and do bad things, then he loses."

Jack is ready for her line of thinking. "Okay, he loses. But do you really win?"

Jasmine sighs, and her eyes take refuge behind her long fingers. "I may not always win," she mumbles, "but he loses. That's what's important. I have the power over my life, and he doesn't—even if it comes at the expense of a Pyrrhic victory."

"Isn't there some middle ground where you can shun your dad's power over you while still practicing good self-care?" Jack inquires. "The way it is, you do drugs and sleep around and get wasted—if, in fact, you do all those things—not because you necessarily want to do them, but because then you're making a statement to your father that he can't control your life."

Jasmine's eyes peek out from between her fingers. "You've just described my whole existence," she admits grudgingly.

"Can't you just tell yourself that you're doing the good things for yourself and not for him?" Aly asks.

"It's not that easy," Jasmine snaps at the young woman who so easily triggers her irritability. "It's like I'm trying to trick myself, and I'm too self-aware to fall for that."

"Well, it sounds like you're destroying yourself instead," Armando comments. "Would you rather do that or trick yourself?"

"It's like I can't escape from how I think," Jasmine says in frustration.

She removes her hands from her face and adds, "I'm an Ivy League student—or was—so I'm not totally stupid. I've thought about this dilemma thousands of times, especially at night when I have trouble sleeping on the park bench or in a cardboard box next to the train tracks. Sometimes I arrive at the conclusion that I made a promise to myself when I was a child, and now I can't go back on that promise."

"What promise?" Aly asks.

Jasmine takes a gulp of her coffee and attacks her fourth muffin with a bite that a great white shark would be proud of. Eventually, she says, "I already told you," she says with an exasperated sigh between chewing and swallowing. "I made a promise to never let my daddy have the satisfaction that he's controlling me."

"So, part of keeping that promise is doing just the opposite of what he wants you to do and who he pressures you to be," Jack reflects to the young woman.

"Yes."

"I think your dad is still winning," Jack observes as he leans back in his chair.

Curious, Jasmine locks her eyes on the young man with shoulder-length, straw-blonde hair and blue eyes. "How so?"

"As I said earlier, your father has a lot of power over you if you've dedicated your whole life to rebelling against him," Jack says quietly.

The woman tilts her head to one side and narrows her eyes, attempting to absorb the full impact of what Jack said. Finally, she speaks words that are probably meant only for herself. Her voice is so soft that the three Academy students strain to hear what she is saying.

"If I obey my daddy," Jasmine mumbles as she stares over Jack's right shoulder, "he wins because I'm letting him have power over me. But if I spend my life disobeying him, he wins because I'm giving him power over me by always striving to do just the opposite of what he wants...Either way, he has power over me. Either way, he wins, and I lose...So, what do I do? I'm in an impossible bind."

The young woman falls silent for a long time. Nobody at the table says a word. They know that Jasmine has come to an unprecedented intersection in her mind that she needs to resolve. Sounds of scraping chairs, buzzing conversations, clanking coffee mugs, and grating coffee grinders fill the cozy café. None of them register in the awareness of the four young people sitting at the table.

Eventually, Jasmine's eyes float over to Jack's face, and she says hesitantly, "You said there's a middle ground, possibly. Where do I find that?"

"That's the right question," Jack replies. "But you need to discover the answer for yourself. If it comes from us, you'll think we're telling you what to do. And you know how well that works for you."

Jasmine gazes at Jack for a while, then nods her head slowly.

"I'll throw one more wrench into things," Armando announces. "I hope it won't gum up all your gears. I was just wondering, Shorty, do you think your daddy is an ignorant man or an evil man?"

When Jasmine appears puzzled, Armando explains, "My mentor, Juan Ortega, taught me there's three types of parents. I'm just going to mention two of them now. The first type is ignorant. They don't know how to be a parent, how to show love, how to comfort, how to teach, how to lead. They can do great damage to their children, not just by the bad things they do, but by the good things they don't know how to do. Deep down, however, they love their children.

"The other type of parent is evil," Armando continues. "They intend to harm their children. They will even kill them. Almost always, not physically, but emotionally. You might be familiar with the old saying about breaking a horse or a child without harming a hair on its head. These parents may never harm their children physically, but they're willing to break their children emotionally, even to the point of killing their spirits."

Armando pauses for a moment and then says, "I believe my own father was a combination of the two: ignorant and evil. What do you think about your father? Does he hurt you out of ignorance, or does he try to harm you because he's evil?"

Jasmine pauses in the middle of chewing and rolls her eyes toward the tin ceiling. "I can't say my daddy is evil," she concludes, still looking up at the ceiling, "as much as I'd like to. But I hate him, nonetheless. It did seem like he killed my spirit to a great degree."

"Do you know his motive?" Armando inquires as he touches his goatee with his thumb and index finger.

"Are you asking me if he killed my spirit on purpose like that was his end goal? If yes, I'd have to say no," Jasmine says.

"Okay," Armando says, "then your daddy isn't evil—at least not more than the average sinful parent. Yet, it sounds like he was controlling and shaming. I wonder what that was about."

Jasmine shrugs. "I guess I'll have to ask him next time I see him—at his funeral probably," she says sarcastically.

When a short silence falls over the small group, the young woman with the beautiful but fatigued face slaps her hands together and says, "I'd better get going."

"Are you going to be okay?" Aly asks. "Do you have enough food and clothing? I could probably arrange for you to stay in my dorm room back at the Academy on real cold nights."

"At the Teleios Academy?" Jasmine asks, throwing up both hands in protest and sliding off her tall stool. "Oh, no! No, no, no! Not a chance, girl. Remember, I already refused my daddy when he pressured me to go to Bible school. So, I'm certainly not going to set foot in any Christian school at this point. Remember, I have to be free. At all costs, I guess, as you guys pointed out today."

The rebel with a cause pauses and looks at Jack. "I'm off to strategize another Pyrrhic victory," she says without humor. Her face is a study in resignation.

"It was good to meet you, Jasmine," Jack says, rising to his feet. Armando and Aly do the same.

"Now that you know me better, you can call me Jazz," the young woman says.

They all shake hands with Jazz and share their hope that they will see her at the Bridge again soon. A moment later, the young woman walks out the door of the coffee shop, taking Susan B. Anthony with her.

The three students sit back down at their table and exhale collectively.

"Why do I feel so heavy and exhausted?" Armando asks.

"You feel the weight of Jasmine's lonely and depressing life," Aly suggests.

"Wow!" Jack exclaims, shaking his head, "Jazz used exactly the right word today. She's in a bind if I ever saw one. If she obeys, she feels controlled by her father. So, then her oppositional self takes over, and she refuses to obey—ever. Either her father or her own stubborn self are her masters at the two opposite ends of the continuum. Both masters prevent her from being the woman God created her to be. It may not be true, but I wonder if

Jasmine is even more controlling of Jasmine than her father ever was."

"She's definitely not free," Aly says sadly. I hope she finds that middle ground,"

Armando nods his head and says, "She's enslaved, all right. I wouldn't be surprised if she's addicted to crack and alcohol and earns her dinero by selling herself to men on the street." Then he looks at Jack and asks, "What is the middle ground she needs to find, Juan?"

"Where it always is, mi amigo," Jack says with a smile. "Smack dab in the middle of the love of Jesus. He sets us free from slavery to others, the enemy, and even our own selves. Only in Him are we truly free."

Jack glances back and forth at his two friends and then clarifies, "You guys are on the same page as me. We're not going into the world proclaiming some trite magical answer to the problems of life, some pie in the sky by and by, right? We believe that the God who became flesh like us, who suffered and died in our world, is the one true God who empathizes with our weakness and supports us in our suffering. He's the only God who walked in our shoes and knows how much we struggle and groan in this painful world. He's the only one who can break through Jasmine's thick defenses and woo her toward His amazing love."

"Wooing sounds much better than controlling," Aly comments with a smile.

"Amen to that," Armando says, "amen to that." Jack's roommate pauses and sighs deeply as his face falls. "By the way," he adds, looking down at his empty plate, "I'm going to order another muffin before we go. That girl ate both of mine."

CHAPTER 24

Emily and Embee

"Sometimes I feel like I have a prosecuting attorney inside my head," Emily announces in a voice remarkable for its flatness. Dr. Livingstone, who is sitting cross-legged on the overstuffed chair across from her, simply nods her head.

"I can't seem to escape the constant cross-examination," the Academy student continues. "I'm accused of being shameful or stupid or selfish. There's always some reason I'm bad. So—" she elongates the word, "so I try not to look inside. I distract myself from knowing myself. Then the prosecuting attorney leaves me alone because the condemning searchlight has no crimes to litigate."

The sagacious mentor nods her head and comments, "The enemy's intent is to deter you from looking inside your heart by repeatedly accusing you whenever you dare to be self-aware. His goal is to divorce you from your own heart, but he accomplishes this by first making you obsess about the badness of your heart until you can't bear to do so any longer. It's too depressing and punishing to look inside.

"Eventually, the punishment gets so overwhelming that you change your outlook from inside to outside. When you look outside, you're free from the condemning voice and the accompanying shame but at the cost of being disconnected from yourself and the saving awareness that you need to be rescued from your sin.

"Always remember, Emily: Satan accuses you about the darkness of your sin, so you'll run away and hide, whereas Jesus sheds light on your sin, so you'll run toward Him for love and forgiveness. Satan's end goal is isolation. Jesus' aim is relationship. Always."

Emily nods her head abstractedly and glances around the homey office with its cozy rugs, colorful decorations, and barn-wood walls that give it a rustic ambiance. She is still looking around the room when she asks Embee offhandedly, "Do you think I'll go to heaven?"

The mentor, whose silver hair is braided and wrapped in a bun on the back of her head, is caught off guard. She gazes at Emily for a while and then replies, "Do you want to go to heaven?"

"I don't know," the young woman says as her eyes continue to drift around the office, avoiding Embee's gaze. "Part of me doesn't seem to care—honestly. Another part of me is afraid of not being in heaven. But that part of me also knows I probably don't deserve to be there."

"None of us deserve heaven, Emily. It's never a matter of deserving it."

"I know the right answer," the mentee says with an edge in her voice. "It's just that I...I've done bad things. Of course, only part of me believes that. See how divided I am?"

"There's always a war inside," the professor says.

"That describes me," Emily admits dryly as she examines a picture on the wall displaying a younger version of the woman sitting in front of her. One of the daughters, she thinks to herself.

"Jesus said we're like a house divided against itself," Embee says.

"If I remember correctly," the younger woman responds, "Jesus said a house divided against itself cannot stand." She pauses and then inquires as she turns her eyes toward the professor, "Am I destined to fall?"

"Why do you wonder that, Emily?" the spelunking guide asks as she leans toward the student in front of her.

"Sometimes, I believe that God will cause me to fall because of what I've done," Emily answers.

"Do you mean the things you've spoken about in the past?" Dr. Livingstone inquires.

Emily nods and sighs. "The drinking, the drugs, lying, sleeping around, yada yada," she says dispassionately as if talking about what she had for lunch.

There is a long pause. "But there's more," the young woman finally says as she performs the customary flick of her hair over her shoulder—her "tell." Her green eyes flee Embee's gaze—another "tell." The mentor has observed that these behaviors consistently predict that her mentee is going to reveal something from her vault of secrets.

Abruptly, Emily gets to her feet and walks over to the window. She looks down on the snow-covered scene below her and mumbles as if she is speaking only to herself, "I wonder what it's like to feel as white as snow? To feel clean, even pure. I left that feeling behind years ago. Now I live with my new normal that is no longer new, and neither does it feel normal. I try to convince myself that I like my new normal, but I really don't like it much at all. If I'm honest, I pretend to like it because there's no going back to the old normal, to the naivete and innocence that used to embarrass me about myself. I was such a girl scout in high school," she says with disgust.

The young woman sighs as she continues to gaze on the winter scene below, silent and sparkling in the fading light. "My parents overprotected me," she muses aloud. "Especially my father. It's like he believed that bad things would happen to me if he didn't protect me all the time."

"Was he wrong?" Embee asks quietly.

There is silence for a while. "I guess bad things did happen to me," Emily speaks slowly, almost wistfully. "Sometimes...sometimes I wish I could go back. But I know I can't. I'm not her anymore. A huge canyon yawns between who I was then and who I am now. It's too late for me."

"Jesus is the bridge," the mentor risks as she prays that her words will not offend her listener.

Emily continues talking as if she hadn't heard Embee's comment. "Aly says her brother may have killed some people in Thailand. I don't think I've ever met a real killer before except...except me."

Embee sighs inside herself. There is a long silence. Eventually, she inquires softly, "How many were there, Emily?"

The young woman wheels around and glares at the professor. She doesn't say a word, but her eyes are serrated daggers. After a while, she turns back to the window and folds her arms. It appears to Embee that the girl is hugging herself.

In a lifeless voice, Emily finally answers, "One abortion. Two babies. Twins."

"So, you're confessing that you took the lives of two babies," the older woman says.

"Yes, of course, I am," Emily snaps scathingly. "I may be a murderer, but I'm not a liar or a hypocrite!"

"Did you tell anybody? I mean, besides me just now?" Embee inquires, clasping her hands under her chin.

Emily tilts her head as she watches two young men initiate a snowball fight with several other classmates. "The father knew. He gave me the money. A few of my friends knew."

"How about your parents?"

"Are you kidding?" she exclaims harshly, her back still turned to Embee. "Of course, I didn't tell them. They'd never look at me the same way again. My sins would be too heinous for them. Unforgivable, most likely."

"I wonder who really doesn't forgive you," the mentor comments quietly.

"What's that supposed to mean?" Emily asks as she turns to look at Dr. Livingstone. "Are you saying that I haven't forgiven me?"

"Do you think the prosecuting attorney you spoke of earlier originates primarily from the outside?" Embee inquires. "From your parents or some pastor or God? Or could the harshest indicting voice be your own?"

The young woman stares defiantly at her spelunking guide. "You think you're always right, don't you," she snaps. "You think you know everything about me. Well, you don't!"

Dr. Livingstone doesn't back down from her words. She sits quietly—waiting and praying. With soft eyes, she looks at the highly defended young woman at the human castle who a long time ago built an impenetrable wall around herself to keep the bad things out but, in so doing, inadvertently kept the good things from getting in.

Emily doesn't back down either. "How easy it must be for you to sit there smug and cozy on your self-righteous throne!" she accuses sharply, her face a study in hate. "You have no idea what goes on inside of me!"

Emily takes a step toward her professor and keeps venting. A crimson hue floods her face. "This is exactly what I hate about Christians!" she yells. "You're all so ready to judge those who are sinning! Well, let me tell you, more judgment is the last thing I need! I'm already up to here with condemnation," she cries, raising a horizontal hand above her head.

"And where is this judgment coming from if only your boyfriend and a few friends know about the abortion?" Embee asks softly.

Just when she is ready to fire another salvo at the midsection of Embee's ship, the young woman pauses. "I—"

"I'm assuming your boyfriend and your friends didn't judge you," the spelunking guide reflects aloud. "So, who are all these people—these Christians—who are judging you if no one even knows what you've done?"

The young woman stares at Dr. Livingstone and lets out a loud, hissing noise. Then she falls silent.

Embee continues, "Can you bear with me while I mention just two things to you, Emily?"

The spelunker glares at her professor with flashing eyes but says nothing.

"I'll take that as a yes," the older woman says as she gazes at Emily with a compassion that the younger woman cannot bring herself to attack. "First, I don't doubt that there are Christians out there who make it a practice to condemn other people for their sin while ignoring their own. Some of these people may not even be true believers. Jesus had frequent encounters with these hypocrites back when He walked the earth. You know who they are—they were called the Pharisees. Jesus reserved His strongest anger for these judgmental people who condemned everybody's sin but their own."

The matronly professor assesses Emily's response to her words. Sensing no immediate rebuttal, she continues. "But while there certainly are Pharisees out there in the world who can't wait to point a finger at you, I don't think they're judging you, Emily, since they don't even know what you've done. It's my belief that the judgment you're experiencing comes from another source—either yourself or the dark one who is the accuser of every creature who is made in God's image. I tend to think you're being judged by both you and him."

Dr. Livingstone pauses again and gently tilts her head as she watches her listener carefully. When there still appears to be no forthcoming reprisal, she says, "If right and wrong do exist in the universe—flowing from the character of a perfect and holy God—then all of us will feel bad when we do something wrong, something unholy. But as you know, Emily, you don't have to run and hide or blame someone else. You can immediately go to Jesus with your sin and admit to Him that you did wrong and ask Him for forgiveness. He'll promptly forgive you and cleanse you from all badness. He'll make you as white as that snow outside you were looking at just a minute ago. Just read 1 John 1:9. It's all there."

Embee pushes a stray lock of silver hair behind her ear and says, "If you don't go to Jesus to be forgiven, your sin and subsequent guilt remain unresolved inside of you. It's not forgiven and washed away. It becomes fodder for the prosecuting attorney you mentioned earlier who wants to accuse you and shame you for your badness. At that point, the only escape you have from accusation is to deny your sin or project it onto someone else and focus on their badness. Are you familiar with the concept of projection, Emily?"

"What makes you think—" the young woman stops herself abruptly. She is recalling the day in the hallway outside Dr. Hawkstern's classroom when she and the other members in her micro-cohort discussed projection and projective identification. It dawns on her that in this current application of the term, Embee is saying that she—Emily—is perceiving judgment from people outside of herself when, in fact, she is judging herself for her unresolved sin that she has not brought to Jesus for forgiveness.

Before Emily can offer a response, Dr. Livingstone says, "The second point I want to make, Emily, is that I not only *will* not judge you—I *cannot* judge you."

The matron with the silver hair bundled up on the back of her head sighs and gazes up at the spelunker standing over her. Such an intense sadness spreads over the professor's face that it looks to Emily as if she might cry. The older woman looks down at her lap and asks, "Do you remember the grave that Sunny and I have at Lighthouse Farm?"

Dr. Livingstone looks back up at Emily with eyes that are pools of grief. The younger woman is initially shaken at witnessing such vulnerability in her mentor. Eventually, she nods her head slowly and replies, "Yes, your little boy who died a few days after birth—in your arms, in the swing, under that large tree by the pond."

Embee is surprised that the young woman remembers so much of what she shared a month ago. She goes on in a tired voice, "That's right, Emily. Well, when Abraham died, I was convinced that...God was punishing me. For months after his death, I marched and stomped and trudged over the country roads around our farm day and night, crying and yelling out to God. Sometimes, I didn't get back home until the middle of the night. I was beside myself with so many emotions: grief, sorrow, anger, but especially shame. Sunny was so worried. He anguished over whether he needed to check me into the hospital or even a sanitarium."

Emily's face of stone slowly melts, and her brilliant green eyes scan her mentor's face. Finally, she asks, "Why did you think God was punishing you?"

Embee pauses and then replies, "I was projecting—just like you, Emily."

The young woman makes a defensive face at her mentor, and the familiar edge in her voice returns. "What do you mean?"

"I was placing on God my anger and judgment toward myself," the professor explains. "I was totally unaware that I was punishing me for my sin, so I naturally assumed that it was God who was punishing me. I erroneously believed that in His wrath, He cruelly took Abraham away from me to pay me back for my sins in the past."

Emily examines Dr. Livingstone's face again. The younger woman's right eyebrow is raised slightly above the other. Finally, she turns and walks over to her chair, and sits down slowly. "What was *your* sin?" she asks even more slowly without taking her eyes off her mentor.

Without blinking, Dr. Livingstone answers, "Emily…I had two abortions. Just like you, I killed two babies." The spelunking guide watches her mentee closely as she absorbs the candid confession.

"You?" Emily reacts, her eyes large with incredulity. "You had two abortions?"

Embee nods her head slowly as her countenance floods with sorrow. She reaches over to the tissue box at her elbow and dabs at her eyes.

"Why? When?" Emily demands as she sits forward in her chair. "You?" she repeats.

"I was young…very young," Dr. Livingstone explains. "Only a teenager. Both were with the same boyfriend, who was three years older than me. My parents paid for both abortions."

"Your parents knew?" Emily sounds surprised.

Embee nods. "I told them both times when I discovered I was pregnant. My mother encouraged me to have the abortions claiming that my life would be ruined if I had babies when I was so young."

The woman pauses, and her face turns wistful. "Strangely, I've always wondered if my mother secretly wished she would have aborted me. She was only seventeen when I was born, and I often felt that she treated me as an obligation when I was growing up. Whatever the case may be, she was quick to convince me of the convenience of an abortion."

Emily sits staring at her mentor for a long time; her clear green eyes fixed on her professor. Her previous anger is now tempered by shock. "When Abraham died, you assumed that God was punishing you for the abortions," Emily reasons aloud.

"That's exactly what I thought at the time," Dr. Livingstone confirms, nodding her head.

"So, you're saying that you were the one who was actually judging and punishing yourself," Emily continues, "but then you projected that belief onto God and thought He was the one who was punishing you. He killed Abraham to exact revenge on you for killing your two other babies."

"Essentially, yes," Embee answers. "I was a young believer at the time and didn't know Jesus' character very well. I hadn't yet learned that Jesus came not to condemn us for our sin but to set us free from the guilt and condemnation that naturally accompany our disobedience. So, yes, Emily, I concluded that Jesus was punishing me for killing my two babies earlier."

Dr. Livingstone pauses and adds, "All those nights walking the country roads were about me hating me and me hating God. It was a terrible, terrible time in my life. I was the condemner of myself who then projected the condemnation onto the very one who came to deliver me from all condemnation."

"Does your husband—" Emily begins. "Sorry, I shouldn't be asking that question."

"It's okay, Emily," Embee says reassuringly with a smile that is less sad now. "Yes, he knows."

There is a short silence before Emily asks, "So now you believe that God wasn't punishing you for your sin?"

"As I said earlier, God's Word makes it clear that Jesus didn't come to rub our noses in our sin," the professor responds. "Rather, He came to set us free from the guilt of our sin as well as the condemning accusations that come from ourselves, Satan, and the Pharisees around us."

When her listener is silent, Embee adds, "So you see, Emily, Jesus is not our judge or accuser if we run toward Him with our sin. Rather, He becomes our defense attorney. Then we can declare with confidence, 'If God is for us, who can be against us?'"

Emily examines her mentor's face a while longer, then gets up and walks over to the window again. She keeps her back turned toward her mentor. "There's a part of me that doesn't have to project my badness onto others and then accuse them instead of me," she begins in a voice that sounds hollow and detached. "That part of me declares that I did nothing wrong in the first place; that abortion is not killing a person but disposing of a mass of accidental, unwanted cells; that a baby isn't a baby until it's born; that my rights as a woman supersede those of an unborn embryo."

Dr. Livingstone has so much she wants to say in response to the young woman's words that she places her fingers over her mouth to keep silent. She senses that anything she might say at this point will only arouse Emily's indignation.

The spelunker falls quiet, lost in her thoughts. "I really don't want to admit this to you," she says hesitantly, her back still turned to Embee, "but in my better moments, I realize that those thoughts are pure rationalizations. Deep inside, I know that what I did is wrong and against life. It's just that I can't bear to feel the guilt and accusations, as I mentioned at the beginning. It feels like a dissonance inside that must be quieted. So, I perform some cognitive hocus pocus in my head, and 'voilà!' my badness is no longer bad anymore. After that magic is performed, the only bad person left is the one who accuses me of being bad and sinful—the hatemonger, the judge, the religious fundamentalist."

"That person is the messenger who points out your sin," the professor offers, "and therefore awakens your sense of guilt and shame. You view this messenger as bad and shoot him or her instead of looking inside yourself and owning what you've done wrong."

Emily pauses and says icily to the window, "I suppose you could say it that way. I accuse anyone whom I perceive accuses me. Yes, I focus on the outside, the other person, not the inside."

"Jesus said that those living in darkness want to avoid the light at all costs because it will reveal their sin," Embee says with another prayer racing through her head.

When the young spelunker sighs in disgust, her professor is quick to add, "Hear me out, Emily. Remember, the enemy's goal is to keep you alone and ashamed, so you'll never seek God's help. Instead, you'll secretly hate yourself for being bad and hate others and God for judging you. You'll run away and hide from everybody, even yourself. Then you're forever locked into a dungeon of isolation and defensiveness."

The young woman stares out the window for a long time. She stands as still as the coat rack beside her and just as wooden. Finally, she turns and looks back at her mentor. Her face is alabaster, and her eyes are flat.

Embee gazes at the young woman with eyes that have witnessed the passing of more than five decades. More importantly, her eyes have been looking into Jesus' face for thirty years, and so she sees the world increasingly less from her perspective and more through His eyes. With these eyes, she looks at the young journeyer standing before her.

Outwardly, Emily is a pretty woman. However, her outward beauty is compromised by something that threatens to undo her entire personhood.

Embee never met ten-year-old Emily, of course, but she can imagine what she was like back then: a happy girl who smiled often, still laughed with innocence, maybe experienced some anxiety but was largely free of the heavy anchors of regret, shame, and badness. That was before the fall, of course—before the slow, unrelenting descent into darkness.

Now, sadly, thirteen years later, the lily-strewn and butterfly-inhabited meadow of the innocent and carefree girl's heart has been paved over with a highway of suffocating asphalt. Her spirit is now so bitter and harsh that it is very difficult to approach the young woman without eliciting a defensive reaction that is off-putting to those who desire to draw close to her.

How tragic what the passing of thirteen years can do to a young soul.

The older woman knows from her own journey through the labyrinths of life that two factors are at play in Emily. First, there are the bad things that others have done to her as well as the good things they haven't done. These others include parents, siblings, extended family, teachers, friends, the parents of friends, and maybe even pastors and Sunday School teachers.

Then, secondly, there is the even more important variable, namely, how Emily has reacted over the years to the bad things that were done to her and to the good things that weren't done—in short, how she has coped with the pain and disappointment she experienced from others.

Yes, here is the crux of it all. From what Embee knows of the young woman so far, it appears that her primary coping skill is to erect a force field around her that makes it impossible to approach her heart. She is defensive. She is defending. It is active, ongoing self-protection.

What is it she is defending so vigorously besides the abortion?

Embee thinks she knows.

"Why are we so different?" Emily asks, still standing at a safe distance.

"What do you mean by different?" the professor asks.

"You've been through some of the same things I have, and yet—" Emily stops abruptly.

Embee waits patiently for the young woman to finish her thought. She crosses her legs and irons out the wrinkles in her long dress with her fingers. She senses that Emily is torn once again by the perpetual battle within her—to hide or to be known.

"It's just that—" the young woman hesitates and then continues, "we've experienced similar things and yet ended up in such different places."

"Yes, Emily," Dr. Livingstone says warmly, "but you're young and have time to decide where you'll finally end up in life. Do know, though," the mentor says to her mentee as she narrows her eyes slightly and leans toward Emily, "that you appear to be standing at a crossroads."

The mentee does not disagree with her mentor. "A crossroads," Emily repeats. "Yes, I've felt that for a long time now," she admits. I've thought of it more as a fork in the road of life. Crossroads or a fork—the point is the same, I guess. I have a decision to make."

Embee fingers the tissue that is still resting on her lap and says, "Is there something you need to...resolve before you decide which path to take?"

Emily folds her arms and shifts her weight to her left leg. "Maybe," she replies cautiously.

"Is that one reason you came to the Academy—to hopefully resolve things?" the older woman inquires.

"You who knows everything about me knows that, too," Emily states making no attempt to hide her sarcasm.

"Okay, let's say I know that already," Embee says with a small shrug of her shoulders that are covered by a white cashmere sweater. "So, how is the resolving progressing?"

It is Emily's turn to shrug. "Varies from day to day, I suppose."

The mentor can sense she is beginning to lose all access to the highly defended young woman, so she decides not to probe any further but to consolidate the gains they have already made.

"So, Emily," she says, folding her hands on her lap and looking up at the guarded woman. "You and I both came to forks in the road of life. I could've held onto my hatred toward both myself and God after Abraham died, but Sunny helped me through that nightmare season by being amazingly patient with me. He never gave up on me even though I was walking the edge of rationality for a while. He prayed for me and loved me through it all. In a very real way, I experienced Jesus' love through Sunny's love."

Embee sits up straight and laughs softly. "I still remember the day I came out of the dark valley," she says. "I read the words in 2 Samuel 18, 'For it is you who light my lamp; the Lord my God lightens my darkness.' At that moment, something shifted in me, and I cried out to God to forgive me and to remove the veil of bitterness that had covered my heart. A week later, I found out I was pregnant with our first daughter, Ruth."

"I'm glad to hear it worked out so nicely for you," Emily says flatly. "And then they lived happily ever after," she adds sarcastically.

"What I'm trying to say, Emily, is that He can turn your darkness into light just as He did for me."

"Who says I have darkness?" the young woman remarks in her disagreeable tone as she tilts her head slightly.

There is a short silence before Dr. Livingstone says, "Emily, you and I are exactly alike because both of us were born into a broken world. We are very similar because broken people have hurt us by what they did or by what they didn't do. And we're also sisters from the same family who rebelled against our heavenly father, the one who designed us for the joy and peace that accompanies obedience to him. Yes, we are alike in so many ways."

Embee pauses and purses her lips thoughtfully. "We're different from each other in one regard," she says carefully, knowing that she is in danger of trespassing onto Emily's private minefield that humans are known to defend to the death—usually their own death.

Emily straightens her back with attitude and narrows her eyes to slits, steeling herself for the words that surely will toggle the switch of her defensiveness.

"While both of us have felt deeply angry, betrayed, and alone in this world," Dr. Livingstone observes, "and while both of us have rebelliously pursued created things instead of our Creator, there is a difference between us. You've all but made that observation yourself."

The mentor fingers the cross hanging from her neck and asks aloud, "What is that difference between us? I believe it's that every day I run toward Jesus as if my life depends on Him—which it does—while you appear to run away from Him as if your life depends on avoiding His presence."

The young woman compresses her lips tightly and stares coolly at her mentor.

"The truth is that I'm not any better than you," Dr. Livingstone adds. "Our father doesn't love me any more than He loves you, Emily. It just comes down to that fork in the road again. I eventually chose the path back home to the Father while you linger at the crossroads, remaining a house divided."

The professor pauses and then ends by saying, "It's really not about where we've come from, Emily, or what we've done in the past. Rather, it's about where we choose to go today and then the day after that and the day after that."

Emily finally parts her lips and speaks in a voice that is not as defensively charged as her mentor anticipated. "So, we're both rebels, but you've obediently returned home while I'm still pursuing my plan instead of God's," she summarizes in a detached tone. "I'm Summer, and you're Belle. I'm the one who runs off across the river and into the woods and may never come back to the Master."

"Okay, that works," Embee agrees with a nod of her silver head. "We're both part of the family and can choose to stay home and experience all of the benefits of the Father's house or—"

"Or," Emily interrupts, "we can be lured away by something across the field that sparkles brightly and promises to make us feel so good we can't imagine living without it."

"Exactly," the spelunking guide says, nodding. "The enemy's design is to kidnap us from our father's house and prevent us from returning. He deceives us with so many lies. One of his most treacherous ones is that there is something out there in the world that's better than living at home in our Father's beautiful house."

The young woman admits in a hollow voice, "The last six years have been a battle for my affections." She falls quiet for a long time, and then Embee notices yet another shift in the woman's countenance. It is not for the better.

"Some things feel so good to me, but then I'm told that they're bad for me," Emily reflects as she looks at her mentor. "Others tell me that those things are sinful. I'm often left wondering why something that feels so good can be judged by others as so wrong."

"If sin offered no pleasure, do you think we'd be tempted to pursue it?" Embee asks.

"Probably not," Emily replies slowly without conviction. She pauses and says, "Maybe I believe that I can have Jesus and the pleasurable things that are supposedly bad for me. Why can't I have both?"

The mentor sighs. "Not an uncommon question, Emily, and it's one that deserves an answer." There is another sigh, and then Embee says thoughtfully, "You yourself said that life is a battle for our affections. That means you can't live with both light and darkness, with both obedience and disobedience. You can attempt to marry them together, but in the end, you must choose one or the other. Trying to live with both a husband and a lover results in that divided heart you described. It's kind of like the law of non-contradiction, which says that two contradictory things cannot be true at the same time. You cannot say A is A and A is also B."

Dr. Livingstone tilts her head and gently pulls on one of her dangling earrings. She says, "Open relationships never work well. Why not? We're designed for commitment to one spouse, one God, one self. It's hard-wired in us, Emily, no matter how much you protest. God made us to function that way, just like a bird is made to fly in the air and not in water. We can resist what's natural for us—even demand that it's not true—but in the end, it'll harm us like insisting that we only need two hours of sleep every night.

"Faithfulness and loyalty used to be noble and even pragmatic attributes," the mentor continues. "I believe they still are since they flow from the very character of God. In practice, however, rebellious humans often want to color outside the lines. When we do that, we devalue faithfulness and commitment, to our own demise."

Emily shrugs her shoulders and says, "I seem to be able to live with the dissonance well enough."

Dr. Livingstone studies her mentee for a long time with compassionate, searching eyes. The young woman sitting in front of her is so beautiful but so hard. Embee experiences a deep sadness at that moment because the window to Emily's heart that had opened briefly is now shut. How quickly the young woman can flee to her own private dungeon.

Embee glances at the clock on the wall and says, "I've kept you too long, Emily. It's already past seven. Let me pray for you, and then you can get on with your evening."

Embee closes her eyes and says, "Jesus, I thank you for this young woman. I believe that she and I are much alike. My heart feels knit to her heart. I know you've brought her to this school for a purpose, and I believe you'll accomplish that purpose for her amazing joy! Open her eyes, so she'll see that obedience to you is far more fulfilling than pursuing counterfeits that promise satisfaction but never satisfy the soul's hunger.

"Jesus, if it's appropriate, help her to remember your words from Jeremiah: 'For my people have committed two evils: they have forsaken me, the fountain of living waters, and hewed out cisterns for themselves, broken cisterns that can hold no water.' May Emily and I both thirst for the living water that comes from your fountain, Jesus, instead of attempting to draw water from our own empty wells.

"Also, Lord," Embee prays slowly, selecting her words carefully, "give Emily power to not settle for desires that compete with her desire for you. You know what she's holding on to—it is an affection that steals her away from your house. Yes, Lord, give her strength to forsake every tantalizing counterfeit affection as you open her eyes to see what you have for her. May she see the one thing that is truly satisfying, namely...you, Jesus. You are the one and only."

When the prayer is over, the two women exchange goodbyes, and Emily exits the homey office. As she strides quickly down the wide marble hallway with its tall ceiling, she asks herself, *Does Embee know my secret affection? How could she? But then again, she seems to know so many other things about me.*

She knows!

CHAPTER 25

Journal Reading at the Joyful Java

The Screaming Eagles have gathered for another reading from the journal of JLS. Tonight, they are gathered around a table in a quiet corner of their favorite coffee shop, Joyful Java, only a mile from the Academy. A cold rain mixed with sleet plinks against the windows and the metal roof of the small building. Thanksgiving is a week away.

Rachel sips her hot chocolate that is topped with a generous dollop of whipped cream. She holds her cup in her hands to warm her cold fingers. She is wearing a multi-colored infinity scarf that tastefully complements her brunette hair and rosy cheeks. Her eyebrows are curved into an expression of sadness.

"The news about Violet Windsor is so heart-breaking," she says.

"Yeah, I can't believe she's already in hospice," Jack comments with a shake of his head. "It seems like just a week ago we were over at their house."

"What was that, three weeks ago now?" Emily asks.

"Three weeks ago, yesterday," Stewart confirms, "just after our homeless outreach under the bridge when Andrew Jefferson had to be rushed to the hospital due to low blood sugar."

The plinking of the icy rain grows louder until it sounds like the furious tapping of hundreds of fingernails. "She's only fifty-eight years old," Rachel laments. "That's way too young to die."

"Where I come from, fifty-eight is considered old," Armando reflects matter-of-factly.

"You're talking about people in gangs," Jack states.

"Yes, Juan, the gang bangers. Especially the males, of course."

"We should go visit Violet," Aly recommends.

"Yeah, the sooner, the better," Jack says as he takes a swallow of his iced tea, a beverage he drinks year-round, whether it is sweltering summer or freezing winter. "You never know how long a person will last at that point." An ancient memory, uninvited and unwelcomed, lumbers across his brain.

"How about this weekend?" Aly asks. "Are we all off from the hotel Saturday night?"

They glance around the circle at each other until Armando says, "The bad news is that I'm scheduled to work 'til 10. The good news is that Jonathan owes me a shift, so I think I can talk him into covering for me."

"Okay, let's plan on going to St. Joseph's at 7:00 then," Rachel says.

"Is that where the hospice is?" Armando asks.

"Yes, it's right next to the main hospital."

"Rach, can you organize that visit for us?" Jack asks, looking at his classmate, who has the gift of hospitality. "Could you also think of a gift, a card, or something like that? Maybe even something for Dr. Windsor."

"I can do that," Rachel says, nodding and smiling warmly at Jack.

There is silence for a long time as everyone listens to the precipitation outside that sounds increasingly like hail and less like rain and sleet. "Just think," Aly observes, "Mr. Fagani's wife lives to be eighty-nine years old, and Violet won't even make it to sixty."

"And then there's Armando's brother who died at eighteen," Jack offers.

Armando nods his head but says nothing.

"We never know, do we?" Emily remarks hollowly, staring out the window at the dark night.

"No, we don't," Aly agrees. "But He knows. Jesus knows. That's an immense comfort for me—a woman who used to serve a god who never felt personal to me."

"I heard one teacher say, 'We're invincible until God calls us home,'" Stewart offers.

"I've always liked that truth," Jack says. "If we trust that Jesus knows when and how we're going to die and that He'll be with us as we take our last breath, there's really not much to fear."

"I'm not so much afraid of death as I am of dying," Rachel offers, adjusting the scarf around her neck. "Cancer kind of scares me. I don't like the thought of dying slowly with lots of suffering. If a person could just get cancer and then die in a few days or a week, it would be a lot easier to deal with. I've decided that I want to die like Dr. Greenlay's grandfather—in his sleep."

Emily laughs a rare laugh that summons her dimples. "Yes, asleep at the wheel of his car while his four passengers scream."

Everyone laughs along with Emily.

"I don't like the idea of suffering either," Aly confesses. "But I'm comforted by God's words in Isaiah 43 where it says, 'When you pass through the waters, I will be with you;

and through the rivers, they shall not overwhelm you; when you walk through fire you shall not be burned, and the flame shall not consume you... Fear not, for I am with you.'"

Jack observes the eyes of the young woman who has a Thai mother and a Saudi father. They smolder with passion as she speaks. He finds her conviction impressive.

"I've always been comforted by Psalm 23," Armando interjects, "where it says, 'Even though I walk through the valley of the shadow of death, I will fear no evil, for you are with me; your rod and your staff, they comfort me.'"[1]

Jack nods his head and takes a swallow of his tea. "The presence of Jesus changes everything," he says. "When He is with us, we can face anything. Really, the only difference between the unbeliever and us is simply Jesus. That's it."

"Which is always," Aly says. The young woman pauses and then clarifies, "You said when Jesus is with us. I just wanted it to be clear that He's always with us."

"Yeah, of course," Jack agrees, not surprised by the young woman's almost obsessive need for precision.

Stewart clears his throat in his loud, familiar manner that announces that he is going to speak. Often, what he says is not relevant to the current conversation. This occasion is no exception.

Turning to Aly, he randomly comments, "I observed that when you first came to the Academy, you wore your hijab religiously, but now you rarely do. Why the change?"

Aly reflexively reaches up, and her fingers run over her black head-covering. Then she looks over at Stewart and explains, "My Muslim faith was all-encompassing. It dictated what I wore, the words to use when I prayed, how often I should pray, what the role of a woman is at home and out in the world, what I should think, and that I could not drive a car. As a Sunni Muslim, Sharia law directed all the details of my life. Wearing a hijab

5 Ps. 23:4 (ESV).

was mandatory. Not doing so would have resulted in censure or something worse—especially in a country like Iran where it's not just the family system but the theocratic government that controls the religious behavior of Muslims."

The young Muslim woman who fell in love with Jesus less than two years ago adds, "Yes, Islam permeated every aspect of our lives. That's why we saw the casual faith of most Christians as merely an extracurricular activity for them—one of many values in their world, all of which possessed equal importance."

Aly pauses and looks around at her new friends with her large brown eyes. "When I was a Muslim, it often appeared to me that the Christian in the west would define themselves by saying, 'I'm an engineer; I'm a father; I have three sisters; I like The Bachelor on television; I prefer Caribou over Starbuck's; I love Jesus.' All these defining characteristics seemed to be of equal importance in the eyes of the western believer. Therefore, as a Muslim, it was easy for me to despise Christians for their impotent faith and their lack of love and respect for their God.

"Now, of course, I'm free from all the burdensome laws of my faith," Aly explains. "When I was still a Muslim, it was always law, law, law. So many rules. By obeying them, I believed that I would honor the Chief of the Prophets, Muhammad, and maybe please Allah enough to be allowed into heaven on the day of my death."

The young woman with the honey-colored skin and heart-shaped face looks at Stewart and says, "Today, I wear my hijab not out of obedience to any law. I wear it only when I wish to. I'm free to choose now. Sometimes I wear it because it's comfortable and familiar. Sometimes it reminds me of my mother and sisters, who my heart aches for every day."

Aly falls silent, and her eyes mist over. Eventually, she says, "I never said goodbye to them when I fled Thailand. I know they worry about me and miss me, especially my mother. But I dare not communicate with them—as much for their safety as for mine."

"You're afraid of your brother," Emily states more than asks.

"I fear him, and I don't fear him," Aly replies as her eyes flash with emotion and her jaw tightens with resolve. "If I must die, then I must die. If Jesus gave His life for me, then how can I not give my life for Him? I fear rather for my sisters' safety and my mother's."

Jack notices that when the young woman is filled with passion, she speaks with a harsher voice that must favor her Saudi background. Most of the time, her voice reflects the softer tonal inflection of the Thai language.

"You must understand," Aly continues, "I was living enslaved to spiritual darkness. Allah was a distant god who was to be feared. He was never portrayed as a father who loved me but as a rule-keeper who I could never please. When I finally surrendered to the unconditional love of Jesus," she exclaims, her face brightening with joy, "the darkness lifted. Yes, all my life, I lived under dark, foreboding clouds. Every day. Then, the Holy Spirit entered my heart, and I was filled with light! Now I experience a personal relationship with God, with Yahweh. I actually consider Him a dad. I sense Him close to me even when the storm clouds gather on the horizon."

Rachel reaches across the table and touches the smaller woman's arm. She expresses the sentiments of everyone in the micro-cohort when she says, "We're so glad God brought you here, Aly. You've amazed us at how God can change even the life of a person dedicated to the Muslim faith. I don't think I ever knew anyone who turned from Islam to Jesus until I met you."

"It's a good thing your brother doesn't know where you are," Armando adds. "It sounds like he's a bit—radical. Can't say I'm a big fan of radical.

Been there, done that."

Stewart glances at his NASA watch and clears his throat. Then he announces, "It's getting late. I'm going to read the diary entry now since I need to be back at the citadel for spelunking later tonight." The Intellect opens the journal and informs the others, "This entry is dated May 19th of 1899.

My musings on this night are focused less on my behaviors and more on my life philosophy. Now that I have jettisoned everything that constrained me from doing whatever I desired, I find that the morality instilled in me in childhood through family and religion is fading from my being. Increasingly, I am now driven by pleasure. I find rules burdensome and guilt old-fashioned. The only question that remains is if I am altering my values by intellectual choice or if my profligate lifestyle is quietly eroding my prior moral position. Currently, I favor the latter explanation even though I am loath to confess it since that suggests I am at the mercy of something other than my will.

Yes, I am at the mercy of my desires. But why not be controlled by my desires? I find it appealing to exchange rules and morality for freedom and desire. My previous way of life would label my present behaviors as sin. But as I distance myself from morality, I no longer view what I am doing as violations against God but simply as the freedom to make autonomous choices. I am simply choosing to do what's right in my own eyes, not God's.

Do I still maintain that God exists? Possibly. However,

I view myself as less of a theist now and more of a deist who believes that God may have created the world but that He then walked away to leave us to our own devices. God may exist, but He is impersonal, uninvolved, detached from our lives. If God exists and He wishes to correct me, why does He not do so? Up to now, I've heard no voice from heaven (I have dismissed the Bible as God's voice) or seen any handwriting on my parlor wall or had a vivid dream in the night in which the divine intelligence railed against my amorality. Accordingly, I will proceed with my new course in life.

Do I possess any morality at all? Yes, although I am inclined to call it "ethical guidelines." I will not murder anyone. Murder is clearly wrong. I don't plan on robbing the bank or stealing my neighbor's new horseless carriage. I may covet my neighbor's wife, but that's not the same as murder or theft, is it? If our affection is mutual, I am not stealing anything but simply taking whatever is given to me by her free will. My gain and her husband's loss. It is quite transactional. I call on the idiom that all is permissible in love and war. (Although I remain uncertain how I will react if anyone dares touch my wife). I will not cast lustful eyes on children or set fire to my competitor's business. I will not succumb to greed, although I will continue to earn a tidy income but only to provide for the welfare of my wife and three children—and sundry private pleasures, of course.

I have decidedly become the navigator of my life. Just as the Cunard shipping line is talking about designing two giant ships called the Lusitania and the Mauretania, which can never be sunk, so I am a ship captained by me that will never be sunk. I will never be deterred by the currents of an obsolete morality or be run aground by the storms of guilt. I will sail where I wish and when I wish.

On a personal note, I believe my wife is ignorant to my recent liberties except maybe for my indulgence in liquor—its odor is too difficult to mask fully. The cough syrup—which some refer to as heroine—she believes is simply an innocent expectorant. She knows nothing of my flirtations or investments in other women either by hire or by mutual dalliance. I will do all I can so that she will not be privy to these undertakings. Isn't our city large enough that I can hide my deeds in the anonymity of the masses? Life is too short to limit myself to a small paddock when the open field beckons me to run free at my whim and fancy.

The longer I conduct the experiment, the more I am aware that belief in a god with moral expectations is incompatible with my new style of living. How can I resolve the lingering discomfort I feel when I transgress the boundaries I formerly considered to be sin? My relief lies in softening the expectations into relative truths that vary from person to person—or in embracing the notion I mentioned earlier, namely, that deity has walked away from us and no longer sees or cares.

I have not committed deicide—not yet.

My only hypocrisy is that I expect more from my own children in terms of obedience than I permit God to expect from me. I have rules for my children, such as no cats or dogs in the house—especially not on the oriental rugs—and no disrespect toward their mother or myself. I want them to obey me. What if they adopted the same stance toward me that I have adopted toward my Father in heaven? Should I ponder such inconsistency?

Even as I write these words, I am aware of an emerging shift in my thinking. Increasingly, I find it advantageous to believe that God simply does not exist. No God means no rules and no guilt. Deicide quite possibly is not the worst scenario. I am developing a strong appetite for what formerly were the sinful things in life. I will allow nothing to interfere with these indulgences. Carpe diem! Anchors away! Yes, no more anchors. I have cut the chains, and they have sunk to the bottom of the ocean.

In sum, my beliefs are evolving (optimistically said) or devolving (pessimistically said) into a new paradigm wherein I am free to choose what I wish. My view of God is also evolving. Maybe Darwin was correct. Only the fittest survive. Soon I will be left standing while God will be eradicated through my own willful (as opposed to random) "mutations" of who I manipulate him to be. This process is not Darwin's natural selection but an artificial selection of which I am the designer. I am a breeder selectively breeding the God of Christianity into a god who will serve my purposes.

Alas, my time has fled. Martha expects me by 6:00. If

I arrive at home at the proper time most nights, she questions less my late arrival on other nights. What a clever man I have become! I indeed am evolving into a higher being!

Stewart closes the century-old journal carefully—as if it is a sacred relic—and places it ceremoniously into the tin box.

"How sad that he considers drug addiction and unfaithfulness to his wife as attributes of a clever man," Aly comments with mild disgust in her voice.

"Such is the way of evil," Armando states, "a way that I used to know very well. Denial is a convenient coping skill for someone bent on ignoring the voice of conviction."

"It sounds like cognitive dissonance to me," Rachel comments. "Embee told me once that when we love both God and sin, we experience a dissonance in our minds and hearts that cannot go on forever. We will embrace God and eradicate sin, or we will embrace sin and eradicate God. It's impossible to live with God and sin as equal masters. We must denounce one of the two. It sounds like our Mr. JLS has decided to resolve his dissonance by reducing God to a disinterested deity or...to a nonentity."

"Wow, excellent point, Rach!" Jack observes. "Clearly, this man's love for sin has led him to slowly downgrade his concept of God. I wouldn't be surprised if in one of his future journal entries he totally replaces his deism with atheism."

"I hate to break up the party," Emily interjects, "but Stewart needs to get going."

"Yeah, we need to call it a night," Jack agrees.

The six students get up from their table and file out into the dark, icy night. They have no awareness that their departure is observed by eyes that have nothing to do with the world of the material.

CHAPTER 26

The Watering Trough Cantina

Appropriately, JLS sits in the darkest corner of the saloon known as the Watering Trough Cantina. A shrinking part of him is still ashamed of his recent choices, and so he feels a compulsion to hide in shadows. It is a dying part, throttled almost to the point of nonexistence. Soon, it will no longer possess any authority to convict, to interfere, to resist.

Good riddance to bad rubbish.

While his wife is home bathing their three children and preparing them for bedtime, he sits here muddle-headed and bleary-eyed, under the influence of heroin and alcohol. He is alone at the table, but the saloon around him is chaotic with activity: raucous laughter, loud voices—some celebrating and some irritated, men sitting anxiously around tables gambling at cards as if their future depended on their winnings—or their losings—colorfully dressed saloon girls strutting back and forth laden with libations and food, a piano brightly plunking out the notes of Clementine in the background, smoke everywhere. Several floozies who provide special services beyond those offered by the saloon girls flow silkily from table to table. Jacob is familiar with several of them.

As his eyes survey a woman ironically named Victoria, a man dressed in a snappy gray sack coat with matching vest and dark trousers slithers into the chair next to him. His brown hair is neatly trimmed, and his small beard juts downward sharply like the head of a spear. In fact, all of his features appear sharp, including his nose, the lobes of his ears, and his chevron eyebrows. He presents himself as relaxed. His eyes and mouth speak of quiet confidence.

"I've seen you cavorting around this groggery many a night, my good sir," the gentleman says as he fingers the brass gargoyle head positioned on the top of his ebony cane, "but I've never had the opportunity to make your acquaintance."

Jacob turns to look at his inquirer with narrowed eyes. A voice in his head screams at him to run. Instead, he stays and replies, "Name's Sutherington—Jacob. Who are you?"

"I'm Philip DaFoe," the man replies with a tight smile. "I had a hankering for some old orchard tonight, so thought I'd mosey on over and partake a bit."

Jacob nods his head but says nothing. His faculties are quite foggy, but he is still aware that something about this man awakens a deep uneasiness within him. He looks away and fixes his gaze on Victoria.

"I reckon you have eyes for that young hussy," Philip DaFoe observes as he rests his arm on the back of the leather-upholstered chair next to him. "Are you going to pony up for her? Take my word, Sutherington; you'll sour on her quickly. Used to be a schoolmarm, I'm told. Very bossy."

Jacob nods his head and continues to eye the object of his covetousness. Eventually, he offers regretfully, "Couldn't if I wanted to. After a long evening of pleasure, I'm as poor as Job's turkey."

"Ah," Mr. DaFoe says with a smile, "a man after my own heart! Indulgence is king, my good man."

Jacob turns and looks at his new admirer more closely. In a moment's time, the warmth of the man's affirmation transforms his heart from suspicious to trusting. He becomes an open book.

"In the past," Jacob confesses, "I foreswore pleasure and immorality, but in recent months, after much thought and calculation, I radically altered my course. After choosing debauchery, I've since taken a cotton to liquor and ladies." He tries to sound certain, experienced. But the fact of the matter is that inside he feels like a schoolboy speaking to the headmaster.

"Do tell!" DaFoe exclaims excitedly. "A babe in the woods has become a fox in the henhouse!" He strikes the floor loudly with the end of his cane to display his admiration. Four men sitting at the table next to them turn with lazy curiosity to consider the man with the noisy cane.

A brief silence lingers between the two men as they observe the carryings-on around them. Eventually, Jacob glances over at the man sitting next to him and notices his tattoo.

"What's the symbol?" he asks offhandedly, nodding his head toward the man's arm just above the wrist.

"The hexagram?" Philip DaFoe asks, pulling up his shirt and jacket sleeves. "It's an icon that represents allegiance to my lodge. I belong to a small group of men knit together by a common...purpose."

His curiosity aroused, Jacob asks, "Oh? Some type of secret society?"

"One could call it that," Philip replies, raising his eyebrows. Jacob notices that when the man's mouth speaks, it causes the spear on his chin to thrust downward. "Although, we have few secrets," he adds.

The man pauses for a moment and gazes out at the busy room. "Our society is called the Devil's Lodge," he volunteers matter-of-factly.

"Sakes alive!" Jacob exclaims as he sits up straight in his chair. "Your society exists to worship the devil?"

DaFoe coils both hands around the gargoyle on the end of his cane and shakes his head. "Very few of us even believe the devil exists," he comments. "In fact, most of us don't even believe in the supernatural. We believe that there's no god, no devil, nothing beyond physical matter in the whole universe, and we despise those who are foolish enough to believe in any manifestation of the supernatural."

The speaker hesitates and looks directly into Jacob's eyes. "A Christian in our eyes is as mad as a March hare." His tone is sharp and distasteful. It is not inconsistent with the sharpness of his beard, nose, ears, and eyebrows.

"So why in tarnation do you call it Devil's Lodge if you don't even believe in Satan?" Jacob asks, crinkling his forehead.

"For us, the devil, like this hexagram, is nothing but a symbol," DaFoe explains, "not a living being. He's merely a symbol of man's true object of worship: his own self with his fleshly passions. We believe that a man is a beast—although a noble one—with animal desires that need to be properly fed with little to no denial or delay of gratification. We're opposed to men of any spiritual persuasion who insist that we must disavow our natural inclinations and wield morality against us like a fire hose dousing a blaze."

"Man alive!" Jacob exclaims. "My encounter with you is proving to be serendipitous indeed! Did I not reveal but a moment ago that I myself have recently been making the transition from God and morality to hedonism and self-direction?"

"That you did," the man remarks as he leans back in his chair, "Yes, I agree that it's almighty fortuitous that we crossed paths tonight. You don't seem to be one of those narrow people I despise."

Phillip pauses and rubs the point of his chin spear with the back of his hand. "Maybe," he says, examining Jacob as one might view a potential investment, "you could join me at the meeting later this night."

Jacob blinks his clouded eyes against the smoke in the room. "Your lodge meets tonight?" he inquires with some hesitation.

"Yes, directly at midnight."

"Why the Sam hill do you meet so late?" Jacob asks with more irritation than he feels. *Must be the liquor,* he says to himself. "Are you all plum crazy?"

DaFoe shoots a severe look at Jacob that turns his blood cold. "I can assure you that we're not a society of insane men with one-horse intellects," he snaps. "I'll have you know that every last one of us hails from upstanding walks of life."

Jacob rips his eyes away from the man's intense gaze and extracts a handkerchief from his coat pocket. For some reason, he finds himself perspiring profusely. Wiping his forehead, he says, "I'm not certain I want to attend a meeting involving Satan, whether it be him in person or him as some symbol representing your principles of indulgence. I've always believed in the devil, myself—although much less so recently. I reckon I'd prefer to avoid sacrifices and blood and incantations and all of that ritual."

"We don't do much of that, my friend," says the man. "Remember, we're high society men who don't mess with humbug matters. We're outstanding citizens in this city—men of honor."

When Jacob sighs and looks down at his hands, DaFoe says, "So are you going to vamoose with me or not? I'm about to hang up the fiddle here and mosey on over to that meeting. It must be approaching the eleventh hour by now."

When Jacob continues to alternately wring and examine his hands as if looking for a message written on his palms, DaFoe gets to his feet abruptly and inquires, "So are you fixing to come with me, or are you going to remain all night at this bucket shop?"

Jacob shakes his head in frustration and rises unsteadily to his feet. "I'm not deaf!" he exclaims. "I heard you the first blamed time! And yes, I'll come with you as long as there's no shecoonery or skullduggery at this meeting." It is only then that Jacob notices the large gold ring on DaFoe's left hand.

"What have we here?" he inquires of the mysterious man. "You have a cross on your ring? I thought you said you believe in no god."

"It's a cross to you," the man replies and licks his lips. "But from my perspective, when I'm looking down at it, it's an inverted cross."

"Inverted? Whatever for?" Jacob asks.

"If I told you that," the man says with bemused eyes, "you might ride me out of town on a rail, so religious you have been in the past."

"You've nothing to fear from me," Jacob insists. "Remember, I've now chosen the left path instead of the right. Religion is done hornswoggling me with its provincial grip."

"Ah," DaFoe says with a wink, "I discern that the long arm of the church won't catch this weasel asleep again. You once were imprisoned by rules but now are liberated to be a man of the world."

"So, what does the inverted cross on your ring signify?" Jacob persists.

"I suppose I could tell you that it's none of your funeral," DaFoe comments with a wicked smile. "However, as I said earlier, I have no secrets."

The man repositions his cane and rests both hands on top of the leering gargoyle. "The inverted cross symbolizes the very reason for the existence of the Devil's Lodge, my friend. As I alluded to earlier, we're hostile to the supernatural—no—we're downright contemptuous of it. We oppose Christianity for its repression of humanity and for how it rails against the animal appetites and condemns them all as sin. Who the blazes do those totalitarian scalawags think they are, after all, attempting to restrict our freedom? Blazing bullies is what they are!

"Yes, we in the lodge oppose Christian values and pursue the inversion of all that God stands for," the man declares with increasing passion. "Instead of holiness, we pursue indulgence, self-assertion, sexual freedom—all the satanic virtues. We live to rebel against any and all authority, religious or otherwise, that seeks to limit individual autonomy. We will permit no man or god to impose their will on us!"

When Philip DaFoe concludes his impromptu diatribe, his voice is at a volume just short of yelling. His eyes are ablaze with emotion, and his hands grip his cane as if throttling his worst enemy. Jacob can see a vein, like a small snake, bulging out of his neck.

The man, apparently aware of the intensity of his harangue, inhales deeply and relaxes his jaw. "As you can see," he says in a more subdued voice, "I've had run-ins with religion and other sources of authority that have soured me badly. I'm wrathy because too many tyrants have attempted to imprison me in their jails of morality. No more, I say, no more.

"And you," he adds, pointing a sharp finger at his listener, "you're cut out of the same cloth as I. You're weary of getting the little end of the horn in life and have a mind to change all that. Well, good for you, Jacob Sutherington! Good for you, I say! Bravo!"

Jacob's uneasiness returned in full force during the provocative man's verbal tirade. Nonetheless, he hesitates to part company with his new acquaintance. After all, is not the man simply giving vent to what he himself has felt over the years, albeit in the privacy of his heart?

"So, are you with me, then?" DaFoe inquires, narrowing his eyes.

"Yes," Jacob replies after only a brief hesitation. He does not want the supremely confident man to think him weak. "Yes, I'm with you. And I can ride us to the lodge. I have in my possession a horseless carriage that can take us there lickety-split."

"My lucky day," the man with the spear-shaped goatee remarks, chortling. "Think of that—serendipity and luck encountered in the same place on the same night! What the dickens does that happenstance omen for us? There's only one way to know—let's venture forward and find out!"

Jacob imagines the Devil's Lodge convening at some deserted business or in the back room of another saloon in town—maybe even in the basement of the new Carnegie library. He is somewhat disconcerted but also intrigued when DaFoe directs him to the edge of town where the castle-like Congregational church is silhouetted against the night sky like a crouching behemoth. In the darkness, the edifice does not inspire peace in Jacob's chest—quite the contrary. Secretly ashamed of his recent departure from faith in God, he imagines the huge turret of the church rising up against him like an angry reverend accusing him of apostasy.

The man with the hexagon tattoo and the inverted cross directs them past the condemning clergyman as well as the foreboding cemetery. They continue to drive farther down the gravel road aided only by the meager lights of the carriage until they pass the huge hill that is partially gutted by a large quarry.

A short while later, DaFoe directs Jacob to turn right onto a narrow road—a path, really, only two horses wide—that veers off from the main road and trails off into the trees. As they bounce through the forest, they are quickly enveloped by a darkness that Jacob oddly thinks is too thick to be accounted for merely by the late hour of the night. He is uncertain whether to blame the trees that blot out the stars overhead or if there is another, deeper and unspeakable darkness in this place that cannot be perceived by the physical senses.

Two hundred yards later, after following the narrow path as it snakes through the woods, DaFoe instructs him to stop the carriage. When the bouncing vehicle comes to a rest and the motor is silenced, both men get out, and the Satan man, as Jacob has come to think of his new acquaintance, leads him toward a hulking mound that is a shade darker than the surrounding night.

As they penetrate the Stygian darkness of the forest, Philip DaFoe comments over his shoulder, "I feared you'd be too drunk to navigate a horseless carriage, but you did better than I expected. The cool air must have revived your faculties."

Yes, Jacob thinks to himself, the night air is partly responsible for his reinvigoration, but even more potent is the mingled curiosity and dread that accompanies an invitation to Devil's Lodge.

Shortly, they arrive at a rock outcropping partially hidden by what appears to be a stand of small firs. As they make their way forward through the trees, Jacob feels them and smells them more than he sees them. He follows the man as he pushes through the trees and then disappears.

Behind the camouflage of the firs, Jacob finds himself standing before a dark oval shape. It is an entrance to a cave. Groping his way into the portal, Jacob hears the other man making scraping noises in the darkness ahead of him. Soon his guide lights a match and holds it up to a torch that he must have extracted from a niche in the entrance. In a moment, the torch ignites, and light floods the cave. Jacob is now able to see that he and the Satan man are standing in a small sepulchral room no larger than his den back at home. The ceiling is not high—seven feet at the most.

With a tilt of his sharp beard, Philip motions Jacob to follow him. In the otherworldly light of the torch, Jacob thinks the man's visage has changed. He looks forbidding, even monstrous. *My eyes have not adjusted to the light*, Jacob reasons to himself.

The two men pass through a doorway that is so small they have to bend low to navigate it. Soon, they are in a larger room about the size of Jacob's parlor. Here they encounter a man—Jacob assumes it is a man—wearing a hood over his head. The hooded figure nods at DaFoe and hands him a matching hood—as red as a cherry with holes cut out for the eyes. The man does not offer a hood to Phillip's guest. When Jacob opens his mouth to inquire about the matter, the Satan man says, "You're not initiated."

Against the protests of a voice in the back of his mind, Jacob follows his guide through another narrow doorway that opens into a long tunnel. The floor is uneven in the passage, and Jacob stumbles and falls hard to his knees several times in the torch-lit shadows as they move forward. The smell of smoke grows stronger in the tunnel. Mingling with the smoke are other smells: Kerosene. A rotting odor. Dankness.

After what seems to Jacob like a very long time, the passage gradually doubles in size and then opens into a larger space. Stumbling into the room, Jacob stops and gazes around at the eerie scene that meets his astonished eyes. At least twenty hooded figures are standing around in the gloomy cave like so many stalagmites. A few are holding torches like the one DaFoe wields. The figures turn, and their eyes peer at the intruder through the holes in their masks. They continue to stare at him for a long time. Jacob feels naked before their gaze—especially without a mask.

A sudden, disturbing thought possesses Jacob: *I've been lured here to be sacrificed to the prince of darkness.* His fear is further intensified when he notices the long freakish shadows cast on the walls of the cave by the hooded figures. He has a fleeting sense of being in hell, surrounded by grotesque demons. His heart begins to gallop in his chest, and a drop of perspiration rolls slowly down his back.

Jacob tears his attention away from the ghastly shadows, and his eyes focus instead on vivid images that have been painted on the cavern walls. In the uneven light of the torches, he makes out images of black crows, their ragged wings spread and their eyes burning with balls of fire.

As his nervous eyes scan the room, he also sees horned goats, serpents with long fangs, the severed heads of bulls with rings in their noses, six-pointed stars, men and women in various stages of undress, and words written with symbols he cannot decipher.

On the far side of the cave, he espies what looks like an altar with horns jutting up from each corner. Something resembling black paint streaks the sides of the altar.

Jacob swallows hard. The walls and ceiling of the cavern begin to close in around him, and he finds it difficult to breathe. He fears that he might pass out. He curses the foolish pride that prevented him from declining DaFoe's invitation all because he feared being perceived as weak.

Remembering the man with the spear beard, he wheels around to locate his escort but does not see him anywhere in the cave. What meets his panicked eyes is the eerie throng of stalagmites wearing blood-red hoods.

Just when Jacob is about to flee the room, he hears the familiar voice of the Satan man addressing the hooded people. "Good evening, and welcome to our fortnightly meeting, fellow hedonists," he says, laughing softly. "I'm thankful for you citizens of earth who have chosen to shed the shackles of restricting morality and embrace instead the cornucopia of carnal desserts offered by this world.

"We're here because we agree with Darwin about the evolved human animal. We agree that all humans have not evolved equally. Some are stronger than others. The fittest will dominate the weaker, and the superior will lord it over the inferior. We believe that we represent the fittest in our society. Ergo, we're the ones who will survive.

"We scoff at the supernatural and the Christian fairy tale of life after death. We believe that we can attain ultimate satisfaction during our years on this earth not by restraining desire, but by liberating it."

In response to the man whose spears are now hidden beneath his hood, lusty cries fill the room and echo off the walls.

When the Satan man begins speaking again, Jacob feels his body relax. It appears that he has not been lured to the cave to be sacrificed after all. He has simply been invited to attend the lodge and witness their meeting. So far, he does not disagree with what he hears.

After Philip is done addressing the lodge members, several other hoods speak. Jacob is almost certain he recognizes one of the voices but cannot be sure. After the third hood is done speaking, a fourth man leads the group in a chant: "We worship you, O lord of the dark, and offer our hearts to receive your mark. We serve you forever with abandoned souls until that day when the bell tolls."

After the chant is repeated several times, a chalice is spirited into the cavern and is passed among the hooded lodge members. Each figure partakes of the mysterious liquid by lifting his hood. Jacob stands on the fringe of it all, observing the ritual and wondering what liquid is in the chalice. Blood? Exotic ingredients mixed into some magical elixir that induces an elevated state of consciousness?

When the chalice has been passed to everyone except the outsider, the members of the lodge drift toward a doorway in the far wall of the cavern. One by one, they are devoured by the dark orifice.

Jacob is about to follow when the last hooded person wheels around and, without a word, extends an arm toward him and makes a fist with his hand. The gesture is a clear warning to remain where he is. Jacob can only stare helplessly as the last person disappears into the passage. The room is now significantly darker since it is illuminated by only two torches left behind in the crevices of the wall. All the other torches have accompanied the hooded ones into the mysterious mouth.

Jacob stands transfixed near the entrance to the room. He has not moved since he entered the cavern. He begins to feel cold.

He looks around the room with sobering eyes. Here and there, in the grotto, stalactites extend down from the ceiling like giant icicles. Beneath the icicles, smaller stalagmites reach upward, created by the drippage from their counterparts above. Fingers of water vein the stone floor of the gloomy room and flow toward a pool on the left side of the chamber.

Jacob hears distant chanting as he stands in the gloomy abyss. It sounds far away, eerie. He has a fleeting thought that his life has taken a bad turn in recent months, but the thought is flimsy and is soon pushed aside by more compelling stimuli—such as the large white rocks he sees submerged in the pool. Willing his legs to move, he shuffles stiffly over to the water and focuses his eyes on the objects.

A shudder involuntarily rolls through his body when he sees that they are not large rocks but skulls. Most of them look to be bovine or porcine. One or two of them are submerged in a deeper part of the pool. Upon closer examination, Jacob identifies the skulls as unmistakably...human. Instinctively, he takes several steps back from the small body of water and puts the back of his hand over his mouth.

"What in the blazes is this all about?" Jacob whispers into the deep gloom of the underground chamber. For the second time that night, he feels an instinctual desire to run. Before he can act on his impulse, he hears a muted voice carry into the room through the mouth that swallowed the lodge members.

"I don't care beans for your gentlemanly hesitations, Charles!" the muffled voice challenges. "It's imperative to our way of life that we get all-fired up against that new church. After all, they insist that the Bible is God's truth written to direct our lives. Now I'm not suggesting we burn their building to the ground. That's too almighty obvious. But we do need to go the whole hog in resisting their influence in our city. We must stop frequenting their businesses! We must prevent them from gaining public office! We must expose their narrow-minded judgmental attitude and undermine their high falutin' dogma designed to restrict our human expression!"

Jacob hears several other muted voices respond to the first voice, but none of them are distinct. Eventually, he hears more words from the louder first voice travel out through the dark hole.

"I can tolerate a church that keeps to itself," the voice declares, "one that doesn't hone into the public forum—especially if they believe that God is only some fairy tale phantom who doesn't actually exist. Several churches in town are of that ilk. What I can't oblige are those orneries who believe that God exists as a supreme being who makes claims on our lives. Those people are plum dangerous! They should be wiped off the face of the earth!"

Other voices again respond to the first voice. The boisterous conversation continues for a long time. Then Jacob hears more chanting. Occasional words are discernable: "Molech...sacrifice ...torture ...rebellion ...pagan ... black masses ...Satan ...suppressed ...indulgence ...unfettered freedom ... magic ...council of nine ...Walpurgisnacht ...way of darkness ...dark evolutionary force ...hidden ...mystery ...individualism."

Time passes. Jacob massages his face and swollen eyes with the fingers of both hands. He wants to leave, but something dissuades him. It is as if an invisible hand bars the way out of the cave. His heart whispers to him that he is crossing a line from which there will be no return. His brain wills to run out of the cave and flee in his carriage. His body remains frozen several feet away from the pool of the skulls.

An awareness slowly possesses him: there is a presence in the stone room. It is thick and dark, like a black fog. It muddles his mind, makes it hard for him to think. He grinds the palms of his hands into his forehead to clear it.

As time passes, he realizes that the presence is now inside of him. Desire ignites like a match within him, and the image of the saloon girl, Victoria, materializes in his mind's eye.

At this moment, he does not devote even a fleeting thought to right and wrong. He thinks only of what he wants, and when he can get it, consequences be damned. He is beyond reason. He has forgotten everything but the object of his desire. He is in a trance. He is being summoned and has no desire to resist. He has lost his identity. He no longer is Jacob Sutherington. He has become desire.

Somewhere in the deep recesses of his rational mind, he wonders if the hooded figures have spoken some sort of enchantment over him...

The sound of approaching voices awakens him from his intoxicating reverie. Now it is too late to flee. He has made a life-altering decision by making no decision at all. He should have fled when he was still able to resist the draw of desire. Now he is its prisoner. How delightful it is to imbibe the enticingly sweet elixir even though it promises the death of so many things. The pleasure of the moment is so...provocative and...enslaving. Irresistible and...deadly.

When the hooded figures return with flaming torches in their hands, they file silently into the large cavern. They do not tarry but trudge past Jacob and exit through the passage that leads toward the entrance of the cave. Several of the Devil's Lodge members eerily pivot their hooded heads to stare at him as they walk by. Two of them appear to stagger as they leave the cavern. The last person in the unholy procession removes his cherry-red hood revealing the face of Philip DaFoe.

"Shall we?" his escort says as he gestures with his hood in the direction of the retreating figures.

Jacob turns his back on the Satan man and leads the way out of the cavern and into the subterranean hallway. As they move forward, his wretched imagination pictures the man behind him, crushing his skull with a jagged rock. Once again, he stumbles several times as he makes his way through the dismal passage by the inconsistent light of the torch behind him.

On the journey out of the cave, they pause twice, once at the keeper of the hoods and once at the exit so Philip can douse his torch in a bucket of water and throw it on the floor with a dozen other extinguished torches.

When the two men finally squeeze out of the cave through the narrow crevice, Jacob feels like he has just emerged from the underworld. The pitch-back night is alive with the welcoming sound of chirping crickets, hooting owls, and leaves flickering in the gentle breeze. None of the other lodge members are in sight. It is as if they evaporated into the night like specters. Were they only a collection of apparitions all along?

When the two men reach the horseless carriage, Jacob carefully cranks the small engine to life. Then he climbs over the wagon wheel into the driver's seat. Soon he is navigating the motor car with its high center of gravity through the pitch-black forest. Three lights guide them—one on each side of the carriage and one in front.

"Ironic," his passenger comments, speaking over the sound of the engine.

"What's that?" Jacob asks, glancing at the man sitting next to him in the darkness.

"The name of your motor car maker—Armstrong—that's my mother's maiden name," the man announces. "No relative of mine, unfortunately."

"Yes," Jacob replies distractedly, "how ironic."

"I have yet to be convinced of the value of a horseless carriage," the Satan man volunteers as the vehicle dips into a depression in the forest floor. "I find them noisy, smelly, and unreliable."

"All true," Jacob replies. "But unlike an ornery horse, it's never going to run away from you."

The man next to him laughs. It is not the pleasant laugh most people would express at such a moment. It is harsh and cold. Out of the corner of his eye, Jacob looks at the man in the dim illumination of the carriage light. For some odd, terrifying reason, the face with the spear-shaped beard and severe nose remind Jacob of the devil himself. He shivers and attempts to concentrate on the serpentine trail in front of him.

There is an extended silence until the passenger announces, "The members of the lodge would like you to join us. We have unanimously agreed to extend you an invitation to enter our fellowship."

"What is the cost of membership?" Jacob inquires. Without thinking, he carelessly adds, "Medusa's head or a newborn child?" He regrets his words as soon as he has spoken them.

His passenger laughs darkly and says, "Nothing quite so exotic or costly, my good man. Just a commitment from you to attend meetings and to come to the aid of any lodge member when you are asked to do so."

"Are there no rules?" Jacob asks as he steers around a fallen tree.

"Yes," the man concedes slowly and then hesitates. "There are a few privileges that accompany membership in the lodge. We find it in bad taste to refer to them as rules. The word is...too confining and restrictive. Too reminiscent of religion and authority. But yes, there are privileges."

"And what might those be?" Jacob wonders aloud.

The man beside him pauses before he replies, "Why don't you come over to my manse this Friday eve. You can meet my wife, Madeline, and my children. Then we can retire to my study, where I will introduce you to the privileges of the lodge. I have taken a cotton to you, Jacob Sutherington. I see you as a man of grit and fortitude—a good egg. I reckon you'll fit into our little society quite tidily. We are progressive, liberal, and committed to the goddess of choice. You're clearly a man of choice, are you not, Jacob?"

Jacob steers the horseless carriage onto the gravel road that runs toward town. His ambivalent sentiments wrestle in the dungeon of his mind. Finally, he announces, "Very well, DaFoe, I will meet with you on Friday. My only condition is that there be no shecoonery or skullduggery. I want you to be forthright with me at all times."

DaFoe laughs his devilish laugh again and replies, "I will do what I can, Jacob. But the life you chose to pursue long before I ever met you is beset on every side with shecoonery and skullduggery. In truth, you already are a dark and deceptive man. Your wife undoubtedly has no awareness of your activities on this night or any other night. Tell me I am wrong. So, do not be a hypocrite, my good man. I absolutely despise hypocrisy. Don't ask of me what you don't even ask of yourself."

Jacob watches as a deer runs across the road in front of the motor car and disappears into the darkness. As he resigns himself to the future meeting with the strange man named DaFoe, he feels a raindrop strike his hand. Tarnation, he thinks to himself. *Why didn't they give this carriage a roof? People never think ahead these days, do they?*

He also wonders with a shiver if Philip's wife, Madeline, is the Madeline with whom he is already acquainted. *No, it cannot be,* he thinks as he glances briefly at his passenger.

Jacob navigates his horseless carriage forward through the present darkness and toward the future darkness that will soon rob him of everything he holds dear.

CHAPTER 27

Isaiah and Violet at the Eleventh Hour

"So, what's it like, Vi?" Isaiah asks his wife as he stares straight ahead. "What's it like for you right now?"

The Windsors are reclining on lounge chairs on the concrete patio in their backyard. It is only 4:30 in the afternoon, but the early December sun is already low in the sky, peeking timidly through the pine trees. The air temperature is cool and pleasant, but the breeze that gusts occasionally has an edge as cold as steel. Violet is covered with a heavy blanket from her toes to the middle of her chest.

The husband turns to look at his wife and says, "I only ask because you and I have shared everything else in life: the joys and the sorrows; the bright days and the dark days; the birth of little Jack and...his death." The colonel's voice trails off as he speaks the last few words.

Violet turns her wan face toward her husband and nods her head. The perfect black wig only partially camouflages the toll of months of chemotherapy. "Yes, we've shared so much, haven't we, Ize?" she says nostalgically. Her voice is weak but clear. "And to think that I almost divorced you twenty-five years ago. Thank God that He spoke some sense into the impulsive head of that foolish young woman."

"It wasn't you, Vi; it was me. I was gone too often and too long back then," Isaiah says, shaking his head. "I regret it now, in so many ways."

"Don't go there, hon," Violet says softly, her sunken eyes radiating compassion. "It wasn't only you who signed up for the army, remember? We both enlisted. 'Sides, I made so many friends along the way at the different posts. I wouldn't have wanted it any other way. It was the adventure of a lifetime."

"If I hadn't been gone for six months at a time, we might've had more kids," Isaiah says wistfully.

"Isaiah Windsor, I said, don't go there," his wife repeats with as much intensity as she can generate from her cancer-compromised body. "You're puttin' yourself on God's throne when you do that. He's in charge, not you—least last time I checked."

Isaiah chuckles softly and shakes his head. "If my soldiers had known how often I looked to you for wisdom and reassurance over the years, they would've made you CO in the blink of an eye."

The man pauses, and his eyes search his wife's face, memorizing it in preparation for her imminent departure. "You've been so strong, Vi," he observes in a soft voice. "So strong for so long. That's one reason I'm asking you what it's like to be dying. I want to be strong for you, for a change. I want to walk with you every klick of the way on this journey."

"You get right to the point, don't you?" Violet comments as her mischievous eyebrows manage to arch upward, just not as high as they used to before her illness descended. She sighs, and her brows fall. "You've never said the word before."

Isaiah's eyes turn away from his wife and gaze out at the stand of pine trees that mark the end of their property. "I don't mean that God can't still heal you, sweetheart. I—"

"No need to explain," Violet says quietly as she fingers the thick blanket that lies over her body like sod. "I'm at peace with whatever God has for me. Yes, He could still heal me, but—I don't think He will. It's my time to go home. He's callin' me, Ize. He's callin' me."

Isaiah turns back toward his wife and reaches over to hold her hand. "So, what is it like?" he asks in a voice husky with emotion.

Violet licks her pale lips and replies, "I don't have much pain—least not yet. Mostly it's a discomfort that tells me somethin' else is comin' down the road. But I'm tired," she says. "Never been so tired before. That's the hardest part by a country mile. Up until a month ago, my mind would always tell my body what to do. Now my body tells my mind what to do. Most of the time that's to sleep. So, I'm sad because I don't have much time left, and I spend too much of it sleepin'."

Isaiah swallows hard and looks back into the eyes of the woman he has known for forty years. Her eyes look the same as the day he met a younger version of her at a small church in Alabama.

"Of course, I do think some about what dyin' will be like," Violet admits as her fingers slowly run back and forth over the edge of the blanket. "I wonder what it will be like a week from now when I wake up in the morning. How bad will the pain be then? Will the cancer spreadin' in my brain make me blind? Will the tumors begin to erupt through my skin? Will I be strong enough to handle it?"

Isaiah looks deep into the eyes of his soulmate and nods his head slowly. He does not trust himself to speak.

Violet attempts to pull the blanket up higher on her chest with her free hand but makes little progress.

The ex-colonel releases his wife's hand and rises to his feet quickly as if a sniper bullet struck the concrete patio. "Let me get that for you, Vi," he says.

He is relieved to have a reason to get up and move—to do something. Sitting and talking feels so powerless, so much like surrendering. He is used to issuing a command and having it executed immediately, not sitting around and waiting. He is accustomed to attacking and defeating the enemy, not passively watching while it arrogantly strides into his compound in broad daylight and massacres everyone in sight.

Isaiah pulls the blanket up until it touches his wife's fleshless chin. He is thinking about Jesus' anger toward death when He was standing at the mouth of Lazarus' tomb. He can relate to Jesus' anguish so intensely he can taste it.

Before Isaiah sits back down, he turns his lounge chair so it faces his wife. He wants to look at her as much as he can while he can. He does not lay down in the chair but rather sits on the edge of it and leans close to his wife.

"I'm not afraid of death," Violet says. "I know where I'm goin'. There are times, though, when small waves of anxiety roll over me. The longer my runaway brain rehearses thoughts of dyin', the bigger the waves grow until they become so large they threaten to knock me off my feet. About then, I begin to feel a rumblin' beneath. Panic rises in my chest and grips my throat."

Violet closes her eyes, and Isaiah wonders if she is falling asleep. But she soon opens them and says, "At those panicky times, I think of good ol' King Jehoshaphat. When the enemy was comin' up against him, and his heart was alarmed, he said, 'We do not know what to do, but our eyes are on you.'

"When I put my eyes on Jesus and not on those waves of fear, I feel peace—a peace that passes understandin'. Dyin' shrinks from a scary giant to a door that opens to eternal life. That's when dyin' no longer serves the Devil but God. Dyin' is still a lion, but God has pulled out all its fangs and claws. I'm not afraid for a second of a toothless lion. Never heard of no lion gummin' someone to death."

Isaiah stares at his courageous wife and nods his head slowly. "You sound like Peter when he walked on the Sea of Galilee," he observes. "When he looked at the waves, he began to sink, but when he kept his eyes on Jesus, he was fine."

Violet nods her head but says nothing.

The Warfare professor steeples his fingers and covers his nose with them, "I've asked God so many times to take me instead of you," Isaiah says. His chin trembles slightly, but it is hidden behind the steeple. "I don't understand it all, Vi. Why you? Why now?" He pauses and then adds, "The only comfort I have is knowing that if you die first, then I won't have to worry about leaving you behind when it's my time."

Violet licks her lips, and her eyes grow moist. "It's right for me to go, Ize," she says. "I really want to see our little Jack. I've missed him so much. I suppose I still blame myself for him fallin' into that well. I want to see him and tell him I'm sorry for not watchin' him close enough."

"Now it's my turn to tell you not to go there," Isaiah says sternly. "Little Jack dying was not your fault. We both know how quickly he could slip away and run all over kingdom come, just like his daddy. My goodness, we had to put a leash on the little bugger so we wouldn't lose him. And do you remember how I decided to look at Jack's death? He died doing what he enjoyed the most—exploring the world."

Violet shifts uncomfortably and grimaces. She mumbles to herself, "This is my last time on this lounge chair." Then she sighs and announces, "Yes, Isaiah, I'm definitely goin' to see Jesus and Little Jack before you do. I'll let Little Jack know that you'll be comin' sometime in the future. He'll be glad to hear that."

Isaiah tries to put on a brave face. He says, "Soon, no more tears, Vi. No more pain. No more regrets. All wrongs will be made right. Best of all, Vi... no more death."

It strikes him, at the moment, that he is using his wife's diminutive name more frequently than usual. He knows why. Soon, she will be gone, and he will never be able to speak the affectionate pet name to her face again. At least, not in this world. He swallows hard.

"Mm-hmm," Violet responds. "All because of what Jesus did for us."

Silence hangs in the chilly backyard for a while like an invisible, ominous noose. The sun falls behind the trees, and the backyard is overrun with dusk. Isaiah pushes the thought out of his head that this is his last autumn with his wife. His last month. Maybe even—

"You know what else I've been thinkin'?" Violet says in a voice that is noticeably weaker than fifteen minutes earlier. She does not wait for her husband to answer but goes on to say, "I've been tryin' to put myself in the shoes of someone who doesn't know Jesus and try to feel what it might be like to face death alone."

Isaiah shakes his head and exclaims, "You're the one who's dying, and you're spending your time wondering what someone else might be feeling? Vi, how do you even have room in your head to think about others at a time like this?"

Violet ignores her husband's question and says, "I've wondered how they comfort themselves when they don't know what's goin' to happen when they die. They don't know if they're ever goin' to see their loved ones again, and they certainly don't know that Jesus will be waitin' for them on the other side. I can't imagine facin' death not knowin' those things."

"You'd have to be mighty good at denial or distracting yourself with other thoughts," Isaiah reflects aloud. "Or maybe you'd have to believe that you're going to be reincarnated or flow into the great circle of life and death. But those beliefs are...so impersonal and lonely. Jesus isn't in them."

Violet closes her eyes and winces. Her husband sees his wife's facial expression and asks, "Time for more pain meds, Vi?" His eyes observe the insignificant displacement of the blanket that rests on his wife's body, and he mourns at how emaciated she has become.

The woman shakes her head and says, "Not yet. They make me so tired, and my mind is fuzzy enough the way it is—'chemo brain,' most likely. I want to stay awake and talk some more, Ize. I just don't know how long I have, and I want to spend time with you while I can still communicate. Just you and me."

Violet draws in a deep breath very slowly and then comments, "I've got the harder job right now, dyin' and all. But soon, you'll have the harder job, hon. I'll be gone on a permanent vacation to heaven, and you'll be left behind here in the house by yourself. It's always harder bein' the one left behind."

"I used to always be the one leaving," Isaiah observes. "Now, Vi, you're the one doing the leaving. The tables have turned."

"Yep, I'll soon be leavin' my earthly tent and movin' into my eternal house that'll never need repairs," Violet says. "And it's mortgage-free. Jesus paid for it all."

The recumbent woman closes her eyes and does not move. Isaiah sighs and rests his hand on his wife's arm. Very softly, he recites, "So we do not lose heart. Though our outer self is wasting away, our inner self is being renewed day by day. For this light momentary affliction is preparing for us an eternal weight of glory beyond all comparison—"

Her eyes still closed, Violet finishes the passage her husband is quoting. She speaks slowly and softly. "As we look not to the things that are seen but to the things that are unseen. For the things that are seen are transient, but the things that are unseen are eternal."

There is a long silence before Violet whispers, "I'm sorry, Ize, but I don't think I'll make it to Christmas. I hate the thought of not spending it with you, but God has a reservation for me at His banquet table."

As the woman begins to drift off again, she mumbles quietly, "I'll be home for Christmas."

This time, Violet falls into a deeper sleep, even without her medication. As she lies under the heavy blanket, her husband begins to reminisce out loud. His voice is subdued and filled with passion.

"Remember our first date, Vi? I made that picnic lunch for us, and we went and spread out the blanket down by the river. First, the ants came and then the honeybees. I got stung on my nose, and it swelled up like a big old beet. You tried so hard not to laugh, but finally, you busted out until you cried. Then I started laughing, too. I've never laughed so hard since. Best picnic I ever had."

If only I had enjoyed those moments more, he thinks with a sigh. If only I had known that some things would never come again. I would have been so much more intentional about sucking the marrow out of them.

The warfare professor considers his sleeping wife with blurry eyes and then says, "We were so young, back then. Where did the years go, my sweetheart? Where did the years go?"

The colonel wipes his eyes with the sleeve of his cardigan sweater and then says, "Do you remember our wedding day, Vi? First, my cousin forgot the rings, and then that old black Lincoln Town car from Fred's wouldn't start. I didn't feel nearly as awkward as you did when your father had to drive us to the motel."

The man with the heavy heart laughs softly, then falls silent. He continues to gaze at his wife. When the sadness constricts his throat, and he cannot breathe, he clenches his jaws and squeezes his hands together until they ache.

After gently running the back of his hand over his wife's cheek, Isaiah gets up and walks out onto the grass that is buried under leaves he normally would have raked and composted by now. He stops in the middle of the yard and looks up into the sky. His shoulders are unusually slumped, and his strong legs feel wobbly beneath him. The light of the first star travels to his eyes. He sighs deeply.

"Father, it hurts so much to love in this broken world," he says softly. "But I guess the hurt tells us how much we love the other person. I can only imagine how much you hurt for all your children who turn their backs to your love and walk away."

Tears begin to make a silver path down his dark cheeks as he says, "I'm going to need your help with this, Jesus. I haven't lost anyone this close to me since mamma twenty years ago...and Jack, of course. Little Jack. Beloved Jack."

The colonel swallows a sob and places the back of his hand over his mouth.

As Isaiah continues to stare up into the heavens where more stars are appearing, something envelops him. At first, he feels it only on the outside, like the embrace of a warm blanket, but soon it is on the inside as well. It is the Presence he has known since he was sixteen. It is the comforting Presence that has been with him whenever he encountered something dangerous, frightening, or sad—whether on American soil or on battlefields overseas. The Presence was even with him when the small coffin with its special cargo was lowered into the ground on that cruel day so many years ago now.

He knows what it is. No, he knows who it is. It is the Spirit of God who has never left him since the day he surrendered his life to the Commanding Officer of the universe over forty years ago.

The tears of grief on his cheeks are soon mingled with other tears. They are tears of joy, the joy that not even sadness and loneliness and fear can overwhelm because this joy is not a chuckling brook of happiness. It runs far deeper than a brook. It flows up from a spring that originates in the very heart of God and becomes a river—deep and wide.

The man standing alone in the middle of the darkness remains where he is for fifteen minutes, his face still turned upward toward the heavens. The wind is cruelly cold, but the Presence warms him inside and outside.

Eventually, something shifts within him.

He is no longer grieving. His thoughts are not on the imminent death of his dear wife. He is worshipping his Savior, who has made so many promises to him, not the least of which is that He will come back one day and take His children to be with Him in His Father's house—the house where Little Jack already lives. Death does not have the final word. His Daddy does. The One who made it all has also promised to make all things right.

Isaiah sits down next to his wife and again touches her cheek with the back of his hand. She stirs but does not awaken. He gets down on his knees and gently lays his head on his wife's chest. He feels the rise and fall of her shallow but regular breathing. He can even hear the muted beating of her heart.

"We're not home yet, Vi," he whispers as the sadness returns like a wave. "But you're going home soon, and then I'll follow."

After a silence that is deep in the dark backyard, Isaiah says, "Yes, Vi, please hug Little Jack for me and let him know that I'll see him before he knows it. And...I love you, my dear wife. I love you, Vi. Always have, always will."

The husband falls asleep with his head next to his wife's face. His last conscious awareness are words from the Spirit. They are spoken ever so softly but flood his mind and heart with peace: "Blessed are those who mourn, for they shall be comforted...He will wipe away every tear from their eyes, and death shall be no more, neither shall there be mourning, nor crying, nor pain anymore...Weeping may tarry for the night, but joy comes with the morning."

Yes, the glorious morning.

CHAPTER 28

Clyde the Glide Kildaire

Clyde Kildaire inadvertently crushes the two hands he is holding when the woman who is the sole object of his attention opens her mouth and begins to speak. Her voice is gruff and unnaturally deep. He had been instructed beforehand to keep his eyes shut throughout the "receiving of the message" no matter what happened in the dimly lit room. But Clyde is a man severely lacking in self-control. Predictably, then, as soon as Serena begins to cough, gurgle, and eventually speak, Clyde's eyes spring open and fixate on the exotic necromancer and her contorted countenance. The six other participants sitting in the human circle appear entranced. Their eyes remain obediently and firmly closed as they huddle around the small wooden table with the single candle flickering in the middle.

"I am here," Serena speaks slowly but not in her customary high-pitched voice. "Your desperation is remarkable if you must disturb me."

Clyde's body shakes with excitement beneath his long, brown trench coat that smells like sauerkraut and engine oil. He squeezes the hands on either side of him even more tightly. The woman on his left whimpers quietly, but Clyde is oblivious to her discomfort.

"I am Jacob Sutherington," the medium utters in the deeper voice, "and I know what you want with me—Clyde Kildaire."

The man's big body trembles again, but this time with excitement as well as with a tinge of fear, speaking to the dead and all. As he studies Serena, the woman's body seethes in her chair until her head abruptly jerks backward so that her face is staring at the ceiling. A grimace twists her mouth, and her throat emits an awful groan.

"I have no loyalty to you," the voice coming from Serena says slowly, gruffly. "But summoned I am, and so I will divulge my secrets veiled for generations."

Abruptly, Serena's head snaps forward so that her face is now suspended over the round table. The locks of her long, wild hair hang down like the ragged strands of an old mop.

"You will find what you're looking for in—" the voice of Jacob Sutherington via Serena pauses, and Clyde cannot contain himself any longer.

"Where?" he cries out. "Where?" His neck cranes forward from his body in an unnatural manner, and his eyeballs protrude from their sockets. His forehead and the bald front half of his skull are beaded with sweat.

The medium interrupts her summoning of Jacob Sutherington and hushes the impatient man with an upraised hand.

Eventually, the woman speaks again in the low voice that is ghastly incongruent with her physical presence. "What you seek is buried under sod and dirt—" the woman pauses— "beneath the ash tree." Another pause. "In the place nearest...the north. One hundred paces from...the river. It is adjacent to—"

Clyde is not exceptionally intelligent, but he's not downright stupid either. In his mercurial fashion, he throws away the two hands on either side of him and jumps to his feet, overturning the table in the center of the human circle. The chairs of three of his fellow message seekers tip over backward, and their occupants sprawl onto the floor. The medium, Serena, shrieks and jumps to her feet, a look of utter horror on her face.

Clyde stabs a thick, trembling finger at the necromancer and shouts, "You're a chameleon (he may not be downright stupid, but since he's not very book-smart either, he doesn't realize that he means to say 'charlatan') and a fraud! You might be able to pull the cotton over someone else's eyes, but not mine!"

The man with the long, stringy hair, yellow teeth, and crooked nose spits in the direction of the summoner of spirits and screams, "You're not getting a dime from me! Take your three-ring pony show somewhere else! I'm done here!"

The man, who has always looked most naturally attired in a single-piece orange jumpsuit, wheels away from the demolished gathering, cursing loudly. He storms out of the house and into the blinding daylight. He stomps more than he walks as he lumbers down the sidewalk. His feet land so widely apart that he leans from side to side as he strides forward.

He is muttering to himself—"nearest the north"—when his cell phone comes alive with the tune, "A Country Boy Can Survive." He fishes the device out of the pocket of his trench coat and squints his eyes as he looks to see who is disturbing him. As usual, it is his cousin, Donnie. His cousin is the only person who ever calls him, so he really does not need to check to see who is trying to reach him, but Clyde is a man of many unnecessary habits.

"Whadda ya want?" he growls into the phone.

"Jeepers!" the voice on the other end exclaims, "I must've caught you goin' into court or talkin' to your P.O."

Clyde ignores Donnie's attempt at defusing his anger and barks, "That necroromancer you told me to go see—she's nothin' but a lyin' fake! That's the last time I listen to anythin' that comes outta your ugly mug!"

"Hey, ya gotta chill," his cousin counters in his best placating voice. "Ya win some, ya lose some, Clyde. You know that, bro'."

"Shut up!" Clyde yells into his phone. "I told you not to call me bro'. You're my poor excuse for a cousin, not my brother!"

Donnie closes his eyes and shakes his head on the other end of the line. He sighs away from his phone and then returns it to his face. "You better be nice to me," he says.

Clyde stops walking and tilts his head into the phone. Then he replies slowly, "Because I should or because you got somethin' for me?"

"You know me, cuz. I always got somethin' for you," Donnie says with a self-satisfied smile. "This time's no different. My well never runs dry. Why do ya think I'm callin' you in the first place, Clydesdale? To whisper sweet nuthins in your ear?"

"Whadda ya got?" Clyde demands. "This better be good, or I'm gonna tat your face with my fist."

"Promises, promises," Donnie chides.

"So, what is it already?" Clyde yells impatiently as he throws his free hand into the air.

"You know my sister's boyfriend? The dude we call 'Porker'?"

"Of course, I know Porker, you idiot!" Clyde retorts. "I only shoot billiards with him every Friday night at Red's Tavern."

"Okay, okay," Donnie says as he raises his free hand as if to fend off an approaching bull. "You don't have to be so nice to me."

"You'd be as angry as a buzzard if you were me, too!" Clyde retorts. "After wastin' my time with that phony neck-romancer, you set me up with!"

Donnie holds the phone away from his face again and silently mouths curses in the other direction. His whiskered face is twisted in such a way that it resembles The Scream, Edvard Munch's famous painting. How he despises dealing with Clyde the Glide when the man is irritable—which is all the time.

He only returns the phone to his ear when he hears his name being taken in vain.

"I'll tell ya what I've got, big guy," Donnie says hurriedly into the phone before his cousin can launch another string of insults. "Like I was sayin', my sister's boyfriend, Porker, has a sister, Sally, and Sally has a friend named Brandi who works at that little coffee shop on Walnut."

Donnie hears a loud hissing noise through his phone that sounds like air rushing violently through clenched teeth. "What's this got to do with the price of tea in Chinatown?" Clyde growls.

"As I was sayin'," Donnie says again, attempting to ignore his cousin's characterological impatience, "Brandi was workin' at the coffee shop several weeks ago and heard a bunch of students readin' somethin' together. She told Sally, who told Porker, who told my sister, who told me just today that she thought they were students from that religious school on Oak. And"—Donnie pauses before he delivers the golden nugget—"She said they were readin' some diary they'd found in that big church next to the cemetery where people are dyin' to get in."

Donnie breaks out in loud guffaws at his attempt at humor. Clyde, who is locked in like a bird dog trying to flush out a pheasant along a fence line, ignores the humor and demands impatiently, "Tell me about this diary."

"Okay, dude. Brandi says that when she went to refill their coffees—or whatever they were drinkin'—it might have been hot chocolate, too, come to think of it..."

"Donnie, shut up and focus!" Clyde yells. "What else did Bambi say?"

"*Brandi*," Donnie corrects emphatically. "Her name is *Brandi*."

Clyde curses into the phone and fumes, "So what happened when that Brandi girl went to their table?"

"Dang, you don't have to be so huffy about it," Donnie says, sounding offended. He snorts into the phone but then continues. "She saw somethin' in the open journal when she went to the table. She said they were initials. They were...JLS."

Clyde leans his whole body into his cell phone. "You said they were JLS," he repeats loudly.

"I think I hear an echo," Donnie says, once more unable to resist an attempt at humor.

"Again, Donnie, shut up! Did Bambi hear—that woman—did she hear anythin' that they said? Did she say anythin' else?" Clyde inquires breathlessly.

"Only that the diary looked real old. 'Mythological' was her exact word, I think. No, maybe she said 'legendary.' It's possible—"

Clyde doesn't hear another word as his cousin blathers on. He is lost in thought. He drops his phone to his side and mutters to himself, "I'll bet that kid, that Jack Sutherington, was at that coffee shop. He must've found the diary that Damon was talkin' about. Maybe that's why he came to the school in the first place. And I'll bet that good old Jacob wrote about the hiding place of the treasure right in that there diary."

Clyde the Glide turns his attention back to his cousin, who is still jabbering away on the phone. "Donnie, shut up already!" he demands gruffly. "You and I got a job to do. Call Porker, and then you two meet me at the river tonight at 8:00. Not a minute late! I think we're about to find the pin in the haystack."

The large man dressed in the shin-length trench coat laughs loudly and begins stomping down the sidewalk toward his pickup truck.

CHAPTER 29

Jack's Past

It is the middle of the afternoon on a cloudy day. The pewter skies make the world feel simultaneously cozy and gloomy. The three professors are sitting around one of the large round tables in the Agatha Room, sipping coffee. Raindrops tap-dance on the cupola glass high above their heads.

"I don't think he has any idea," President Milner McNeely comments in his deep bass voice. "How could he?"

"I don't think he does either," Dr. M. B. Livingstone agrees.

Isaiah Windsor cradles his cup in strong hands. "We know this for sure?" he inquires, studying his colleagues with tired eyes.

"Louis Fagani brought it to my attention back in October," the president of the Academy explains as he fingers his close-trimmed black beard. His deep-set eyes that are hiding in caves beneath his protruding brow turn toward Dr. Windsor. He says, "He informed me that he stumbled over it by accident."

Embee smiles, then shakes her head. "If anybody could unearth it, Louis would be the one. After all, he knows the complete church history along with the names of all its members. We're talking over a century of history! I'm convinced he has a photographic memory." She pauses and adds, "Sure, he's gotten a bit slower in recent years, but he still has an amazing recollection of those details."

There is silence for a while as the three faculty members drift off into their private thoughts. The sound of distant thunder grumbles like a slow roll on a giant kettledrum, and the tap-dancing on the cupola grows louder.

"What are the odds of him ending up here, at the Academy, in an old church where his forebears were prominent members over a century ago?" Milner asks, raising his eyebrows.

"It wasn't chance," Isaiah Windsor states as he levels his steely gaze on his colleagues. "God brought him here for a reason."

"I agree," Embee says, leaning forward, her elbows resting on the table. "But why? To learn the tragic truth about family members he doesn't even know existed? What are we talking about here, anyway? Great-great grandparents? Great-great-great grandparents?"

Milner McNeely stares into his coffee cup as if the answer to his colleague's question is floating in the dark liquid. "I think Louis mentioned that Agatha and Joseph were the great-great-great-grandparents," he clarifies.

"That's a lot of *greats*," Isaiah Windsor says.

"Tell me about it," the Academy president says. His coffee cup eclipses his mouth and nose as he takes another swallow of his strong brew.

Embee absent-mindedly wipes the table with her napkin. Her brow is furrowed, and her lips are contorted by deep reflection. "So, Louis made the connection because of the last names, of course, and then traced the family history back to Jacob," she half states, half asks.

"That's what I understand," Dr. McNeely says. "Jacob, then, is his great-great-grandfather."

"And he was the lone survivor," the Warfare professor offers.

"Yes, he was the only one," Milner McNeely confirms gravely.

"So, remind me why nobody has told him yet," Isaiah Windsor asks as he slowly rubs his closed eyes with his long fingers.

Embee Livingstone shakes her head and is silent.

The Academy president shrugs and says, "None of us are convinced he would benefit in any way from knowing that information. And I suppose there is still some doubt that they are related."

"I see God's fingerprints all over this," Isaiah Windsor says with conviction. His face is haggard, but his voice is strong. "There's a divine plan unfolding. God's boots are on the ground, here," he says. "And everywhere else in the universe," he adds quietly.

Embee nods her head in affirmation. "Yes, something is clearly afoot here. Jesus definitely has my full attention, too."

"So, it looks like we wait to tell him and pray in the meantime," Milner says as he slides his cup aside with the back of his hand. "Something will eventually come of all this."

The president pauses and then says, "But before we go to God, please give us an update on Violet, will you, Isaiah?"

The man who looks cut out of stone with his square shoulders and sharp-featured face sighs deeply. He examines his folded hands for a long time before he looks up at his colleagues. "I'm headed over to the hospital immediately after this," he says quietly, glancing first at Milner and then at Embee with eyes that are deep pools of sorrow.

He pauses and sighs again. His eternally strong shoulders slump a bit as he says, "Violet is being moved to hospice." He falters a bit over the last word.

"Oh, Isaiah," Embee says, placing a hand on his arm. "I'm sorry. I'm so sorry."

CHAPTER 30

Cousins and Brothers in Crime

They meet at a hole-in-the-wall bar near the Farmer's Market that still permits smoking—against city regulations, of course. The redbrick walls inside the establishment are littered haphazardly with sports memorabilia and automobile antiques from a by-gone era. The grill of a '57 Chevy Impala bursts through the wall above the corner table where the four men sit nursing their drinks. An ancient jukebox blares out an even more ancient country song crooned by a dead man.

The lights are so low and the smoke so thick that the vision of the four men is severely compromised—an optometrist would encounter better eyesight in an octogenarian patient afflicted with late-stage, milky-white cataracts. The full moon peeking in through the single window in the bar offers better illumination to the four men speaking in low voices. But then, light is the last thing these men desire. Darkness is their medium, on the outside and, even more sinisterly, on the inside. They do not simply dabble in it. They are dedicated to it.

Especially two of the men.

Donnie peers at Clyde through the gloom. His typically brash blowhard cousin with the misshapen nose and the crooked teeth is ostensibly humble around the two other men, almost obsequious. Donnie is mystified by his cousin's deference toward these men who he has never seen before.

The two strangers are wearing gray dress pants, matching suit coats, and muted button-down shirts with long sleeves and no ties. One of the men has an athletic build with broad shoulders and a face that verges on being handsome despite its flat nose. He is big but not as big as Clyde. The other stranger is medium-sized with no outstanding features except for protruding eyes and no neck. His head appears to grow out of his chest. The men sport matching crew cuts but no visible tats or scars. They look like run-of-the-mill businessmen, not the usual mobsters and ex-cons that Clyde the Glide would have met during one of his involuntary stays at the state-run resort—the one remarkable for its barred windows and armed housekeepers.

As Donnie continues to study the two suits, he soon becomes aware that they exude an aura that makes him feel extremely uncomfortable. They smile and laugh like ordinary people, but their eyes are reptilian—flat and unblinking. Donnie decides he'd rather encounter an assassin in a dark alley than deal with these two men. But here he is, sitting at a table with the two cold-blooded creatures because his obnoxious cousin has demanded that he be present. It is one among many perilous adventures Clyde has roped him into beginning in the fourth grade when his cousin dared him to throw a cherry bomb into a school latrine.

The larger of the two reptiles sitting across from Clyde smiles. It is not a warm smile, certainly not even a genuine smile. Donnie doesn't trust it for a second. He can't help but remember his father's oft-repeated warning from his childhood: "Son, never trust a smile. Never. Faces lie." These wise words always came after his father had just disciplined him with a 2x4.

The smiling man says, "So, Mr. Kildaire, help me understand the situation. You've been on our payroll for six months now with no material progress to justify your compensation except for a journal that—"

"A diary," Clyde corrects, unable to stop his mouth from saying what his brain is thinking. "It's a diary."

The man obviously does not like being interrupted. His flat eyes stare coldly at the stringy-haired ex-con with the straggly beard and bloodshot eyes. Clyde falls silent, and his gaze drifts to the brick wall behind the two men. He sees but does not register the message of the neon light flashing in soft blue tones, "Cenosillicaphobia."

The suit with the lying face speaks to Clyde again. This time there is no smile. "To clarify, all you have is a lousy diary that some kids were reading in a coffee shop near the school. That's the sum of your progress to this point."

"I tell you, it's a breakdown," Clyde insists, displaying yet another example of his faulty mastery of the English language.

Donnie shakes his head ever so slightly and looks away. Between clenched teeth, he whispers, "*Breakthrough*, you idiot. It's called a *breakthrough*."

"Bambi says the diary is important," Clyde insists.

"Who the heck is Bambi?" the larger reptile inquires as frustration mingled with disinterest slithers into his flat eyes.

"She's...she's—" The ex-con sits frozen for a moment, then roughly elbows his cousin in the ribs and says, "You tell 'em, Donnie."

Donnie gives his obnoxious cousin the evil eye and sighs in disgust. Then he says, "It's Brandi, remember? Not Bambi. Brandi is my sister's boyfriend's little sister's friend."

The man with broad shoulders shakes his head and glances over at his companion, who also shakes his head. "This just keeps getting better and better," he growls.

"Listen!" Clyde exclaims way too forcefully. He catches himself and calms down. "Listen," he says with a rare display of disciplined evenness as a current of fear flows through his face. "The diary they was readin' was old. The initials written in it were JLS."

Donnie watches the two men as closely as he can in the gloom. Their faces remain unaltered by their lowbrow protégé's words—they are masks of stone—but their eyes narrow, and the talking man's tongue flicks across his lips. Disinterest has finally been eclipsed by curiosity.

"JLS, you say," the man with a neck repeats.

Clyde nods his big, balding head that has always reminded Donnie of the Half Dome rock formation in Yosemite Valley, which, incidentally, he has only seen on the history channel. "You told me to look for anythin' relatin' to Jacob Sutherington or Philip DaFoe," he says. "You know, those old stiffs."

"Cold-eyes" glares at Clyde and retorts, "One of those old stiffs is Jacob, my great, great grandfather," he lies. "I must insist that you refer to my family with respect. Understand, idiot?"

Donnie's eyes slide over to watch his cousin's blood pressure climb. His face is already a bright shade of crimson. Donnie grips the table, ready to run if he needs to make a quick escape from the bar brawl that is on the verge of erupting. Amazingly, Clyde holds his temper in check, a temper that has a long and storied rap sheet of indiscretions that attests to the man's outrageous impulsivity.

Clyde grunts and repositions his big body on the black faux-leather chair. Ignoring the man's insult, he says, "There's more."

"More. What do you mean, more?" the businessman asks, his face impatient but his eyes still betraying thinly-veiled interest.

Clyde is slow to respond to the man's question. Donnie knows that his cousin is taking sadistic pleasure—or revenge—in the power he has over his two superiors by tantalizingly withholding the coveted information as long as he can.

"Well, what is it?" the snake-in-a-suit demands with growing impatience.

Clyde hesitates a bit longer. Donnie pictures the businessman molting his skin right before their eyes in his utter frustration.

Finally, Clyde reveals the withheld information as if announcing the combination to a bank vault. "My resources tell me that one of the people at the coffee shop who was readin' the diary signed his 'John Henry' on the credit card receipt. His name was Jack Sutherington."

There is silence as the two men in suits absorb their hired hand's words. Donnie can read in their faces that Clyde's revelation is potentially the missing link to the whole safari—whatever its final objective might be. Even the masks of stone betray a hint of excitement.

The two reptiles have chosen not to practice full disclosure with their henchmen. All that Clyde and Donnie know is that their handlers have been paying them decent money to root out any information they can find about the dead men, Jacob Sutherington and Philip DaFoe. Clyde and Donnie have been around the block enough times to know that revenge or money or both must be involved, but most likely not revenge since the men in question died a hundred years ago. That only leaves money—big money, likely.

The two cousins always take a deep personal interest when big money is on the table. They listen carefully for what is being said between the lines and also for what is not being said. Neither of them is particularly book-smart, but they're both street-smart, as savvy as two old hound dogs on the hunt.

The large man with the flat nose who is the designated speaker finally smiles—as falsely as before. He says, "Get me everything you can on this Jack Sutherington. Everything. And don't let him out of your sight."

"I'm a leap year ahead of you," Clyde laughs through his straggly beard, flashing his crooked, yellowed teeth. "I've already been followin' him and his friends. Just call me a tick on a warthog."

There is a short pause before the designated speaker insists flatly, "And bring me that diary. Get it any way you can as soon as you can." He locks eyes with Clyde. The big-ex con holds the crocodile's gaze admirably for a few seconds until he finally averts his eyes.

"You can go now," the broad-shouldered man says with a wave of his hand as if dismissing children. "You know how to reach me when you have what I want."

Clyde nods his head and slaps the table loudly. "Okay, I guess that's all he wrote," he announces with a loud laugh that draws stares from several other bar patrons. The two cousins awkwardly linger a moment longer in their black faux-leather chairs. Then they get up and, without any words of parting, make their way through the smoky haze toward the front door. Clyde's large frame leans back and forth in harmony with his unique stomping gait.

After the two cousins have left, the talking suit rattles the ice in his empty glass. "I was ready to say, 'never send two idiots to do a man's job.' But now it sounds like they finally found something, Aamon."

The smaller man with the protruding eyes and no neck nods in agreement. "They're uneducated and stupid, but hopefully, they have just enough gray matter to accomplish what we're using them for. You don't want them too smart, of course, but then you don't want them too dumb, either. But I agree. It looks like they've finally picked up the scent, Damon."

"Now we'll wait and see if Laurel and Hardy can stay on the trail or not," the larger man says with a grunt.

The one named Aamon says, "I have to admit, that diary has me salivating."

Damon nods and says, "We can only hope that good old Jacob made mention of the coins in his diary—if indeed it is his."

"I feel confident it's his, all right," Aamon claims as his head bobs slowly on its shoulders. "JLS has to be Jacob Lane Sutherington. Who else would it be?"

Damon sets his glass down precisely in the center of the paper coaster and looks at his brother. "We can only hope that the housekeeper's granddaughter was right about Philip's missing coins," he says.

"We wouldn't be putting all this time and money into this little endeavor if we didn't believe she was right," Aamon comments.

"True," Damon concurs. "After all, we did discover one of the coins in the attic of the old house—only after we removed the current owner, of course. And we can't forget that the old stiff, Philip, wrote that letter before he disappeared stating that Jacob Sutherington had killed his wife and stolen his collection of Seated Lady Liberty Silver Dollars."

Aamon smiles and stares off into the gloom of the dimly lit bar. "Remind me again, brother, how many of the beautiful ladies are missing."

"Two baker's dozen," the large man with the flat nose replies as he picks up his glass again and rattles the ice.

"And how much are those ladies worth in today's market? Tell me again, Damon."

"Numismatic value or intrinsic value?" he says with a wicked laugh.

"Both."

"Intrinsic value—a little north of $13 dollars apiece," Damon states with a deadpan face. "Numismatic value to the right collector—one point nine five nine million dollars."

"Remind me, is that for all twenty-six combined?"

"You know, Aamon."

"Yes, I know, but I like hearing you say it. Tell me again."

"One point nine five nine million...apiece," Damon announces.

"Fifty-one mill total," Aamon says with a low whistle. "I'd be willing to kill for that much money."

The older brother turns to his younger brother and looks him squarely in his reptilian eyes. "You already have," Damon replies. "And kill again you will," he states matter-of-factly as he lifts his transparent glass and examines the ice as if it is an exhibit in an aquarium. "Once those two buffoons point us to the location of those coins, we'll have to off them, of course. They may be idiots, but they're curious idiots. Much too curious for my liking."

"Clyde and Donnie—almost like Bonnie and Clyde," Aamon says sardonically. "What classic names for two dolts from the hill country. Two dolts who will meet a tragic demise and whose bodies will never be found."

The man without a neck pauses and then adds, "Maybe one other dolt will meet a tragic fate if it turns out he's here to collect the coins for himself. What's the kid's name again?"

"Jack," Damon says flatly. "Jack Sutherington. A babe in the woods, no doubt."

As the two brothers conspire in the dark corner of the bar, two other individuals sit beside them in the chairs that Donnie and Clyde recently vacated. The two newcomers have no names. They are not known or seen. They are there only to perform their wicked functions. If they succeed, there is no approbation. If they fail, they are reviled.

They exist to carry out the will of their master: to steal, destroy and kill. Their purpose is to ensure that those still breathing in the land of the living will soon join them in the shadows, in the nothingness. Their job is relatively easy at times. So many of the image-bearers willingly embrace philosophies like nihilism and secularism and theologies like agnosticism and atheism. It's like shooting sleeping elephants.

The first shadow-being who quivers like an ethereal 3D image in the chair speaks in a gravelly voice, "*These humans are dead where they sit. They're so insatiably hungry for the idol of money that they will never see the Glory—ugh—the One they are made for.*" His voice quavers as much as his "body" quivers, for he is not solid; he is not alive as one might think of being alive. He exists, yes, but what an unbridgeable abyss yawns between existing and living.

The other being agrees. "*These humans are made to worship, so all we must do is lure them away from Him by tempting them to worship something else.*"

"*The concept is really quite elementary,*" the first being says. "*It's all about The Exchange. We are here to tempt them to satisfy their hearts with primitive lusts instead of with Him, to exchange Him for material pleasures and intellectual philosophies that are rampant with self-sufficiency and devoid of Him. Yes, it's all about The Exchange. The Exchange. The Exchange.*"

The other being laughs coldly and remarks, "*It's beyond me. I can't comprehend how they are so witless as to exchange the Maker of the universe for round shiny things that cannot comfort or love or befriend. How incredibly insane that they choose baubles and beads over the eternal Treasure. These creatures settle for so little when they could have so much more."*

The other dark presence exclaims, "*The definition of hell: Exchanging the presence of Him for fleeting pleasure. Of course, one doesn't get to hell in a moment,*" the being says knowingly. "*Ten million decisions over eighty years either move a person toward Him or far, far away from Him until they can't even tolerate His presence. Ten million exchanges. Ten million regrets one day when it's too late. Too late. Too late.*"

"*How ironic,*" the other fallen one says as his mouth quivers like a failing hologram, "*that some of their religious leaders claim that He is love and therefore no one will ever end up in hell. How can they not see that many of these creatures simply detest the presence of a being who asks for their obedience and their worship? They cannot even obey their own parents or any other authority in their lives, so why would they ever wish to spend forever with Him who is the Authority above all authorities?*"

The other being smirks and says, "*And how many of these fallen creatures brazenly declare that they hope there's no God because they want to be free to do whatever they wish, accountable to no one, unfettered by law or morality? No law or morality. No law or morality.*"

The other dark one opens his mouth to speak again to his fellow demon when he realizes that he is alone. The whole time, he has been conversing only with himself. Oh, the absolute emptiness of rejecting the One who is the author of intimacy and love!

Oh, the deep, deep, aloneness.

Oh, the utter isolation. Isolation...Isolation

A block away, Clyde and Donnie are sitting in the gray Silverado pickup. "These are the type of hoods who leave no tracks," Donnie says as he wipes his mouth with the back of his hand. "If we help 'em find what they're lookin' for, you know they're gonna tie up every loose end."

"Already thought about that, cuz," Clyde grumbles as he flashes the whites of his eyes at Donnie in the dark cab. "You just might be right. You just might not be right," he adds in his enigmatic way. "But we've got to prepare for the worst-case cinema."

"Scenario!" Donnie snaps, ever amazed at his cousin's verbal miscues. "It's case scenario, Clyde, not cinema."

"Shut up!" the big man retorts angrily as spittle flies out of his mouth and onto the steering wheel. "Stop correctin' my words! I know what I mean, and you know what I mean, so that's all that matters!"

Donnie mumbles something under his breath, but fortunately, Clyde doesn't hear him. The big man has already moved on in his mind.

"We've got to get our hands on that diary, ASAT," Clyde insists. Donnie rolls his eyes and turns to look out the window into the dewy gloom that has turned the parking lot into a silver sheet. "We gotta see what's written in there. Maybe there's a treasure map or a riddle that will help us find whatever they're so hifalutin' about findin'."

"Now you're talkin'," Donnie agrees as he turns away from the truck window and looks at his cousin. "Then we'll keep it all for ourselves. Finders, keepers!" he exclaims as he slaps the dashboard with an open hand and laughs loudly.

Clyde turns his head slowly toward his animated cousin and stares at him. His jaw is tight, and his eyes are narrowed in deep disgust. "How many times do I gotta tell ya to respect the truck, Donnie?" he screams. "Ten times? A hundred times? Don't touch my truck!"

Donnie curses loudly but only in his head because he knows that he's in too-tight quarters with his crazy cousin to say anything rash. He knows that the big man will backhand him if he says anything too smart like, "My butt is touchin' your truck this very minute." Or, better yet, "I'm drooling on your precious seat even as I speak."

When Clyde has cooled down, Donnie turns back to his cousin and says, "Save your anger, big man. Save it for the two dudes back at the bar. Save it for Jack Sutherington. Who knows, you may need to beat information out of him before all this is said and done."

"I can do that, cuz," Clyde says as he reaches down and turns the key in the ignition, and the engine growls to life. "I can most certainly do that."

CHAPTER 31

The Tip of the Spear

Jack shifts the Jeep Wrangler into second gear, and the vehicle accelerates smoothly. With the roof, windows, and doors secured in place, the passengers stay toasty warm on this early December day that is seasonably cold at 39 degrees. Aly relaxes in the front passenger seat while Armando and Rachel sit in the back seat of the four-door vehicle. Emily and Stewart are working shifts at the hotel and so are unable to participate in the bi-monthly Tip of the Spear outreach.

Jack shakes his head and laughs as he recalls Stewart's last ride in his vehicle. Unsolicited, his micro-cohort friend had volunteered a detailed review of his Wrangler, including anticipated gas mileage, vehicle safety testing results, roll-over danger, reliability, the integrity of the interior hardware, and the substandard comfort of the ride. Stewart had concluded his evaluation with the familiar criticism that Jeep stands for Just Empty Every Pocket because reliable evidence suggested that maintenance costs were not for the faint of heart.

Jack responded to the Intellect by educating him concerning the unique features of a Jeep, including its amazing relevance to the back roads of Colorado as well as the priceless intangible of being a member of the worldwide Jeep family.

At a four-way stop, Jack makes a left turn and thinks further about Stewart. In his estimation, the bespectacled member of the Screaming Eagles has begun to speak a little more from his heart and less from his brain. His encounter with Miriam, his experience in the Cave of Dread, and even his ongoing spelunking with McNeely all seem to be working together to crack open the safe of his heart—albeit rather slowly.

"So, how do you guys feel about today?" Jack inquires, glancing into his rearview mirror.

There is a short silence. The only sound comes from the rugged tires of the Jeep as they growl softly over the paved street.

"I find it more challenging than the Bridge," Rachel observes, referring to the regular outreach to homeless people near the downtown area.

"Yeah, the people at the Bridge have been humbled by life more than the students at the university," Armando states as he inserts his head between the front seats of the vehicle. "They seem more open to admitting that they need help."

Aly pulls her jacket around her small body more tightly and says, "Many of them are even willing to admit that they need God's help. They remind me of Jesus' comment that He came for the sick, not for those who think they're well and have no need for a physician."

"I'm probably not a huge fan of the Tip of the Spear approach," Armando acknowledges. "It reminds me of a job I had in college cold calling for a financial planning company. I got burned out in the end by all the rejections," he says with a deep sigh. "I only lasted three weeks."

Jack nods and says, "No doubt about it. Cold calling is a lot tougher than waiting for someone to come up to you and ask you about Jesus," he says with a smile. "Obviously, it is a lot less intimidating to share the good news with someone you already know. Under most circumstances, at least—unless it's your future father-in-law whose favorite authors are Richard Dawkins and Sam Harris."

"At least we're not responsible for the results," Rachel offers. "We're just called to share the good news of Jesus' love and let the Holy Spirit do the rest. He's the only one who can soften hard hearts that are set against God."

"I still feel a bit embarrassed about sharing the gospel with strangers," Armando says with a big sigh. "And then I'm embarrassed that I'm embarrassed. You'd think I would be more courageous about witnessing for God after all the violence I faced in gangland. I shouldn't have any stage fright, one would think."

"In your defense," Aly says as she turns her head to look at Armando, who is leaning halfway into the front seat, "when you speak to people about Jesus, you're engaging in spiritual warfare. I remember how angry and offended I felt whenever people online shared their faith in Jesus with me before I was a believer. You wouldn't have wanted to be on the other end of my verbal attacks, Armando." The dark-haired woman with large brown eyes crinkles her small nose and shakes her head. "I was a genuine fanatic—a hater."

"Thanks for that, Aly," Armando replies. He chuckles and adds, "Call me stupid, but I just can't picture you as a fanatic female jihadist."

The young man from LA slides into the back seat and announces to Jack, "Just an FYI—if you hadn't already noticed, we're being followed."

"What?" Jack exclaims as he glances at his friend in the rearview mirror.

"We're being tailed," Armando repeats in such a casual voice that it sounds like an everyday occurrence for him.

Jack looks in his rearview mirror past Armando and then into his side mirrors.

"It's the gray Chevy Silverado with the winch," Armando comments without turning around.

"Okay, I see it," Jack says with a nod of his head. "The extended cab. How do you know it's following us?"

"I saw it sitting next to the cemetery on Lincoln Drive when we left the Academy."

"How do you know it's the same truck?" Rachel asks.

"I notice things without trying," Armando replies. "Back in La Puente, the only way we survived was having eyes in the back of our heads." He pauses and then mumbles, "Even then, it didn't always save you."

"I have no idea why anyone would be following us," Jack says as much to himself as to his passengers. He looks in the rearview mirror again and announces, "But it's still there—three vehicles back."

"Does anybody here have any known enemies or owe back taxes to the IRS?" Jack asks half-seriously as he keeps his eyes on the road ahead.

His three passengers glance at each other. Armando offers, "I don't think any gangsters from the Left Coast are still looking for me six years after I walked away from the barrio. And I'm almost certain I made no enemies at the Christian university I attended up in the Twin Cities. Minnesota Nice, you know," he says, winking at Rachel.

Jack turns his head to look at the woman in the front passenger seat. "Sorry to ask, Aly, but I know at the amphitheater you shared about your... your radical brother."

Aly shakes her head confidently and asserts, "No, it can't be Mahmoud. He doesn't even know I'm in America. He thinks I'm still back in Thailand somewhere, probably Bangkok."

"Okay," Jack says with a slow nod. Then he turns on his signal and says, "Well, here we are at the university. I'll park in our usual spot, and we'll see if the truck still follows us."

Jack negotiates the black Wrangler into a parking spot and kills the engine. All four of its occupants watch as the gray Silverado cruises past them and continues down the road.

"A false positive," Rachel sighs with relief as she pushes her auburn hair off her cheek.

"Maybe," Armando says cautiously. "I still think that truck was tailing us."

Jack takes a deep breath and blows it out quickly. "Well, let's do this. Let's get on campus and break up into our witnessing dyads and go about our business as usual. Just be vigilant about what's going on around you since we might have a tail."

Jack pauses, then says, "Aly, I'm pairing you up with our ex-gangster, Syko Loco, today. You'll be especially safe since you're with the guy who has the eyes in the back of his head."

"That's me," Armando says loudly. "The one and only."

After they get out of the Jeep, they pause under a towering eucalyptus tree that has relinquished its leaves to the never-sated demands of autumn gravity. They pray that the Holy Spirit will guide them to someone with whom they can share the good news of God's amazing love. Then Jack and Rachel set off in one direction and Aly and Armando in the other.

After speaking briefly to several random students, they encounter on the university lawn, Jack and Rachel spot a lone male sitting on a bench beside a sign that reads, "Pillsbury Fine Arts Center." Jack and Rachel glance at each other and wordlessly agree that they will go over and talk with the young man.

As they approach the bench, Jack prays in his head, *Jesus, prepare this man's heart for us to speak with him. May he be receptive to your word of love and truth that will change his life forever.*

When Jack's shadow falls over him and lingers there, the young man looks up from his phone. "Hey," Jack says agreeably. "How's it goin'?"

The student, whose curly brown hair frames a broad pale face, replies, "It's goin'." He holds Jack's gaze for a moment, then turns his attention back to his phone.

Jack clears his throat and says, "This is Rachel, and my name's Jack. We hang out on campus a couple of times a month and discuss the topic of God's existence with people. Are you cool talking to us for a few minutes?"

The bench-sitter looks up again and narrows his eyes. He asks, "Are you Jehovah Witnesses?"

Rachel shakes her head and says in her northeast accent, "Not a chance. We're here simply because Jesus loves us, and we want to share that love with others."

The young man seems to enjoy Rachel's presence. He looks at her with an awkward smile and comments, "I'll talk with you about God, but I'll warn you, I'm a hard nut to crack."

"Probably no worse than I was," Rachel replies without hesitation. "I'm a stubborn, independent girl from New England."

"Do we have your permission to join you on the bench?" Jack inquires. "Unless you'd rather talk someplace else."

The student hesitates, and then his fingers begin to fly over the keys of his phone, "I'm going to ask my roommate if he wants to join us."

Ten minutes later, Theo—the young man on the bench—and three other students from his dorm are sitting together in a small lounge in the student commons building, only twenty feet removed from one of the campus cafeterias. The distinct smell of pizza and French fries permeates the lounge.

"This should be good," a student named Pete comments quietly to his friend as he rubs his hands together in anticipation. "Nothing like fighting off the Christian missionaries."

Jack looks at the four university students sitting around him and Rachel and asks, "Any of you guys into sports?"

"We all play sports," Theo replies as he looks at his friends, who all nod their heads.

"What do you play?" Jack asks.

The biggest athlete in the group jabs a thick thumb into his chest and remarks in a deep bass voice, "Me, I play O-line on the gridiron. Pete, here, is the kicker, the smallest guy on the team. I call him 'mini-me.' Theo and Paul play hoops, the second-best sport in the world."

"Great!" Jack says with a smile. "You guys will connect with what I'm going to talk about." He pauses and looks at the big football lineman. "What's your name?" he asks.

"Andrew," the man who looks to be all of 6'6" and 300 pounds replies in his deep voice. "'Drew' for short."

"Okay, Drew, Pete, Theo, and Paul," Jack begins, "the first thing I want to ask you guys is if you've ever been on the field or court when your team won the big game."

"Mini-me" a.k.a. Pete is quick to respond. "In high school, I booted a 38-yarder to win the section championship against Greenburg."

Paul, a dark-skinned student who is the tallest of the four men, says, "Just last week, I drained a twenty-five-foot jump shot in OT to win our first conference game."

"Way to go, dude!" Jack says with genuine enthusiasm. "That's an NBA three-pointer!"

Theo and Drew look at each other as they attempt to remember their big moment. Theo offers, "Obviously, Drew and I were on the field or court during an exciting win. Maybe not as big a game as what Pete and Paul referred to, but still a big game."

Drew chuckles and says, "Honestly, I think my big game goes all the way back to sixth grade. Believe it or not, I was a running back in those days. I was built like a fire hydrant—a man among boys—which is still true today," he announces as he looks around at his peers with a sneer on his face.

After some head shaking and a few "whatevers" from the other three guys, Drew continues. "I scored seven touchdowns in my first game as running back," he announces with a broad smile. "After the game, I stayed up half the night replaying every touchdown in my head until I finally fell asleep from sheer exhaustion. I must have scored two hundred times in my head."

"You had the game of a lifetime that day, but I'll bet you never scored more than three TDs in a game after that," Jack says with a smile.

"How do you know that?" Drew responds with raised eyebrows.

"Because any coach worth his salt would instruct his players to hit you low instead of high after that first monster game of yours," Jack replies. "The secret to tackling a fire hydrant is to hit him below the knees and hope a teammate will wrap him up."

Drew smiles and says, "Man, you got that right. My production went downhill after that first game. I had brute strength but no moves."

"Yeah," Pete says with a smirk, "you've always made a better gravel truck than a Lamborghini!"

Everyone laughs, even Rachel, who seems to be tracking the sports talk just fine.

"The reason I bring up the big game is because I was fortunate to play in a few of them," Jack goes on to explain. "The biggest was the DII football college championship game."

Rachel glances at Jack with mild surprise in her eyes.

"What position?" Drew asks.

"QB," Jack replies.

All four young men nod their heads. Pete lets out a quiet whistle and says, "Props to you." If Jack had failed to earn the respect of any of the athletes earlier, he definitely has it now.

"I had great teammates," Jack says. "Seriously, my O-line was the best in the nation at that level. You know how important those guys are, right Drew?"

The big man raises both arms and displays his biceps for all to see. "Anchors of the team!" he shouts.

Theo and Paul punch the big man in his exposed ribs. Pete retorts, "Shut up, Drew! Everyone knows the kicker is boss!"

"Yeah," Drew parries, "the boss of the loss!"

"You're just jealous, Drew, because you never got to touch the pigskin after the sixth grade," Pete retorts.

"Not true!" the huge O-lineman disagrees. "I once recovered a fumble and ran it in for a score!"

"In the seventh grade," Theo jabs.

"And you ran it the wrong way, fool," Paul laughs.

Everyone hoots as Drew reaches out his long arms and puts Theo and

Paul into matching headlocks.

"Okay, listen up," Jack says, interrupting the scrum in the lounge. "The championship game I played in certainly was not a defensive struggle. We were down 45-41 with seven seconds to go in the fourth quarter. Our ball. Fourth and eight. Their thirty-five-yard line. I get the snap and immediately drop the rock."

"Crap!" Drew cries out as if he has some vested interest in the game. He releases his two friends from their matching headlocks and leans toward Jack.

"My O-line protection is excellent," Jack continues, glancing at Drew, "so I have time to grab the ball and roll right. The 'D' is running a zone blitz, so I know one of my receivers has to be open. I sidestep the blitzing Mike linebacker and roll right. It's then that I see Bucky streaking down the right sideline. The strong safety is in my face, so I throw off my back foot. It's a wing and a prayer, guys. Mostly prayer."

By now, everyone is locked into Jack's story. Rachel smiles and shakes her head. *Boys will be boys*, she thinks to herself.

"The corner plays the zone too loosely," Jack says. "My receiver has a step on him. My duck of a pass falls into Bucky's arms at the fifteen-yard line, and he races in for the score. Boom! Game over. We win the championship!"

"Truly awesome!" Drew exclaims as he sits forward on the couch.

"What a feeling!" Paul remarks, staring at Jack with respect written all over his face. "You must've been buzzed like never before!"

Jack smiles and says, "Here's my point, men—and Paul, you're exactly right." The four friends fall silent and rivet their eyes on Jack.

"The emotion I felt at that moment was unlike anything I'd ever felt,"

Jack says, his eyes flashing with intensity. "A chill literally ran through my body as my teammates rushed toward me. I stood there, frozen, for a second, then started laughing hysterically and screaming. I ran and jumped into the arms of my left guard," he says, smiling at Drew. "I felt like we'd won the Super Bowl!"

"No doubt," Pete says, nodding his head.

"Just like you, Drew, after your seven TDs in sixth grade," Jack says, "I was up half the night watching that play over and over on my phone."

Jack shakes his head and then adds a bit grimly, "I was also up half the night because after I released the ball on that last play, the strong safety speared me, and I hit the ground awkwardly. I ended up tearing the rotator cuff in my throwing arm."

"Dang!" Pete says, his face twisted in dismay.

"Not the injury you want as a QB," Drew responds as a look of anguish replaces the excitement that had been on his face.

"Didn't even know I tore it," Jack informs them, running his fingers through his haystack hair. "The adrenaline had me pumped so high."

There is a moment of silence. Then Jack leans toward the four young men sitting on the couch and confides, "Many professional athletes won the biggest game on the biggest stage. They threw the game-winning pass, caught the game-winning ball, intercepted the should-have-been game-winning-pass, made the key block, split the uprights for the Super Bowl win, hit the three-point shot to win the NBA championship, or sank the sixty-foot putt on the last playoff hole."

Jack pauses and looks into the faces of the university students with his piercing blue eyes.

"All these winning athletes experienced the rush," Jack eventually says.

"You guys know what I'm talking about."

All four men nod their heads.

"And you all know what's true about the rush after it peaks, right?" Jack inquires.

"It doesn't last," Theo replies without hesitation.

"Yeah, you always come down from the high," Drew says.

"Exactly," Jack says. "Some of those professional athletes I referred to have talked publicly about that experience. They've described that when the rush was over, and they crashed emotionally, they felt extremely empty inside. In fact, one football player who won the Super Bowl said that several days later, he went out and bought a $275,000 Lamborghini to try to fill the emptiness."

Jack looks at Theo and says, "But even after buying that amazing vehicle, he said he still felt so empty inside that he couldn't be happy. Something was missing."

Rachel can see by the expressions on the athletes' faces that they are intimately familiar not only with the rush but also with the subsequent crash. All joking has been set aside. The students are in lockstep with the young man who is four years their senior.

"This star cornerback who buys the Lamborghini eventually meets a fellow NFL player over a meal, and they talk about the emptiness," Jack says. "Then he goes home.

"In the middle of the night, this Super Bowl winner wakes up and senses that God is in the room with him. He lies in his bed, shocked and amazed. After a while, he gets up, opens his Bible, and reads a passage that talks about confessing that Jesus is Lord and believing that God raised him from the dead.

"At that moment, he knows he has finally found what his heart has been longing for. He asks Jesus to come into his heart and fill his emptiness. Jesus answers him in that very moment and transforms his life forever," Jack says with passion in his voice and on his face.

"This Super Bowl winner is just one of many people over the years who tried to fill their emptiness with fleeting pleasures only to find that they're still empty," Jack says. He pauses and then adds, "As one man said centuries ago, 'You have made us for yourself, O Lord, and our heart is restless until it rests in you.' There's a hunger inside all of us that nothing in this world can satisfy. Only God can do that."

When Jack is done speaking, the four athletes stare at him awkwardly. The lounge area is quiet, but a constant waterfall of noise spills out of the adjacent cafeteria.

Eventually, Theo sits forward on the couch and cracks his knuckles. Pete clears his throat, and his eyes find refuge on the carpeted floor. Tall Paul and big Drew continue to look at Jack with eyes that reveal nothing.

Rachel clears her throat and says, "So, guys, we're here on campus to share the love of Jesus with you. His love changed my life and filled my emptiness, and now I want others to have the same abundant life I've been given. As Jack said, only Jesus can fill the emptiness of the human heart. We're made by Him and for Him, and nothing else will ultimately satisfy us."

The young woman's face flushes with a red hue that resembles her vivid hair. She is not accustomed to having the attention of four young men.

Theo looks at Rachel and frowns. "Isn't that a bit arrogant," he comments with an edge in his voice, "claiming that Jesus is the only one who can satisfy people? What about Mohammed and Buddha and the gods of Hinduism and all the other paths to God?"

"Muhammad, Buddha, and the Dalai Lama never claimed to be God," Rachel says without hesitation. "Jesus did." Although Rachel is nervous, there is also a part of her that enjoys the attention of the small audience in front of her.

"How do you know Jesus even existed?" Pete chimes in. "That was like two thousand years ago."

"You can check it out, Pete," Rachel says. "There aren't many historians who doubt that Jesus walked this earth and was crucified."

"Crucified?" Drew asks. "What's that?"

Jack and Rachel glance at each other, aware of what the other is thinking. Dr. Greenlay is right. Only thirty or forty years ago, he said, most everyone in America knew who Jesus was and what He did on the cross. Increasingly, however, as God becomes more marginalized in the postmodern world, the contemporary culture is ignorant of Jesus and the details around His life, death, and resurrection.

Rachel rolls her head to move her hair from her face and says, "Crucifixion, you could say, is the Roman version of the electric chair. They decided that Jesus was guilty of something deserving death, so they nailed Him to a cross by His hands and feet, and He hung there for hours." She swallows hard and adds, "He slowly suffocated to death and may have died of blood loss or exposure. Crucifixion was a cruel means of execution, but Jesus loved us so much that He chose to die for us in that horrific way."

"If Jesus claimed to be God," Paul inquires with sincerity, "how could He die? Why would He die?"

"Those are the right questions," Rachel says, taking a line she had heard from Jack. "Jesus had to die to build a bridge between us and God the Father. Our sin, our disobedience, and our desire to live our lives outside of God's will had separated us from the Father, who is perfect and cannot allow anything unholy to approach Him. As sinful people, we could no more reach God than walk to Australia.

"When Jesus died, He paid the penalty for our rebellion and disobedience. In exchange, He gave us His perfect goodness so that when the Father looks at us, He sees Jesus in us. Because of this amazing exchange, we can now be friends with God. We can approach Him and be close to Him—just as it was back in the beginning."

Drew asks, "So are you saying that we can't get close to God by doing good works, that we can't make ourselves good enough to earn our way to heaven?"

"Exactly, Drew," Rachel says, nodding her head in affirmation. "That's why God the Father sent Jesus the Son to our planet to initiate a rescue operation that led to the Great Reconciliation between us and God the Father."

"Now we can walk to Australia," Drew comments, clearly tracking with Rachel. "Jesus is the bridge."

"Yes," Rachel says with more vigorous nodding, "and the emptiness that Jack was talking about can be filled in us because when we believe in Jesus, He sends His Spirit to live in our hearts. We will never be alone again."

"It's been real, boys and girls," Theo interjects with a mirthless chuckle as he glances at his phone. "I gotta get to P-chem, pronto. Maybe I'll catch up to you Jesus freaks another time," he says as he gets up and nods curtly in the direction of Jack and Rachel. Before either Academy student can say a word, the young man turns his back and walks away. Paul and Pete are quick to excuse themselves as well. Left behind by his friends' quick exit, only Drew remains.

The massive young man, whose squarish face sits atop a thick neck between two hulking shoulders, glances from Rachel to Jack. He is not unhandsome. "I need to run, too," he announces in his bass voice that fits his body size perfectly.

As the O-lineman gets to his feet and grabs his backpack as if it is an empty milk carton, he says to Jack, "Give me your phone number. Maybe I'll give you a call sometime."

After he has entered Jack's contact information into his phone, Drew pauses and looks at the two Jesus believers. "Thanks," he says in a surprisingly soft voice. "To be honest, I know I'm empty. I know I need more than what I've got going right now. Beer doesn't fill the emptiness. Neither does smoking a dime bag with my buddies or random hookups, for that matter. None of it is ultimately satisfying. I just don't know if I'm ready to give it all up for an unknown commodity—because even though none of those things last, they do bring some pleasure for a while. Something's better than nothing."

He looks away from his two listeners toward the cafeteria. Then he says so quietly that Jack and Rachel can barely hear him, "Pray for me. I need help." Then he strides away and is gone.

Ten minutes later, the four Academy friends rendezvous at the Jeep and climb in. They spend the drive back to the Citadel praying for Drew and a girl named Skyler, who Aly and Armando had spoken with in the library. They are so engaged talking to Jesus and each other about the two university students that none of them notice the gray Silverado with its two passengers following them.

Not even Syko Loco.

CHAPTER 32

Mahmoud Rising

Mahmoud Ahmed's flight from Bangkok via Narita, Japan, to the United States is uneventful. He clears customs at San Francisco International Airport with relative ease replicating his past experience and subsequent belief that arriving from Bangkok generates much less scrutiny than a flight originating in Saudi Arabia.

"Allahu Akbar," he says repeatedly in his head as he gives thanks for his US citizenship that he obtained at the time of his birth in California. Even though he has lived most recently in Saudi Arabia and Thailand, he has maintained his citizenship in America. At one point, not long after beginning his road to radicalization, he considered pursuing the affirmative action of renouncing his citizenship in the country of the infidels. However, he is now thankful that he never followed through on his plan. Being a citizen of the United States can have many benefits.

Mahmoud looks into the rearview mirror of the nondescript rental car and sees a totally different face staring back at him than the one he saw three days earlier in Thailand. He is confident that he made the right choice to shave his long, thick beard because he now looks younger, more innocent, and appears to be of Mediterranean extraction. He should encounter no trouble moving around the United States. The full black jihadist beard would not have done him any favors in a nation that has increasingly grown wary of the appearance of the stereotypical terrorist. *If they only knew*, he laughs to himself sardonically.

He decided to drive to his destination instead of taking a domestic flight. To minimize complications, he feels that it is safer to avoid the airways and stick to the highways. His name on a flight manifest will place him at the scene of the crime. Driving into the city will be noticed by no one. There will be zero proof to suggest he was even in the area. Besides, it affords him ample opportunity to purchase the needed weapon for his holy mission for Allah.

Relying on the research he had done weeks before his arrival in San Francisco, Mahmoud follows the GPS directions to drive to the specialty shop he had located near Fisherman's Wharf. Since he knows exactly what he's looking for, it does not take long to make his purchase. Less than fifteen minutes after he enters, he emerges from the store with a Jambiya Khanjar knife that cost him just under $400.00. The knife reminds him of the ones he collected in Saudi Arabia and those he still has in his personal collection back at his home in Yala, Thailand. It has a curved blade that will cut deep if thrust into a human abdomen, eviscerating vital organs and slicing through major arteries.

Shortly after departing Fisherman's Wharf, the familiar sound of adhan—the melodious chanting calling him to prayer—fills his rental car. Without looking down, he knows that the muezzin on his phone app is calling him to the third prayer of the day called Asr. Mahmoud looks for a place to stop and fulfill his religious duty. Since he used the restroom before he left the airport and so is unclean, he needs to engage in ritual ablution and purify his body before he can pray.

The young man soon locates a city park with a public restroom. Parking his car, he enters the restroom and begins the necessary ablution known as *Wudhu*. Using the water from the sink faucet, he washes his hands and mouth three times, breathes water in through his nose three times, washes his face three times, and does the same with his arms. He cleanses his head by running a wet hand through his hair from his forehead back to his neck. Lastly, he washes his hands and his feet. A man who enters the restroom eyes him curiously when he sees Mahmoud's right foot hoisted up onto the lip of the sink.

Having purified himself in preparation for salat, Mahmoud returns to his car. Retrieving his prayer rug, he locates a private spot under a tree near the restroom and rolls it out. The prayer app on his phone shows him the direction of the Kaaba in Mecca. Orienting his rug in the prescribed direction, he performs the ritualized prayer routine he has been practicing since he was five years old.

Over the next ten minutes, he recites various prayers in Arabic, including passages from the Quran. While praying, he positions his body in different postures. He alternates between standing with his hands raised up to his ears, bending over at a ninety-degree angle, placing his head, knees, and hands on the ground—a position called *sajdah*—sitting on his knees, then returning to the *sajdah* position, standing up, and then ending the prayer time by turning his head to the right and then to the left. Throughout *salat*, Mahmoud often repeats the words "Allahu Akbar" which means "God is most great."

When he has completed his prayers, Mahmoud rolls up his prayer rug and returns to his car. The five times a day prayer routine has become such a familiar practice in his life that he organizes his whole day around it. Was it not his father who taught him years ago to plan his daily life around the five salat instead of planning the salat around his daily life?

Mahmoud navigates onto I-80 and begins his journey east. He has decided to allow three days for his trip to Aliyah's location. It might be less if he feels rested enough. Either way, his plan is to find a motel near his sister's school and then decide how to contact her. He will give Aliyah one opportunity to return to Islam. If she renounces her Christian faith, he will spare her life but demand that she return to Yala with him, where she will be punished for her unfaithfulness. If she refuses to admit her apostasy, he will have no choice but to execute his sister according to the Wahhabist tradition he learned in Saudi Arabia and continues to practice in southern Thailand.

Mahmoud hates the Ahmadiyya sect of Islam, strongly dislikes Shia Muslims, and tolerates moderate Sunnis. Buddhists and Christians are infidels that deserve death. He views himself as a follower and propagator of the strict purist interpretation of Islam. Allah and the Prophet would be pleased with him. The eternal Quran and the Hadith are the mystical basis for his faith, and Sharia law is his practical living out of the eternal truth of Allah. He will uncompromisingly obey the Prophet even if it means executing his sister, who has abandoned the faith of her ancestors and committed idolatry by embracing Jesus as God.

There is no other alternative. His sister must recant or die!

Mahmoud wakes up three days later in the city where his sister's school is located. He had done enough research a month before he left Thailand to discover that the Silver Bay Lodge Hotel is owned by the school, so he purposefully ruled it out as a place to stay. Instead, he selects a chain motel located five miles from the Teleios Academy.

After he has eaten lunch and said noon prayers, he pulls out a burner phone he purchased in San Francisco to ensure that no one will be able to identify him as the caller. He dials the last known number of his sister's phone several times. She does not answer. Since there is no personal message in the voice mailbox, he does not know for certain that the number is still Aliyah's. He dials the number a dozen more times over the next several hours. Still, no response. He leaves no messages.

Suddenly he has an inspiration. He sends the following text to his sister's phone: *Hey, Aly, this is Sarah, Sean's sister. Passing through your area later today on my way to visit a friend in Chattanooga. LOL! Hope I can c u. Text me ASAP!!*

Half an hour later, he receives a response from his sister's phone: *Sarah! Why didn't you tell me you were coming through town! I would've spent several days with you. If today is all you have, I can meet tonight after work. Done at 8:30. Meet you at the coffee shop on Walnut and 49th? The White Owl. If I don't hear from you, I'll see you tonight!!!*

At 8:00 that evening, Mahmoud navigates his rental car through the neighborhood where the White Owl is located. Assuming that his sister does not own a vehicle, he locates the nearest bus stop and decides to keep vigil for her there. It is a damp, breezy night, so much colder than hot and humid Yala. Illumination from the half-moon peeking through broken clouds and a handful of streetlights provides the only light in the darkness. The cold and darkness are not an issue for Mahmoud. Passion for his mission provides both warmth and light to his heart.

At 8:45, he spots her. She is getting off the bus. It both surprises him and angers him that she is wearing her black hijab. He gets out of his car quickly and runs to catch up to her. He overtakes her half a block from the coffee shop.

"Salaam, Aliyah," he hisses quietly as he comes alongside his blasphemous sister.

Initially, Aly doesn't believe her ears. Her hijab is covering her head, and the night wind is gusting around her. She decides that the terrifying voice she heard is her imagination playing nightmarish tricks on her. But then the voice comes again, only louder, "Salaam, Aliyah."

This time there is no mistake. Even as she turns to look at the man walking beside her, the blood in her veins turns cold. Her body shudders involuntarily. Initially, she does not see Mahmoud because the man walking beside her is clean-shaven. Gone is the bushy black beard that had obscured his face for the last four years. But she recognizes the eyes immediately. Cobalt scorpions would be more inviting than the steely gray eyes partially shrouded in darkness. Aly immediately stops walking because her legs no longer work. Her eyes are wide with horror.

"Allahu Akbar!" Mahmoud utters through lips twisted into a sneer. "I have found you according to his will, my sister."

Aly cannot speak. Something has stolen her voice. She cannot produce any sounds from her throat. An invisible viper has coiled itself tightly around her neck, and she cannot breathe or swallow.

"Do you know what great evil you have committed against our family?" her brother snarls. "Do you know how much shame you have cast on me, a leader among the brothers in Yala? How could you do such a thing to us, Aliyah, vile betrayer of faith and family?"

At this point, Mahmoud grabs her left arm and squeezes it so hard that a cry of pain attempts to rise in her throat.

"You need not speak, sister," Mahmoud utters in a low voice as sharp and cruel as a knife's blade. "I am here to inform you that you have but two choices: Repent of your despicable apostasy and return with me to Yala or remain here and continue to embrace your shameful blasphemy.

"You *will* be punished either way," her brother announces in such a dispassionate voice that another wave of fear surges through Aly's body. Mahmoud grips her arm even harder, and his eyes burn holes into her face. "But as you must already know, one punishment will be far more severe."

Aly's legs are shaking, and she fears she will collapse. She discerns at that moment that she is looking into the eyes of her executioner. If she was not certain of it in the past, she now knows that Mahmoud has killed before—her beloved brother, who she used to idealize with the awe generated in the heart of a younger sister.

She is now fully convinced that she has lost her brother. He has been swallowed by deep darkness. All of him.

Aly has a fleeting thought that Mahmoud must feel the same way, that he has lost his dear younger sister, who he used to play with and carry around on his shoulders. Initially, a wave of sadness caresses the edges of her heart. But then a harsh thought follows on the heels of her soft emotion: *Mahmoud has lost his little sister to what is unlawful and prohibited in his eyes, so he has come to kill me.*

"I will contact you tomorrow with a location where we will meet," he informs her, his mouth pressed hard up against her hijab. "We will meet, and I will discover what you have decided, my sister. Your fate is in your hands. I hope you choose wisely, foolish one."

Mahmoud pulls away from her ear and stares at her one last time. In the moonlight, she can see that his hands are at his sides, balled into fists that are opening and closing. Suddenly, he reaches up and rips the hijab from her head, and spits out the words, "You disgrace your people and your God, Aliyah!" Then he strides off into the night and, like a demon from hell, is swallowed up by the darkness.

Aly can no longer stand. She staggers over to a nearby tree and collapses against it. She breaks into convulsive sobs that last for several minutes. A handful of people approach her to see if she needs assistance, but she waves them off.

Eventually, her ragged breathing calms, and she looks up into the night sky. The clouds have completely covered the moon. The vault above is as dark as her brother's heart. Tears roll down her cheeks, and her legs quiver with cold and fear.

"How, Jesus?" she asks of the heavens in an anguished voice. "How did he ever find me?"

Later that same night—long after midnight—the six members of the micro-cohort are together in the huge sanctuary. They are in the belly of the massive turret sitting on the raised platform that looks down on the rows of pews rippling back into the darkness of the castle. Dim lights high above the platform are the only source of illumination in the room. Rachel and Emily are sitting on either side of Aly, who is not wearing her hijab. The young woman with the auburn hair has her arm wrapped around her shaken friend. Jack, Armando, and Stewart sit in front of the three women, eyeing Aly with concern.

"How did he find you half a world away?" Jack asks incredulously, shaking his head.

"At first, I had no idea," Aly admits. "Then I realized he must've contacted Sean, a family friend living in Los Angeles who I spoke to about six months ago. My mistake. Sean knew he wasn't supposed to let Mahmoud know that I was back in America. Somehow, he must've let that slip out. Today, my brother texted me posing as Sean's sister. Stupidly, I believed it."

"He wants you to recant and return," Armando says, summarizing the woman's earlier communication.

Aly turns large brown eyes on Syko Loco. She feels safe in his presence, in the safe fellowship of the whole group. She nods her head and takes a deep breath. "Yes, recant and return or remain an apostate and—"

"Do you really think he'll try to kill you?" Rachel inquires.

"I saw it in his eyes," Aly says as she levels her gaze on Rachel. "There's no doubt of it. He will kill me."

Jack shakes his head and grimaces. Stewart adjusts his glasses and says, "He sounds very much like a jihadist."

Aly nods.

"Why does he think he has to kill you?" Emily asks. "Why is it such a terrible thing that you're a Christian?"

"Being a Muslim is such an all-encompassing identity," Aly explains. "It impacts every area of our lives and determines what is halal—permissible—for us. There are so many rules that tell us what is haram, or unlawful, that apply to food, drink, dress, prayers, preparation for prayer, family life, and how we should approach Allah in a manner that pleases him."

Aly pauses and shivers slightly. "Mahmoud wants to kill me because he believes that to do so is the will of God, and he wants to please Allah above all things. I have forsaken the one true God with all of his proscriptions for my life and therefore deserve the punishment of death."

"It sounds like some people might remain in Islam because they fear what will become of them if they leave," Armando says.

"That is true," Aly agrees as she repeats her new ritual of reaching up to touch her hijab. "But most Muslims are not so radical as to kill their own family members if they forsake the faith. Apostates are often cut off from their parents and siblings as if they are dead. Other times, the apostate is coerced to come back to the family in the hopes that over time he or she will return to the true religion. In some cases, they are tolerated."

"I'm so thankful that Jesus is a merciful God who is full of grace and forgiveness," Rachel offers as she rubs the smaller woman's arm.

Aly smiles for the first time that night. Her face lights up so brightly that Jack cannot help but see Jesus in her. He quietly thanks the Holy Spirit that His presence inside of Aly serves to strengthen his own faith.

"Mercy and grace and forgiveness are what drew me to Jesus," Aly confides with eyes that glow with joy. "Those attributes of His character convinced me that Jesus was the one true God. As amazing as they are, they captured my heart, and I could not help but believe.

Yes," she says as her large eyes shine in the dim light of the cavernous room, "I could not help but believe. What else could I have done when I was captured by that kind of love? It's almost as if I had no other choice," she says, her voice trailing off as she stares into the darkness of the massive sanctuary. A deep silence fills the huge space. Nobody feels led to disturb it.

Eventually, a determined look settles over the countenance of the Saudi-Thai woman, and her fellow students know that she has arrived at a decision.

"What is it, Aly?" Rachel inquires.

"I know what I must do."

"What's that?" Emily asks.

"I must meet Mahmoud tomorrow. It's what Jesus wants me to do," Aly says, nodding her head.

"You will not renounce and return?" Emily queries.

"Of course not. I cannot stop loving Jesus any more than I can decide to stop breathing," the woman with the honey-colored skin announces as a smile spreads over her heart-shaped face. "I will meet my brother tomorrow at the place and time he chooses."

"But you said he'll kill you," Rachel says. She tightens her hug around Aly's shoulders.

The young woman confesses, "In my own strength, I'm terrified of Mahmoud." She hesitates and then admits, "I felt his knife when he pulled me close to himself. It was a Khanjar, a dagger with a curved blade. He has many back in Yala. He collects them like you and I might collect seashells. So, yes, I am terrified," Aly concedes as she turns her eyes to look at Armando and then at Jack.

"But in Jesus' strength, I will go and face my brother," she continues. "It's what God wills me to do. I must show Mahmoud that my faith in Jesus is so real and true that not even death is to be feared. His perfect love casts out all my fear."

"We'll come with you," Jack announces.

"Yes," Stewart agrees, "even Jesus had His disciples with Him in the Garden of Gethsemane."

Aly shakes her head, and her long black hair glides over her cheeks. "No, I must go alone."

"Are you crazy?" Rachel exclaims. "He'll kill you!"

"It's what God has told me to do," Aly repeats, her face resolute.

"Would God ask you to walk into an ambush?" Emily asks, an edge in her voice.

"It's not an ambush," Aly responds quietly. "I know the danger I'm walking into."

"Do you want to die?" Rachel demands.

Aly shakes her head. "Unlike Mahmoud, I have no desire to die. I have no wish to be a martyr. I only want to obey my Savior who died for me so that I might live."

Jack places his chin on a fisted hand and considers his fellow Screaming Eagle. The lights shining down from far above cast a soft glow on her dark hair like a heavenly radiance. In one moment, her face looks so young, so innocent. In the next, the conviction in her face appears as large and immovable as a mountain.

"Aly," Jack says, "I agree that you need to meet your brother tomorrow. But...you can't go alone. Stewart is right; even Jesus had His closest disciples with Him to watch and pray with Him—feebly, at best—in the moment of His greatest danger. We don't have to be right next to you, but we need to be close by."

Aly is silent as she searches Jack's eyes. Finally, she nods her head and says, "What you say sounds wise. But if Mahmoud discovers I'm not alone, I'm certain he'll turn around and leave. He needs to see me alone. But if you're hiding somewhere nearby, I think that would be acceptable."

"If he reaches for his knife," Armando interjects, "you can tell him he's surrounded by your friends. We can show ourselves then, so he knows you're not alone."

"The only problem is that Aly's brother has yet to inform her where they'll be meeting," Stewart says. "It might be difficult for us to hide our presence if he decides to meet in a very private location."

"Good point, Stew," Jack agrees. Then he turns to Aly and says, "We need to pick a good public place for you two to meet. Then you need to insist on meeting him at that specific location."

"We also should let Windsor, McNeely, and Embee in on this," Emily says. "I don't think it's wise for the six of us to manage this situation alone."

Jack nods his head and looks at Emily. "Another valid point. We need to fill them in on everything first thing in the morning."

"Do we need to contact law enforcement?" Rachel asks.

"That's a question for our esteemed professors," Jack acknowledges. "Right now, though, I think we need to pray for Aly and Mahmoud."

Everyone agrees. They sit in a circle around Aly so that they can all touch her shoulder, arm, or hand. Then they approach God's throne with passionate hearts.

They pray for an hour. Armando concludes the time of intercession.

"Father God, we thank you that you have heard our pleas," he says as he lifts his hands toward the towering ceiling. "How good that you, our all-powerful Father, love us so much that you listen to every word we speak. If it wasn't for you, some of us here would have never had a father," he says in a husky voice.

"Your word has told us that we're in a battle between light and darkness," Armando continues, "and we acknowledge that all of us, at one point in the past, lived in the darkness and practiced its ways. So, we can't judge Mahmoud or lift any stones to throw at him. Instead, we pray that you might lift the veil that covers his face and open the eyes of his heart so that he might see you. In the power of your name, Jesus, we bind and rebuke Satan from this man's heart. Set him free from the prisoner of war camp where he is imprisoned.

"Father, we also ask you to protect our sister, Aly. Just as the mountains are round about the city of Jerusalem, we ask you to be a shield around your daughter to keep her safe from harm. Give us faith to believe in you, the One who has promised Aly that you will be with her in trouble."

Armando squeezes his eyes shut even tighter as he prays more loudly,

"We claim for our sister one of her favorite passages, the words written in Isaiah: 'When you pass through the waters, I will be with you; and through the rivers, they shall not overwhelm you; when you walk through fire you shall not be burned, and the flame shall not consume you...Because you are precious in my eyes, and honored, and I love you, I give men in return for you, peoples in exchange for your life. Fear not, for I am with you...'"

Armando pauses and lifts his face toward the dark cupola above them, "Deliver Aly tomorrow, Lord Jesus—I guess it's technically tomorrow already. Why do we ask for her deliverance? So that we might never forget what you did on this day and praise your name all the days of our lives for your great faithfulness. Amen."

The believers gathered in the small circle open their eyes and look at Aly. She gazes back at her five prayer warriors, her face glistening with tears. "I have missed my family back in Thailand so much, including Mahmoud," she says in her high-pitched voice, "but now I am reminded that God has adopted me into a new family. To think that four months ago, you weren't even in my imagination. Now I feel like I've known you forever! I thank God so much for all of you!"

As the members of the micro-cohort get to their feet, Jack feels a familiar cold presence settle over him. He shivers involuntarily.

"Armando, Stewart," Jack says as he looks over his shoulder into the dark recesses of the huge sanctuary, "let's walk the women back to the dorm and inform the security guard that he needs to be especially alert tonight—just in case."

"Sounds good to me, Juan," Armando replies so loudly that his words echo in the massive sanctuary.

The Screaming Eagles stretch cramped legs and tired arms and then descend the steps of the platform. "We're on the verge of something big,"

Jack announces quietly without looking at his companions. "As my grandmother used to say, 'I can feel it in my bones.'"

"Throw down a gauntlet around the man from Thailand so that anyone who attempts to approach him from any side will be thwarted." The voice speaks slowly, ominously, and sounds like the low grumbling of an awakening volcano. "Strengthen his hand so that he will accomplish what he has been summoned to do; so that his blade will pierce the worthless heart of the apostate and liberate the walking dust from her animal body. You must not fail."

CHAPTER 33

THE SHUFFLER OF HEARTS

After the surprise visit with his sister, Mahmoud parks his rental car in the Vacation Express lot, enters the motel, and takes the elevator up to the fourth floor. Just after he left Aly, the muezzin on his phone app alerted him of *adhan*, the fifth of the daily prayers. Accordingly, when he arrives back at his room, he engages in *Isha'a*—the night salat—by reciting five *rak'ah*. Then he retires for the night. As he drifts off to sleep, he gives thanks yet again that he has been called to serve in the holy jihad for the name of Allah. Tomorrow will be a day unlike any other...

Even before he wills his eyes open, he senses something is amiss. He can't explain it. He just feels it.

When he finally forces one eye open, he sees the red digits of the clock radio on the nightstand announcing the time: 2:34.

It's the middle of the night, so why is there a bright light in the room, he wonders in his sluggish brain. Not aroused enough to fully awaken, he closes his eye and drifts into full unconsciousness again. It is only then that he is torn from his repose by the most unlikely and unwelcome interruption.

"Mahmoud."

The young man's eyes fly open.

"Mahmoud." The Voice that speaks is deep and rich, and it vibrates the whole room. A light is shining behind him.

"Mahmoud." The Voice is soft but so loud that it strikes something deep within him—something that has never been touched before.

A giant tuning fork in his chest has been struck by an unseen agent. It is resonating within him, vibrating throughout his whole body. He hears a pure musical tone within himself. It feels warm, terrifying, intimate. It is so inundating that he feels immersed in it as in a river. No, it is something broader and deeper than the ocean. There is something amazingly familiar about it yet something so totally unknown, so incomprehensible.

"Mahmoud," he hears the deep, sonorous voice repeat yet again. It is not one voice. It sounds like many voices, like the sound of cascading water rushing over rocks. The young man does not dare to turn and look behind him. He is incapable of not turning. As if being summoned, he sits up slowly and swings his legs over the edge of the bed. His back is still turned to the Voice and the Light.

At that moment, something strikes him as truer than he can understand with his intellect alone: His face is and has always been turned away from the Light. Yes, the Light. Shockingly, tears moisten his eyes. They begin to flow down his cheeks. Soon, he is weeping uncontrollably.

Somewhere in his head, a voice cries out, "What is happening? This is pure irrationality! Go back to sleep, Mahmoud, and...sleep forever." The words are faint, barely perceptible. The words are irrelevant, and he ignores them.

The young jihadist turns around slowly and sees...Him. The figure is so dazzlingly brilliant that Mahmoud raises his hands to shield his eyes against the glorious presence. The tuning fork in his chest explodes, and his whole body begins to shake violently. He collapses to the floor as if struck by lightning. He lies there on the carpet for a long time, unable to move or think.

"Mahmoud."

Immediately, as if in obedience to a divine command, the shaken man gets up on his knees—a very familiar prayer position—next to the bed. He beholds the figure of a man. But he is no ordinary man. He has been changed...altered...transfigured. His presence floods the room. No, more than that. The room cannot contain Him. Mahmoud senses that the light emanating from the Being's body is penetrating the four walls around him and bursting out into the adjacent rooms, the hallway, the parking lot, the entire city, and the surrounding countryside.

Worst of all—best of all—or both, the young Muslim knows at that moment whom he is beholding. He simply knows.

He also remembers in his throbbing brain what they say. They say that just before you die, your life flashes before your eyes. At the moment, he entertains the strange sensation that he is going to die, but his life does not flash before his eyes. Rather, he experiences something within him that feels like shuffling—everything inside him is being shuffled like a deck of cards. Shuffling. Shuffling. He is a deck of cards, and he is kneeling in the presence of the Great Shuffler of hearts. He sinks down on his knees and legs as low as he can behind the bed to hide from the Presence that is undoing him from the inside out.

"Mahmoud Ahmed," the water-over-the-rocks voice resonates, "I have been pursuing you, and you have been fleeing from me to a far country. Tonight, I have come for you, my lost son. There will be no more running from my face. I am calling you to turn and come home." The words are not an inquiry or a suggestion—they are a statement of fact.

Mahmoud lies flat on the floor behind the bed and attempts to sink down and hide within the fibers of the carpet. Another part of him—the summoned part—responds quite differently. He gets back up on his knees and reaches his arms above the edge of the bed toward the object of his soul's deepest affection. His head and body remain hidden behind the bed.

If Mahmoud's heart is impenetrable steel, the Being who has invaded the room is a massive magnet pulling him inexorably toward Him. Indeed, Mahmoud finds the bright figure irresistible. Yet, something in his soul holds him back and prevents him from running toward his visitor. Then there is the sound of sinister, urgent chanting coming from some distant place. Thousands of voices warn him, "Flee from Shaytan! Flee from the liar! Flee!"

"Approach me, Mahmoud," the beautiful voice invites with no hint of demand, only a gentle beckoning reminiscent of his mother sweetly holding out her hands to him when he was a three-year-old boy.

Without hesitation, Mahmoud jumps to his feet and hurries over to the figure that throbs with brilliant light. Mahmoud is overwhelmed with impatience because he cannot reach the Being as quickly as he would like. As he draws close, he glances into the face of the sun standing before him. Immediately, he crumbles to his knees.

"I cannot be in your presence!" Mahmoud cries out with a loud groan as he continues to weep and bury his face in the carpet. "I have esteemed you as a prophet and a good man but have defied you as the God of the universe. I'm not worthy of your visitation."

"You speak the truth, Mahmoud," the transfigured Being affirms in the beautiful voice that rushes through his body like streams of cool water. "No one is worthy of being in my presence, or that of my Father, or the Spirit. No son of Adam can ever be holy enough by his own efforts to stand in our midst. Yet, my desire for the glory of the Father and my love for you bring me here this night. I have come to draw you to myself."

"You love me?" Mahmoud cries out in muffled anguish as he grinds his forehead into the carpet until his skin burns. "What must I do?"

The jihadist feels the hand of the Ancient of Days rest gently on his head, and the turning fork in his chest resonates once again so intensely that he cannot contain its vibration. He fears that his body will crumble to dust.

"Today, before the sun sets, you must go and meet your sister at the Academy," the rich, rushing voice speaks to him. "She will come to you and pray for your soul. Rejoice, Mahmoud, my dear son who I designed and in whom I take great delight, for today is the day of your salvation."

Then—too immediately to be comprehended by physical senses alone—the Light is gone, and Mahmoud finds himself alone in the now desolate room. The absence of the Presence makes the room feel far darker and emptier than it had been before the visitation.

In one sense, Mahmoud feels like he can convince himself that nothing happened in the last few minutes. An old and formerly dominant part of him prefers that to be the narrative of the night. No, that part of him fights to insist that nothing happened in the motel room. Denial is the most primitive and powerful defense mechanism of them all. Another phrase for denial is the positive presence of unbelief. Mahmoud's level of unbelief is massive and beyond every intervention except the miraculous.

In another sense, everything has happened that night, and Mahmoud knows nothing will ever be the same. Nothing. The decimated man with the shuffled heart rolls onto his side and curls up into a fetal position. He moans and mumbles the name of his nighttime visitor over and over. A part of him curses the name while the other part blesses the name. He is torn, a house divided. He is undone, and he is terrified.

Mahmoud lies motionless on the floor long after the Light of Life has departed. He is in unspeakable turmoil. He is sobbing. He hears his voice crying out plaintively, "Leave me alone, Jesus. Please don't leave me alone."

As he continues to weep uncontrollably, his wild eyes roam the room and fall on the nightstand next to the bed where he had been awakened only five minutes earlier. Incredibly, the three red digits on the small clock now read 9:31. Seven hours have passed since he had first heard the VOICE! *How can this be?* Mahmoud whimpers in the room that is bright with the morning sun.

An hour later, the young man is still lying on the floor, listening to himself mumble. "Leave me," he says. "Please, don't leave me."

It is early in the afternoon of the same day. The six members of the micro-cohort are gathered in the official campus prayer room adjacent to the fireside room. The small space that has a statue of St. Francis of Assisi in one corner is full of folding chairs and a few tables.

The Screaming Eagles never did make it back to the dorm earlier that morning. As they exited the sanctuary, they decided to call Dr. Windsor even though they were tortured over whether to bother the man who was tending to his ailing wife. Urged on by Violet's wise and selfless counsel, the professor decided it was imperative to meet his students at the Academy within the hour.

When the Warfare professor finally arrived—closer to 4:00 a.m.—they prayed for Mahmoud and Aly until the sun was rising.

At 8:00 a.m., Dr. McNeely, Dr. Greenlay, Dr. Livingstone, Miriam, and several other professors joined the students for additional strategizing and prayer around Aly's dire situation.

By 1:00 in the afternoon, more than three-dozen people are crammed in the prayer lounge with St. Francis like sardines in a can. They are talking, listening, drinking coffee, eating donuts, worshipping, and praying in small groups. A few individuals refuse to eat or drink as they feel led to fast for their fellow student. The unexpected arrival of Aly's brother has turned into a full-blown community event at the Academy. The campus is abuzz with tension and excitement.

The final plan had been finalized hours ago. When Mahmoud contacts Aly, she will insist that her brother meet her at Paseo Park in the rose garden. The Screaming Eagles, several professors, and Bill, the security guard—along with his brother Bud, who is in law enforcement in a neighboring city—will all be inconspicuously scattered around the rose garden prepared to act at a moment's notice. Bill insists that he will conceal and carry. Bill's older brother, who knows how trigger-happy his younger brother can be when out bird and deer hunting, reminds Bill to draw his weapon only if Mahmoud demonstrates that he is a material threat.

Aly rises from her spot on the couch for the twentieth time and begins pacing around the room. "Why hasn't he contacted me yet?" she asks aloud as she folds her hands and gently touches them to her lips. "I don't think I'm scared. I'm just getting a bit anxious about this whole meeting. Jesus, I don't think I can wait much longer."

"You don't need to, daughter," the authoritative voice of Miriam pronounces as she enters the lounge. "Your brother is here. He's in the sanctuary."

"What!" Aly cries out. "He's here?"

"How do you know?" Rachel inquires of the elderly woman. "Did the

Spirit reveal it to you?"

Miriam smiles and replies, "No, daughter. I saw him walk in the front door just as I came out of the downstairs restroom."

A few people in the prayer room chuckle quietly. Then everyone in the chapel gathers around the young Saudi-Thai woman.

Aly swallows hard and says, "All that worrying and planning, and he ends up right under our noses."

"So, this is it, then," Dr. Windsor announces like a general addressing his troops before the invasion begins. "God has brought Mahmoud here, into His house. Such a development is not the strategy of the enemy. God has an amazing plan in place for the salvation of this young man."

"I agree," Embee says in a calming voice as she strokes Aly's arm. "Jesus has clearly answered our prayers."

"We still need to approach this situation with utmost caution," Dr. Windsor advises. "Bill and Bud, take up position in the choir loft to keep an eye on things from above. I'll slip into the sanctuary and hide myself behind the last pew."

Aly nods her head and says, "I know Mahmoud well. If I sense any immediate threat from him, I'll let him know I'm not alone." She pauses and shakes her head. "I'm still very confused. I don't understand why he came here, to the Academy."

A new thought strikes her, and her brown eyes open wide in alarm. She asks in a trembling voice, "Miriam, he didn't have a briefcase or backpack with him, did he?"

"No, chosen one of God," the elderly prophetess replies, her faded green eyes smiling. "I checked him out closely as he walked by. He was carrying no explosives."

Aly exhales loudly and nods her head slowly at Miriam.

"We're heading out now," Dr. Windsor announces, gesturing at Bill and Bud as he moves toward the door. "Give us two minutes to get into position, and then you can come in."

Aly nods her head and sighs. Jack watches as the young woman's delicate fingers absent-mindedly search her head for her absent hijab.

Embee leads them all in one final prayer. She asks the Holy Spirit to protect Aly and to scatter all the powers of darkness from both her and her brother. Then the young woman turns to depart for the sanctuary and her rendezvous with Mahmoud.

Just before Aly reaches the door, Jack intercepts her and reminds her of Violet's dream. He reminds her that just as in the dream so now she is being pursued by a lion who is intent on killing her. However, God has a superior plan that supersedes Mahmoud's plan: He is going to deliver her from the jaw of the angry lion. In fact, He is going to completely disarm the power of her pursuer by blinding him and shattering his teeth.

The small woman with the giant-sized spirit smiles at Jack and thanks him for his words. "I know Jesus is going to protect me," she utters with complete confidence. Then she departs the room, a woman on a holy mission for the God who gave His life for her.

Several minutes later, Aly opens the door of the sanctuary and closes it carefully behind her. It shuts with a click that echoes throughout the cavernous room.

She carefully scans the mammoth church that is dimly lit only by the natural light streaming in from the cupola far overhead and from the stained-glass windows. It doesn't take long for her to locate her brother sitting in the front row of the sanctuary—a long way removed from the choir loft and her protectors. But Aly does not hesitate for even a moment since this rendezvous is not about her being safe but about Mahmoud seeing Jesus in her.

Aly walks slowly past the back pew where Dr. Windsor is kneeling and makes her way forward to where her brother is sitting. As she draws close to him, she notices that his head is bowed toward the floor—how unusual. He does not appear to be performing salat, so what is he doing? She hesitates five pews behind her brother and observes him closely. His whole body is shaking. Is it rage that has possessed him or maybe...an emotion altogether different, something far removed from anger and hate? She cannot tell if he has his knife.

"Mahmoud, it's me, Aliyah," she speaks quietly but firmly. Her voice sounds small in the mammoth room of worship.

Her brother lifts his head slightly but does not turn to look at her. It is then that she hears sounds of weeping. With slow, hesitant steps, she makes her way to the front pew and then hesitates again.

"What is it, brother?" she inquires softly. "Why are you crying?" A strong wave of compassion floods over her. She does not remember ever hearing her brother cry.

"My world has been turned upside down," Mahmoud mumbles as he stares straight ahead at the platform where Aly had prayed only twelve hours earlier with the members of the micro-cohort. "Everything I have known and believed...has been washed away in an instant. I...I am undone."

Her older brother finally turns to look at her. His face is haggard and swollen, and his eyes are bloodshot. He looks as if he has been beaten. Shocked, Aly puts the fingers of her right hand in front of her mouth and exclaims, "What happened to you, Mahmoud?"

Her brother sighs and says, "I'm a prisoner in a no-man's-land I never knew existed. It is a space somewhere between joy and despair," he says wearily. There is a brief silence before he adds almost cavalierly, "Oh, by the way, you should know that you no longer need to fear me, sister. I'm not going to kill you. My Khanjar knife is at the bottom of the river—along with my sanity."

"What is it?" Aly asks as she walks to the steps leading up to the platform and turns to stare at her disheveled brother.

Even though tears are still streaming down his face, Mahmoud laughs loudly in such a strange departure from his normal character that Aly fears that he is deranged. "No, sister, the correct question is not 'what is it?' but 'who is it?'" he replies. Then he laughs even louder and declares, "Indeed, the mystery of mysteries in the universe comes down not to 'what,' my dear sister...but to 'whom.'"

The Saudi-Thai woman sweeps her hair behind her head with both hands and kneels in front of the troubled young man. "I don't understand, my brother."

"On that count, you are wrong," Mahmoud says with a tired smile, shaking his head with its wavy black hair. "You do understand, Aliyah; it is I who do not. However, I think that before I leave this place today, I also will understand. At least that's what He led me to believe."

"What are you talking about?" Aly inquires as guarded hope begins to rise in her chest. "Who are you talking about?" She leans toward her brother and waits for his response. She is vaguely aware that she is holding her breath.

"This time, you have asked the correct question," Mahmoud says with a staccato laugh that makes him sound drunk. Aly finds it so ironic that he sounds inebriated since her brother never drinks alcohol in strict obedience to the rules of sharia law. It is haram for him and every pure Muslim.

"He came to me last night," her brother states, turning serious. "He came to me and told me I needed to come and speak with you, that you would pray for my soul."

Aly's heart floods with excitement. *Could it be? Could my brother have been visited by the One who transformed my life?*

Aly waddles on her knees toward her brother until she is so close that she can reach out and touch him. "Mahmoud, are you saying that...are you telling me that...Did Jesus come to you?"

Her brother stares at her for a long time from the tops of his eyes. Finally, after winning his battle with internal reluctance, he nods his head. "He didn't tell me who He was, but I knew immediately that it was Him—whether I wanted to know or not. He did not give me that choice."

The younger sister reaches out to the older brother and touches his cheek with her hand. He is still weeping softly, and his shoulders are shaking. "Jesus revealed Himself to you!" Aly announces excitedly.

Mahmoud nods wearily, and Aly sees something different in his countenance beyond the exhaustion. His face is no longer hard like a rock. Something has softened him like summer rains falling on a drought-hardened field. Furthermore, it is apparent to Aly that seeds have been planted in the plowed field and that they are ready to sprout.

"God's Word says, 'Behold, now is the day of salvation,[1]' Mahmoud."

"Yes, I know," her brother acknowledges. "He came to me and informed me of that truth in the middle of the night. I don't know whether to be joyful or terrified or—enraged."

Aly beams at her brother and says, "You will be overcome with joy, Mahmoud. Nothing compares to being a friend of Jesus."

The young Muslim stares at his sister and shakes his head. "I have

6. 2 Cor. 6:2 (ESV).

already noticed one problem that comes from being around Jesus; simply being in His presence awakens a painful awareness of my—evil." He pauses and then admits, "I have done bad things, sister."

Aly looks at Mahmoud with sadness in her eyes. At that moment, she loves her broken brother deeply. She also understands why God is insistent on repentance being a condition of salvation—it is only the broken, humbled, repentant heart that is willing to surrender to the Creator of the universe and cry out to Him for salvation. How attractive is a heart that is genuinely contrite, beautifully overcome with godly sorrow.

Aly takes one of her brother's hands into her own and smiles at him. "I will pray for you, Mahmoud. If the words I speak are words you agree with, repeat them in your head or aloud to me."

The broken and shuffled man groans and pulls his hand away from his sister's grasp. He shakes his head and buries his beardless face in his hands. He seems suddenly resistant, and Aly wonders if her optimism was premature.

"I don't know what to do, Aliyah," he moans into his fingers. "How can I simply turn and walk away from three decades of what was my truth. I don't believe I can change that quickly, that *radically*. In the deepest part of my being, I am a Muslim who serves Allah and reveres the prophet Muhammad. Islam is my identity. It's who I have been, who I am, and who I—."

There is a long silence. Aly feels fear and disappointment take up residence in her throat. But then she does what she has always done since the day Jesus found her: she prays. She prays in her heart for her deeply conflicted brother. Minutes go by.

Mahmoud wraps his fingers around the back of his neck and shakes his head back and forth. He sighs loudly. He groans even more loudly. He jumps to his feet and paces frenetically back and forth in front of the platform. He wrings his hands violently. He chews on the knuckles of his right hand. He holds his head between his hands. He recites the words of a prayer from the hadith louder and louder until he is shouting. He grabs his shirt beneath his chin and rips it open all the way down to his waist, and lets out a guttural scream.

Aly does not have to guess what is happening inside her brother. She experienced it herself not all that long ago. There is a war being fought for her brother's heart. It is the most crucial battle of his lifetime. Spiritual forces are vying for his heart at the seat of his being. She discerns that any words she might speak will only give Mahmoud something to push against. The presence of Jesus is the only thing that matters at this point. Aly remains silent as she continues to pray fervently for her brother.

Eventually, Mahmoud throws his arms up toward the lofty ceiling with its constellation of huge timbers and cries out, "Why did you choose to pursue me, Jesus? Didn't you foresee that you would devastate my life like a Tsunami thundering in from the ocean? Why? Why? Why? You've destroyed in thirty seconds what I built in a lifetime!" The young man with the distinctive Saudi nose and olive-hued skin is incensed. He shakes a fist toward the ceiling and grits his teeth like a rabid animal.

"Do you see what you've done to me?" he screams at the darkness above. His raised voice echoes throughout the vast room. "You, who say that you love me! How can this be love, when you strip away everything I have and leave me only yourself? What kind of exchange is that, Jesus?" he cries out bitterly. "You are nothing more than a thief who robs me of everything I have and then asks me to follow you! Do you think I find that appealing? No, I find it cruel and repulsive!"

Tears form in Aly's eyes. She presses her hands together and touches the tips of her fingers to the bottom of her nose. She is genuinely afraid. She fears that her brother is going to be trapped forever in the dark tempest of his rage. She begins to cry out in her head, "Jesus! Jesus! Jesus!"

"And you!" Mahmoud yells, stabbing a trembling finger at Aly. "You're the one who prayed for Him to pursue me like an assassin bent on taking my life! You're a willing accomplice in this scheme to destroy everything that's holy to me!"

The unhinged man strides up to Aly and drives his finger into her forehead. "You are to be sacrificed for your apostasy!" he spits out. His face is twisted by malevolence; his teeth are barred, his eyes are wild. Anger vibrates off his body. Aly closes her eyes and winces, steeling herself for the blow that is certain to come.

For a long time, the crazed man stands over her, drilling his finger into her skin and literally growling. His breaths come quickly through his teeth and sound like the hissing of a snake. His cheeks, angry bellows, puff in and out violently.

As quickly as the madness had arrived, it is over. Mahmoud's finger falls from Aly's face, and he pivots away from his trembling sister. He stumbles twenty feet away and then turns to face her again. His chin falls into his chest, and his shoulders suddenly slump. The vibrating rage has been replaced by utter weariness.

Aly thinks he looks like one of the rag dolls her grandmother used to make for her when she was a child in Saudi Arabia. She begins to weep openly for her brother, who has never looked so fractured. Still, she does not speak.

Mahmoud begins talking to the floor. His words are soft, difficult for Aly to hear. "I am a monster," he says in a voice that is so flat and emotionless that he sounds dead to Aly.

"I am hate," he mumbles. "I am rage. I am murder. I deserve...to be... executed." He pauses a long time, and total silence fills the sanctuary. At one point, the undone man staggers forward a few steps. Aly fears that he might collapse.

"Why don't you kill me right now, Jesus?" he groans. "An eye for an eye and a tooth for a tooth, right? No? You love me and forgive me, you say? How could you ever forgive me, a man who even—" His voice trails off until Aly can no longer hear him.

As she watches him with large eyes, Mahmoud's body crumples, and his knees hit the stone floor hard. He stares straight ahead toward Aly, but she knows he is looking right through her. His head tilts a bit to one side so that he looks...insane. His arms dangle lifelessly toward the floor. He resembles a puppet on strings, passively waiting for some marionette to awaken him to movement and purpose.

When he finally speaks, he again sounds drunk to Aly. "Yes, yes, yes!" he says in a subdued voice infused with growing passion. "You win," he says, throwing one hand toward the ceiling. "I surrender. I can't fight you anymore. I can't resist you, the cosmic bully who—"

Mahmoud shakes his head at this point and squeezes his eyes shut. He says, "No, you're not the bully. I am. I must stop hating and blaming you and admit that I am the rebel and that I can no longer refuse your invitation to love me. So, yes, I surrender to you...Jesus." He says the name slowly as if it is difficult to get it out of his mouth.

He pauses a moment before he straightens his head and places his hands up by his ears as if he is engaging in salat. "You do know what this means, though," he says softly, speaking to someone other than Aly. "It means I must say goodbye. A divorce is unavoidable here, in this transfer of allegiances," he says with a mirthless chuckle. "All because of you."

The young man's chin falls to his chest again, and he moans, "Goodbye, Allah...Goodbye, Muhammad...Farewell, my childhood faith, as close to my heart as my most trusted brother. So familiar—so severe. Farewell, Thailand, for I cannot return to you. Goodbye, my father and my brothers in Islam."

There is a brief silence before Mahmoud lifts his head and announces, "I give it all away for you…you who pursued me and found me and revealed yourself to me."

The man whose heart is still being shuffled pauses and shakes his head. His face is twisted in bewilderment. "I never would have believed it until last night. Never in ten thousand Arabian nights. Ten million Arabian nights! Now, twelve hours later, I have no choice but to believe in you, Jesus…for I have met you face to face."

Totally unraveled, Mahmoud sighs deeply and laughs softly. Then his eyes focus, and he sees his sister kneeling fifteen feet away. "Come here, Aly," he says. "Come here, my sister—please. I'm too tired to move. He told me that you would pray for my soul."

The former Muslim woman, who had met Jesus only eighteen months ago, leaps to her feet. Joy explodes in her chest and drives away the fear and grief that had all but extinguished her hope. She runs over to Mahmoud and falls to her knees in front of him. She smiles even as tears flow like twin rivers down her silky cheeks. She takes her brother's hand in hers for a second time and presses it up against her cheek. From the choir loft, she hears the faint sound of sniffling.

"I will pray aloud," she informs Mahmoud. "Repeat any of the things I speak that you can honestly agree with in your heart." Then she begins to pray words that send shock waves rumbling through the spiritual atmosphere in a three-hundred-mile radius.

"Jesus, I can't believe it's you," Aly says softly, sweetly. "You're the God of the universe. You're the One who has loved my heart and my soul. For so long, I have believed that you were only a prophet, and not even the prophet, and certainly not God. Today, you have surprised me. You have shocked me! You have thrown my whole world into disarray. You're the One my heart has been seeking all along. I just didn't know it until today."

Aly pauses and peeks at her brother. His eyes are closed, and his lips are moving. She smiles into the hand that is pressed against her cheek and continues to pray.

"I confess that I've sinned against you, Jesus," she says softly but with a growing passion in her voice. "I refused to believe in you, and I hurt other people with my words and actions. But today, I approach your throne and ask you to have mercy on me and forgive me. Please wash away all my sin with your once-for-all-ablution of my heart that was accomplished not by water but with your blood.

"I choose to believe in you, Jesus, and confess with my lips that you are the crucified and risen Lord of the universe. I bend my knee to you and ask you to be my Savior and friend. Yes, my friend!"

Aly peeks again and watches her brother's lips as they repeat her words. Aly opens her mouth to keep praying, but Mahmoud takes over where she left off.

"Yes," the young man says with a shaking voice and a bowed head, "I now believe in you, Jesus. I cannot help but believe that you are God, and I cannot fathom that I can call you friend. This truth is too difficult and too wonderful for me to understand that you are both the Sovereign One who is above all things and that you are right here with me as my closest friend. But I want to believe that, Jesus. Help me believe that."

Mahmoud takes a deep breath and then looks up at his sister. Aly immediately notices that her brother's eyes are clear—as if scales have fallen from them—and that the corners of his mouth are turned slightly upward.

"Do you know what this means?" Aly asks the man kneeling next to her, who is now her brother twice over, once in flesh and now in faith. "You've been delivered from the kingdom of darkness and transferred into the kingdom of God's Son, brother," Aly informs him with a smile. "You're a new creation, and the Holy Spirit has entered your heart. You're forever adopted into the family of God. Your name is written in the book of life!

"And best of all," she begins to announce and then hesitates to accentuate the importance of the words that follow, "your salvation doesn't depend on you being good enough for God. It only depends on you believing in the name of Jesus. Our hope of salvation rests only in His grace and mercy and not our attempts to be good."

Aly is grinning so broadly that the muscles of her face begin to ache. There has been only one other time in her life when she experienced such amazing joy.

Mahmoud gazes into his sister's face. The jihadist eyes that formerly were as sharp as Khanjars are now deep wells of peace. The initial, turbulent transition from death to life and darkness to light has passed. Smiling, he extends his arms and pulls his sister close to him, patting her hair with his hand. At that moment, Aly knows without a doubt that her brother has joined her in the family of God.

The two siblings begin to laugh softly. Then they disengage from their embrace. They pull away and stare at each other as if they are looking at one another for the first time. Finally, they break into loud laughter that echoes through the vast reaches of the sanctuary. Aly can picture all the angels in heaven rejoicing now that the veil has been lifted from Mahmoud's eyes. He who once was blind can now see. Oh, what things he can now see—and will see!

Mahmoud abruptly lifts a hand, and silence fills the sanctuary. A serious look spreads over his face, and he says, "I have only one question, my sister."

He pauses as Aly squints her eyes at him in curiosity. A thimbleful of fear stirs in her chest. "My only question is...what do I do now ?"

Aly studies her brother's face for a few moments before Mahmoud bursts into giddy laughter. A second later, she joins him, and they laugh until they cry.

No brother and sister in time immemorial have been filled with more joy than Mahmoud and Aly at that moment. It is a beautiful moment. It is a holy moment. The universe pulses with a spiritual glory that is unleashed when a lost child is reunited with the Father. After all, there is no greater miracle that can occur in the human heart than when it is reborn.

Even as Aly laughs with Mahmoud, she is thinking that she wants to freeze this moment in time. She wishes that she and her newly found brother could live in the safety and joy of this sanctuary for the rest of their lives. She knows that faith in the Creator God does not guarantee smooth seas ahead. In fact, it often entails difficulties and suffering as they sail onward against the dark tides of the universe. Was not Jesus Himself a man of sorrows?

Fortunately, Aly also knows that even when their course takes them through deep darkness and fierce tempests, Jesus will be their navigator. He will guide them every day, indeed every hour, as they journey forward on the most amazing adventure imaginable that begins in this world and continues into the next.

CHAPTER 34

After the Visitation

The day Mahmoud's veil is lifted, and he enters the kingdom of the eternal Son falls toward the end of the semester, the day before final's week. The Academy is already abuzz with the relief that comes when the end of the term is in sight, with the burgeoning anticipation of Christmas, with the excitement of holiday home-goings, and with amazing Spelunking adventures, Narrative Nights, and journeys into the Cave of Dread. The news of a dedicated Mujahid miraculously surrendering to Jesus spreads across the campus like wildfire and fuels the holiday jubilation at the Academy until it rises to unprecedented levels.

Few professors and even fewer students have seen or even heard of a Muslim bowing his knee to Jesus. If one adds to that miraculous event the fact that it occurred when that same man was on a mission to kill his sister in obedience to the law of apostasy, it is absolutely an unprecedented event for all who hear about it. Faith soars. Joy abounds. The celebration of the advent of Jesus into this world coupled with the celebration of the arrival of Jesus into the life of His previously lost son, Mahmoud, infuses the Academy like a living thing.

After his confession of faith in Jesus as God, Mahmoud's question, *what do I do now?* is amazingly appropriate. To help him address this question, Aly invites her brother to meet with some of the professors at the Academy.

Although Mahmoud admits that he dreads the prospect of gathering with believers from a faith he so recently despised, he concedes that he desperately needs guidance to navigate the foreign territory into which he has been summoned. In addition to feeling lost in a strange land, he fears that its inhabitants will doubt his new faith.

Within the hour, Mahmoud, the six Screaming Eagles, and professors Livingstone, Windsor, McNeely, Greenlay, and Miriam all descend on the prayer room to welcome the new believer into the family.

When the ten Christ-followers enter the lounge to meet with Aly and her brother, they have little idea what to expect. What they encounter is a man about thirty years old of medium height with wavy black hair and the complexion and facial features of a middle easterner. His nose is large but complemented well by high cheekbones and a resolute jaw. He is wearing jeans and a gray pullover.

All in all, the young man's presence is not very remarkable except for the expression on his face. Even though he's not smiling, something that can only be described as an unusual illumination radiates from his face. Some of those who enter the lounge shake hands with the young man while others embrace him warmly. Everyone present finds it unbelievable that only several hours ago, this same man was intent on murdering his sister.

When all twelve people are settled in their chairs, the members of the micro-cohort and their professors introduce themselves to the new believer. As a part of their introduction, they all share a brief testimony about how they came to know Jesus, or more accurately, how they came to be known by Jesus. They want Mahmoud to know that he is not alone in his journey from the darkness into the light.

The primary message communicated to the new believer is that at one time, they all had been blind to God as well. The eyes of their hearts had been covered by the obscuring veil so that they could not comprehend and much less believe in the Triune God. Then along came Jesus. Out of His great mercy, He removed the obstruction.

When everyone has had a chance to speak, Dr. McNeely asks Mahmoud if there is anything he wishes to share with his new brothers and sisters.

Despite strong discomfort, Aly's older brother opens his mouth and begins to speak. His face is still glowing, and the tone of his voice is like one who is disoriented by amazement.

Mahmoud begins by admitting that he feels like a lion turned into a lamb, which is now sitting in the middle of a pride of strange lions he hated only hours ago. Everyone in the room laughs and nods their head in understanding.

Mahmoud goes on to describe his astounding encounter with Jesus in the motel room earlier that morning that left him feeling like a door unhinged from its frame. All eleven lions in the small room sit mesmerized by his account. Seven of his listeners cannot help but feel a special level of amazement as they remember Violet's dream pertaining to Aly and the lion that was pursuing her.

Jack feels a strong desire to let Dr. Windsor's wife know about the fulfillment of her dream.

Mahmoud admits to his listeners that he had heard of miraculous appearances by Jesus to Muslims in the past but that he had dismissed them as fictions created by his dishonest followers. Now the very fiction he had despised in the past has become his personal reality. He is still in disbelief at all that has occurred in the previous twelve hours. No, he is in complete and utter shock.

Mahmoud relates that Jesus' appearance to him was so vivid and emotionally powerful that he would never forget the encounter at 2:34 in the morning, even if he lives to be as old as Methuselah. He states that it was so different from a dream—or a nightmare, for that matter—that no one will ever be able to convince him that it was caused by some bad chicken he ate the day before.

"I have never, in all my life, experienced anything so real," he tells his attentive listeners. "Never. Without doubt, I was fully awake."

At this point, Miriam begins to sing quietly, worshipping the Creator who chose to manifest Himself so beautifully to the young Muslim man sitting in their presence. Dr. Greenlay prays excitedly about how, in His great love, God pursued and revealed Himself to a man who wasn't even looking for Him. Embee picks up on that same idea and gives thanks to Jesus that He came and died for all men and women even when they were still sinners and their hearts were set against their Creator.

Dr. Windsor, who has taken several hours of leave from the hospice his wife only recently entered, intercedes for Mahmoud that he will powerfully realize that he is now a part of God's family. He also prays that the young man will know that he will be in heaven one day with all other believers who have chosen to embrace Jesus as their Lord. This is a fact, not a wish or a hope. Mahmoud never needs to doubt that truth.

After more spontaneous prayer and sharing, Dr. McNeely turns to Mahmoud and says in his deep voice, "We need to discuss where you go from here, son. You've experienced a life-altering conversion and must feel upside down—or, better said—feel like you've gone from upside down to right-side up," he says. The Academy president flashes a broad smile that pulls back the curtain of his mustache and beard. "The reality is that right-side-up probably doesn't feel very natural to you at all. It has to be completely alien to what your world was like earlier today."

Mahmoud leans forward and places his elbows on his legs. He sighs deeply. "What you say is true," he says, looking up at Dr. McNeely from the tops of his eyes. "I don't know who I am, where to go from here, or what I'm going to do. I'm a tree uprooted from its old soil and transplanted into new soil. It is rich soil and beautiful, but so new and unknown to me. At the same time, oddly, for the first time in my life, I sense that I'm home."

Aly, who is sitting next to Mahmoud, reaches out her hand and rests it gently on her brother's shoulder. She smiles through tears of joy and comments, "Just like me, Mahmoud trudged along the old familiar road until he encountered a new path whose truth was too compelling to dismiss."

Embee nods her head and says, "Jesus told the parable about a man who found a treasure in a field that he did not own. He valued that treasure so much that he sold everything else he had and bought the field so that the treasure could be his."

The silver-haired professor pauses and then smiles her radiant Embee smile. "Today, you're that man, Mahmoud. You've found the treasure, or, more accurately, the treasure has found you. Now you've forsaken everything else so that the treasure can be yours."

Mahmoud hesitates and then nods at Embee's words. "It is odd for me. On the one hand, yes, I feel like I've lost everything. On the other hand, I feel like I've gained everything and have really not lost anything."

"I can't begin to imagine what it's like for you to walk away from everything," Rachel interjects in an uncharacteristically quiet voice.

Without hesitation, the former jihadist replies, "The only way I ever would have turned my back on everything in my past is if Jesus Himself appeared to me in person. That's the only way I would have even considered leaving Islam." Mahmoud laughs wryly and then says, "And wouldn't you know, that's exactly what Jesus did."

There is a short pause before the new follower of Yahweh says, "I do want to ask Jesus why He appeared to me and inconveniently overturned my life like a watermelon cart in the marketplace. I also want to ask Him why He decided to love me of all people."

Mahmoud sits up in his chair and looks around at his captivated listeners. "I never thought I would say the word 'love.' Never in the past did that word appear in my vocabulary. It still is most difficult for me to say—it's too soft, too womanly, too vulnerable."

Dr. Greenlay suddenly shows signs that he has something to share. His mouth takes on the familiar round shape that presages a release of intense pressure from his brain in the form of a verbal avalanche.

"You must read about Saul as soon as you're able," the professor says quickly. His words cannot come out of his mouth fast enough to keep up with his brain. "He was a man who was guilty of imprisoning Christians and even being an accomplice in their deaths, but he was surprised by Jesus much like you were. Out of nowhere, when Saul was on his way to arrest some believers, Jesus shockingly appeared to him out of the clear blue sky and asked him why he was at cross purposes with Him. He specifically said, 'Saul, Saul, why do you persecute me?[7]'"

Mahmoud is mesmerized. His eyes open wide, and his thick black brows arch upward. He leans toward Dr. Greenlay as if communicating confidence and asks, "What did Saul do? You said he imprisoned and killed believers in Jesus?"

"Yes, yes," the professor almost shouts in his high-energy style. "Jesus went one step further with Saul than He did with you, however. He blinded him and then ordered him to go and wait for what was to happen next. For three days, Saul couldn't even see the nose on his face—which, arguably,

---

7. Acts 9:4 (NIV).

I suppose, is difficult for any of us to see, blind or not. He had to wait in darkness until Jesus sent a man of God to pray for him."

"Did Saul believe in Jesus?" Aly's brother asks, riveted on the professor's words.

"He did!" Dr. Greenlay replies animatedly. "Then when God's man, Ananias, came, he prayed for Saul. Immediately, something like scales fell from his eyes, and he could see again—physically, that is. Spiritually, of course, he was able to see for the first time in his life, just like you, today."

Dr. Greenlay pauses to breathe for the first time in a while and says, "Ananias was not very pleased with Jesus when He told him to go and speak with Saul. Understandably, he was deeply afraid of the man. His violent reputation had preceded him."

No one is prepared for what happens next. Mahmoud abruptly begins to weep and groan loudly. The groans are so primal that everyone in the room knows that they come from the deepest recesses of the young man's heart.

"I am Saul," the young man chokes out of his constricted throat.

"Even my own sister doesn't know the transgressions I have committed against God and His people." Mahmoud glances at Aly, whose hand still rests on his shoulder. "I, like Saul, have done violent things. I'm ashamed to even speak of them," he confesses. He looks away from Aly, and his eyes seek the refuge of the floor.

No one speaks. Only the sounds of the clock ticking on the wall and a vibrating cell phone interrupt the silence. Those gathered in the room would agree that they are in the presence of a modern-day Saul. The sudden transformation in Mahmoud's life is as miraculous as it had been in his first-century counterpart. Nothing short of God's intervention could change a heart of stone into a heart of flesh.

"I have threatened people; I have beaten people," Mahmoud begins his confession, still staring at the floor and weeping. "I have driven people out of their homes." He pauses and lets out a long sigh. "I have even been an accomplice to...to the killing of men and women, some with the blade of a knife or sword. Some with explosives."

For a long time, the contrite man is silent. Finally, he turns to look at Aly, whose face is etched with deep sadness. "So why, of all people in the world, would Jesus appear to me?" the modern-day Saul asks, his voice anguished. He drops his head into his hands and groans again.

"There are two reasons," a voice announces with authority. It is Miriam who speaks. Everyone turns to look at the old woman with the snow-white head and the face of a thousand wrinkles. Her countenance is resolute, defined by her burning Irish eyes and her set jaw. Her whole body vibrates with such intensity that there is something terrifying about her.

"First, Jesus died for you because He loves you deeply and wants to be the bridge of intimacy between you and your Father," the prophetess declares in her no-nonsense fashion. "Second, He has a plan for your life, young man. You are going to proclaim Jesus to people who otherwise would never have an opportunity to hear His name."

The wizened woman pauses for a moment and then adds gravely, "Your proclamation of Jesus will come at great risk and high cost to you."

Even while the gravity of Miriam's words is still settling over the twelve people in the room, Dr. Greenlay begins gesturing animatedly with his hands. Eventually, words follow. "That's exactly what Jesus said about Saul!" the professor exclaims excitedly. "He said about Saul—who He renamed Paul after he believed—that he would speak about Him to people who had never heard Jesus' name."

Dr. Windsor looks at Mahmoud, and a smile disturbs the lines of fatigue engraved on his face. "Yes, you have an amazing future ahead of you, young man," he proclaims. "Unlike any other. Trust me; there's no greater adventure than when a man or woman totally surrenders to God and says, 'Here I am. Send me.'"

Mahmoud nods at the words of the former colonel whose troops—unbeknown to him—fought against several of his distant relatives in Iraq. Then he gazes slowly around the room at his eleven mentors. Finally, he comments, "I can say one thing without doubt—I don't ever remember so many people looking at me who actually appear to like me."

Several people smile while others laugh loudly. "I have been the person who people fear and hate," Mahmoud admits, pursing his lips together. "I do not want to be that man for even one more day. I desire to be the new creation you told me about, Aliyah." He looks at his sister with eyes softened by grief. "I want to be a new man."

Dr. McNeely clears his throat and says, "The minute—no, the second—you declared your belief in Jesus, you became that new man, Mahmoud. You now sit before us a new creation. The old has gone...and the new has come."

"Then there are many things I need you to teach me about this faith," the young Saudi-Thai man says. "I need you to explain the Father, the Son, and the Spirit to me since I have always believed that God is one, not three."

Dr. McNeely nods his head and replies, "Yes, the Trinity of God is amazing—amazingly beyond our ability to fully understand but also amazingly beautiful. It is so awesome to me that these three persons who are one in nature have lived together forever, loving each other and communicating with each other and glorifying each other. They've been part of a relational triad that I believe is reflected in human relationships as well. At His core, God, just like us, is relational. Love that flows from the heart of God is what is meant to motivate us in this world, not power or materialism or selfish pleasure."

Mahmoud nods his head and says, "This is exactly what I must learn." His voice is subdued. He speaks as a man who has been broken and humbled and is now willing to submit to authority. A teachable spirit has replaced his heart of stone.

"You speak of relationships," the new believer says as he turns to look at his sister. "I believe I have gained a friendship with Aliyah, but in the same breath, I have lost relationship with my father and my Muslim brothers. This loss is already weighing very heavily on me because, in our culture, family and religion are of utmost importance. Allegiance to both is the highest value in our lives."

"Mahmoud," Embee says in a gentle voice.

The young believer looks at the woman with long, silver hair and shivers a bit. The last time he heard someone call his name in a similar fashion was in the motel room at 2:34 that morning.

"I've been hesitant to say too much," the professor says with a smile. "I wasn't certain how you would receive the voice of a woman—and in this case, a woman without a hijab—coming as you have from the conservative Sunni faith, but God has made it clear that I need to speak."

The matronly woman pauses momentarily and then says, "Jesus will teach you that you are to seek Him first—above everything else—even above family and religion. As you seek Him first, He promises that He will take care of everything else for you. He will provide for you since He already knows what you need."

Embee tilts her head slightly to one side and comments, "I see that you are confused. Ah, you wonder what I mean by seeking Jesus above even religion. Yes, that is a bit perplexing."

The woman's hand finds the cross that hangs from her neck, and she fingers it without awareness. "In the Christian faith, we don't believe in religion, Mahmoud. We see religion as men and women attempting to reach God. We don't need to do that with Jesus. He has reached down to us. He has pursued us with love and truth and has taught us that there is nothing we can do to earn His love. Good works are desirable, but they don't put us in relationship with God. Only believing in Jesus opens the door for us to be friends with God."

"So, you see," she says, "religion is nothing to us. Our faith is all about relationship. We are not as driven to know *about* God as we are to know Him personally as our Father, Savior, and friend. Yes, we do want to know the truth about who God is. We do value theology—the study of God. But that head knowledge is worthless if we don't know Him personally. And knowing Him personally is a higher priority than family, as Aly showed you a year ago."

Mahmoud shakes his head and glances at his sister again. "This faith in Jesus is so different from Islam. In our religion," he says, looking back at Embee, "God is distant. He is so high above us that we can never know him personally. What we do know very well are his rules and his prescriptions for how we should conduct ourselves in this world."

Mahmoud transfers his gaze to Dr. Greenlay and says, "I have never perceived Allah as a father. He has never been that approachable. Already I see and hear that you have a close friendship with God. How amazing! I have always believed that God is too powerful and majestic for us, that we should never assume we can come into his presence. I picture a street sweeper approaching the King of Arabia and expecting an audience. How disrespectful! What impudent sacrilege for a human to assume such intimacy with the sovereign God who dwells high above all!"

Dr. Greenlay nods sympathetically and vigorously squeezes his hands together as he waits to talk. "The transcendence of God and the immanence of God!" he exclaims. "Oceans of ink would not suffice to write about these two complementary truths about God's character."

The shorter man cannot remain seated. He jumps to his feet and begins to pace around the small confines of the room. "You are correct, Mahmoud—the God who created light to travel at 186,000 miles per second is far above us!" he announces as if he is speaking in his aquarium classroom. He then lowers his voice just above a whisper and says with no less fervency, "But God is also so close to us that He knows the number of hairs on our heads and sees us when we lie down and get up!"

The animated man abruptly stands still and gazes at Mahmoud, his face incandescent. Reverting to a louder voice, he exclaims, "He is so holy and majestic that we dare not even look into His face!" And then, in the quieter voice, he adds, "Yet He commands us to approach His throne so that we might receive grace and mercy in time of need.

"Mark my words, my young friend," Dr. Greenlay says in a confiding tone. "Yahweh is the sovereign Creator of the universe and...He is our Father and friend, closer to us than our own skin."

The professor places one arm across his stomach and rests the elbow of his other arm on top of it. He places two fingers on his upper lip and rolls his eyes toward the ceiling. "I do believe that to some degree, Islam does a good job portraying the majesty and transcendence of God." Looking back down at Mahmoud, he adds, "However, your old religion does not at all communicate the closeness of God. I mean no offense," the professor adds quickly, putting his hands up toward the young man.

Dr. Greenlay walks back to his chair and turns as if to sit down. "Do you know why Islam does an inadequate job of expressing the intimacy of God?" he inquires, looking at Mahmoud.

The young man pauses to think for a moment, then shakes his head with its thick black mane.

"One reason," the short man says very quietly. "They don't have Jesus." He pauses and raises one hand with an extended index finger to communicate the saliency of his next point. "John tells us in his gospel that Jesus is the eternal Word of God, who became flesh. He became one of us. The One and Only came to live among us! The God of the universe became a man so that we might see the unapproachable Father, so that we might fall to our knees in fearful worship of His majesty but also approach Him and cry out to Him as our loving daddy."

There is a silence before the professor concludes, "The transcendence and immanence of God. What an incredible co-existence. Unfathomable. Unheard of in any other faith."

Dr. Greenlay sits down, and the room is quiet.

"My old heart is hostile to such talk about God," Mahmoud eventually admits. "After all, is not The Holy One so high above us that He is unknowable to our finite minds? But my new heart...my new heart thirsts for a relationship with such an approachable God. I desperately want to know Him as a Father and a friend. It is yet too much for me to believe!"

Aly pats her brother's arm and says, "It is too much to believe. But your eyes have now been opened, Mahmoud, and your heart longs for Him, the great lover of your soul. Soon you'll begin to experience Him as your best friend."

The conversation among the members of the small circle continues for another forty-five minutes before Dr. McNeely finally says, "We need to pray for this young man who has crossed over from darkness into light. Let's give thanks to the Most High God for His saving love and also pray for Mahmoud's growth in his new faith."

Dr. McNeely asks Mahmoud if he would be comfortable sitting on the floor so everyone in the room can gather around and pray for him.

"I am very accustomed to praying on the ground," the young believer says with a wide smile. "I will certainly kneel here even though I am without my prayer rug."

Dr. Windsor chuckles and says, "By the way, Jesus doesn't care if you pray toward Mecca or Monterrey. What He values most highly is the position of your heart, not the position of your body."

"Ah," Mahmoud says, "that does sound like something that would be true of Jesus. I am rapidly discovering that He is more concerned with the inside of a man than with his external rule-keeping."

All the brothers and sisters in the room gather around the young man who had traveled from so far away to execute his sister only to have Jesus show him that he needed to die to himself.

Many in the room pray for Mahmoud. Dr. Greenlay thanks God for the obedience of the young man. Miriam gives praise to Jesus for being the changer of hearts. Jack prays that the Holy Spirit will help the new believer grow quickly in his faith. Embee prays that God the Father will hold Mahmoud close to Himself as he navigates the difficult challenges that lie ahead, including likely separation from his parents and sisters back in Thailand.

Dr. McNeely asks God to show the young man where he should go and what he should do to grow in his new faith. Aly weeps loudly as she lays her head on her brother's back and praises the name of Jesus for pursuing her lost brother. "What a wonderful Savior you are, Jesus, and what a beautiful name you have!" she exclaims. "And thanks for hearing our prayers!"

When the time of talking to God is over, Mahmoud rises to his feet. "I sense deep in my heart that I know God for the first time!" he declares loudly, raising his hands toward the ceiling. "I know Him! I know Him! I'm a new creation! Thank you, Jesus! Thank you, my friend above all friends!"

Everyone in the room is aware that they are witnessing a miracle. Seeing Jesus raise Lazarus from the tomb might rival and possibly surpass their wonder and joy at what God has done in this young man's heart. But not by much.

Nobody wants to leave the room that has been made cozy with love and joy. Everyone feels like they are back in first-century Jerusalem gathered as new believers in a house church. They are all family. They have been adopted by the Triune God. They are brothers and sisters in Christ. The Holy Spirit flows through the prayer lounge and through the hearts of those who are one in Jesus. Jack feels something powerful travel from his brain and down his spine.

It is with mixed emotions that Dr. McNeely announces that the professors must return to their classes.

As everyone turns to leave, the professor adds, "Please keep praying for Mahmoud that God will give him the wisdom to know the first step in his journey of faith. He's more than welcome to remain here, of course, or he could possibly attend an institute in Atlanta that might be a perfect fit for him. I'll be contacting the staff there within the hour."

A handful of those gathered in the prayer room remains with Aly and Mahmoud late into the night. Conversation, worship, prayer, Scripture reading, and laughter are in rich abundance. Everyone is so caught up in the Spirit that they forget to eat or drink. It is Armando who finally exclaims, "Caramba! Am I the only one who's spiritually stuffed but physically starving?"

Decades later, many who gathered in that room on that special day will say it was the richest spiritual experience of their lives.

CHAPTER 35

Violet Windsor Crosses the Jordan

The single-story hospice care facility is located on the edge of downtown in the shadow of the much larger seven-story hospital. It is not attached to the larger structure, Jack observes, possibly communicating albeit unintentionally that the hospital is for the living while the hospice is for the dying.

The hospice building resembles a large cottage with its white shutters, robin-egg blue siding, and flower boxes situated under latticed windows. The six Screaming Eagles enter the double glass door and find themselves in a cheery community room replete with overstuffed chairs, couches, floor-length curtains, and a warm earth-tone carpet. Other students and faculty members populate the cozy living room standing or sitting in small throngs. They are speaking softly among themselves.

Greetings are exchanged along with hugs and the frequent sighs that so often accompany dying and death.

Always the sighs.

A woman with a nametag on her chartreuse blouse that reads, Sue Proctor, Hospice Director, strides up to them. When Jack glances at her face, he gets the feeling that he parked in front of a fire hydrant and the policewoman is approaching him to issue a citation. The Director has a long, sharp nose and blue horn-rimmed glasses that serve as mini windshields for her two vigilant eyes that peer out at the world. The woman nods at the students in a type of formal salute and states, "I assume you're here to visit Mrs. Violet Windsor."

Everything about the woman is precise. Jack imagines that she is a straight shooter who lives her life by searching out the rules and then enforcing unbending compliance to them for herself and others. There is no coloring outside the lines with this woman. Her life is black and white, with no tints or hues allowed beyond her incongruous vivid blouse that somehow evaded the color censor.

"Yes, we are," Rachel manages to squeeze out from a throat that is tight with grief.

"Her husband notified me earlier today that you might be coming," Director Sue announces, her tone firm and even. "You may go in and see them. Just be vigilant to their needs at this delicate time, or I may have to ask you to step out of her room."

The six members of the micro-cohort nod their heads slowly and exchange glances, not entirely certain what behaviors might get them exiled from Violet's room. Sue Proper, as Jack has already begun to think of the hospice director, escorts them across the living room toward a door in the far corner of the large common area.

The woman comes to a smooth, professional halt at the entryway and gestures for them to keep going. "Remember to be vigilant to their needs," she repeats before she wheels to return to the proper management of her kingdom.

The six students swallow hard in unison and then enter what looks to Jack like a large bedroom suite that was most likely not decorated by Sue Proctor. The colors in the room are bright pastels, including the peach-colored blinds and carpet. There are no intrusive tubes or wires or wall-mounted containers for sharps, or commodes, or intimidating medical machines with blinking lights and beeping sounds like there had been in the hospital room he was in when he was a boy. His tense shoulders settle a bit, and his neck muscles relax. He is not a fan of being in the room.

When Dr. Windsor looks up from his chair beside his wife's bed and sees his students, his face brightens with recognition, and he rises to welcome them. His typically ageless countenance carries dark divots beneath his bloodshot eyes. His whole face appears haggard as if he has been in a months-long trench battle during WWI on the western front in France—one he appears to be losing. There is little doubt that in this ostensibly pleasant but deathly hospice room, the colonel is engaged in the most difficult battle of his life even without the presence of sniper fire and IEDs. The fierce siege mounting minute by minute against the body, mind, and heart of Violet Windsor is, of course, even more daunting.

In an unusual gesture of welcome from the typically measured former army officer, the weary man reaches out both of his hands to welcome the students. He warmly shakes each of their hands in turn. He is genuinely pleased to see them.

More than a dozen people are sitting in chairs around the periphery of the large bedroom. The professor introduces the Screaming Eagles to the sitting visitors who rise to greet them. They are members of the Windsor's church. The warm welcomes that are exchanged between the church members and the micro-cohort are tempered by the quiet grief communicated by moist eyes and feeble smiles.

Jack's attention finally turns to the woman in the bed. He is not excited to look at her.

The woman is motionless. She is not flesh and blood but porcelain. Her eyes are closed. Her dark hair sprawls across the white pillowcase too evenly. Jack is certain the hair is not her own. It glistens too brightly under the hospice lighting to be natural. Her face is wan, and its flesh has sunk down into her neck. Her skin is stretched across her face like the membrane of a drum. The bones of her face protrude harshly, unnaturally. Violet Windsor's age is just south of sixty, but she looks to be eighty. This is not the same woman he had met in October.

Jack watches the colorful quilt that lies over the woman's chest. It rises and falls too infrequently. Death lurks nearby—not in the parking lot or in the large common area, but in this very room. Jack knows. It strikes him as incomprehensible that less than two months ago, this kind woman cooked up a feast for the students that must have taken her a full day to prepare.

As he recalls that wonderful day with the walk in the leaves and Violet's amazing dreams, Jack is reminded how much he hates death. The great interrupter. The thief that steals, sometimes cruelly, slowly, a day at a time, until its object is engulfed by dying looks and smells. The terrible, uninvited intruder that appears where it is not welcome and takes what it did not give without asking permission. Inside, he groans, and Jack thinks of Jesus being troubled in His spirit outside the tomb of Lazarus.

As Jack observes the dying woman, something moves beneath the quilt. A second later, a small head with hairy ears and a black button nose pops out. Jack nearly jumps in surprise. Rachel and Emily do jump and take a step backward. It does not take them long to recognize Brown Sugar, the honey fleeced Goldendoodle they held and petted and kissed at the Windsor's house on several occasions over the last eight weeks.

Rachel, who has grown close to Dr. Windsor and his wife since the day in the amphitheater, folds her arms across her chest and chides in her sternest Bostonian tone, "What have we here, Dr. Windsor? A dog in the room? This action is clearly a violation of all the rules and regulations found in the field manual!"

Despite the heavy cloud that hangs over the room and the sad occasion that has summoned all the men and women to share in this temporary community, everyone laughs. Sugar barks excitedly. Isaiah Windsor smiles in embarrassment, revealing his perfect, white teeth. Out of nowhere, but not entirely unexpected, Director Susan sweeps into the room like a bracing gust from the north. With her hands on her hips, she asks, "Was that an animal I just heard?"

Everyone stares blankly at the proper woman as if they are all guilty of a crime but are not willing to confess. Eventually, one by one, they all turn and look at Dr. Windsor, the perpetrator of the crime. Armando is the one who puts into words what everyone else is thinking. "Did our professor smuggle an animal into this room without getting prior permission from nurse Susan?"

"Director Sue," the prim and proper woman corrects Armando.

"I think in the army they call it AWOP—animal without permission," Stewart remarks as the right corner of his mouth tilts upward. The smile is almost imperceptible, but it is such a rare facial expression for the Intellect that his classmates notice it immediately.

Everyone shifts their attention from the strait-laced colonel to the young man from Minnesota. "Stewart Olson," Aly says, "what amusing words have come forth from your mouth!"

Rachel raises her fist and punches Stewart in the arm.

Sugar, who apparently has some German Shepard in her somewhere, quickly extracts herself from the flowered patchwork quilt that reminds Jack of Violet's living room furniture that she will never sit on again. The small dog jumps to the floor and begins a barking tirade, scolding Rachel for her assault on Stewart.

Director Susan's mouth drops open when she sees the four-legged intruder. Everyone in the room glances at the proper woman's shocked countenance and then at Dr. Windsor's sheepish face. Laughter breaks out in the room for a second time. Within moments, people from the living room area rush into Violet's room to check out the commotion.

For several minutes, the dying room is transformed into a cheery pandemonium punctuated by animated chattering, more barking, laughter, and some crying—not due to grief but to the distracting laughter that is enthusiastically welcomed as a brief respite in the face of deep sorrow. Everyone watches, amused, as Isaiah Windsor attempts to explain the presence of the unauthorized canine visitor to Director Susan, whose folded arms and frowning face communicate her consternation.

It is remarkably amazing, then, with all the general disorder that is occurring in the room, that during a brief interlude—as might happen at the theater when someone is talking to a friend during a loud scene in the movie only to have the audio fall silent so abruptly that the talking person is heard by everyone in the theater—a whisper is heard.

Isaiah Windsor snaps to attention like an officer to an air raid siren and strides over to his wife's bed. Violet's eyes flutter open even as everyone stares at the dying woman. A hush falls over the room. Brown Sugar glances up at Director Susan, barks her displeasure one last time, then runs and leaps back onto the bed. She settles herself into a valley in the quilt between the woman and the attentive husband.

Violet attempts to raise her head off the pillow, but its weight is too much for the atrophied muscles of her neck. "Ize, am I in heaven, my love?" the reclining woman asks in a voice so quiet that everyone in the room holds their breath to hear it. "I thought I heard the angels singin'."

There is a pause. Thirty people in the room swallow hard in unison. Violet's body labors to draw precious oxygen into her lungs. She turns her head ever so slightly to locate her husband. She looks up at him for a long time, as if examining his face for the first time—or for last time.

Before her speechless husband can respond, Violet answers her own question in a voice just above a whisper, "Nope, I'm not there yet. Your right ear is...still higher than...the left one." Her face has no ability to show emotion, but her dimming eyes are smiling. The exertion of speaking wears her out, and her eyes fall shut.

Isaiah takes Violet's hand in both of his. Then he bends over and kisses his wife's forehead ever so gently. His touch is that of a father with a newborn baby.

Speaking as if they are the only two people in the room, the husband confides to his wife in a voice husky with emotion, "I love you, sweetheart and—" The man falls silent for a long time before he recovers himself and says, "and I don't know what I'm going to do without you."

Violet does not respond. Jack notices that the woman's breathing has become more ragged. Every labored breath is accompanied by a grating, gurgling sound that reminds Jack of another dying room he had been in long ago. The sound of soft sniffling begins to fill the crowded room. Thirty pairs of eyes are fixed on Isaiah and his wife. Some people think of leaving the room to give the couple some privacy in this intimate moment, but no one moves. Brown Sugar licks Violet's bony arm. Amazingly, the woman opens her eyes again.

Violet rolls her eyes ever so slightly to look at her husband. She has no more strength to turn her head. She licks her lips slowly—so slowly. She opens her mouth as her gaze remains fixed on her lover. Everyone stops breathing for a second time.

"I saw him...my love..." the woman whispers in a breathy voice. "Our little Jack."

There is silence for a long time, and Jack thinks that Violet has slipped into a coma since her eyes have closed once again.

More sniffling. Louder sniffling. Isaiah Windsor's shoulders are shaking without making a sound.

The next time Violet speaks, she does not open her eyes. She is beyond even that now, it seems. Somehow, the dying woman musters enough strength to whisper, "He was...with Jesus. Smiling. Said he'd...see me...today."

Jack watches from the foot of the bed as the man whom he has always experienced as larger than life chokes back a loud sob and covers his mouth with the back of his hand. He is still holding his wife's hand in his other hand.

Surprisingly, more words find their way out of Violet's mouth. "Say... goodbye to the...eagles...and the others." Her whisper is so quiet and breathy now that only those directly next to the bed can hear what she is saying.

Jack is one of those who hears. He knows she is referring to the six members of the micro-cohort and all the other students the woman has loved at the Academy over the years. He feels a wave of emotion rush upward into his chest. He grips the bed railing firmly. It is cold and hard against his fingers and reminds him of the presence of death. He has felt that presence somewhere before.

"Love...you...Ize."

Some people in the room are openly weeping now. Still, no one moves. Jack glances out of the corner of his eye at Director Susan. Even the wooden hospice sergeant, undoubtedly a veteran of many dying moments that unfolded in this very room, is dabbing at her eyes with a tissue. She is not such a bad egg after all.

Jack counts fifteen seconds between Violet's breaths. The next time, it is twenty seconds before she sucks in a short breath. Dr. Windsor's wife of thirty-five years is at the end of her life.

Then the most unexpected thing happens. Violet opens her eyes wide, and a smile spreads across her face as bright as the morning sun when it breaks above the horizon. To everyone's utter amazement, the woman lifts her head off the pillow a few inches. Her eyes are fixed on the ceiling.

"I knew you'd come for me," she says. Her words are not loud, but they are more distinct than anything else she has said in the last few minutes.

Now there's not a dry eye in the hospice room. Some people are hugging each other, several are praying in whispers, and a few are raising their arms silently upward. One woman is laughing, her face as radiant as Violet's.

At that moment, Jack senses that the massive doors of heaven have swung open. He is standing with one foot on earth and one foot in eternity. A chill travels down his spine, and goosebumps break out all over his body. He closes his eyes and feels himself swelling inside as if he is going to burst. He knows he is witnessing a rare event, one that only happens when a believer enters the presence of God.

Without even willing it, he says, "I love you, Jesus, and I thank you for coming for your beloved daughter." Nobody hears him above the noise in the room, but it would not have bothered him if they had. He is reminded again of one of the many amazing benefits of believing in Jesus: Death does not have the final word. It is merely the door that opens to life eternal.

When Jack opens his eyes, Violet Windsor has already abandoned her earthly body. Her head has sunk back into the pillow. One of her lifeless hands is resting on Brown Sugar's fluffy head while the other is still in her husband's hands. Isaiah Windsor's head is bowed over his wife's body. His forehead rests on her cheek.

Someone begins singing "Amazing Grace," and soon everyone joins in. The hospice bedroom swells with the sound of voices rich with intermingled grief and joy.

Jack smiles to himself—Violet has her angel voices after all. Everyone present knows that while Violet's body is resting on the bed, she is home with Jesus, her Savior, the One who had found her when she was thirteen, two years removed from her mother's sudden death. Her fragile earthly tent has been struck. Now she is in her eternal house in heaven.

Jack glances at Emily. She is not actually singing, only half-heartedly mouthing the words, but her cheeks are streaked with tears. At that moment, she looks over at him and holds his gaze for a while before she closes her eyes and turns her face away.

Jack looks back at the bed where the body of Violet Windsor lies like the molted exoskeleton of a cicada. The moment feels... misplaced. It is so powerful that it feels almost tangible. A minute ago, he sensed the woman's presence in the hospice room as real as the bed railing he is still gripping with both hands. Now there is an emptiness here that cannot be explained.

For years, he has believed that something unusual happens at death. But now, he is more convinced than ever through his firsthand experience. Clearly, the human body is not all there is. There is a spirit inside every person that exudes a powerful presence into the physical world around it while it resides inside its physical vehicle. But once the vehicle dies, the nonmaterial person leaves for other climes. Violet's spirit has now left her vehicle, and the vacuum she leaves behind is astounding to Jack.

As is true of many dogs, Brown Sugar is aware that something is wrong. She is alternately licking her grieving master's face and then the face that Violet left behind. "Amazing Grace" is coming to an end. The mystery of the astounding confluence of the temporal world with the eternal still lingers in the room like a beautiful fragrance. No, more like a rumbling earthquake.

If Jack had possessed entrenched doubts about his faith before he entered the hospice room, they are now dispelled.

It is not simply that Violet has left. Not at all. It is much more than that. It is that someone has been in this place to greet her and escort her home. Someone so infinitely huge that He created everything in the universe with a single word from His mouth. Someone so intimate that He is Violet's closest friend. Someone indescribably holy, perfectly loving, and larger than the universe.

Someone named Jesus.

CHAPTER 36

Violet's Homegoing Party

Violet Windsor's homegoing celebration takes place five days after her death in the hospice center where her husband, the Screaming Eagles, Director Sue, miscellaneous other friends, professors and students, and even button-nosed Sugar were in attendance to send her off. Today, all the same people—surprisingly, even Director Sue—are present along with many other mourners and celebrants. Only Sugar is absent, and not by her choice.

The celebration is held in the Citadel sanctuary, the same place where only six days earlier Mahmoud Ahmed was introduced to Violet's best friend. Now Violet and Mahmoud are brother and sister—family. While Violet is now beholding Jesus' face by sight, Mahmoud is still on this side of the grave, just getting to know his Savior by faith.

The home-going service lasts two hours primarily because student after student—former and current—make their way up to the raised platform inside the towering turret and share their memories of the woman who embraced them as her children during her husband's eight years as a professor at the Academy. Jack and Rachel are two of the students who share fond memories of Violet. People cry at the stories told about Violet, and people laugh at the same stories. Songs are sung. A portion of the "Cherubini Requiem" is played by the Academy Orchestra with Rachel on the organ. Prayers are prayed. Dr. McNeely delivers the meditation that throbs with the promise and the reality of heaven. The service ends with Isaiah Windsor speaking the final words.

"Jesus," the bereaved husband begins, "I thank you that because of your resurrection, I have no doubt that my dear Violet is in your presence." Jack is amazed that the man's voice is so steady, so sure. "And I know that I will see her again. Today, it is perfectly appropriate for me not to bid my soulmate 'goodbye.' It is much more accurate for me to say, 'I'll see you, later, Violet, lovely flower of my life.'"

Isaiah Windsor stops praying, and his eyes drift down to the casket. After a long pause, during which the expansive sanctuary is amazingly quiet, the professor says, "Jesus, I miss my dear wife fiercely...Yet, I know she's in good hands, the best hands. So, I'm sad for me and overjoyed for her... Thank you for creating such an amazing woman and sharing her with me for thirty years."

The grieving man pauses to wipe his eyes and nose with a handkerchief, then prays, "Jesus, I'm a better man because of Violet's love for me. I look forward to seeing both of you in the not-so-distant future. Death will be so much easier for me now because I know that the three people I love the most are waiting for me on the other side. But until that day arrives, I make an oath before all these people gathered here today to serve you with all my heart. Be glorified this day in your servant, Father God."

When the service is over, eight pallbearers solemnly walk to the front of the massive sanctuary and wheel Violet Windsor's casket down the long main aisle and out through the double doors at the back of the church. Once outside the sanctuary, they navigate the coffin carriage out the side door of the Citadel and onto a crushed rock path that leads up to the cemetery. Here the pallbearers lift the casket off the four-wheeled cart and commence the gradual ascent toward the graveyard. The procession follows a man playing "Amazing Grace" on a bagpipe and Louis Fagani. Fortunately for all, he is in a wheelchair pushed by an Academy student.

The mid-December day is clear and crisp. A steady breeze makes the air feel even colder. The micro-cohort, along with the other individuals who are attending the graveside ceremony, follow the casket through the cemetery gate. As they pass under the arched entryway, Jack looks up and reads the now-familiar words: "The dead will be raised imperishable."

He has always felt a bit uneasy in cemeteries, but this one stirs an even more intense discomfort within him because of his nightmare about the demented man with the long stringy hair—the same man, strangely enough, that had appeared in Violet Windsor's dreams.

At the gravesite, the white casket with gold trim is placed above the vault on the green straps that Jack has seen at every graveside ceremony he has attended. They have become so associated with burials for him that every time he sees green straps, even when he is not in a cemetery, he is reminded of death. Is not green a color that should be associated with life and not death? Jack shakes his head to clear his mind of such irrelevant musings. He steers his mind to thoughts of Mahmoud, who flew to Atlanta just two days after his rebirth to meet with a professor from the Middle East, who himself is a believer in Jesus.

A pastor from the local church that the Windsors attended conducts the brief graveside ceremony. Jack and his fellow students stand under and around a canopy behind a row of white wooden folding chairs where Dr. Windsor, along with several family members, sit.

As the pastor commends the departed woman's spirit to her God and Savior, Jack's mind drifts back to Violet's words she spoke back on that October night in her home: "For me to live is Christ, and to die is gain." He can't help but smile at the unwavering faith Violet displayed even in the lengthening shadows of the illness that would claim her life.

Jack's eyes drift across the cemetery that sprawls over the gradually sloping hillside. He considers the domino-slab monuments that populate the grassy knoll for fifty yards in both directions and the small stands of hardwood and fir trees scattered among the graves. Most of the hardwood trees are barren. The once-green leaves that clothed them are long dead and have fallen to the earth from their lofty perches, never to rise again. Such is life. Even the mighty, the beautiful, and the glorious fall into shadows and return to the dust. Until He says otherwise.

In the corner of the cemetery, not more than fifty feet away, Jack's wandering attention is captured by three large trees—they appear quite old—growing so closely together that they appear to sprout out of the same trunk. *Three sisters,* Jack thinks to himself, and he is reminded of his younger siblings back in Colorado. He will be traveling to see them in just a matter of days over Christmas break.

The brief ceremony ends. Everyone is on their feet, waiting their turn to extend personal condolences to the bereaved Isaiah Windsor. Some people shake his hand, others embrace him, and a few simply nod at him silently while their eyes convey wordless messages of comfort mingled with grief. Tissues and handkerchiefs are as numerous as the domino-slabs of death.

While the other Screaming Eagles line up to speak with Dr. Windsor, Jack decides to take a closer look at the sister trees. Afterward, he cannot recall what exactly summoned him to that spot. He just knows that the urge arose within him, and he acted on it.

When he arrives at the old trees, he discovers that there is actually a fourth tree hidden behind the others. All four trunks touch at the ground level like they grew out of a common seed. Jack inserts his head into the small interior space between the trees and looks up toward the blue expanse above. The spacing of the arboreal constellation is such that the afternoon sky pours down through the leafless trees roughly in the shape of a cross.

How providential, Jack thinks—*a special sign on Violet's home-going day.*

Jack backs away from the trees and examines the adjacent gravesite. He counts six small memorial stones that have sunk into the cemetery floor like floundering ships. They are almost entirely obscured by the encroaching grass of the cemetery lawn. Behind them, a large, lichen-coated monument rises four feet in height. Roughly a third of one side is missing, broken off by some force of nature, Jack assumes.

He approaches the six markers and gets on his knees so he can study them more closely. With some effort, he makes out the words *grandfather, grandmother, mother, son, son,* and daughter engraved on the weathered stones. No personal names are inscribed on any of them.

After further examination—and with some difficulty—Jack makes out numbers and months. The date of death on the grandfather marker is 27 November 1905, while the date of death on the grandmother stone is 13 March 1899. The year and day of death on the other four stones are oddly all the same—7 April 1899. *How sad,* Jack thinks. *Probably a house fire or maybe even some type of plague. But what about the father? Why isn't his grave here? Did he and some of his other children survive the unknown tragedy?*

Jack's eyes shift from the six sunken gravestones to the fractured monument. Unlike most of the other gray headstones that stand in the cemetery like so many tired sentries, this one is cut out of a darker stone. *Black granite,* Jack thinks to himself. No doubt this family was wealthy.

Jack gets to his feet with the intention of returning to the burial party, but something captures his attention. He looks back at the upright black slab and sees the letters Eccle inscribed near its base. Intrigued, Jack approaches the oversized black monument and stops in front of it.

It does not take him very long to make out the word, Ecclesiastes.

Getting on his knees again, he attempts to read other words etched in the black stone above Ecclesiastes. They are almost entirely worn away by over a hundred years of exposure to the elements. Jack shakes his head, trying to imagine in his twenty-four-year-old mind the passing of 120 years.

Jack closes his eyes and attempts to trace the faint letters with his fingers. With great difficulty, he is able to tactilely read the phrase, There is a time for everything, and a season— Here he is forced to stop because the rest of the words are missing, inscribed on the part of the monument that had been broken off.

He picks up the scripture verse on the next line with his tracing finger. *A time to be born and a time to die*—he reads with his laborious Braille method. Again, the rest of the sentence is missing. The next two lines read, *A time to kill and a time to heal, and A time to weep and a time to laugh—*

Jack leans away from the monument and stares at it with unseeing eyes. *Where have I heard these words before?* he wonders. *Recently, that is.* He opens several drawers in the file cabinets of his brain before realization dawns. "Of course," he says aloud. "Violet Windsor. She mentioned these words in her dreams about me."

Jack's interest spikes. It is only then that he recalls Violet's reference to the four sisters standing tall in fields of death. Could it be? Could Violet's dream about the four sisters and the words from Ecclesiastes refer to this gravesite?

His interest in the deformed monument now further galvanized; Jack leans forward on his knees and examines the *Rosetta Stone* wondering if it contains secrets that will irrevocably alter his future. Above the Ecclesiastes inscription, he eventually makes out larger but even more weatherworn letters engraved in the black stone. The letters are so faint that he would never have discovered them had he not been looking for them.

After further tactile reading of the surface of the worn stone, he eventually deciphers that the letters are *S-U-T-H-E.* The remainder of the word, which must be the family name, Jack assumes, is forever lost, inscribed into the piece of the monument that had been displaced by some act of nature or vandalism.

Jack rises from his kneeling position and slowly backs away from the deformed slab. His brain is swimming with the unfathomable implications of Violet's dream. *Four sisters. A time to die. Dead relatives. Sutherington.* Yes, he knows that the family name on the monument is his own. *Sutherington.* This gravesite is what Violet's dreams were pointing to. But what does it all mean? And how did he end up at a school with an adjoining cemetery where relatives of his are most likely interred? What are the odds of that happening? Clearly not a coincidence.

Jack interlaces his fingers behind his head, and his eyes drift past the black monument and out across the cemetery. He tries to put all the pieces together in his brain, but his attempts prove futile. *Why, God, would you want me to come here to this cemetery where my great-great-great somebody or other is buried?*

He stands there a long time, then slowly backs away even further from the gravesite. Eventually, he turns his back to the monument and walks thoughtfully over to the thinning group of mourners who are gathered around Violet's casket.

The micro-cohort is preparing to leave the gravesite. Jack approaches Armando and touches the arm of his somber-faced friend. "Tell the others to wait," Jack comments quietly. "I have something to show you guys."

Jack hears his friend reply, "Sure thing, Juan," and then Jack is past him and standing in front of the imposing Dr. Windsor, who has become more approachable in recent weeks.

"Thanks for being here, Jack," the retired army officer says with moist eyes that stand in sharp contrast to his hard, chiseled face with its high cheekbones and square jaws. He shakes Jack's extended hand and pats him firmly on the shoulder in such a way that Jack feels like a man. "Your visit to the house was the last time Violet cooked a meal for anybody. You six were very special to her—with the dreams and all."

Jack begins to speak, but the warfare professor interrupts him. "I want to explain why I've been heavy-handed with you, Jack."

"No need," the young man replies. "I know you want me to get a haircut."

Both men laugh. "The army in me says, 'Yes, get a haircut,'" colonel Windsor agrees in his most intimidating voice without even trying. "The rest of me," he muses aloud thoughtfully, "says that appearances don't matter squat."

"I share your son's name," Jack interjects. "Maybe that has something to do with it."

"Yes, I suppose you could be right about that, at least partly," the grieving man says with his eyes fixed on Jack like two 50-millimeter Barrett sniper rifle barrels situated three feet from his face. "If you're saying that I'm subconsciously singling you out because you trigger some overprotective parental instinct related to my deceased son—maybe. I can't prove that theory or disprove it."

"And then the dreams..." Jack trails off.

Dr. Windsor nods his head and says wistfully, "Yes, Violet's dreams. As you discovered that night at our house, she was telling me about some of those dreams as early as July. Those dreams—which I put great stock in, by the way—indicate that your life is in danger, son. I've been harder on you to prepare you for the battle, just like I did with the men and women under my command in the army.

I see great potential in you, Jack, and...I see a soft side in you that's vulnerable to great harm. You need to have stronger defenses in the war against darkness. You're too nice, Jack." The professor pauses and then clarifies, "Nice has nothing to do with love, by the way."

Jack nods his head and wonders if he should inform the colonel about his discovery in the cemetery that is surely related to Violet's dreams. On this day of all days, he decides not to bother the grieving man. It can wait for another time. Before he can ask the professor what he means by his "soft side," a couple approaches the Warfare professor and engages him in conversation.

Jack smiles and takes a step backward. "Later," he mouths to the colonel. Dr. Windsor winks at him and says over the shoulder of the man in front of him, "Yes, later, Jack. Definitely."

Jack turns quickly only to bump into Stewart and the other members of the Screaming Eagles, who are gathered in a small semi-circle behind him. Despite the sadness of the occasion, he smiles broadly at his four-month-old friends and announces, "Do I have something to show you guys? I've got something to show you guys!"

"It can't be that important," Rachel comments facetiously.

"Follow me," he says as he turns and strides away.

His five friends look at each other and shrug their shoulders. Then they follow Jack as he leads them across the cemetery lawn to the four sister trees. In a matter of minutes, he explains everything to them. Soon they are all examining the six half-buried grave markers and what remains of the black granite Sutherington monument.

"This is incredible," Emily remarks as she traces the large letters on the monument with her long fingers. Then she looks up at Jack with shining green eyes that not even her mysterious melancholy can fully extinguish and comments, "You coming to this school certainly doesn't appear to be an accident, Jack."

"My thought exactly," he says, looking back at Emily.

"So, what does it all mean?" Aly inquires, her detective skills whetted.

"I don't know," Jack replies. "I'm hoping we can put our heads together and figure it out."

"Mrs. Windsor's dreams certainly pertain to this gravesite," Stewart reflects as he adjusts his glasses. "I suppose it's possible there's some elusive and enigmatic message hidden in the markers and the monument."

"And don't forget the four trees," Rachel adds. "They must be the ones Violet referred to in her dreams."

"Maybe their only purpose is to lead Jack to this gravesite," Armando says, "meaning that they simply point to the location of the message and are not part of the message themselves."

"I like that idea," Emily says, nodding her blonde head.

"So, where do we begin?" Aly asks. "All we have are six lonely gravestones and one broken monument over a hundred years old that tell us a mother and her three children all died on the same day."

"And we can surmise that all four of them are Jack's progenitors," Stewart says in way of reminder.

"Also," adds Armando, "it may mean nothing, but the mother and three children all died only several weeks after the grandmother. Maybe all five of them died of the same disease."

"Possibly," Emily remarks, drawing out the word to express some doubt about Armando's comment. "It's just hard to believe that the mother and four children all died from the same disease on the same day. What are the odds of that happening?"

"So, what am I supposed to do with all this?" Jack thinks aloud more to himself than his fellow students.

"Maybe it has something to do with what Embee said at the orientation meeting in August," Emily suggests. "Remember what she said about the urban myth around the Academy involving treasure and murder and worshippers of darkness."

"Yeah, I remember. I just haven't thought much about it," Jack admits.

"Do you think all of Violet's dreams have a spiritual dimension to them?" Rachel asks.

Jack nods his head. "Doesn't everything in this world have an underlying spiritual meaning?" he asks. "It does appear that Violet's dreams involve real events in this earthly world, but so far, they also seem to have to do with the world beyond sight. Just yesterday, we discussed Violet's dreams about Aly, where she was leaving the palace and was protected by Jesus, the rising sun. That dream certainly had a clear spiritual theme."

"Yes, Juan," Armando says, "it couldn't have been more obvious that the dream was about Aly fleeing Thailand and the spiritual darkness of her Muslim faith and running toward the true God. The lion with the sharp tooth, of course, was Mahmoud with his knife. Fortunately, Jesus shone the blinding light of His love into the eyes of that lion to protect Aly but to also save the lion."

Aly turns away from the monument and gazes at Jack with scrunched eyebrows. She has been so engrossed in her thoughts that she did not hear what her peers had been saying. "I think you need to speak with Dr. Fagani," she observes. "If there are any mysteries hidden among the graves of this cemetery, he would be the one to ask."

Everyone agrees with Aly's suggestion. Stewart nods his head along with the others, then adjusts his black horn-rimmed glasses and fingers the pens in his pocket protector one by one. "There is one other possibility," he states in the know-it-all manner that frustrates Armando to no end.

"What's that, Stewart?" Jack inquires as Armando shakes his head and rolls his eyes.

"The final piece of the puzzle might rest beneath your feet," the Intellect speculates.

"What do you mean?" Rachel inquires as she brushes away strands of her auburn hair that have blown into her mouth.

"I'm suggesting that the missing piece to resolve this mystery could be buried beneath us in one of the Sutherington caskets," Stewart states in his flat tone.

"That's a real stretch, Stewart," the voice of Armando says edgily.

"Well, we're in the brainstorming phase right now," Jack reminds Armando, defending his bespectacled friend. "When people brainstorm, they consider every possibility no matter how incredible it seems at first blush. I think we need to add Stewart's idea to the list of possibilities."

"Wouldn't that be something if we had to dig up an old grave!" Rachel exclaims. She hesitates and then says, "I suppose we'd have to get some kind of license to do that."

Jack laughs. "Probably more like a court injunction," he says.

"Unless we come here under the cover of night and surreptitiously exhume the coffin or coffins from the ground," Stewart says, his large childlike eyes fixed on Jack.

"Let's not get ahead of ourselves," Jack replies with a smile. "I'm not ready to go CSI just yet. We need to do a little research on the Sutherington family first to find out if I really am related to the people buried here."

Emily shakes her head and remarks, "I never thought at the beginning of the school year that part of our education would be solving a mystery. First the journal, then Violet's dreams, then the truck that followed you guys to the university, and now the cemetery and the Sutherington family."

"Maybe they're all linked together somehow," Rachel offers.

"How would the journal be connected with—" Aly stops in mid-sentence. She gasps and puts a hand over her mouth.

"What is it, Aly?" Jack inquires as he places a hand on the young woman's shoulder.

"The journal . . ." she begins to say.

"What about it?" Emily asks.

"The initials in the journal," Aly expands on her previous thought. "Remember how we thought it was kind of strange that the initials were the same as Jack's—JLS. Except for the middle initial, of course." The Thai-Saudi woman taps her forefinger on her chin and says, "What if the S stands for Sutherington? That would mean the journal and this monument are somehow connected."

"Are you thinking that the author of the journal could be the man buried here under the grandfather marker?" Emily asks. "Or that he's the husband who isn't buried here beside his wife?"

"I certainly wonder," Armando interjects as he massages the teardrop tattoo beneath his right eye and turns his back to Stewart. "The journal was written back in what—1899—and these gravestones are from the same year. I have to believe there's some connection between the two, my fellow journal readers and future grave diggers."

There is a brief silence as the six men and women eye each other under the cool mid-afternoon December sun. "I think we all know what we have to do next," Jack says slowly, decisively.

"We have to eavesdrop on someone's private journal as soon as possible," Rachel says with a cunning smile.

"That's exactly right, Agatha Christie," Jack comments with a laugh. "But we don't have much time before Christmas break, do we? What are we down to now, about five days before we're done with the semester?"

"There's only four days left of Finals Week," Stewart comments without hesitation.

"Between finals, spelunking, and work at the hotel," Aly interjects, "we don't have much time to read the diary—all of us together, I mean. Maybe we'll have to wait until after we get back from Christmas holiday."

Rachel turns her head slowly to look at her classmate. "Who are you, Aly?" she asks in an animated voice full of mock frustration. "No self-respecting woman can wait a month to read that journal, not with this recent development. Where's your sense of curiosity, girl?"

Aly smiles, and her large Thai eyes twinkle. "How do you say it here in America? 'My bad.'"

Jack glances at the woman whose shiny black hair sans hijab flows down over her shoulders like liquid basalt on the slope of an active volcano. "Nice," he comments with a wink. "You're learning American slang quickly." Then he scans all the faces of those gathered around him and says, "I think Rach has the right idea. The sooner we read that journal, the better. I vote for tonight after we're done with academics and work responsibilities. Can all of you get together around 11:00?"

"That's a bit late for me," Armando quips. "My primary physician tells me that as a growing young man, I need to get eight hours of sleep every night."

Jack gives his friend a stiff-arm shove. "Yeah, right. I doubt that you've even been to a doctor since you got shot in that drive-by shooting back in high school."

"What are you talking about?" Emily asks, obviously not privy to Armando's near-death experience six years ago.

"It's a long story that's going to have to wait," Jack says gently. "So how about it? Tonight at 11:00 in the fireside room with Moses and Hawkstern?"

"Don't even joke about it," Rachel replies. "I know the painting of Moses does uncannily resemble Hawkstern, but their personalities are nothing alike."

Everyone laughs, and then they all agree to meet at the fireside room that evening.

As they begin to drift away from the gravesite, Jack says, "Hey, let's quick pray. I just want to make sure we're putting this adventure into God's hands. Who knows how much darkness is connected to this whole thing."

When Jack finishes praying, Emily turns to him and confides, "This is getting...interesting. Very interesting."

Jack nods his head but says nothing because, in his mind, he's still praying, only now for the young woman standing beside him. He prays that this recent development will be enough to lure her back to the Academy after the winter break. Her return to the school seems anything but certain in his mind. *But then, all things are possible with you, Jesus.*

CHAPTER 37

The Journal of Revelations

The six members of the micro-cohort settle into the couch and overstuffed chairs in the Fireside room far from the painting of fiery Moses at the Red Sea that resembles Dr. Hawkstern. It is 11:30 at night. Stewart removes the old leather-bound journal from its protective box and sets it carefully on the coffee table.

"So, where do we start?" Armando asks, rubbing his hands together.

"I think Jack should choose," Rachel suggests, "now that we know that the diary—journal—may technically belong to him as a Sutherington." No one disagrees with her recommendation.

Jack looks around at his five Academy friends and says, "I think we should read the last journal entry prior to the death of the mother and the three children. If this JLS person really is, or was, a Sutherington, I'm sure he would mention the illness that killed his family."

"Sounds good to me, Juan," Armando says, rubbing his hands together again.

Jack turns to Stewart and instructs him to find the journal entry dated just prior to April 7th, 1899.

The bespectacled man, who is always eager to help, opens the journal with the same care as he had set it on the table. Then he begins to page through the one-hundred-twenty-year-old journal. It doesn't take him long to find the correct entry.

"Jack," Stewart says, looking up at his friend. His eyes are peering over the top of his glasses. "The entry I found is three days after the grandmother died and approximately three weeks before the mother and children died."

"That sounds perfect," Jack replies with a grim smile. "It's hard to believe that what you're about to read, Stew, might be about my family a century before I was born. Like you said, Armando, this could be interesting."

Stewart looks down at the diary and then back up at Jack with his passionless eyes. "The handwriting in this entry is much larger than the previous entries, he observes. "Larger and...wild."

"Okay," Jack comments with some hesitation, elongating the word. "Go ahead and read, and we'll find out what that's about."

Stewart directs his attention back to the journal of JLS and begins to read. The pace of his reading slows down dramatically when he gets to the last sentence, pausing between each word.

> 16 March 1899. It is finished. My misdeed is secreted. My inadvertent trespass is removed from the face of the earth. I have buried her where no one will find her.

Stewart stops reading and stares at the page. The room is quiet except for intermittent crackling and popping from the logs burning in the huge fireplace. Finally, Emily clears her throat and asks in a soft voice, "Is he saying what it sounds like he's saying?"

"It sounds like your great-great somebody or other could be a murderer, Juan," Armando says with a chuckle.

Jack swallows hard and replies, "Again, there's only one way to know for sure. Keep reading, Stew."

The designated journal reader begins again.

The events of the past three days have been unspeakable—the content of a nightmare. It all began with my mother's untimely death. My sorrow was unbearable! I strove to comfort my deep grief with liquor and the special syrup and then went to visit Madeline at her house. Her crazy husband was away in St. Louis.

I think I was inebriated when I arrived. No, I know I was inebriated. Why in the blazes did I ever choose to go there? My wife and children were back at my father's house with other relatives grieving my mother. So why did I concoct the lie that I had to return to the office and complete plans for my business travels the following week? I do know why—but I am loath to confess it. I've become a callous man who thinks much of himself and little of others.

My desires have ruled me for months and months now. Agatha has been increasingly suspicious of my activities outside the manse and questions me daily until I grow weary of it. I have learned how to lie. One lie has led to another until I now have a tower of lies built one upon the other. If I misspeak, but once, they will all come toppling down. Undeterred by this possibility, I have continued to feed my growing lust for fine food, drink, pleasure, and women. And then tonight—

I had no evil intent in my heart when I went to her house! I swear to God that's the truth. I was full of spirits and out of my natural mind. In my rapacious love for her, I grabbed Madeline's arm when she refused me comfort. She pulled away much more violently than my grip warranted—this is true. I swear to it! Foolish woman! She easily freed herself from my playful grasp and, in doing so, caught her foot on the Persian rug in the parlor.

Since she was in the act of pulling away from me, she lost her balance and fell backward. I watched her fall as in a dream. The look of surprise on her face! The dull thud when her head impacted the edge of the stone hearth and—I yet cannot believe it! Her body was taken by unnatural tremors, and I quickly took her up in my arms!

There was no saving her. There was nothing I could do. Her convulsions were the convulsions of death.

I held my beloved Madeline to my chest for a long time after her body grew still. I wept bitterly! God knows how remorseful I was! But then it came to me that her two children were in their beds sleeping. In horror, I jumped to my feet and began pacing the room. What was I to do? Who should I notify? I had not killed her! No! Never! My hand had hastened her tragic demise, possibly. But she is the one who pulled away from me! It was all a senseless accident.

In the end, I was not guilty of murder, so I deemed it unnecessary to contact the constable. What was I then to do?

Eventually, I was possessed by the irrational thought that I had to hide her body! Remember, I was drunk! I was out of my mind! I ran and frantically searched her bedroom for something to cover her body so the children would not see their mother in such a state. I found some blankets in the closet and quickly wrapped her body in them. There was little blood—only a dark flow from her nostrils and a trickle from her right ear—none on the rug.

I carried Madeline out to my horseless carriage and then rode to the cemetery simply because it was the first place that came to my mind and because I had to escape the watchful eyes of men. In some corner of my muddled brain, I suppose I also hoped that my dear deceased mother would find a way to tell me one last time what to do. She did not fail me.

At the cemetery, I sat in my carriage beside myself with sorrow. I wanted to die. Indeed, I thought of taking my own life. But how? Then it came to me in the blink of an eye. I must bury the body. (Again, I attest that I was not in my right mind. I was momentarily deranged). Since I had served as a deacon two years earlier, I still had a key to the church in my possession. I quickly retrieved a shovel from the church cellar and carried the body to—to the grave and—buried her.

My conscience is less burdened because before she fell, Madeleine had been showing me the rare coins that belonged to her husband. I knew the box that held the Libertys was in her pocket. Yet, it did not even enter my mind to dispossess her of them. I left them in her clothing. I am no thief! Neither am I a murderer! What befell me this night is a terrible misfortune!

What am I to do now? Will I fall under suspicion for the disappearance of Philip's wife? I am convinced that no one saw me at the DaFoe house last evening. The children were in bed. Philip himself, as I wrote, was in St. Louis. My wife and family were at my father's house and believe—I am certain of this—that I was detained at the office as has been my custom. There is nothing out of place that would lead anyone to think it was me.

No, I will not be suspected. Was not Madeline severely discontented with her husband and entertaining dalliances with any number of men? Will it not be assumed that the dissatisfied wife ran off with another man—especially when no body will be found. Additionally, there is nothing amiss at the house that will betray signs that a death occurred there. I will not be under suspicion by the authorities! Quite to the contrary, I am above suspicion.

My fear is that I will be severely discomfited by the voice within! Already, I dread that I will experience the fate of the murderer in the Tell-Tale Heart, who is haunted by the beating of the old man's heart after his dark deed was accomplished. Thankfully, the ears of my mind do not hear the literal beating of a human heart. However, I am plagued by an uninvited voice in my head. It chants to me at every importune moment, "Two in one. Two in one. Two in one." I condemn this voice to hell from whence it came! I will whistle and sing and drink and do everything else in my power to mute this voice since I have done nothing wrong. I was merely chosen by fate to be an unwitting agent in this woman's untimely demise.

Madeline is free from the icy currents of this world that bore her on their sharp shoulders to places she did not wish to go. I remain at their mercy.

I will return to my house and carry on as if nothing ill has occurred. Was I not at my place of business, detained longer than I had anticipated? All will be well. Most assuredly, all will be well.

My trembling has mostly eased. My galloping heart has slowed to a trot. My breathing is no longer that of a crazed animal fleeing the presence of the devil himself!

I will be calm. I will be at ease. After all, it was an accident, was it not? Perchance, it was providential that I was present with Madeleine in her dying hour. None of us desire to be alone at such a time. I was surely destined to be there for her.

Life is a series of accidents, a string of determined events. I was party to one last night—no, I was a witness to one! Dust to dust. Ashes to ashes.

Bar none, all of us will sleep beneath the sod of eternal rest that knows no waking interruption. Madeline is now asleep. She has entered her rest.

I must seize each day and drink life to the dregs while I still have breath in my lungs.

I fear Philip DaFoe more than I fear the constable or even God Himself—did He exist. May Madeline's devil-worshipping husband never discover what transpired that night!

Heavens, no.

When he stops reading, Stewart's eyes remain fixed on the pages of the journal. The room is as silent as the proverbial graveyard. Even the dying fire is soundless. Like a dark shroud, a heaviness settles over the room.

Aly shifts uncomfortably in her chair. "Do you think it's true?" she asks the room quietly.

"Who's to know for sure?" Emily replies. "It certainly sounds like it could be true. Unless the man was psychotic or something."

"He does sound kind of crazy," Rachel offers.

"Crazy like a fox," Jack clarifies, glancing at the brunette from the east coast. "He does sound crazy, but also calculating and in massive denial, not to mention devious. It sounds like his experiment that launched the journal in the first place went totally awry. He threw his life to the wind and crossed the line of no return."

"Poor Madeline," Aly says sadly, "and her poor kids. I wonder whatever happened to them?"

Armando stands up and stretches. "I think we need to do some research. Let's get on the Internet and check out the date of March 16th in 1899—or whatever it is—and see if there's any information about this alleged murder."

"I already have it up," Stewart announces while slowly dragging his finger up the screen of his phone. The five other students look over at the man whose middle name should be the title of a search engine. "There's one reference here to a Madeline Anne DaFoe in an old archive," the Intellect informs his fellow detectives. "It says that she went missing on March 17th of 1899. Her body was never found. The mystery of her disappearance remained unsolved."

"It's true, then," Emily breathes, her eyes large with incredulity.

"Jack," Stewart says quietly.

"So, someone with the initials JLS killed—we'd call it manslaughter—killed a woman named Madeline Anne DaFoe and buried her body somewhere in the very cemetery we were in this afternoon," Armando summarizes.

"Jack," Stewart repeats with notable urgency in his customarily flat voice.

"What is it, Stew?" Jack replies impatiently without looking at his friend. He is lost in his private thoughts.

"Jack, there's more," Stewart says gravely as he looks up at Jack. Something threatens to animate the man's Stoic face.

Jack sits forward in his overstuffed chair and stares at the reader of the journal. "Do I want to hear this?"

"Yes and no," Stewart answers as he adjusts his "Clark Kent" glasses by squeezing the bow between the thumb and forefinger of his right hand.

"Go for it, Stew," Jack says as he rests his chin on his fisted hands. "Let's get all the skeletons out of the closet, figuratively and possibly...literally."

The man from Two Harbors, Minnesota, hesitates a moment, then begins to read the Internet article word for word: "Last evening a local woman and her three children were primitively slaughtered in their own home as they slept."

Emily gasps and covers her mouth with a hand. "The grave markers!"

Stewart continues to read, "Dead are Martha Sutherington, thirty-nine years of age, and her children Ezra, James, and Delilah aged eleven, eight, and six respectively. Husband and father, Jacob Lane Sutherington, was out of town for business at the time of the killings and is not a suspect in the heinous deaths."

Aly speaks before Stewart can continue. "JLS stands for Jacob Lane Sutherington!" she exclaims. "He's the writer of the journal!"

"Yes," Jack observes as he leans back in his chair and runs his fingers through his hair. "For better or worse."

"It's becoming perfectly clear," Emily observes. "Jacob Lane Sutherington admits in his journal that he was involved in the death of Madeline DaFoe, right? Then about three weeks later, Jacob's own wife and children are murdered. Isn't it obvious that Madeline's husband discovered that Jacob was responsible for his wife's disappearance and then went after the people who were dear to his wife's killer?"

"A revenge killing," Armando says as he punches his fisted hand against the palm of his other hand. "I've seen too many of those," he admits with disgust in his voice. "You know they're coming. You just don't know when or how. It makes life very...unnerving."

"If it was Philip DaFoe who killed Martha Sutherington and her children out of revenge, how did he discover that Jacob Sutherington was his wife's killer?" Rachel wonders aloud.

"Good question," Jack says.

Stewart looks up from his phone. "It's obviously a murder that was driven by intense passion."

"Why do you say that?" Aly asks in a hesitant manner that makes it clear she may not want to know the answer.

"An article in the same local newspaper dated several days after the first story says the murderer entered the Sutherington house under cover of darkness and killed his victims by first bludgeoning them into unconsciousness with a ball-peen hammer and then...cutting their throats."

Rachel and Emily gasp, and Jack groans softly. Armando simply says, "Dios, have mercy."

Stewart goes on to share a few more pieces of information. "The ball-peen hammer was left at the scene but could not be connected to anyone in the community. Philip DaFoe is mentioned as the primary suspect in the multiple homicides primarily because he disappeared after the killings. Like his wife, later articles indicate that he was never found."

"What a terrible, terrible tragedy!" Rachel exclaims with tears in her eyes.

"Maybe Jacob got revenge on the avenger," Armando offers with a smirk.

"I think we're forgetting one thing," Aly points out.

"What's that?" Jack asks.

"We need to read the diary to see if there's additional entries after the mother and children were killed," Aly explains like a true forensic detective. "Maybe Jacob himself will tell us what happened."

"Wow, girl," Jack says, "you're right!" He turns to Stewart, who is already bent over the old journal. Within seconds, the designated reader looks up slowly and eyes everyone wordlessly.

"Obviously, there's more," Jack says, torn between curiosity and resignation.

"April 14th, 1899," the journal curator says evenly.

"A week after the murders," Emily observes.

Silence falls over the fireside room again. Jack stares into the distance at the tempestuous face of Moses. *The messiness of life*, he thinks to himself. *The evil in the world. Whoever claimed that humans are basically good and are only corrupted by society is smoking something.*

Stewart clears his throat and says, "Jack. Do you want me to start again?"

Jack pulls his eyes away from Moses and considers his friend for a few seconds. "Yeah, Stew," he finally says, "keep going."

Stewart turns slowly through a number of pages in the journal and says, "There are seven, eight, nine pages here with unintelligible scribbling, expletives, and crude drawings of what appears to be knives, guillotines, and various handguns. It is only on the tenth page that the writer records an entry that's decipherable."

Rachel says, "I think we're witnessing the irrationality of a man whose wife and children were savagely murdered only seven days earlier. What can a person write under those circumstances that would be sane?"

When no one adds anything to Rachel's comments, Stewart starts reading:

I am a man forever divorced from peace.

I am bereft of any hope in the world.

I have nothing.

I have no one.

"There's a drawing of a large noose on the next page," Stewart interjects in way of commentary before he continues reading:

I ponder why I have not taken my own life. I have entertained the thought and imagined the deed a thousand times.

Grief and rage keep me alive. The grief is so total that I have no strength to take my own life, much less the life of the Satan man. The thief! The murderer! The devil from hell itself!

I am adrift—a ship without a rudder.

I have swallowed the ocean and am sinking into the depths.

I do not eat. I do not sleep except when exhaustion overtakes me, and I am incapable of resisting it. I stumble about like a drunken man who is not drunk with liquor... but with grief and rage and inconsolable regret.

Never. Never. Never. Never. N-E-V-E-R did I give a thought to losing my wife and children!!! It was an unimaginable thought! Incomprehensible! Outside the realm of possibility!

"More scribbling and ink blots all over the page," Stewart informs the others.

I was out of the city on the night the devil broke into my house like a wraith from hell!! He knew I was not home. I told him myself at the monthly gathering at the Devil's Lodge several days earlier!

He gave me no sign that he knew of my involvement with his wife. Absolutely none! I was not informed of that truth until after the—fact.

His letter came in the post two days later. Demonically, he composed it before that night. He mailed it only hours prior to his—

The rage! It tempers my grief. It robs me of sadness.

Twice over, he is a thief. He stole my wife and children from me, and now he steals my peace—eternally.

No, he has stolen my mind! I cannot quiet its unbridled agitations.

They are all dead.

I want him dead. I have murdered him in my mind over and over in every way imaginable!!

The pathetic truth is that...I could never kill my enemy besides on the stage of my mind. I am incapable of murder—mouse that I am. I hate myself for this lack of intestinal fortitude. Alas, I am condemned to forever rehearse in my mind what I am unable to execute in the world. This itself is a type of hell! I am a man tortured.

I must find a way to summon forth the power to kill him.

The letter. He told me. I was seen with Madeline the night she died.

His youngest child—four years old—told Philip that mommy was with the man who rode the noisy horse. The deceptive Satan man knew all along that I was in the house with Madeline that night! I am one of only a handful of men who own a horseless carriage in the entire city, so he deduced it was me.

He informed me in the letter that I had accomplished for him what he was about to do himself—kill his wife. He knew of her many indiscretions with other men and hated her for it. He was going to make her pay for her unfaithfulness. Nonetheless, my action was still unacceptable to him...especially since his wife was with child! Madeline had never spoken to me of her condition. I have since wondered if the child growing within her was...not Philip's. Do I dare ponder that I have lost four children?

He told me in the last sentence of his letter that I, too, would have to pay. Because I had taken from him, he would have to take from me.

So here I sit in the dark belly beneath the church. I am alone. Everyone I loved is in the graveyard. I lost them all in a period of weeks. I lost them all: Wife, children, mother, Madeline. In the rich, joyful economy of love, I am bankrupt.

Strong Ezra. Sweet James. Beautiful Delilah. They are all gone—in the ground.

I cannot bear to think of them being consumed by bugs and worms. I become crazy with grief when I think of them.

But I cannot bear not to think about them...My mind is held hostage by memories of them and—by thoughts of repaying him.

All is lost.

What have I done?

I am Jonah. I am Samson. I am King Saul. I have been cursed by the God I forsook.

How the mighty have fallen.

Stewart looks up and announces, "Here ends the diary of JLS."

The six students sit in shocked silence, lost in their own thoughts as they attempt to absorb the magnitude of what Stewart just read. The grandfather clock in the room chimes twelve times. The last chime reverberates in the stillness for a long time until its attenuating sound dies to nothingness.

"Just think," Armando finally reflects aloud, "we're talking about six murders here, two women and four children—one unborn."

No one comments on Armando's words until Emily looks over at him and says, "Are you thinking what I'm thinking?"

"I don't know," Armando replies straight-faced. "Tell me what you're thinking, and then I'll think about telling you if what you're thinking is what I'm thinking."

The attempt to lighten the heavy mood in the room proves successful, and everyone relaxes a bit. Their minds come back from their private wanderings into the circle of friendship.

"What I'm thinking," Emily pronounces slowly as her eyes squint with concentration, "is that Jacob is telling us that he buried Madeline's body in the Sutherington family gravesite."

"I haven't thought that yet," Armando replies with a twinkle in his brown eyes, "but if you had given me a little more time to think about it, I would have thought that."

"Ha, ha," the young woman says. "Seriously, though, isn't that a strong possibility—that he buried Madeline next to the other Sutherington graves?"

"Do you want to hear what I heard him saying in the diary?" Rachel interjects.

"Sure, Rach," Jack says.

"Two for one," Rachel says, and then repeats it again, "two for one."

"I heard that, too," Aly says, nodding her head.

"Okay, so we all heard those three words," Rachel agrees. "But what do they refer to?" she asks. She leans in toward the coffee table and looks around at the others conspiratorially.

"Two for one," Stewart repeats Jacob's haunting thought as he stares over at Rachel. For once, the Intellect is at a loss.

"Who was buried the same day Madeline died?" Rachel asks, looking around at her fellow Screaming Eagles with expectancy.

"Jacob's mother," Emily answers, her eyes widening.

"There was already a fresh grave in the cemetery that Jacob was intimately familiar with," Rachel continues, offering another clue to the conclusion she has reached.

"Yes," Armando says, elongating the word in a manner that encourages his friend to share more.

"I see where you're going, Rach," Jack states with dawning realization.

"What am I missing?" Armando inquires as he looks from Jack to Rachel and back to Jack again.

Rachel hesitates just a moment and then says, "I believe that the 'two for one' thought that haunted Jacob Sutherington refers to the possibility that he buried Madeline in his mother's grave. Two bodies end up in one grave and maybe even in the same casket. Two for one."

"Exactly," Stewart agrees with a rare hint of passion in his voice. "What better way to hide a body than to bury it in a pre-excavated hole that contains an already occupied coffin buried far from curious eyes. Who would ever think of looking for Madeline there?"

"Ay!" Armando exclaims. "We may be on the verge of solving a one-hundred-twenty-year-old murder mystery. Talk about a *cold* case!"

"Well said, Ese," Jack says with a tired smile.

"So, Jacob took the body to the cemetery," Emily begins summarizing more for herself than for the others around her, "and waited in a panic until his dead mother told him to bury Madeline in her—the mother's—grave. Then he removed the fresh dirt that covered the grave, opened the casket—or not—and placed Madeline's body on top of his mother's body. Finally, he backfilled the grave so that no one would be any wiser about what he had done."

Emily pauses briefly and then announces to her classmates, "What a perfect solution for a crime! Just bury the evidence."

"Literally," Jack adds.

"I guess Jacob proved once again that you should always listen to your mother," Armando quips.

"Who put a quarter in you?" Rachel laughs as she throws a pillow at her fellow student.

"It's after twelve o'clock, my dear," the ex La Puente gang member exclaims. "I lose all sanity after midnight."

"No wonder they called you Syko Loco," Jack says.

"You're not the only one who's exhausted," Aly remarks. "My eyes are so tired that I'm beginning to see two of all of you."

"Two for one," Armando says.

Everyone groans as Aly follows Rachel's example and uncharacteristically throws a pillow at the unrelenting joker.

Jack massages the back of his neck and says, "I can't believe that this Philip guy actually sent a letter to the man whose wife and children he would murder later that same night."

"What a sick man," Armando says.

"What an evil man," Jack responds. "He devised and carried out a premeditated quadruple murder! He was undoubtedly planning his actions for several weeks. What he committed was not a crime of passion but a cold, calculated, diabolical execution that included the murder of three children!"

Jack feels a shiver travel up his spine. Emily says, "I hope we never have to meet any of Philip's descendants—if there are any."

"People do change," Aly says optimistically. "Look at what happened to Mahmoud."

"There's no arguing that," Emily agrees. "But sometimes generational patterns get passed down for hundreds of years."

"And how would you know that?" Armando says, poking fun at the woman who rarely smiles. Emily looks away and says nothing.

Jack knows something has been touched inside Emily that she keeps hidden beneath a thin veneer. "The girl in the dungeon" is how Jack is beginning to think of her.

"Do we call the police?" Rachel asks.

Jack rubs his chin for a while and licks his lips. "Let's wait, Rach," he replies. "These murders have been unsolved for over a hundred years, so a few more days won't matter. Let's get some sleep and meet again tomorrow to figure out what we do next."

"We probably should notify our professors about this," Aly counsels.

"I think we should definitely include Mr. Fagani," Emily suggests. "He knows all the history about the church and the cemetery."

"He might be able to inform us what happened to Jacob Sutherington and Philip DaFoe," Stewart suggests as he slides his fingers over the mechanical pencils in his pocket protector. "Without any more journal entries, the trail ends so abruptly. We have no idea what happened to those two men."

"There's nothing more on the Internet?" Rachel inquires.

"Nothing that I was able to find," Stewart answers.

"I'm with Emily on this one," Jack comments as he looks at the young woman with the long blond hair and the perennially subdued countenance. "Fagani will have information for us; I'm almost certain. We need to bring him on board. He can probably help me figure out if I'm related to Jacob or not."

Jack gets to his feet and yawns. "I'll quick pray, and then let's adjourn for the night."

The other five friends get up, and they gather in a circle. Rachel takes Jack's hand and Emily's hand in her own, and soon they're all holding hands.

"Jesus, we thank you that you've adopted all of us into your family irrespective of race, country, gender, or our past actions," Jack prays. "I praise you that you have a special place in your heart for the orphan, the fatherless, and the lost. I'm so grateful to you for giving me these five brothers and sisters who have become my family. Guide our steps as we leave for Christmas break later this week. Amen. Oh—and give us the wisdom to solve the mystery of these five dead people."

"Six, if we count Philip, who disappeared," Armando adds with his eyes closed.

Jack laughs loudly out of his fatigue and shakes his head. "Six," he says, correcting himself. "Father, give us the wisdom to solve as many as six murders."

"Seven, if we count Madeline's unborn baby," Aly says.

"Yes, Lord," Jack sighs and amends his prayer yet again, "give us the wisdom to solve the murder and or disappearance of seven individuals whom you created and you loved. May we meet some or all of them in heaven one day."

CHAPTER 38

Fagani Meets the Journal

It is late in the afternoon, two days after the journal reading in the fireside room. Long shadows are melting into the unrelenting dusk. Despite the size of the Agatha room with its towering ceiling, the atmosphere in the Academy cafeteria feels cozy. Contributing to the hominess is the heavy snow falling outside and the warmth of the fellowship inside.

The man wearing the chocolate-brown fedora takes the last bite of his donut and, in slow motion, wipes his lips with his napkin. A minute passes. Finally, he finishes chewing and swallows. After a sip of coffee—which is always an adventure due to the elderly man's shaking hands—he lifts his watery, red-rimmed eyes to consider the small audience gathered around his table.

"Yes," Mr. Louis Fagani finally answers in a hoarse voice, "I'm familiar with both of those men—Jacob Sutherington and Philip DaFoe. Never met them, of course, since I didn't show up on the scene 'til '22. Both men attended Redeemer Church for a long time. Grew up here; they did. My grandfather knew them some."

The members of the micro-cohort glance around at each other with growing excitement in the wake of the unveiling of the journal to the elderly man. "Jacob was your great-great-grandfather, Jack," Mr. Fagani says as he slowly turns his head and looks at the young man who shares the same last name as Jacob.

Surprised by the confident pronouncement by the resident historian, Jack inquires, "How do you know this?"

The older man takes several breaths and pauses. It appears as if he is resting after a major exertion and requires some recovery time. Eventually, the man is able to speak again. "When your name appeared as an applicant to the Academy, I was very intrigued since Sutherington is a common name in...the annals of Redeemer Unitarian Church. Accordingly, I decided to do some research which, I...might add, is what I do best."

Mr. Fagani pauses and removes his glasses. He wipes his eyes with his napkin and grunts, "The older I get, the more my eyes water without provocation."

Replacing his glasses, he licks his lips slowly, methodically, and looks at Jack again. "You don't know your family history," he states matter-of-factly.

"On my mother's side, yes," Jack replies. "On my father's side, hardly at all. He died when I was very young, and my mother never talked much about his family."

"David," the church cemetery historian utters. "David is your father's name." It is not a question but a statement of fact.

"Yes," Jack says, nodding his head, "yes, that's right, Mr. Fagani."

"Your grandfather was Gabriel, and your great-grandfather was Michael," the old man announces as he points a crooked finger at Jack. He breathes and then says, "Michael was Jacob's son by his second wife. You didn't know that Jacob remarried, did you?"

"No, we didn't," Rachel interjects in her typical assertive manner. "The diary ended with that last entry about three weeks after the murder of Jacob's family."

The old sage shakes his head ten degrees to the right, then ten degrees to the left. "I'm saddened that it was Philip DaFoe who killed them. There were rumors...of course...at the time."

"So, whatever happened to him, to Philip DaFoe?" Armando inquires.

"Disappeared," the cemetery professor replies as he looks at the young man from behind, eyelids drooping under the impact of almost ten decades of gravity and aging.

"When?" Emily asks. "When did Philip disappear?"

"He was never seen again after the murder of Jacob's family," Mr. Fagani replies. "I think that's the primary reason he was...suspected of it. People assumed he murdered them and...fled."

"I wonder if Jacob killed him as a revenge killing for a revenge killing," Armando reflects out loud, "enacting the ethic of gang warfare."

"In the journal, he does refer to Philip's letter," Aly says. "Since Jacob knew that Philip had murdered his family, he could have decided to repay him for his terrible deeds. But Jacob wrote that it wasn't in him to kill the man."

"If we can believe that," Rachel says.

Emily observes, "What is strange to me is that Jacob never mentions in his diary that Philip disappeared, does he? His entry is a week after the murders, so by then, Philip could have been long-gone, so why doesn't Jacob mention that? Maybe because he killed him."

"But Mr. Fagani here," Jack says, nodding at the professor, "says that Philip was never seen again immediately after the murders. Jacob reports in his journal that he didn't get the letter until a few days after the murder of his family. So, if he was the one who killed Philip, he wouldn't have done it until after he had received the letter."

"Maybe Philip did flee after he committed the murders and moved to

Timbuktu, totally vindicating Jacob in the man's death," Rachel says.

"Unless Jacob somehow knew even before he got the letter," Emily suggests.

There is a pause before Stewart offers, "We can be almost 100 percent certain that Jacob knew it was Philip DaFoe who had murdered his family even before he received the letter. Who else would've had reason to commit such a heinous crime against Jacob's family unless motivated by revenge?"

"Let's say that Jacob did kill Madeline and then her husband," Aly offers, "and buried both of their bodies. He could have buried Philip in another pre-occupied grave like he did with Madeline."

"Now that just doesn't seem right," Armando says with furrowed brow and a crinkled nose. "I know Jacob was a sick man but was he that sick?"

"If he knew Philip had murdered his family, why didn't he turn the letter over to the police? He didn't notify law enforcement that we're aware of, right?" Emily says.

"There's a lot of loose ends here," Jack says. He turns to Mr. Fagani and asks, "Is there anything else you know that we don't?"

The elderly man massages his lips between the thumb and forefinger of his right hand while his left hand grasps the cane standing between his legs.

Finally, he clears his throat loudly and offers in a raspy voice, "My grandfather, who was a police detective from St. Louis...he confided that... the chief investigator reached a conclusion about the case...Maybe it was mere speculation."

Mr. Fagani pauses, tilting his cane back and forth in front of the table. He takes several deep breaths and finishes his thought. "The chief investigator agreed with you detectives," he says, his eyes smiling at the six students. "He decided that Jacob was responsible for the mysterious disappearance...

of Madeline DaFoe. But there was no evidence. None...He also concluded that Philip had...exacted revenge by killing Jacob's family but...but that Jacob didn't come forward with any accusations against Philip because... he didn't want to draw any attention to himself. He feared that he might then...be investigated for...the disappearance of Mrs. DaFoe."

The cemetery professor takes another sip of the coffee that trembles in his hand. A wave of the dark brew sloshes over the rim of the cup and spills into his lap. Fortunately, several napkins have been proactively positioned for such an eventuality. "The investigator believed that Philip DaFoe fled the area after his heinous crime or...even suicided in some remote location... where his body would never be found. Why would he do this?"

"Possibly so the authorities would believe that Jacob was responsible for the disappearance of Philip as well as Madeline," Stewart suggests, answering yet another rhetorical question. "Maybe, even so, people would believe that Jacob was guilty of the DaFoe disappearances and the murder of his own family."

"Correct," Mr. Fagani says with a slow tip of his omnipresent fedora. "That was the...speculation, at least. The only problem with accusing Jacob...of killing his own family is that he had an alibi...He was out of town the night of the murders but...only four hours away. Conceivably, he could have...come home during the night and then returned to where he was staying...for business. Even with a horseless carriage...that would have been a tall order back in 1899."

"But now we appear to have the truth directly from Jacob Sutherington's own diary," Aly says. "Aren't diaries a safe depository for true confessions of the heart?"

"I suppose Jacob could have been lying about things," Rachel says. "His experiment could have taken him way off the deep end to the point that he killed six people, including Philip."

"I don't know," Jack counters. "My great-great-grandfather certainly was carnal, but I don't think he was crazy."

Silence falls over the small group. Darkness has extinguished all the light that had been peeking into the windows of the Agatha room. The six Screaming Eagles and the professor are the only individuals in the expansive cafeteria that could seat five hundred people.

Eventually, Armando asks what everyone is thinking. "So, what do we do, then, with the information we have?"

Jack toys with his Styrofoam cup and says, "Let's review all the facts—or conjecture—that we know at this time. First, Jacob was involved in the accidental death of Madeline and possibly buried her in his mother's grave. Second, we have no idea what happened to Philip DaFoe—he disappeared into thin air—but the evidence is very compelling that he murdered the Sutherington family. Lastly, we discovered that Jacob remarried sometime later and produced a son named Michael."

"The man who is your great grandfather," Emily adds.

Stewart clears his throat, the ever-reliable precursor to him speaking, especially when he has an observation no one has thought of yet. "There's one other matter," he states blandly.

"What's that, Stew?" Jack inquires of the journal keeper.

"Jacob mentioned burying the Libertys with Madeline," he says. "I've done some research on valuable coins in the nineteenth century, and to the best of my deductions, the Libertys he is referring to are most likely coins depicting an image of the seated figure of Liberty. Depending on if they're dollars or half dollars and on the location of their mintage, some of them could be worth a large fortune today. Their value is contingent on their condition, of course."

"What dollar amount are we talking here?" Armando inquires as he massages his goatee.

Stewart glances briefly at his confirmed critic before his eyes flee to his phone screen. He replies, "One version of the Seated Liberty Silver Dollar, if it was minted in San Francisco, is worth anywhere from $177,000 in poor condition to around $2 million dollars if it's in excellent condition."

"In other words," Rachel says, "there's a coffin out there in the cemetery that might contain a fortune!"

As Armando looks sidelong at Stewart, he comments, "Depending on how many coins there are."

Jack smiles tiredly and shakes his head. "This just keeps getting more convoluted, doesn't it?" He turns his attention to Mr. Fagani to ask him what he knows about Seated Liberty coins. The old man's head is bent over his cane like a shepherd weary from tending his flock.

Before Jack can ask his question, the shepherd says, "Philip DaFoe was a numismatic and a coin collector. His collection...primarily, purportedly, included coins from...the Roman, Greek, and Byzantine eras. But he also focused on...nineteenth-century American coins, especially from the Civil War period."

Rachel opens her mouth to speak, but the old man holds up his cane. His nonverbal gesture speaks loudly, Wait, I'm not done yet. Let me breathe, and then I'll finish what I'm trying to say.

"I don't know for a fact," Mr. Fagani begins again in a voice that is fading in volume, "but I would say there is a high probability that...Philip had Seated Liberty Silver Dollars in his collection."

"So, Jack, your great-great-great grandmother might have a lot of other women in her coffin with her—Madeline DaFoe and a bunch of Seated Libertys," Armando declares. "Talk about a communal burial site."

"Do we need to call the police and get the coffin exhumed?" Rachel asks.

"I don't know what other step we would take," Jack admits.

Mr. Fagani holds up a wrinkled hand. He takes a deep breath and states, "I wouldn't advise that course of action."

"Why not?" Emily asks.

"Things might get a wee complicated," the cemetery historian says. His face grimaces under the brown fedora.

"How so?" Jack inquires.

The old man raises his bent head and announces, "The police commissioner in this city happens to be...a man named Draegan DaFoe. By all accounts...he is a very dangerous man."

"A descendent of Philip DaFoe," Stewart offers.

Mr. Fagani nods his head ever so slightly and briefly chews on his lower lip. "He has the reputation of being...half cop, half criminal," the old man says in a manner that sounds like he's forcing the words out against some type of resistance. Jack has the mental picture of a trombone with a mute in it.

"Would his reputation impact this situation?" Aly asks.

The church historian cups a hand over his right ear and says, "Say that again, young lady."

Aly repeats her question, only louder this time.

The cemetery professor laughs in response to the young woman's question. "Very much so, I'm afraid," he says, resting his chin on the top of his cane. “Like Philip DaFoe, he is also known to...collect coins. But unlike a numismatic like...his great-great-grandfather, he has no...desire to study coins. He’s driven only by a...by a desire to amass great wealth and even greater power.”

Jack leans toward the nonagenarian and says, “It sounds like this Draegan DaFoe guy would be very interested if he discovered that someone with the Sutherington name wanted to dig up a grave in the old church cemetery.”

“Undoubtedly,” Mr. Fagani agrees as he puckers his lips. “My grandfather mentioned that one...of the rumors that circulated at the time...was that a portion...of Philip’s coin collection was missing...and probably had been stolen...by whoever was responsible for the disappearance of the DaFoes.”

Jack looks up at the darkened cupola as he runs fingers through his hair. When he looks back down, he asks, “So, what should we do, Mr. Fagani? Should we just walk away from this mess and not disturb the past?”

The historian takes off his glasses and dabs at the corners of his eyes with his napkin for the tenth time. Then he situates his glasses back on his leathery face and stares at Jack for a long time. At one point in the long pause, Jack wonders if it is possible for the cemetery professor to fall asleep with his eyes open. The constant trembling of the professor’s head continues unabated.

Eventually, Mr. Fagani lifts his chin and straightens his back so that he appears more confident and stronger than his ninety-eight years typically communicate. “Jack,” he says. “Jack Sutherington. God loves justice and truth.”

The Academy students nod their heads at the sage’s words and wait for what is to follow. They wait quite a while.

"Dig up the grave of Agatha Sutherington!" the elderly man finally announces, pointing a bony finger at Jack. "Let the truth of this whole matter...come to the light," he says with impressive volume and resolve. "Do not doubt that you were brought here by God at such a time as this by divine design...Discover your purpose and never waver from fulfilling it! Never!"

Not long after Mr. Fagani has shuffled off to his office with the assistance of his third leg, the six friends get up from the table and stand just outside the arched doorway of the Agatha room. They are discussing what to do, when, and how. The where is more obvious to them, of course. Jack's great-great-great grandmother's grave is clearly the focal point.

"So, when do we pull the trigger on this grave-digging adventure?" Armando asks. "I'm dying to open that coffin," he says wittily. His pun is just subtle enough that the distracted students miss it entirely.

"I think we need to talk to Windsor, Embee, and McNeely before we do anything," Rachel advises.

"Agreed," Jack says. "The more counselors, the better. And realistically, we're not going to do anything until after the break. We just don't have enough time. Besides, we don't want to rush into this whole thing without some advanced planning."

"Are you saying we have to wait until February to solve this mystery?" Aly asks.

"It looks that way," Jack replies, raising his eyebrows and nodding his head.

"When does the ground freeze in this part of the country?" Armando asks, introducing a new variable. "That might be a concern if we attempt to dig up the coffin."

"Wait," Aly interjects. "Are you saying the ground actually freezes here?" Her large brown eyes are wide with wonder.

"You're not in Thailand anymore, Dorothy," Jack can't resist saying. "I'm guessing you never saw any frost in Yala."

"Dorothy?" the Thai woman inquires as her brows knit with puzzlement. "Who's Dorothy?"

"Just a fictional girl from Kansas who killed witches and conquered wizards and fought flying monkeys," Rachel says as she pats the smaller woman on the shoulder.

Aly's delicate face wrinkles with confusion, and she opens her mouth to ask another question.

"Stewart?" Jack speaks first as he turns toward the walking search engine.

The Intellect adjusts his glasses and stares at Jack. "The ground here certainly doesn't freeze to the depth it does in northern Minnesota, but it will freeze—even with the urban heat effect generated in a larger city. A person probably couldn't dig without frost in the soil until sometime in March or April, I would estimate."

"So that means we'll have to wait 'til spring?" Rachel asks.

"Not necessarily," Stewart replies. "A person could find a way to heat up the ground and drive the frost out of the soil, probably even in January if you know what you're doing."

"Okay," Jack says, "so maybe we won't have to wait until spring—just early February when we return to the Academy."

"At least, we'll all have something to think about during the break," Armando says.

"By the way, are you still going back to LA?" Jack asks Armando.

"That's the plan, Juan."

"And you're headed to Connecticut, right, Rach?"

The woman with the short brunette hair and meadows of freckles nods her head.

"I just spoke with Mahmoud yesterday," Aly volunteers, her face beaming. "I'll be going with him to the state of Georgia near the city of Atlanta. You know, where he traveled last week to meet with that professor at the international institute. We've both been invited to stay with a family there over the break."

"Aly, that's great," Rachel comments. "You'll be so helpful in Mahmoud's growth."

"If your plans are still the same," Jack says, glancing at Emily and then at Stewart, "you guys are traveling to opposite climates. Northern Minnesota with blizzards and ice fishing for you, Stew, and Fort Myers with hot, humid weather and beaches for you, Emily."

The young woman with the dimples that have all but disappeared as the semester wore on turns a serious face toward Jack and asks, "How about you? I don't think I've heard where you're going for the winter break."

"I'll be in Colorado with my mother and sisters," he replies. "Apparently, they can't wait to see me."

"Are you going to tell your mom about the latest developments in the Sutherington family history?" Rachel asks with a smile.

"It's all so new, I haven't even thought about it yet," Jack says, "but probably not. Mom can get a bit—worried about things. Sometimes, the less she knows, the better."

"I hope you have a good time with them," Emily replies quietly.

There is a pause before Armando announces, "Hey guys, I've got to blow this pop stand! I have one last journey into the internal cave with McNeely before I leave for sunny California tomorrow."

"Oops," Emily says, putting a finger to her chin. "Thanks for the reminder. I've got Embee in ten minutes as well."

"Hold on a second," Jack says as he puts one hand on Armando's shoulder and one on Stewart's. Bowing his head, he prays briefly for each of his friends as well as for Mahmoud. The pray time ends with Rachel initiating the first Screaming Eagles group hug that lasts a full ten seconds to the obvious discomfort of the Intellect.

As the six students turn to walk down the hallway, Jack touches Emily's arm to detain her. When she stops and looks at him, he inquires, "Are you returning? I mean to school—after winter break."

When she doesn't reply right away, Jack adds, "I hope so." He pauses and then volunteers, "I've come to like you, Emily Joy Parker. I'll miss you if you don't come back."

The young woman shakes her golden mane and says, "I can't believe you remembered my middle name."

Jack thinks it but does not say it: *I don't forget anything about you.* To Emily, he says, "Joy is a beautiful middle name."

A whisper of a smile plays on her lips even as her eyes are still held hostage by something else. "Pray for me, Jack Paul Sutherington. Please pray for me," she says quietly as she turns and begins walking down the dim hallway that is illuminated only by small sconces attached to the walls. Something in her voice worries Jack.

Before she is out of sight, Jack calls after her, "I can't believe you remembered my middle name."

Emily stops and hesitates before she turns and looks back at him. "Paul is a beautiful middle name," she says, flashing a rare smile that displays both of her dimples. Then she turns and disappears around the corner.

Jack wonders if he will ever see her again.

CHAPTER 39

Flying Solo

The sanctuary with its imposing turret is dark and silent. In the attached citadel building on this late Thursday evening, a single lamp protests the night in Dr. McNeely's third-floor office. Jack is comfortably situated in the ancient leather chair in the corner of the office. His feet are resting on an equally ancient leather ottoman that matches the chair. His hiking boots are resting on the floor beside the ottoman.

Jack pushes back his shoulder-length straw blonde hair and replies to his mentor, "So you believe all of us have some kind of secret we need to discover and deal with while we're here at the Academy."

"'Secret' is not quite the right word," Dr. McNeely says. His dark eyes are examining Jack from beneath his prominent forehead. "Let's call it an internal obstacle for lack of a better term."

"So, something inside of us that needs to be identified and resolved," the younger man from Colorado offers. His face is streaked with bands of light and shadow in the dimly lit office.

"Yes, as a part of the growth journey," the mentor affirms, nodding his head. "Everyone has obstacles within them that oppose their intimacy with God, others, and even themselves. It comes down to if a person sees them, owns them, and then makes the intentional choice to grow beyond them."

"What's my internal obstacle?" Jack inquires. "Am I fixated back somewhere in the Oedipus complex?"

Dr. McNeely's teeth emerge from his brown beard, and the man laughs. "Nice try, Jack. Sorry, that's not my department. The identification of your internal obstacle is the job of the Holy Spirit. Besides, Freud's theory of sexual development misses the mark. I think he formulated his whole theory based on his own limited, godless experience. But nice attempt at humor."

Jack turns his head and gazes out the tall, arched window of the office. He watches large, lazy snowflakes drifting silently from the night sky. "If snow was black," he ponders aloud, "we'd never see it in the dark of night."

Eventually, he looks back at the president of the Academy, who has felt no need to respond to his mentee's random observation. The professor is leaning back in his chair.

"I know I'm an unusual guy," Jack volunteers. "At least, that's the way I feel inside. I don't tell anybody that, of course. We've talked earlier this semester about how I had to grow up quickly to care for my mother and my three younger sisters after my father died."

"We have," McNeely replies with a nod. "You had a lot of exposure to females in the first eighteen years of your life. If I remember correctly, you also had your grandmother living with you off and on over the years. More on than off."

"That's right," Jack affirms. "I think that's one reason I feel unusual. I see the world differently than a lot of men. Sometimes, I believe that I see it from both a male and a female perspective." He pauses and then adds, "I'm not sure that's a good thing or not. I don't feel like I fit into either world extremely well, even though I can talk to just about anybody. Maybe that's a strength. I can sense the anxiety of a woman a mile away, and then the next minute mix it up with my teammates on the football field."

There is a brief silence as Jack's eyes focus on the bookshelves that rise up ten feet high behind the professor. "I think sports saved me in many ways," he finally comments toward the books.

"How so?" Dr. McNeely inquires as he rubs his bearded chin over his interlaced fingers.

"Sports brought me into the world of men that I didn't have at home. It introduced me to a lot of coaches who pushed me and held me accountable," Jack reflects. "God knew I needed male influence. My three uncles weren't involved in my life much at all—they were afraid of my grandmother, believe it or not. I didn't know Jesus until I was sixteen, so the men I met later in the church weren't a part of my life yet."

"Coaches were father figures for you," the professor proffers.

"Exactly," Jack confirms. "Some for better, some for worse. At least, they all challenged me in one way or another. They helped compensate for what I was lacking.

"Of course," Jack continues, "when I asked Jesus into my heart at that summer camp near Estes Park, God blew me away. His presence was so real to me. He became the Father I had lost and so much more. I can honestly say I opened up to God the Father more than I had to any human before that."

"That was the summer before your junior year of high school," Dr. McNeely recalls.

"Yup," Jack affirms. "I don't know if it's the typical experience, but I had never felt as close to a human as I felt to God that first summer," he says as his eyes return to his mentor. "It was incredible! Up to that point, I had no clue I could ever get that close to anyone. I still feel closer to God than to people," he adds. "Jesus is definitely my best friend. But those first twelve months with Him were phenomenal."

"Isn't that amazing," his mentor observes, shaking his head slowly, "to feel closer to the God you cannot see than to the people around you that you can see."

Jack nods his head and stretches out his legs on the ottoman. "Actually, I think there are three primary distinctives about me. First, God is my best friend, which is certainly counter-cultural. Second, I feel a bit outside the mainstream male world because I grew up in a female world and learned to be highly attuned to the emotions and needs of the women around me. Third, since I was seven years old, I've been inclined toward self-sufficiency because of the absence of my father. Since I was so intensely independent, I'm still amazed God ever got into my heart."

The president of the Academy laces his fingers behind his head. He says nothing but looks intently at Jack, nonverbally inviting him to keep talking.

"So those are the things that randomly come to mind when I think about my internal obstacles," Jack comments with a shrug.

"Anything else?" Dr. McNeely inquires.

Jack pauses and examines his hands, contemplating, debating. He is not sure how vulnerable he wants to be with this man—with any man, for that matter. In the end, he decides to share the secret that no one knows.

"I do have panic attacks in the night—if that's what you call them," he divulges.

His listener releases his hands from behind his head and leans forward in his squeaky chair. "Panic attacks," he repeats.

Jack nods his head as he takes a deep breath and lets it out slowly. "They come most nights. Two hours after I fall asleep. Like clockwork." He takes another deep breath and says, "I call them panic attacks because they certainly feel violent. I'm not lying to you when I tell you they're vicious."

"Ugh," McNeely says. "Sounds like torture to me."

Jack looks at his mentor and says, "Spot on, man! They're like torture. I never thought my brain could ever experience anything like it. To be honest," Jack says evenly, "they feel like what I'd imagine ECT to be like."

"Electroconvulsive therapy?"

Jack nods his head. "I've read many Internet articles about nocturnal panic attacks, but none of the descriptions fully capture my experience with the jolt of electricity that explodes in my head."

"Have you tried meds?"

"Nope. Don't want to depend on them."

"I get that. I don't either," Dr. McNeely replies, nodding his head. "I certainly believe there's a time and a place for medication, but I think far too often our culture believes they're the be-all-and-end-all. They're seen as the first line of defense against mental illness. Many times, we don't even take the time and effort to listen to what the symptoms are saying. We silence them before we even hear their message. Feel better is the mantra instead of listen to what the pain is saying and grow."

The young man sitting across from him looks as vulnerable as Dr. McNeely has ever seen him. Jack's eyes are large and his face expectant as he inquires, "So what do you think my symptoms are saying?"

The middle-aged man sits up straight and uses the fingers of both hands to massage his chin, then his eyes, and finally his forehead. Eventually, he peers over at Jack between fingers that partially cover his eyes. He opens his mouth and begins to say something, but then interrupts himself and says in words muffled by his palms, "We need to talk to God about this."

Closing his eyes, the professor begins to speak to God as he might speak to a friend: "Holy Spirit, you are the Great Counselor, the Wise Teacher.

Open our ears to hear what Jack's mind and body are saying. He is made by you, the Awesome Designer, so when he begins to malfunction, and the *check engine* light comes on in his heart, there's always a reason. Great Physician, open our eyes to see what we need to see for Jack's joy and your glory."

Dr. McNeely places his hands in his lap and opens his eyes. He sits quietly, gazing at Jack in the semi-dark room. The snow has stopped falling. The stars are beginning to appear through the retreating, thin veil of wispy clouds. They wink brightly against the black backdrop of the night sky. A minute goes by.

"How long have you experienced these panic attacks, and who else knows about them?" the mentor eventually inquires.

Jack's eyes narrow, and his whole face twists with concentration. "Oh, man. Maybe three years now. And to answer your second question—you're the only one."

"I'm the only person who knows," the professor repeats back to his mentee. "Three years."

Jack nods his head and purses his lips.

Dr. McNeely looks up at the ceiling briefly, then looks back down and levels his gaze on Jack. "Do you always fly solo?"

"What do you mean?" the young man asks.

"You're tortured for three years, and you don't ask anyone for help," Dr. McNeely states flatly. "To me, that's what I call flying solo."

Without hesitation, Jack replies, "Who would I tell? There wasn't anyone I could confide in."

"Okay, well, that's one side of the coin," the professor acknowledges. "Maybe there was no one to confide in, although I find that hard to believe. At the very least, you could have gone and consulted a pastor, an M.D., or a counselor. They're all there to serve people in pain, after all."

He pauses and then says, "The other side of the coin is the internal obstacle we alluded to earlier."

The professor pauses. Jack says nothing, waiting to hear any insight that might, at a minimum, increase his awareness and give him hope that his grueling symptoms might not be a hated acquaintance for the rest of his lifetime.

"The other side of the coin is that you were correct when you described yourself as self-sufficient. A less euphemistic way of stating it is that you're a stubborn son of a gun."

Jack stares back at the Academy president, bristling inside.

Dr. McNeely continues. "Let's say your night panic attacks, or whatever we might call them, are an expression of anxiety. I think that's an obvious thing to say about panic, that it has a lot to do with anxiety. Do you know what drives a lot of anxiety?"

Jack shakes his head.

"Aloneness," the mentor states as if it is absolutely true. "You're living very alone inside, Jack. If you don't tell someone about what tortures you, I doubt that you tell anyone much at all about yourself—at least on a deeper, vulnerable level."

"And—" Dr. McNeely says with such a long pause afterward that Jack knows the next words are vital, "I can't help but wonder how much you actually let go and trust God with your life. If you usually fly solo, you not only lack a copilot—maybe you're short one pilot as well."

Jack listens closely to the man's words because they do not sound untrue. How he has lived his life is all that he knows. While it is painful, it is also helpful to get a perspective from another man who sees him from the outside.

I can only presume that somewhere along the way in life, you learned to take care of everyone in your family, including your mother, your three younger sisters, and maybe even your grandmother. But like you said earlier," the mentor pauses and sighs, "no one was there for you."

The professor leans back in his squeaky chair and crosses his legs. "You do have a gift, Jack," he states. "I've seen it in you. You have an amazing ability to observe the world around you and discern what others need. Isaiah Windsor thinks you're also very sensitive to the spiritual world as well.

Yes, you were probably born with a sensitive temperament that equipped you right out of the chute to care for others. But that inborn ability undoubtedly was sharpened and refined to a high degree by your life circumstances—the perfect blend of nature and nurture.

One thing you have to remember about this gift is that it can be a blessing or a curse," the mentor explains to Jack. "The way I see it, you're quick to read the moods and needs of others often before they even know what they're feeling and needing. Then you try to fix those moods if they're negative and meet the needs. In short, you take care of others, Jack.

The only problem with this scenario is that God made you to need someone as well. That's only going to happen if you let them see your heart. As a solo flier, you don't do that very well, if at all."

Jack taps his fingers on the arm of the old leather chair as he considers Dr. McNeely's words. "Are you saying I have night-time panic attacks because I don't let anyone be there for me, not even God?"

The mentor folds his hands in his lap and nods. "That's what I'm saying," he replies. "I'm not a licensed psychologist, but I've worked long enough with people under the guidance of the Word of God and the Holy Spirit that I recognize some things when I see them. In your case, it's written in capital letters—on your forehead."

"What should I do?" Jack inquires. "What you're telling me tonight is news to me."

"For one thing," McNeely says with a wink, "keep doing what you just did now."

"You mean asking for help," Jack says with a smile.

His mentor nods and replies, "Right." He elongates the word as he returns Jack's smile. "Don't fly alone. Even the Lone Ranger had Tonto. Batman had Robin. David had Jonathan. Holmes had Watson. Better yet, God the Father, the Son, and the Holy Spirit have had each other as their *eternal* companions."

The professor pauses and then adds, "Aloneness is a father with many children, Jack. Self-sufficiency, pride, anxiety, depression, self-condemnation, obsessive thoughts and compulsions, even self-harm and suicide, are some of his offspring."

Jack whistles softly and looks down at his hands. "Wow, there's a lot to unpack here, especially your comment that flying solo might mean I'm not even trusting God to be there for me."

Dr. McNeely clears his throat and clarifies, "I don't mean to suggest that you have no faith in God, Jack. Obviously, you're a born-again believer who has trusted in Jesus as your Savior. What I'm saying is that you may try to do too much on your own instead of depending heavily on God for your strength and guidance. Maybe you lean toward self-sufficiency not because you distrust God but because you've never experienced someone there for you. You might also believe that being a godly man means you shouldn't need anything from others."

The professor's dark eyes stare into Jack's soul as he says, "Every man who trusts God with all his heart has been broken to the point that he can't take another step without God's help."

Jack sits in the black leather chair for a long time staring at the president of the Academy. Try as he might, the man's words are not smoothly assimilated into his pre-existing cognitive schema. Rather, they are threatening to produce a shift inside his mind on the level of plate-tectonics. Major accommodations in his view of himself, of the world, and even of God are required. Nothing less than a paradigm shift is demanded.

"Any other thoughts before we call it a night?" Dr. McNeely asks his meditating mentee.

Jack slides his legs off the ottoman and places his feet on the floor. "Two last things," Jack replies as he begins to pull on his hiking boots. "First," he says, "thanks for helping me to witness the power of communication with God. It's so clear to me that He heard and answered your prayer for me earlier tonight. I need to be reminded over and over of the importance of talking to God.

"Secondly," Jack says, "for better or worse, I see that I've got more spelunking to do. I don't think I trust very well."

The professor smiles and says, "We can go deep into the cave system of your heart, Jack—if you allow it. The Holy Spirit is the best spelunking guide in the universe. And always remember, our time together is about removing every obstacle to your experience of God's presence. We're not here just to help you feel better."

Dr. McNeely gets to his feet, and his chair shrieks loudly, as if in pain. The mentor says, "There's one last thing, Jack, before we wrap up with a final prayer. Always remember that God desires relationship, intimacy, and trust. He wants you close to Him. He sent His Son to pursue you. The enemy, however, is always seeking to separate you from others, to get you alone so he can destroy you.

"I know you remember the words of John 10:10, Jack. Jesus tells us there that Satan is a thief who wants you to be sequestered in the caverns of your heart—all alone. So be prepared to fight the battle for love and presence. Every day. Every hour. Every minute."

"*How in the blazes did you allow the conniving teacher to share his lies with the young fool?*" the voice rasps in the darkness. "*Now the Colorado cretin is flirting with one of the unspoken secrets of the universe that we fight to keep unspoken! His heart is in danger of escaping its dark isolation! You've failed again, you bumbling dolt! You know you will pay for this reckless oversight.*"

In that instant, a disturbing rumble is heard in the stygian netherworld. It grows louder as the gathered dark spirits glance at each other furtively. Then, abruptly, the dreaded one is in their midst.

He has no form—at least not to the human eye—but an extremely unpleasant effluvium accompanies him, and a loud, thrumming vibration causes the atmosphere to quiver violently around him.

The dark overlord growls, "*The young one is dangerous. You must not let him rise. If his faith is loosed to the third and fourth levels, he will turn many to the enemy. Many! Throw anything and everything in his path. He must not rise! Never! Drive his face into the ground and grind it into the dust from whence it came! Teach him to despise himself and distrust the One.*"

There is an ominous pause. Then the terrifying being roars, "*You know his weakness, you devils. Exploit it!*"

CHAPTER 40

Jack and Drew

Jack is alone in his dorm room packing his duffel bag for his trip to Colorado when his cell phone vibrates. He does not recognize the number and initially decides to ignore it. Something tells him to answer.

"Hey, this is Jack," he speaks into the phone as he gets down on his hands and knees to dig out his favorite pair of hiking boots from under his bunk.

There is a brief silence on the other end. Then a deep voice replies with some hesitation, "This is Drew."

The voice and the name are familiar to Jack, but he does not immediately register them. He must hesitate too long because the caller goes on to provide more identifying information.

"Remember, you and Rachel talked to me and the other guys here at the university several weeks ago."

"Oh yeah, right!" Jack says with a laugh. "You're the O-lineman!"

"That's me," the voice confirms dispassionately. There is a long pause.

"So, how are you doing?" Jack asks, interrupting the silence as he stands up next to his bed, boots in hand.

"That's why I'm calling. I, uh...I need to talk to someone," the student says, his words choked by emotion. "I need to talk to you."

"What's up, Drew? You don't sound so good," Jack comments as he drops his boots on the floor and leans into his phone, alerted by the urgency in the young man's voice.

"Can you meet me on campus?" the student asks.

Jack squeezes his eyes shut and massages his forehead slowly. *I'm getting ready to drive home tomorrow,* he protests in his head. *I don't have time now, dude.* To Drew, he simply says, "When?" as he sighs silently in his head.

"As soon as possible," the voice croaks.

Jack pulls the phone away from his ear and checks the time. Then he puts it back against his ear and says, "It's 3:15 now. I can meet you in, let's say, twenty minutes."

"Perfect, Jack. I really appreciate this."

"Where do we meet?" Jack inquires. "Back at the student commons?"

"Text me when you get on campus," Drew says with some hesitation. "I'll let you know where to meet me."

"Works for me," Jack replies. "See you soon, man."

Jack pockets his phone and sighs out loud this time. He wrestles with the irritating feeling of being inconvenienced as he grabs his keys and wallet and then throws on his insulated vest. The thought enters his mind that being self-sufficient has its advantages. Namely, he can distance himself from the needs of others.

"Jesus," he says with exasperation as he heads out of his room, "I'm a selfish man who wants life to happen on my schedule. Forgive me for my resistance. No, I haven't forgotten what Bill told me years ago: 'God doesn't want your ability as much as He wants your availability.' So here I am, Lord, willing myself out the door against my own stubborn desire to avoid Drew. Comfort this man. Show me how to love him with your love."

Jack jogs down the hallway of the deserted dormitory. Many students have already left for Christmas break. Once outside, he almost runs down several of his peers who are walking to their vehicles, laden with backpacks, laptops, and miscellaneous other belongings.

When he reaches the parking lot, he jumps into his Jeep and points it toward the university. He notices that last night's snowfall is melting fast before the still significant countenance of the winter sun. Unlike his roommate, Armando, Jack is not as vigilant of his physical environment. He does not notice the nondescript gray truck parked on the street adjacent to the cemetery like a lurking shark.

After he pulls into the lot at the university and kills the engine, Jack immediately texts Drew. He does not have long to wait before his text tone, which sounds like a bell in a monastery, alerts him to Drew's response that says, "Commons. SW corner. Study room."

Jack slides out of the Jeep and strides across the campus lawn that is blanketed with a green and white patchwork quilt. Five minutes later, he enters the huge student commons building and makes his way past the familiar lounge area, the cafeteria, and the coffee shop. On the far side of the building, he walks down a hallway engorged with students animatedly discussing finals, all-nighters, and their optimism or pessimism about achieving a 4.0 for the semester. All of them sound wired with caffeine, Jack observes, and he is briefly summoned back to memories of his own undergrad days.

When Jack arrives at his destination, he finds the door ajar. Pushing it open, he peers into a dim study room. He observes a Formica-top table, four plastic chairs with silver-metal legs, several small tables in the corners with matching lamps, and two overstuffed vinyl chairs. Only one of the table lamps is on—none of the overhead fluorescents. The solitary lamp casts a pale-yellow pool of light in one corner of the 12x12 study room.

Initially, Jack does not see anyone. He is reaching for his phone when he hears a quiet groan.

"Drew, is that you?" Jack asks the room.

"Over here, man," a voice mumbles from behind one of the overstuffed chairs.

Jack closes the door behind him and walks over to the corner of the small room. Sitting on the floor between the vinyl chair and the wall, he sees the strapping form of the football player he had met several weeks ago. He doesn't look nearly as imposing as the last time Jack had seen him. The young man is slumped over, collapsed into himself. His head is buried between his knees. He doesn't look up when Jack sits down in the chair across from him.

"What's wrong, Drew?" Jack inquires softly.

"My life is in the crapper," the student's muffled reply comes a few seconds later. Jack strains to hear him.

When the broken man is unable or unwilling to volunteer anything more, Jack says, "You've got to tell me, Drew. What is it?"

"It's not just one thing," the crushed man moans.

After another period of silence, Drew finally looks up at Jack. His eyes are red, and his large square face is pale and puffy. Jack thinks it resembles a huge clump of the sugar cookie dough his mom mixes up every year for Christmas cookies. A painful grimace contorts his features. His cheeks are wet.

Jack gazes steadily at the sniffling young man. "I'm listening," he says.

"Okay," the O-lineman says in a forlorn tone that makes Jack feel like he's back in Colorado being a big brother to one of his distraught sisters.

The bulky man rubs his eyes with the sleeves of his shirt and takes a deep breath, letting it out slowly. "My parents are getting divorced," he mumbles with bitterness in his voice. "Should I have seen it coming? Maybe. But they didn't say a word about it—until yesterday." Drew opens and closes his large hands as he talks.

"Out of nowhere, my mother calls and announces it to me. She doesn't even seem that broken up about it. She reports it to me like she's telling me the latest gossip back in our hometown." The young man runs gigantic fingers through his hair and shakes his head. "So, what do I do? I couldn't tell her that I'm torn apart by her announcement since she seems fine with it. I pretend I'm fine, too. I tell her that I'm sorry for her and dad and that I'll see her during winter break in a few days."

Jack winces at the man's words. They touch something old, something familiar inside of him. A wave of emotion rolls through his heart. The intensity of it surprises him. Sadness for Drew, Jack tells himself.

"Then something else happens. This morning—" Drew begins but cannot continue. The man's shoulders shake violently, then become still as he stares straight ahead. He is in a daze.

Jack waits patiently. He reaches out and lays a hand on one of the shoulders that is as big as a watermelon. He watches as the man's face shifts from a grimace to something harder, angrier. He grits his teeth, and his eyes roll away from Jack toward the dim room.

"This morning, I woke up and—" Drew's voice has suddenly become hollow, detached—"and, oh man, he was...gone. When I found him, I knew right away he was dead. He was gray...blue."

"Who?" Jack asks as he leans in closer to the student. "Who are you talking about, Drew?"

"Pete!" the big man cries out the name as he stares at his listener with eyes that flash with unspeakable emotion. "Remember him, Jack? You met him that day we talked, only a hundred feet from here."

Jack closes his eyes and groans aloud. He pictures Pete, the smallest of the four men on the couch that day in the Commons. Next to Drew, he looked like a middle schooler. Jack pictures the young man with the quick smile who was the kicker for the football team. He enjoyed mixing it up with Drew in that masculine roughhouse manner that betrayed his brotherly affection for his big roommate.

"We went to a frat house for an end-of-the-semester party," Drew explains as he wipes his face on the sleeve of his shirt. "We did the usual stuff—booze and pills—and I think Pete did some junk, too. Then we came back to the dorm and crashed."

The O-lineman squeezes his nose and chokes out the words, "The last thing I remember him saying to me was something like, 'See you in the afternoon, buddy. I'm sleepin' really late this time.' His words were slurred, and he mumbled so badly I could hardly understand him, but it wasn't any different than times in the past. I had no idea, Jack."

There is a long pause. Jack continues to rest his hand on Drew's shoulder that is shaking again. He waits.

"I think he vomited in his sleep and...inhaled it," Drew says in as quiet a voice as the big man can manage in his deep baritone timbre. Jack thinks of Drew talking quietly as someone trying to play the tuba softly.

"He was really blue, Jack," the shaken man continues. "It was terrible looking at his face."

Drew looks up at Jack again. His face is young. His eyes look like those of a boy. Jack has seen the look before. The university student is scared, lost.

"I can't go back to the room, man," he adds, his voice full of anguish. "I just can't go back there. You've got to help me, Jack. I got no one here, not really."

Jack gazes down at the young man in front of him and feels deep compassion. "I'm here, Drew," he says reassuringly, firmly. "We'll figure something out."

For the next several hours, Jack sits with Drew as the young man gut-wrenchingly stumbles through processing the death of his parents' marriage and his friend, Pete. Jack groans with the young man as he witnesses his agony. He sighs. He listens carefully. He offers words of comfort. Mostly, he is simply there, present—with him. The line he repeats over and over is, "This world can crush you out of nowhere, Drew."

Eventually, the big O-lineman pushes himself up off the floor and collapses into the chair opposite his new confidant. The light that falls softly from the single lamp next to Jack illuminates half of Drew's face while the other half is in shadows. Jack watches the young man knead the arms of the chair with his large hands over and over as if attempting to extract from them some sort of tangible comfort. He is staring at the floor as if in a trance. He is exhausted.

The room is quiet except for the steady flow of muffled voices drifting past the doorway of the dimly lit study space that has been transformed into a cloister of sorts. Jack decides not to bother Drew with any questions. He sits quietly across from the grieving man who seems to be a thousand miles away in his thoughts.

After a few minutes, Drew removes his hands from the arms of the chair and slaps them loudly on his huge knees. "It's time," he announces as he looks up at his listener with a determined resolve that alerts Jack to an abrupt shift in their conversation.

"It's time?" Jack inquires.

Drew nods his head affirmatively more to convince himself that it's time, Jack thinks, than to communicate anything to his listener. "Yeah, it's time," he repeats. "When I wasn't obsessing about mom and dad and Pete, I was wondering about it."

"Okay," Jack says slowly.

"I was thinking about why I should go on living," Drew responds with candor. "If a quarter-century marriage dies just like that," he says, snapping his fingers loudly, "and if my best friend expires in his sleep at twenty-years-old just like that," he announces, snapping his fingers again, "then what's going to last in this world? Why am I even here?" he asks rhetorically as he shrugs his massive shoulders. "Honestly, is there anything that makes life worth living?"

Drew falls silent as he continues to gaze at his listener. Then he sits up in his chair and leans toward Jack. "Do you know what it does to a man when his roommate who's so full of life suddenly dies?" he demands with anguish in his voice. "Do you know?"

Jack has some idea but says nothing.

"It literally blows up your world!" the football player exclaims. "Nothing is the same. Everything is in pieces. Parties don't matter. Finals don't matter. Football doesn't matter anymore. Heck, life doesn't matter right now."

Drew leans back and collapses into his chair. "I was thinking about killing myself," he announces to Jack matter-of-factly. "The emptiness inside of me just felt so total. It was me. If life was going to feel this way for the next sixty years, why would I even want to get up in the morning, I kept asking myself.

But then," Drew says as his eyes drift to the lamp next to Jack, "but then I realized that my emptiness wasn't just brought on by my parents' divorce or Pete's death. I knew that it had always been there. Girls, booze, drugs, and even gridiron highs were all about filling the emptiness. Emptiness has been my baseline position since I was a kid. Unknowingly, my goal in life has always been to fill that aching vacuum with something—just like Pete was doing up until last night. And look where it got him."

Drew abruptly slaps the arm of the chair once with his huge right hand and exclaims, "Then I remembered what you said about that NFL football player who felt empty even after his team won the Super Bowl. At that moment, I realized that you were right—we're all empty. We're all looking to find something to fill the tank inside of us. The problem is that the tank has holes in the bottom so that everything we fill ourselves with maddeningly keeps leaking out."

The big man falls silent as a pensive look transforms his face. "This afternoon, it hit me that nothing will remain in our perforated tanks except for something from outside this material world. It has to be super-natural since nothing natural works."

Drew sits up again and stares at Jack with eyes that burn with passion. "Then something inside of me said that you and Rachel coming to speak to us guys several weeks ago was not some random coincidence. You were sent to deliver me a life raft to get into when the storm came."

The O-lineman hesitates and then says, "Well, the storm is here, and I desperately need that raft. Now." He begins to choke up, and his voice crescendos as he says, "The only problem is…I don't know how to get into it."

Drew pauses and his large eyes search his listener's face. He pleads, "Jack, you have to help me. You have to help me get into that life raft." The desperate man reaches out with one of his large hands and grabs Jack's arm. His grip is so tight that Jack winces involuntarily.

Jack's head is reeling. Listening to the man's metaphor of the life raft fills him with amazement. He knows from personal experience that offensive linemen are deep thinkers—intellectual types—and Drew is doing nothing to undermine that belief.

Jack returns the young man's gaze and says with a confidence that is not from him, "That's why God sent me—to help you get in."

A look of relief floods Drew's half-acre face. His lips curl upward in a bittersweet smile that communicates both grief and anticipation. He remarks, "Jack, I already know the life raft is Jesus. You convinced me of that several weeks ago. He's the only one who can repair the holes in my tank and fill me with what I've always been longing for. I just need to know how to get into Jesus or how to get Him into me."

Jack nods his head and says, "Wow, Drew—you really seem to understand the greatest mystery of life. Your comments remind me of the old saying that we're all restless until we find our rest in Him, or the similar truth that we're all born with a hunger inside that nothing in this world can satisfy. How right you are when you say that only something from outside this natural world can feed the deepest longings of our hearts. And that something is actually a somebody."

Drew ponders Jack's words and then says, "Do you know what's weird about all this? A month ago, I would've laughed at what you told us three weeks ago over in the lounge. I would've told you that your religious babbling is irrelevant to this world and that Christians are a bunch of judgmental hypocrites who are so pathetically weak that they have to lean on a metaphysical crutch."

"And now?" Jack inquires.

"Three weeks ago, something was beginning to shift in me. I was prepared to see something in you and Rachel that caught my attention," Drew admits. "You weren't judgmental or out of touch with life. You had a joy about you that appeared genuine. I honestly envied you for that because I could tell you weren't drinking or smoking something," the offensive lineman says with a sigh as he thinks about Pete. "I had to conclude that it was Jesus who made you different than everybody else around me."

The brawny man grows quiet and looks down at his massive hands. After a short silence, he looks back up and reveals, "You and Rachel probably saved me, Jack. If you hadn't come and talked with us three weeks ago, I might be carrying out a suicide plan even as we speak."

Jack shakes his head and says, "No, Drew. It wasn't me or Rachel who saved you. It was Jesus—and He hasn't fully saved you yet. He sent us to you, and, by what I hear you saying, it was timely. He pursued you, man. We just made ourselves available to Him," Jack says, smiling on the inside as he remembers his thoughts back at the dorm only a few hours earlier.

"Get me in the life raft, then, before it drifts away," Drew says with desperation in his voice. "I don't want to wait any longer on this side of things. I don't want to sleep on it and change my mind." His grip on Jack's arm tightens, but it goes unnoticed because Jack is distracted by joy.

"Okay, then," Jack says with a controlled smile. "Buckle up, Drew, because your life is about to change forever in ways you can't even begin to imagine."

Jack pauses to pray for the young man in his head and then says, "The way to get into the raft is simply to hear and receive the good news from God's Word. This good news contains a four-fold truth: The first is that you were created by a loving Father who designed you, fearfully and wonderfully. Contrary to what many in this world say, you're not the accidental by-product of a godless, random macro-evolutionary process.

"The second truth is that every man and woman on this planet rebelled against their Creator and burned the bridge that connected them to their loving Father," Jack says. "We wanted to be the authority over our own lives—a god unto ourselves. We rejected the notion of some holy and righteous God telling us how to run our lives. 'Leave me alone' became our mantra.

"Thirdly—and here is the heart of the good news, Drew—God didn't abandon us to our rebellion even though we rejected Him and hated His authority. He loved us so much that He sent His Son to save us from our sin. He wanted to restore the close relationship between Himself and us and adopt us into His family." Jack pauses briefly and then says, "Yes, Drew, this is the good news...He didn't leave us alone. He came for us.

The fourth truth is that if you believe that Jesus is the Son of God and receive Him as the one who came to save you from your rebellion against the Father, then the terrible separation will be over. You'll be welcomed into the family of God forever. Of course, you'll still be living in this broken world, but you'll know where you came from, why you're here and where you're going.

Best of all," Jack says with a smile, "you'll receive God's love in your heart through the person of the Holy Spirit. Then you'll have the power within you to love others with that same amazing love. The depressing emptiness inside of you will be gone forever."

Drew doesn't hesitate but restates, "So, I need to believe those four truths and receive Jesus."

"Yeah," Jack says, nodding his head, "you captured the gist of my long explanation and reduced it to two words: *Believe* and *receive.* You offensive linemen are incredible!"

Drew keeps moving toward the prize. With earnestness in his face and voice, he declares, "I'm so ready to believe and receive, Jack. I have to talk to Jesus right now." The 6'6" man lifts up both hands as if preparing to engage a defensive tackle and informs Jack reassuringly, "Don't worry, I had enough Sunday school as a child that I know how to pray. My parents didn't want me to go, but my best friend's family brought me to church after sleepovers at his house."

Immediately, the big man, who reminds Jack of everything he knows about Peter, the disciple, closes his eyes and begins to speak. "Jesus, I heard your name before, but I never thought you were real, not in the historical sense. I equated you with Santa Claus and the Easter Bunny. Today, I know in my heart of hearts that you're the real thing while Santa and the Bunny are only figments of the imagination."

Drew pauses and his brows wrinkle in concentration. "Jesus, I do believe that you came to die for me to save me from my rebellion against your Father. I believe with all my heart, mind, and soul. Thank you for coming. At this very moment, I invite you into my life. I want to be your child, and I want you to be my Father. I desperately need you to fill the aching emptiness inside me. Help me, Jesus. Help me. I can't do it anymore by myself."

The offensive lineman pauses again and bends his head lower and lower until he slides off the chair and falls onto the floor. From his knees, he cries out, "Jesus, please watch over Pete. He didn't hate you. He even talked to me about you once or twice. I didn't want to listen to him, though. I'm so sorry about that! And comfort Pete's parents, please. They're devastated!

And now that I'm praying about parents, please talk some sense into my parents. They need you just as much as I do." Drew hesitates and then adds, "Please save both them and their marriage, God."

There is another short pause before he adds, "Thanks for hearing me, Jesus. I look forward to what you're going to do in my heart. Amen."

Muffled voices continue to spill into the dim room from the busy hallway. But the two men hear nothing beyond the four walls of the study room because Drew is singing in his tuba voice a Sunday school song he remembers from fifteen years earlier. "Jesus loves me, this I know," the big man sings shamelessly, "for the Bible tells me so. Little ones to Him belong. They are weak, but He is strong."

When Drew is finished singing like a young child, Jack does not know whether to laugh or to cry. A surge of emotion rises in his throat, but he swallows it as he continues to sit quietly across from the kneeling man.

Drew finally pushes himself off the floor and slides back into the chair. He takes a deep breath and looks over at Jack. "Well," the big man says breathlessly as if he had just finished an overtime game on a scorching day, "it's over."

"It's over?" Jack repeats.

"Yeah, the emptiness is over," the hulking young man replies with muted excitement. "No, I haven't felt any intense emotions, and I haven't heard God speak to me audibly, but I can tell that I'm not empty anymore. Jack, I'm no longer alone. He's here," Drew announces, finally releasing his grip on Jack's arm and pounding his broad chest with a fist.

Jack nods his head. "That's the good news of the gospel, Drew," he says with a laugh. "God moves into your heart and never leaves you—ever! That's the way it used to be back at the beginning in the garden: unbroken fellowship."

As the offensive lineman rubs his eyes with huge fingers, Jack leans toward him and says, "Now that you've received Jesus, you need to grow in him because the enemy will come and try to steal your faith. He'll lie to you that nothing ever happened on this day."

Drew finishes rubbing his eyes and looks at Jack with such a teachable hunger that Jack is amazed. *Here is a man who is a danger to the kingdom of darkness*, Jack thinks to himself. *Drew already seems to be one of those believers who will be uncommon—sold out to God completely.*

"There are a number of ways to grow spiritually," Jack continues. "For one thing, it's really important to find a church that teaches and preaches the truth of God's Word and start attending regularly. Going to church helps you in at least two ways—you hear teaching from the Scriptures, and you meet with other believers for support and friendship.

"Also, it's wise to get into God's Word on your own as often as possible so you can grow in love and truth," Jack advises. "You're living in a post-modern culture where people don't believe in absolute truth but claim that everyone can do what's right in their own eyes. So, it's critical to get grounded in the Word that contains absolute truth from the mind and heart of the Creator of the universe. As you mine the gold from God's Word, you'll slowly acquire a compass for life's journey. Studying the owner's manual is far better than guessing at true north and drifting along with everyone else whose truth comes from their own subjective opinions."

Jack looks at the young man sitting across from him and decides to communicate one final truth. "Even as a believer," he says smiling to himself, "a man can go it alone. Be careful not to do that. Someone I know told me that the enemy of your soul wants to get you alone and destroy you. He wants to drive you away from God and other believers into a lonely place where you'll be vulnerable to the enemy's lies and accusations. Don't let that happen."

Drew nods his head, then looks down and studies his hands for a while. Eventually, he looks back up at Jack. "Thanks for showing up, man," he chokes out the words. "Both times. If it wasn't for Jesus—and you—I'm convinced I'd be dead right now. No doubt about it."

"Glad that I could be here," Jack replies as emotion rises in his throat for the twentieth time over the past three hours. "I'm confident you'll be doing the same for many people in the future."

"I certainly hope so," Drew replies slowly, nodding his large, squarish face that is ruggedly handsome.

Both men fall silent. The university student is exhausted. Jack is tired as well. Spiritual battles are wearing, after all.

"What's next for you?" Jack finally asks.

Drew pulls out his phone and looks at the time. "Wow, really! We've been talking for over three hours! I'm sorry, man," he says, looking at Jack and shaking his head. "I gotta run. I'm supposed to meet with Pete's parents in a few minutes." He gets up and stretches his arms to the ceiling.

Jack gets up too, and says, "I'm glad you won't be alone when you speak with them."

"Exactly," Drew agrees. "I've got Jesus with me now."

"One last thing," Jack says as both men move toward the door. "Download a Bible app and begin reading the New Testament. I'd recommend beginning with the book of John."

"Will do, Jack," the lineman says as he looks down at Jack, who is not a small man. "And one last thing from me," he adds, "If it's copacetic with you, I'd like to talk with that Rachel girl again. She really impressed me. Almost as much as you," he says with a laugh.

"I'll let her know," Jack replies with a smile.

Just before they open the door and leave the room that has served as a delivery room for a spiritual birth, Drew turns and wraps Jack in arguably the biggest bear hug he has ever experienced, even bigger than the ones his teammates gave him after the DII championship game.

By the time Jack exits the Commons building, it is dark outside and slippery—the melted snow has turned to ice. The sun has long since set, and the warmed air has surrendered to the winter cold. Jack does not notice the cold or the darkness or, for that matter, the large man stomping behind him. He is overjoyed by his totally unexpected encounter with Drew that climaxed in the greatest possible miracle in the universe: a person languishing in the murky ambiguity of forever darkness has been brought into the brilliant light of God's presence. Jack gives thanks to Jesus as the sidewalk takes him past a thick stand of pine trees.

For joy, he begins to recite Psalm 23. Just when he has spoken the words, "Even though I walk through the darkest valley, I will fear no evil," strong hands seize his arm and shoulder in a vice grip and shove him into the copse of pine trees with violent force. Jack feels himself propelled roughly through the trees before he loses his footing and falls into a gully hidden by the darkness. He rolls down a steep hill and comes to rest on his stomach. He scrambles quickly to his feet, but the iron hands grab him again and throw him roughly to the ground that is covered with snow. On his knees, he turns and looks up at his attacker.

It is dark, but there is enough light for Jack to make out the form of a large man dressed in a trench coat. "Drew?" he asks reflexively.

The large figure is not Drew. "Shut up!" the man growls. "You make a sound, and I'll kill you."

Jack adds up the size of the man, his anger, and his verbal threat and realizes that he is in legitimate danger.

"I don't have long, so I'll get to the point real quick," the man snarls at him. "I know who you are, Jack"—he spits out the name as if it is a putrid taste in his mouth—"and I know you got the diary! I want it, and I want it now!"

Jack's brain falters for just a moment before he realizes that the man is referring to Jacob's journal. "The diary," he repeats. "Why would you want the diary? And how do you know my name?"

"Why wouldn't I want the diary?" the man snaps back at Jack testily. There is a short pause, and the man ad-libs, "The man who wrote the diary is my relative. I want it because it belongs to my family and me."

"Jacob is your relative?" Jack asks incredulously. "Are you a Sutherington?"

There is a pause before the man ad-libs some more. "Why, ah, yes, I'm a Sutherington," he stammers. "My name is...ah, Zeke Sutherington from the...the Montgomery side in Springfield."

"So, how are you specifically related to Jacob?" Jack inquires with growing suspicion.

The man stammers some more, then grabs Jack by his coat and picks him up out of the snow as if he is a child. "Shut up and stop askin' me questions!" he yells. "I'm the one askin' the questions tonight! Now, where's the diary?"

"I don't have it here," Jack replies honestly.

"Where is it?" the big man screams as he shakes him roughly.

Jack's mind races. He doesn't actually know where the diary is. *Does Stewart have it, or Mr. Fagani?* he wonders to himself. He cannot honestly recall at the moment. "I don't know where it is," he finally admits.

"Liar!" the man cries. Jack does not see the man's arm pull back in the darkness, so when the fist closes in on his face, it is too late to defend himself. The blow to his jaw is powerful. Stunned, Jack falls backward into the snow.

Jack shakes his ringing head to make sure it is still connected to his neck. Then he sits up and looks up at his attacker just as the moon emerges from behind a cloud. A cold wave rushes over him when the silver light reveals the face of a man who has made appearances in his nightmare and Violet's dream. Jack sees the familiar half-bald head, the long, stringy hair on the sides and back, and the bearded face with the crooked nose. Jack crabwalks backward to create some distance between himself and the monster from his nightmare.

"Where is it?" the man cries in a louder voice. "I want that diary!"

Jack gets on his knees and then rises to his feet. He feels a bit wobbly standing in the gully. He has done some fighting in the past and knows a few self-defense techniques, but his gut tells him that this man will be more than his abilities can neutralize. So, he resorts to reason.

"I can get the diary for you," Jack says as calmly as possible, holding his arm out as if he is stiff-arming a defensive lineman. "I just don't have it here with me right now."

"I want the diary tonight!" the man yells as he takes a threatening step toward Jack. "You have to get it for me now!"

Jack hesitates and then explains, "I can't get it for you right now. I need to go find it first. Any number of people might have it in their possession at—"

This time the lightning-fast left fist hammers his stomach, and the roundhouse right fist hits him full in the left cheek. He goes down hard. He tries to scramble to his feet, but his head swims, and his legs feel rubbery. He struggles to breathe. He imagines the fight referee standing over him, beginning the ten-second count.

Jack opens his mouth to reason with his attacker again, but no words are willing to come from his throat. The man from his cemetery nightmare yells, "Get me that diary tonight, or I'll kill you, Jack!"

Jack massages his head to rid it of the thick veil that hangs over his brain. His sluggish mind tries to figure out how this crazy man knows about the existence of the journal.

As the veil begins to lift, Jack sees something in the man's hand that gleams in the moonlight. It is a knife. *Jesus, help me!* Jack cries out in his head. The man advances toward him and raises his hand.

Energized by adrenaline, Jack quickly scrambles to his feet. He grabs the man's hand that wields the knife and drives his fist toward the man's throat. His blow finds its mark, and the attacker begins coughing and clawing at his throat.

Jack sees his opportunity to escape. He turns and begins stumbling up the side of the gully toward the pine trees. After only three strides, however, a steel vice grabs his right leg and jerks him backward. Wheeling around, Jack sees the knife swinging toward his abdomen. He wards off the blow with a countermove but is unable to totally deflect it. A sharp pain explodes in his left abdomen.

Fighting for his life at this point, Jack launches an elbow into the man's nose—the crooked nose that clearly has been broken at some point in the past. The big man grunts in pain.

Just then, Jack hears voices from somewhere above the gully. He cries out for help as he backpedals up the hill. Then something completely eclipses the pale half-moon, and the world goes dark. The last thing Jack remembers is falling but never hitting the ground.

CHAPTER 41

Jack Awakens

Jack awakens to a voice murmuring. It sounds far away, muted and distorted, as if traveling through water. Someone is holding his arms down. He feels pain. The murmuring grows louder. This time, Jack understands what the voice is saying. "I want the diary," it repeats over and over with increasing volume. He struggles to sit up, but strong hands still hold him down.

"I want the diary!" the voice demands even more loudly. Then he hears another voice interject, "Calm down, Jack. Calm down."

At the sound of the new voice, Jack finally forces his heavy eyelids open and looks up into a woman's face that is grim but not unpleasant. She is wearing a gray shirt with red letters stitched into the top left quadrant that read, EMT.

"Where am I?" Jack asks as he attempts to sit up again.

Strong hands continue to frustrate his efforts. He looks at the hands and follows them up the arms and into the face of a young man sitting on the other side of him. He is wearing a shirt identical to his associate's. He is smiling.

"I don't have it," the young man says with a chuckle. "I swear!"

"You don't have what?" Jack asks as he tries to blink away the sledgehammer that is pounding relentlessly in his head.

“The diary. You keep insisting you want the diary. I sure as heck don’t have it, and I don’t think Melissa has it either,” he says with a smirk as he nods at the woman across from him with the grim, pleasant face.

Jack closes his eyes as the realization dawns that it was his voice that had been demanding the diary. He wants to laugh, but he knows it will only aggravate the throbbing in his head. Instead, he asks, “How do I look?”

“I’m not the one to be asking,” the smiling man says. “Melissa here, though, she thinks you’re pretty hot. Hopes you ask her out before we get to the hospital.”

Jack opens his eyes in time to see the woman glance annoyingly at her coworker before she turns her attention back to Jack. “Something perforated your abdomen,” she comments as she examines him. “Grazed it, actually. Once they clean you up, the extent of your injury can be assessed more accurately. Doesn’t look like you lost a lot of blood, though.”

“What happened?” Jack inquires as he probes his jaw with tentative fingers. “Did I get blind-sided by a blitzing safety?”

The young man who is still holding him down laughs and says, “There’s our answer, Melissa! He obviously got his bell rung. I’d say a moderate concussion with some memory loss. What do we think he was out for, five, six minutes?”

“Sounds about right,” the woman says, “according to the report of the students who found him.” The grim face looks at him again and asks, “Do you hear any ringing in your ears, Jack?”

Jack pauses to listen and then replies, “A little. Not as bad as my last concussion my freshman season.”

“You know you weren’t injured on the football field, right?” the female EMT asks.

"I wasn't?" Jack says, frowning.

"No, campus security found you down behind some trees," she explains. "He said he heard a commotion and came running down the hill along with some students who heard you crying for help." She pauses and adds gravely, "You were attacked by someone, Jack."

Jack closes his eyes and tries to recall what happened.

"Several students reported that they chased your attacker to the parking lot and saw him get into a pickup truck and drive off," Melissa, the EMT, informs Jack. "Unfortunately, they didn't get a license number or any description of the truck except that it was gray. The only physical description they gave was that the suspect was wearing a long trench coat."

The mention of the pickup truck is the trigger that Jack needs. The memory of the attack comes rushing back to him. He sees the big man with the long straggly hair who had appeared in his cemetery nightmare. He remembers the demands for the diary, the fighting, and the knife.

I need to warn Stewart, he thinks, panicking as he attempts to sit up yet again. *The crazy man might go to the Academy and attack him, too.* A second later, however, Jack remembers that the Intellect flew home to northern Minnesota the night before and should be safely back in Two Harbors by now. Jack breathes a sigh of relief.

"Do your best to reconstruct what happened," the smiling EMT remarks. The young man is no longer holding Jack's arms down. Now he just has one hand resting on his chest. "The police will show up at the hospital, and they'll want a statement from you."

Jack closes his eyes to focus on remembering what happened in the gully. The first thing that comes to his mind is the warning from Mr. Fagani. *What did he say, that a descendent of Philip DaFoe is the chief of police? So, do I talk with the police or not? The whole department certainly can't be dirty,*

Jack reasons. *But maybe, just to be wise, I shouldn't admit to remembering anything yet.*

Even though the ambulance is running without lights or a siren, they arrive at the hospital within minutes. Jack is quickly removed from the vehicle and wheeled into the emergency room. Almost immediately, he is attended by three medical personnel who examine his facial abrasions and the wound in his abdomen. He cannot remember ever receiving such close attention from so many people at the same time—even from his athletic trainers. Something about it feels warm and safe to him. He is deeply grateful.

Two hours later, Jack is sitting in the recovery room bandaged up and ready to be discharged. The knife wound turns out to be—just as Melissa the EMT thought—a superficial laceration. Although the length of his unconsciousness suggests something more severe, his other symptoms point to a mild concussion. Accordingly, he is released from the hospital with the strong recommendation to visit his primary physician the next day to assess his condition after a night's rest.

Jack's first act is to call Dr. Windsor. The faithful professor answers his phone on the second ring. The only thing Jack tells the retired colonel is that he is at the hospital and needs a ride back to his vehicle. The grieving man immediately agrees to the request. He promises that he will arrive at the hospital to pick up his student in half an hour. Jack feels warm and thankful for the second time that night.

His second call is to Stewart in Minnesota.

"Hello, is this Jack?" his amazingly intelligent friend inquires when he answers his phone.

"Yeah, it's me. I suppose you didn't expect to hear from me so soon after you left. I haven't seen you for twenty-four hours, and I'm already missing you," Jack says with a laugh.

Stewart misses Jack's humor and instead educates his friend on the colder-than-usual weather conditions for the middle of December in northern Minnesota. He predicts that Lake Superior will freeze over this year. He also informs his Academy classmate that there is an overabundance of Timberwolves roaming the woods this winter.

When Stewart begins telling his friend about the declining deer and moose populations that are clearly impacted by the aforementioned increase in the Timberwolf population, Jack interrupts and abruptly asks, "Where is Jacob's journal?"

"The journal? I decided to bring it home with me over the break because I want to examine it for any other hidden facts or clues. Why do you ask?"

Jack fills Stewart in on his encounter with the man in the trench coat on the University campus. With his friend's safety in mind, he especially emphasizes his attacker's anger and his persuasive insistence on having the diary. Jack goes on to explain to Stewart that he probably won't have any unwanted visitors way up near Canada but to keep his eyes open just in case since it appears that the purported relative of Jacob Sutherington won't stop until he acquires it—even if he must resort to violence.

Jack ends his conversation with the Intellect on a lighter note by suggesting that he probably has nothing to fear since the freezing weather in Two Harbors will keep the riffraff away.

Jack leaves the recovery room and walks down the hallway of the Overland Prairie hospital. His head and face feel like they had been worked over by a jackhammer. His uneasy stomach threatens to discharge its contents.

When he shuffles into the lounge area near the hospital entrance and looks out the floor-to-ceiling windows, he does not see Dr. Windsor's car.

With a quiet groan, he sits down where he has a view of the circle drive in front of the hospital. He tries not to make eye contact with several people sitting nearby who appear to be staring at his face. After a while, he closes his eyes and wonders why the police have not shown up to question him.

Knowing that Armando is not leaving for LA until tomorrow night on a redeye flight, he decides to call his roommate to see if he is available to meet with him and discuss the most recent twist in the Jacob Lane Sutherington mystery. Armando is excited to get an update and insists that Jack count him in. Jack gives his roommate an approximate ETA and says that he will pick him up in front of the citadel.

Before ending the call, Armando informs Jack that his call is especially timely since he needs to talk to him about something relating to one of Violet's dreams.

When he is done talking to his roommate, Jack contemplates reaching out to the female members of the micro-cohort. In the end, he overrules the idea since all three women are either in transit or already at their winter break destinations. Besides, they are all in the Eastern Time Zone and possibly asleep by now.

Jack decides to step outside and wait for his ride under the canopy that spans the driveway in front of the hospital. The pounding in his head has diminished to a heavy throb, but he still feels like he was speared by the crown of a linebacker's helmet. His left side burns whenever he brushes it with his arm, but it is of little concern to Jack. He is simply relieved that he is still alive.

He sits down on the bench next to the driveway and takes several deep breaths hoping that his queasy stomach will calm down. Closing his eyes, he enjoys the bracing breeze that blows across his face.

Well, Jesus, that was a bit scary, Jack prays in his head. *I sure didn't see that coming. I'm not sure if I should ask you why it happened in the first place or just thank you for protecting my life. I'll do the latter—thanks for saving me from serious harm.*

He pauses and then continues, *Please watch over all the Screaming Eagles while we are apart. Especially protect Aly and Mahmoud from the powers of darkness. I believe there's a target on their backs, so watch over them closely, Father. Grow Mahmoud quickly in his new faith so that he will not falter and fall back into his old beliefs. Walk with Rachel, Stewart, and Armando as well. Guide their steps as they travel to see their families.*

Lastly, be with Emily. Thankfully, you know what's going on in her heart because I certainly don't. Preserve her life and keep her safe from debilitating calamities but also bring into her life whatever it takes to bring her close to you. Get her attention, Lord. Soften and heal her heart. Show your character to her every day so she will come to trust you and choose you above all others.

Lastly, I want to thank you so much for opening Drew's eyes! You're amazing, Jesus! I never cease to be blown away at how you transform a human heart! In a week's time, both Mahmoud and Drew have believed and received. Over the past eight years, I don't think there's ever been a time when I've been as convinced of how real you are as I have been these last two weeks. Thank you for your deep love for two men who had no desire to serve you and weren't even looking for you! You certainly are the God who pursues your lost sheep out of love instead of waiting for them to clean up their act. Teach me how to love others with that kind of love.

Okay, Dr. Windsor is here. I'll stay in touch, Lord. Please deeply comfort this man even tonight as he misses his dear wife. New birth and death—what opposite ends of the spectrum, in some ways. But I thank you that you're Lord over it all. Nothing ever surprises you.

Jack walks gingerly to the passenger door of the waiting van and climbs in with an involuntary grunt.

"You look and sound like an old man," Dr. Windsor comments, his face shrouded by the darkness of the night. "I'd hate to see the other guy," he adds. His customarily stern voice is tempered by concern.

"Believe me; this is one time when the *other guy* line is very appropriate. But before I tell you what happened, I want to ask you if you're open to swinging by campus and picking up Armando and then going to your house. We've got a lot to talk about tonight, and I think we need your ears and wisdom."

Dr. Windsor smiles grimly at Jack and says with a sigh, "I have a lot more time on my hands now than a few days ago. So, sure, let's pick up Armando and head over to my place. The house could use some voices besides me talking to God and Violet. Besides, I'm a bit out of the loop with you and your cohort. I need to do some catching up."

As they pull out of the hospital driveway and out onto the main road, neither of them notices the vehicle that pulls away from the curb and follows them. It is not a pickup truck but a late-model, black SUV.

Fifteen minutes later, Armando climbs into the back seat of the Windsor van that seems like the last vehicle a retired colonel would drive. He is surprised that Jack did not show up in his Jeep and makes some wry comment about not being able to ride in style every day. He also asks Jack if his face got run over by a Sherman tank.

While the colonel shakes his head and grunts, Jack announces to his friend that they will be going over to the professor's house for their late-evening debriefing, where he will explain to both of them about his face. Dr. Windsor comments that the two young men can help him eat the mountain of food that arrived at his house before and after his wife's death. "Enough to feed an army," the professor comments quietly.

When the three warriors of the kingdom of light reach the house, they sit at the same dining room table that the Screaming Eagles had gathered around only two months earlier when Violet had prepared a meal fit for kings and queens. All three men sense a heavy sadness in the room, but they are grateful for the impromptu fellowship on this evening that places professor and students on a level plain. Jack and Armando are amazed to hear the grieving husband quote several times from God's Word that Christians do "not grieve as others do who have no hope."

As they consume meatloaf, ribs, banana bread, corn on the cob, a dozen different pasta salads, cookies, mashed potatoes, rolls, baked beans, and red gelatin with fruit cocktail, Jack informs his two listeners of the amazing conversion of Drew. Then he relates the encounter he had at the university with the man from Violet's dream that explains his bruised and swollen face.

Dr. Windsor studies his student with his familiar steely gaze as Jack relates the drama that unfolded with the cemetery man. Only five weeks ago, Jack would have interpreted the professor's countenance as angry or critical. Now, he understands that the man's serious countenance is his way of showing uncompromising strength for the people in his care. It also reflects how impossible it is for a warrior to be light-hearted when burdened by the invisible war that rages around him day and night. His wife's recent death is just one example of the ongoing war that is being fought on two fronts, or better said, in two worlds.

When Jack is done recounting his contrasting adventures, Armando fumes about the bully attacker and swears that no one will ever hurt his friend on his watch. Jack is surprised at his roommate's intensity.

"Did you call the police?" the professor inquires more rationally.

Jack explains to Dr. Windsor what Mr. Fagani had told them, namely, that they should contact law enforcement only as a last resort since the chief of police was a relative of an unsavory character named Philip DaFoe. Jack goes on to tell the professor everything about the Sutherington gravesite in the cemetery as well as the journal of JLS.

Dr. Windsor shares what Mr. Fagani had said about Jack's connection to the Sutheringtons, and so some of what Jack shares is not new to the Warfare professor. However, the existence of Jacob's journal is totally new "intelligence" for him. He plies Jack with many questions about its contents.

After an hour of talking and grazing over twenty different food options, the three stuffed men roll away from the dining room table and retire to the familiar living room to continue their discussion. Jack senses a quiet heaviness in his chest every time he glances at the flowered reclining chair where Violet had sat during the students' October visit.

Jack's face is still being pounded relentlessly by giant hammers, so he closes his eyes as soon as he settles into the wingback chair with the yellow rose upholstery. Dr. Windsor gives him some painkillers to help reduce his discomfort as the three men continue to talk.

Somewhere along the way in their discussion, Brown Sugar makes a late appearance in the room and makes a nest on Armando's lap. The three men grow quiet as they look at the small dog that was such a good friend of Violet's. Jack thinks the dog is a bit lethargic—probably experiencing the canine version of grief.

"So, you're not going to go to the police," the colonel says, finally interrupting their private reflections about the woman who should be there with them. "I'm not sure that's the wisest course of action," he adds with concern, "especially when you're talking about an assault that could have resulted in your death. Do you at least have a description of the man?"

Jack sits forward and opens his eyes. "Like I said earlier, he looks exactly like the man your wife saw in her dreams about me," he announces. "Exactly."

Dr. Windsor stares at Jack and shakes his head. "My wife, Violet—I took her for granted so often. Little did I know that I was living with the dreamer of dreams sent from God," he marvels. "It sends chills down my spine when we talk about it, and that doesn't happen often."

Even as his eyes grow moist, the professor leans back on the couch and states, "You have no idea why this man wants the journal."

"None, except maybe for some unknown financial gain," Jack replies.

Dr. Windsor grunts. "Yes, I doubt that anyone with a mere interest in family history or an heirloom would resort to what that man did tonight. I highly doubt that he is related to your great, great-grandfather."

Jack looks at Armando inquiringly, asking him a question without speaking. His roommate nods his head once. Jack then goes on to tell the professor about the coins that Jacob Sutherington supposedly buried with Madeline DaFoe.

The widower, who, even in the comfort of his home, sits like he has a steel rod in his back, turns this most recent revelation over in his mind. Finally, he asks, "How would your attacker know about the coins, Jack? And how would anyone know they are worth killing for? They could be worth only ten to fifteen dollars apiece."

"Maybe this man knows something we don't," Jack offers.

Dr. Windsor nods his head and says, "He must believe there's a treasure map in that journal if he's so intent on acquiring it."

The retired paratrooper from the 101st Airborne Division pauses and thinks out loud, "It's possible Jacob left information with someone else regarding what he buried in the coffin along with Madeline. But why would he have done that? Such information would only serve to indict him in the disappearance of Philip's wife."

"Maybe he left the information in a will only to be read after his death," Armando suggests.

"Just so you know," the professor says in his sternest voice, "if this attacker of yours, Jack, ever sets foot on campus *property, I will do everything in my power to* detain him. He will not trespass on school property or gallivant around wherever he wishes. Rest assured that I'll keep surveillance sharp for a gray truck that shows up in my theater of operations during winter break."

The young men nod their heads in acknowledgment of the colonel's vow. They are fully confident that the retired military officer will fulfill his promise with a dedication driven by a desire to protect his people at any cost.

"By the way," Dr. Windsor says, "what is the journal's location at this moment?"

"In Minnesota with Stewart," Jack replies. "Just so you know, I called him earlier and told him about what happened today, so he's informed about what's going on."

"It should be safe, then," the professor reflects aloud, "at least for the next six weeks."

"There is one last matter," Dr. Windsor announces as he levels his authoritative gaze on the two young men that Jack has mistakenly interpreted as an authoritarian gaze in the past. "A decision will need to be made about digging up that grave without—I hate to say it since I am a man of the law—without the police chief being privy to it. But before that decision can be made, the reliability of the journal needs to be established beyond the shadow of a doubt. There's always the possibility that it's a hoax," the man warns. "Maybe it was written by bored adolescent boys back in the 1930s."

"But if it is true, it certainly explains a lot," Jack parries, "like the reason for Madeline's disappearance, the location of her body, and the actual killer of Jacob's family. It also would explain the four Sutherington grave markers with the same date of death."

Armando adds, "The only thing it doesn't tell us is what happened to Philip DaFoe and his two children."

"I believe Mr. Fagani will provide us information about that," Dr. Windsor says with optimism. "He should also be able to follow the tracks of Jacob Sutherington after his family was murdered. In fact, the last I heard, our esteemed cemetery professor was busily researching the Sutherington family line from Agatha all the way up to Jack."

Jack and Armando nod their heads. A silence falls over the room. All three men are exhausted, especially the professor after the events of recent days—and recent weeks and months, for that matter. The heavy late-night meal only serves to further sedate them.

Jack closes his eyes for the umpteenth time that evening and soon finds himself in the cemetery standing in front of the Sutherington monument. A thick fog drifts across the landscape, partially obscuring Jack's vision. Assembled around the large gray monument, Jack's narrowed eyes make out a throng of people that includes Jacob's wife, his three children, Madeline and Philip DaFoe, and a woman he assumes is Jacob's mother, Agatha—Jack's great-great-great-grandmother. There is also a small child standing next to Madeline, holding her hand. They're all staring at Jack with expressionless faces and hollow eyes.

Suddenly, a large man with a crooked nose and bloodshot eyes bursts through the throng of the dead as if they are part of the thick fog. He strides toward Jack with malice twisting his countenance. A knife is in his hand. Jack sits bolt upright and cries out.

When he opens his eyes, he sees another throng before him—a throng of two. Dr. Windsor and Armando are leaning forward in their chairs, staring at him with deep concern. His heart is booming much faster than the tympani drum in his head.

"A nightmare," the colonel states instead of asking. "An acute stress reaction."

Jack nods his head and groans quietly. "All the dead people," he says, "and the cemetery man. Not Fagani. The other one who attacked me today."

Dr. Windsor shakes his head sadly and says, "Welcome to warfare 101, Jack. The enemy clearly has you in his sights. But Jesus won't let him have you. Neither will I," the colonel announces in a voice that surrounds Jack like Kevlar. Jack, who has always been there for others but so rarely experienced others there for him, immediately relaxes. He leans back in his chair and closes his eyes again.

"Juan," he hears a voice say a few seconds later. He ignores it as he begins to slip into unconsciousness.

"Juan," the voice says with more urgency.

"What?" he says, elongating the word with irritation as he opens one eye against his will and considers his roommate.

"Aren't you supposed to stay awake as long as possible after a concussion?" his friend asks.

"It's been six hours," he groans. "Besides, why do I have the feeling that you're motivated by something besides altruism for my welfare."

"Me?" Armando says with feigned innocence. He pauses a moment and then says, "Okay, Juan, as usual, you have found me out. I confess, I have a vested interest in mind. I need you to stay awake a little longer," his friend urges. "Remember, I told you I have something to share with you tonight."

"I remember, though, I'm trying to forget," Jack groans as he attempts to focus on his friend's voice instead of his pounding head and throbbing side.

"Dr. Windsor, you'll want to hear this, too," Armando says with excitement in his voice.

"Oh, I will, will I?" the former Screaming Eagle says sternly. The truth is that the grieving husband is totally enjoying his evening with the two young men. In a strange way, it takes him back to another lifetime. The two men could be his sons—or even his brothers. He has neither.

"Yes, I believe you will," Armando replies slowly as he eyes the professor and attempts to interpret his ostensible irritation.

"Okay, what is it?" Jack says, attempting to show marginal interest without sounding too impatient.

Armando does not hesitate at Jack's invitation but jumps right in. The young man's mood changes from excited to serious as he says, "During my spelunking today, I came to the realization that I need to deal with my anger toward Stewart and...Sniper."

"Sniper?" the professor inquires abruptly. Of course, the gang name that sounds like a military shooter grabs the colonel's full attention. Jack cannot help but smile at the officer's vigilance. He groans at the pain that is awakened by the movement of his facial muscles.

"Yeah, the gang banger from Valinda who killed my brother and gave me my face tat," Armando says, pointing with his index finger at the faint white scar running from just beneath his left eye to his jawline.

"With the help of Dr. McNeely and the Holy Spirit, I'm beginning to recognize that my anger toward Stewart is actually anger toward myself that I'm deflecting toward him. I need to deal with that. I also feel called to be the Tip of the Spear to Sniper. I want to—" Armando hesitates as he tries to get words out of his mouth that are reluctant to be spoken—"I want to share Jesus' love with the gangster I still hate on some level."

There is a brief silence before Dr. Windsor asks, "Is this Sniper character back in LA?"

Armando nods his head. "I'm flying back to LA tomorrow to see my mother. Sometime during the break, I'm planning to drive up to La Puente and track down Sniper."

The young man, formerly known as Syko Loco, grins his dazzling smile and announces, "Juan, the reason I needed to share this information with you as soon as possible is that you're going with me to meet Sniper."

Dr. Windsor's thin eyebrows arch upward, and Jack's weary eyes engage Armando's with sudden alertness. "I'm going with you," Jack repeats to ensure that he heard his friend correctly.

Armando nods and says, "I know you weren't planning on a trip to California over your Christmas break, but God has been unfolding all this in my head over the last few days."

"Well, I'm glad my future is clear to one of us," Jack comments irritably as he massages his throbbing forehead.

"Juan," Armando says and then pauses poignantly, "this plan isn't my idea."

"Uh-huh," Jack says slowly. "I suppose you're going to tell me this is God's plan for me."

"Exactly, it's God's plan," the olive-skinned man says, sounding serious.

"He's been moving me in this direction for months now. He's made it clear that I have unfinished business with my brother's killer that poisons my heart and spills over into my current relationships. Dr. McNeely has helped me see that unforgiveness hardens the softest heart."

"Sounds legit to me, bro," Jack says wearily. "Bitterness is a killer worse than the most dangerous weapon—except it's suicide, not homicide. I'm just not clear how I fit into God's plan to rendezvous with Sniper."

"Don't you remember Violet's dream about me?" Armando asks, looking first at Dr. Windsor, as if garnering support from the warfare professor, and then at Jack.

The professor immediately knows what the young man from La Puente is referring to. He displays a thin smile and steeples his fingers under his nose. He is thoroughly enjoying the conversation between his two young Academy students. It takes Jack a little longer, but soon his face betrays dawning realization.

"You're talking about walking through the forest where those trees are attacking you," Jack recalls through the haze shrouding his brain. He covers half his face with one hand and stares at his friend through one eye.

"Exactamente, Juan," his roommate says, nodding his head. Armando eyes Jack with anticipation, waiting for his roommate to remember more of the dream.

"Okay, okay," Jack mumbles slowly, trying not to move his throbbing head any more than he has to since he is feeling nauseous again. Glancing carefully in the professor's direction, he says, "I remember that Violet referred to a companion who was with Armando on his journey through the dangerous forest."

"Correct again, Juan," Armando affirms with growing excitement. "You're the one who's with me in the forest. God didn't reveal this to me in an audible voice," he explains, "but the next thing to it. As soon as I sensed God's calling to go to Sniper, He showed me that you were the one to accompany me."

Jack looks at Dr. Windsor through his single eye seeking advice or, possibly, rescue, but the man is silent, gazing at him with a look that surrenders nothing—a face without a tell.

After what had transpired only hours earlier at the university, Jack is not excited about pursuing an adventure that will take him into gang territory. He honestly hopes that his professor will intervene and announce the foolhardiness of such a foolhardy mission. He seeks escape by closing both eyes and shutting out the Windsor living room.

Instead of an intervention, Jack experiences an almost tangible peace wrap itself around him like a warm blanket. The discomfort in his throbbing head and queasy stomach subsides abruptly. He hears the same inaudible voice speaking to him that Armando must have heard earlier. He is immediately convinced that he is called to go with his friend. He also discerns that the presence or absence of danger is not the anvil on which decisions must be forged but rather the summons of the Father's voice. If God calls him to go, he must go.

Jack knows that the voice he hears is also the same one that penetrated the stony heart of Mahmoud when he was standing on the threshold of genocide. How can Jack disregard the Voice that called the universe into existence with but a word—creating something out of absolutely nothing? Resistance to this voice is futile, unwise.

The presence of the almighty God, who is as far above humanity as the sun is above the sputtering flame of a single candle, falls like a refreshing morning dew over Jack. He smiles at its invigorating power.

Embraced in the arms of this unapproachable yet invitingly intimate personality, Jack's eyes fill with tears. They are the same tears that have come often since the day he was captured by the love of this comforting and demanding Presence—the one who is both the lamb and the lion, the human and the divine, the obedient servant and the King of the universe.

Jack knows he has been filled with the power of the Spirit of God and that he is strong enough to leap over a wall or advance against a troop. He laughs the laugh reserved for those whose experience of the rumbling beneath the present physical world dissolves into a fleeting mist against the backdrop of the towering *Everestian* mountain of God's eternal character.

Jack opens both of his eyes and looks at Armando. "Okay, my barrio brother," he says out of the internal confluence of peace and power that flows through his soul like a mighty river, "when do you need me in LA?"

CHAPTER 42

The Departure

Two days later, Jack throws his duffel bag into the back of his Jeep and slams the gate. He walks across the parking lot in the shadow of the towering castle-church with its impressive turret and retraces his steps from the day he arrived at the Academy. The December snow that waxes and wanes like the ocean tide has totally melted, and the dormant grass of the expansive lawn stretching toward the lake is a blend of faded green and golden brown.

Jack pauses by the shore of the lake that has molted its thin skin of ice and whose leaden gray waters are almost identical to the dark slate hue of the morning sky, and he remembers. He remembers standing in this very same spot four months earlier. Oddly, it feels like it could have been four weeks ago or four years ago. The dual aspect of time has always amazed him—how true that the days are long, but the years are short.

Jack thinks of bespectacled, intellectual Stewart back in northern Minnesota with the Timberwolves, the deer, the moose, and the journal, and he smiles. He pictures Rachel in Connecticut and wonders if she has heard from Drew in the past thirty-six hours since he gave the university student her phone number. He anticipates his trip to LA in two weeks to enter Violet's forest with Armando. He shakes his head in amazement as he remembers the astounding visitation that precipitated Mahmoud's new birth, an event that most of the world would dismiss as fantasy and superstition. He pauses and says a short prayer for both Mahmoud and Aly that they might grow deep in their relationship with Jesus while they attend the institute in Georgia during winter break.

Last of all, he envisions Emily, the young woman with the prickly exterior who nonetheless has captured his attention; the dimple-cheeked girl with brilliant green eyes, who is guarded by an invisible regiment of soldiers armed with razor-sharp spears and swords. They do not protect her from harm but from love.

He misses her. He fears that she will never return to the Academy.

Jack continues along the lake until he reaches the dock that stretches out toward the aquarium classroom. He pauses there for a short time, then climbs the hill and makes his way through the thick stand of trees. When he reaches the amphitheater, he walks to the center of the floor and kneels on the stone pavement.

"Jesus," he begins, "you are my life. I wouldn't be here without your guidance. I wouldn't know these new friends without you. I would be lost and blind and hopeless without you. Thank you for pursuing me and saving me when I was so clueless to what matters in this universe."

He sighs heavily and then says, "Grow me so I can walk increasingly by faith and not by sight. Reveal your will for my life so I might pursue it unwaveringly. May others come to know you through me so that they, too, may experience how beautiful and meaningful life is with you at the center of it all.

Jesus," Jack prays with his forehead pressed against the cool stone, "nothing matters in this world if you're not my best friend and Savior and your Word is not my guide. Life is reduced to fleeting pleasures and shallow experiences and utilitarian relationships if you're not the cornerstone. You're the one who imbues everything with meaning and purpose for me.

You're the one who tells me where I came from and where I'm going. You're the one who fills me with joy and the ability to love others."

Jack saves the most dangerous prayer for last. He takes a deep breath and hesitates. He knows that if he speaks these words, they may—no, they will—profoundly alter his future only because he serves a God who hears such prayers and takes them very seriously.

"Jesus," he finally says, "take me wherever you want me to go and for whatever purpose you choose. I'm here, Lord. Send me."

Just as Jack already knew, his prayer is heard, and it is honored. The adventure of a lifetime is immediately set in motion.

The next ten months will be the most amazing of Jack's young life.

CPSIA information can be obtained
at www.ICGtesting.com
Printed in the USA
BVHW082354040522
635953BV00002B/2